PUTNEY BRIDGE

Ivana Stancomb

MINERVA PRESS

LONDON
MONTREUX LOS ANGELES SYDNEY

PUTNEY BRIDGE
Copyright © Ivana Stancomb 1998

All Rights Reserved

ISBN 1 86106 832 8

First Published 1998 by
MINERVA PRESS
195 Knightsbridge
London SW7 1RE

Printed in Great Britain for Minerva Press

PUTNEY BRIDGE

Acknowledgements

I would like to thank Sarah Molloy, Margaret Forester, the Andrew Robson Bridge Club and Elisabeth Cliff for all their help and support.

About the Author

Ivana Stancomb was born in Buenos Aires of Croatian parents. She moved to London twenty-five years ago where she still lives with her art publisher husband and their two children. Before starting to write she owned an art gallery in Chelsea.

Chapter One

Amanda drew the curtains and greeted the autumnal sun with a sigh of relief. It was a new year. For Amanda the start of the school term in September was the time for new beginnings. Once the children went back to their routines she would adapt hers. Autumn was the time when she enrolled in evening courses, joined exercise classes, and visited her sister in the country. It was also a time for new resolutions, but this September she felt an undercurrent of apprehension at the prospect of more time for herself. This year would be a landmark. Her daughter, Kate, was leaving for Bristol University and Mark was about to start his last year at school.

Amanda dressed quickly, promising herself that after breakfast, when Douglas and the children were gone, she would return to her dressing-table to put on some make-up. This promise was rarely kept and, throughout the day at the sight of the dark shadows under her eyes, she would once more put down taking better care of herself as a new resolution. As she rushed down the stairs she could smell the toast burning. She was late. Late for what? Late for what she was accustomed to do. Kate and Mark were capable of getting their own breakfast, and yet not being there still worried her. As soon as she entered the kitchen Amanda turned on the extractor.

"Mum, do you have to make that terrible noise first thing in the morning?" Mark kept his eyes on his corn flakes bowl.

Kate, who was talking to her father, turned the volume of the radio up and simultaneously raised her voice. Douglas read the paper and sipped his coffee. He would occasionally look towards his daughter who was recounting a conversation she'd had with a friend the night before. Kate knew her father was listening and reading at the same time. Amanda, who had always found her husband's ability to do two things at once irritating, found herself saying: "Are you listening, darling?"

Douglas ignored her and scraped off with his knife a dollop of marmalade that had fallen on the newspaper. The paper will be all sticky, thought Amanda as she plugged in the kettle. The voice on the radio seemed to be struggling over Kate's and the hum of the extractor. Amanda tried to listen to the radio. She had heard Kate's story before. The newsreader talked monotonously about biblical catastrophes; floods, famine, explosions, and acts of revenge. Except for the bomb explosions, thought Amanda as she spooned some sugar into her tea, news must have always been the same. If the Romans had had radios they would have listened to the same string of events: calamities, intrigue and power struggles. But probably, she reflected, they would have had *Woman's Hour* on at a time of day when women had the time to listen to it, and they would have put talks on premature ejaculation in the evening rather than at teatime.

"Is anyone listening to the news?" Mark protested with his mouth full of milky cereal.

"Yes, I am." Kate gave him the kind of look that had always reminded him he was the youngest.

"You aren't listening! How can you be listening when all you've done for the last fifteen minutes is talk?" He dropped his spoon noisily into the empty bowl and, realising his sister had once again driven him to act like an eight year old, got up sullenly and left the kitchen.

"I can talk and listen to the radio at the same time. Some of us can do more than one thing at a time, you know," Kate said to the retreating figure. As she looked towards the door she met her mother's eyes. Kate is having a dig at me, too, for not listening to her story for a second time, thought Amanda, as she looked in the direction of her son, who was putting on his jacket. She felt like comforting Mark but knew it would only annoy him if she highlighted his defeat with her concern.

"I'm off," said Mark defiantly.

Douglas raised his eyes from the paper and, after saying goodbye to his son, looked at his watch and got up from the table.

"I'll finish telling you what she said this evening." Kate chose to put an end to her monologue before her father did, and began to clear the table.

"What are your plans for the day?" Douglas looked at Amanda and turned off the extractor. Amanda knew Douglas was about to ask her to run a few errands and felt humiliated that her days should be so uninteresting that even giving an account of them to her own family was embarrassing.

"Any chance you could take my tweed jacket to the cleaners?" he asked casually. Douglas didn't wait for her to answer. He felt that giving instructions in the form of a question allowed his wife some degree of independence.

"If you're going to the cleaners, Mum, you could get a few things for me at the chemist. Tania is leaving for Edinburgh next week and who knows when I'll see her next. I must make the most of my last ten days in London. I'll make a list of what I need. It won't take a second." Kate rushed upstairs after kissing her father on the cheek.

"Remember tonight we're expected at the Lockhart's for supper." Amanda opened the door for her husband.

"I'll be back early." He kissed her on the cheek. Looking down at his wife, dressed in a pair of jeans and barefooted, he was reminded how young she was to have a daughter who was off to university. "A cradle snatcher", his best man had said at their wedding reception twenty years ago.

Douglas walked unhurriedly towards the tube station. His thoughts slowed him down, allowing the fresh breeze to filter through his lightweight suit. He remembered that, at the end of the month, it would be their twentieth wedding anniversary and two weeks later, as the evenings started to draw in, he

would be fifty. Amanda, eleven years his junior, was no longer
the outspoken and impressionable girl he had married. Since
motherhood she had become cautious and dependable, which
also had made her unadventurous and less exciting. Douglas
had married late. The success in his business had been his main
concern in the third decade of his life. Once well established,
he had felt marriage would add respectability to his image.
Douglas had also started to tire of lonely evening meals in his
comfortable but dark mansion flat off the Earl's Court Road
and decided it was time to get a large suburban house and have
a family. It wasn't wise to leave fatherhood uncelebrated past
forty, one started doubting one's virility and there was also
one's wife's age to consider. A son. He had envisaged showing
his son round his old college at Oxford, unconsciously hoping
this would perpetuate his own existence.

Douglas had met Amanda at a garden party at his sister's
house. Amanda was the niece of one of the neighbours and had
just come back from America, where she had spent a year
working as a secretary for an advertising company. She was
pretty and vivacious but, most of all, she had the youth he felt
had gently, but irrevocably, started to seep out of him. Amanda
seemed bright enough, and Douglas, in a self-indulgent sort of
way, had pictured himself as the mentor who would lead her to
maturity and a sensible life. The ten years between them, he
had told himself, could be an asset. Amanda would learn from
his maturity and he would be kept on his toes by her youth.
They had started a family straight away, Amanda eager to offer
what she could, and Douglas happy to complete the tableau he
had envisaged. Kate was born, to the slight disappointment of
her father, but as Douglas's natural single-mindedness was
always kept in check by his equally natural common sense, he
greeted the event cheerfully. Amanda was young, their new
home in Putney was large and there was plenty of time for a
son. Mark was born eighteen months later.

Douglas crossed the high street and joined the crowd at the
tube station. Teenagers, he reflected, were difficult and not as

enjoyable and rewarding as small children. They weren't pleased to see you and sometimes made you wonder if you were pleased to see them. Amanda was a good mother and, being closer in age to the children, maybe understood them better than he did. As he sat in the airless train, where the atmosphere was a cocktail of aftershaves and none-too-inviting deodorants, he found himself wondering what had happened to his young wife of twenty years ago. His thoughts turned to Claire, his new girlfriend. He had met her for the first time at last year's Christmas party. She was the PA of one of his junior colleagues. He now met Claire regularly twice a week after work and he always told Amanda he was playing squash. It was easy to lie to Amanda. Since the children were born she had become so absorbed in her role as mother that she seldom noticed any change in his routine. Douglas tried to read the back page of the paper held by the woman sitting opposite and, without his glasses, failed. He wondered grudgingly if Amanda ever read the paper he left on the kitchen table every morning.

*

"Mum, I don't know if I'll be back for supper. Don't forget my shopping list! It's on the kitchen table." Kate's voice carried clearly and with authority up the stairs. The front door was shut with a robust slam, and then the house was silent.

Amanda sat on the unmade bed enjoying the silence in the empty house. In front of the dressing-table she examined the lines round her eyes, then opened a pot of cream and massaged some vigorously into her face. She couldn't remember when these lines had started to appear. She waited for the cream to be absorbed by what the instructions referred to as her "undernourished skin", and then applied an even coat of make-up. The effect was rewarding; the fine lines, even in the bright, unforgiving light of a sunny morning, seemed to have vanished. She took a hair dryer and, with the help of a round brush, shaped her hair into a fashionable bob. One of her new year's resolutions was to take more care of her appearance. It hadn't taken her long, just over five minutes.

After making the bed, she walked aimlessly round the house. Mark's room was littered with clothes, banana skins and tapes. She knew she would find ashtrays with cigarette ends under the bed, which she hoped Douglas never would notice. The children's bathroom, that doubled as a laundry room, was full of dirty clothes, and the ironing basket had twice as many clothes in it than usual.

In the kitchen, she started to tidy away the breakfast, only to be reminded as she opened the fridge, that there was nothing left to eat. The children seemed to get hungry at the oddest times; pounds of cold meats and cheeses would suddenly disappear overnight. Amanda put on the kettle to make herself another cup of coffee. She didn't particularly feel like one, but needed the pause. It was an excuse to delay the moment when she would start picking up discarded clothes, loading the various machines and emptying the rubbish.

She sipped her coffee slowly, clinging to the moment and looking out at the large garden. Douglas liked gardening, which he did meticulously and not unimaginatively. The red berries on the shrubs at the bottom of the garden seemed to glisten in the low autumnal sun. It was a beautiful day, an exceptionally beautiful day; a day people would refer to as "rare" for the time of year. If it is so special, thought Amanda, shouldn't I try and make the most of it rather than just let it be lost in my memory as another Monday, another laundry day. She decided to go out and do the errands before starting with the housework. She might even go to the park on her way back. Another resolution for this new year, she told herself, would be not to miss opportunities. A sunny day was an opportunity to be out, perhaps not in Italy or in other places where the sun shone nearly every day, but it certainly was in England.

She left the mug of coffee on the table and, without looking at the mail that had just been dropped through the letter-box and forgetting Kate's shopping list on the kitchen table, put on her blazer and walked out into the tree-lined street. As she made her way towards the park, she thought of Douglas. He had been very distant in the last few months and was easily irritated by the children. It had also become more difficult than usual to communicate with him. Amanda had tried to talk to him about her apprehension at the prospect of an empty house with both children gone but Douglas had dismissed her worries, as though she had been complaining about a broken dishwasher.

★

That evening when Amanda arrived home, Douglas was already back from his office and having a bath. Kate sat with a sulky expression at the kitchen table, where she was poking at a piece of quiche.

"Had a good day?" Amanda poured herself a glass of orange juice.

"Kind of. Mum, you left my shopping list behind." Kate's voice was reproachful.

"Did I? You're quite right. I'm sorry, I must have left in a hurry."

"Have you been to enrol for an evening class?"

Amanda perceived the sarcasm in her daughter's voice. "No, I met a friend and went for a long walk in the park. It was such a beautiful day, it seemed a shame to waste it."

"Who did you go with?" Kate knew most of her mother's local friends.

"You haven't met her. Someone new in the neighbourhood," she said firmly, wanting to put an end to the conversation.

"I see." Kate raised her eyebrows, shrugged her shoulders, and looked at her forgotten shopping list still lying on the kitchen table. "If Dad and you are going out for supper tonight, what will Mark and I have to eat? There doesn't seem to be much in the fridge," she said, still determined to make her mother feel guilty.

"There's plenty left in the deep freeze. I'm sure you'll find something you both like. I'd better go and change or I'll be late." She pretended not to notice her daughter's tone and left the room.

"I don't know what's come over her. You don't suppose it's one of the manifestations of the change of life," Kate said to her brother who had just walked into the kitchen, while making sure her voice was loud enough for her mother to hear as she went up the stairs. Mark knew his sister wanted a temporary ally against his mother but was not going to allow Kate to use him. He had learned from past experience that she would treat him like a ten year old again the minute it suited her.

Amanda heard Kate's remark as she went up the stairs. One's children always wanted one to fit a particular role. Her primary role so far had been nurturing, providing meals, taking them to school and doing the shopping. In their eyes any deviation meant one was deemed to be having menopausal problems. This unpleasant teenage phase, seemingly necessary for one's young to go through in order to become independent, never ceased to disconcert her. She remembered the day Kate had asked her why she hadn't had a hysterectomy yet, all her friends' mothers seemed to be having them. Kate had been sixteen at the time, old enough to know it was a serious operation. Why had she asked? Was she wanting her to be like her friends' mothers or, more perversely, was she implying it was time to give up her womanhood to make room for her own. The recollection of that day made her chest tighten. Amanda took a deep breath and tried to push away the unpleasant memory.

Up in her bedroom, still preoccupied by thoughts of Kate's difficult and, at times, brusque quest for maturity, she looked at her wardrobe unenthusiastically, wondering what to wear for the dinner party. As though in an act of defiance towards her daughter, Amanda decided to make an effort. Red seemed to be one of the colours in the winter collections. She found an old red skirt and rolled it at the waist so that the hemline finished round her mid-thighs. She then decided on thick black tights and a black jacket. The colour combination was striking and in the evening, with artificial light, no one would notice that the wools were different and that the back of the skirt was shiny from wear. She went to Kate's bedroom and took the pair of large drop pearl earrings she had given her as a birthday present.

She met Kate as she was going down the stairs.

"You've taken my earrings!"

"Darling, I was about to tell you I was borrowing them for tonight. Is it all right?"

"Don't forget to put them back in my room tomorrow." Kate looked at her mother and refrained from flattering her on her appearance.

Douglas and Amanda left in good time for Julia and Henry's party. One always left in good time when invited by Julia, in the same way one thanked her promptly. Douglas, who always became a good conversationalist in the car, today was silent. He had never asked Amanda why his jacket was still bundled on the chair in the hall and had not been taken to the cleaners. One of Douglas's characteristics, she reflected looking at his profile, was that he didn't judge people for their immediate actions, but for their overall long-term performance. Like an accountant, he would analyse how much housekeeping money they spent and how many times they made love on a yearly basis. His jacket could sit in the hall for a week and he wouldn't bring it up, but this didn't mean it wouldn't eventually be weighed as a point against her. Amanda adjusted her seat belt as they turned into the more fashionable part of Putney. "I always forget how much larger the houses are on this side," she said.

Douglas was irritated by Amanda's comment. Was she implying their house was not big enough? Lately, particularly since he had started having an affair with Claire, he often felt that, if anything, they were overhoused. Now, with the children away at school or university for eight months of the year and away on holidays for half of the remaining four, the house seemed to fulfil only Amanda's needs.

Douglas looked at his wife out of the corner of his eye. Her comment had been harmless and, deep down, he knew she didn't want a bigger house; lately everything Amanda said annoyed him. He noticed she had made an effort with her appearance and that annoyed him too. Douglas had found Amanda sexually unresponsive after Mark had been born. Feeling neglected by his wife, he had stopped feeling attracted to her. When this post-natal phase was over, Amanda gave all her energies to the running of the house and the baby, neglecting herself, which Douglas felt was neglecting him too. If Amanda had no time to take care of herself for him, surely her love for him must be questionable. Douglas liked reasoning and lately he had spent a lot of time reasoning about his marriage. The fact he felt attracted to Claire was not entirely his doing, nor Claire's. Surely Amanda was also to blame.

Douglas knew Claire was tiring of her role as a part-time girlfriend. She wanted him with her at weekends and often threatened putting an end to their relationship unless arrangements changed. Douglas would assure her he was planning to leave his wife, that the right moment to do so would come soon, now the children were older. Douglas didn't want to lose Claire and, at times, suspected he even needed her. Her youth excited him and made him feel younger. Claire was only seven years older than Kate, but she always reassured him that the age difference didn't matter.

★

Julia and Henry's house was the largest in the tree-lined street. The gravel at the front of the house was new, as was Henry's large Mercedes. Although they had a large garage, the cars were left outside. Julia also drove a Mercedes, three years old – the one Henry couldn't possibly drive now.

Julia felt that if her guests saw the cars it saved so much explaining over drinks, particularly if they hadn't seen them for some time. This way, it was immediately obvious that, despite the recession, not only was Henry employed but most likely he was a director in his firm. Henry had always been hard-working and reliable, and Julia had always made sure that anyone who could be of any use to Henry's career was asked for supper or Sunday lunch. Each time she looked at the large extension at the back of the house or saw the new registration metallic car, she felt rewarded for her efforts. Henry had bought her a mink coat when he had been made a senior director of the firm, though it now hung in the cupboard unused, for fear someone might throw eggs at her or shout abuse. It had arrived a little late. Had Henry been promoted before the era of animal rights groups, she might have been able to wear it. But having it hanging in the cupboard and complaining about not being able to wear it, gave her nearly as much pleasure.

Julia had not only fought every inch of the way for Henry's advancement, but for Rupert's too. Their only son had gone to the best nursery schools. He had been able to read and write remarkably early. He played the violin and took karate lessons, for which Julia would chauffeur him around London. The whole of Putney and neighbouring Richmond were told of his early academic career and every school interview was discussed with the intensity of a peace treaty. Julia was aiming high. There was only one school in England that would, in her heart of hearts, do for Rupert. She felt it was important to tell people that there were two other schools she liked just as much, just in case Rupert did not measure up. The day the news came that Rupert had been accepted into the alma mater of great statesmen and nobility, she was jubilant. She spent most of that day shopping locally so that when people, as usual, asked her about Rupert, she could give them the momentous news. She had also rung most of her friends and acquaintances that day with some pretext so that they could be told. Julia entertained for months spreading the news. Some neighbours remarked that she even looked different after the event; there was a regal air about her as she talked incessantly about the clothes and picnic baskets she would need in the following years.

For five years Julia drove down to Windsor regularly, watched cricket matches and talked about Rupert's future in a half-whisper, as one does when great things are expected. Henry was made to change his car so that sports events and picnics could be attended in style and comfort. They learnt how to ski so that they could accompany Rupert on holidays to the resorts most favoured by his school friends. She had Rupert's housemaster over to supper once a year and kept in contact with the parents of her son's school friends whom, she felt, could one day give Rupert an introduction into whatever field he chose. When the time came to think about university, Julia fretted and planned. Henry had never been to university and she now resented him for this. She felt that an allegiance to a specific college in Oxford or Cambridge would have been useful. Some parents said that Rupert's school had a higher success rate in getting its boys to Oxford than Cambridge. Once again, Julia's hopes were high, despite the housemaster's warnings that Rupert, although an accomplished school boy, might not be Oxbridge material. The day the news came that Rupert had failed to get into Cambridge, her first reaction was to blame the school and then Henry.

Rupert went to York University laden with his mother's disappointment and after a couple of terms decided to give it up and go to Australia, where a school friend had offered him a job. Julia was devastated. "How is Rupert?" people would ask. Instead of saying "at Cambridge", as she had always assumed she would, she had to say "in Perth".

Soon after Rupert left for Australia, Julia became a shopkeeper. She bought a shop in the high street, from where she sold accessories and costume jewellery and there was now even talk of branching into fashion. Rupert was hardly ever mentioned and, if he were, it was to remind one where he had gone to school. All Julia's energies were now invested in her new commercial venture. She talked about gaps in the market, turnover and profit, with the authority of the Chancellor. Her exterior image had also changed. The regality, with which she had cloaked herself in Rupert's schooldays, was now replaced by a brisk business-like manner. Nowadays, she was always in a rush, with no spare time to talk outside Sainsbury's about her son's progress. The days were gone when her eyes would fill with tears of pride as neighbours rang to tell her they had seen Rupert photographed in some glossy magazine looking dashing at some youngster's ball. She was a businesswoman now, demanding success and recognition in her own right.

When Amanda and Douglas arrived, Julia, who no longer had the time to do her own cooking, was giving last minute instructions to the caterers.

Henry opened the door, relieved the first guests had arrived. Julia would now stop asking him for a third time to check the wine. Since Julia had become a businesswoman, he was made to feel guilty for relaxing in his own home.

Henry was genuinely pleased to see Douglas and Amanda. They were friendly and unassuming neighbours. "How lovely to see you!" he said kissing Amanda on the cheek. "Let me take your coats."

Henry was aware of his own shyness which he had found hard to overcome with the passing of the years. He knew his success in business was not due to his personality or acumen, but because of his hard work and consistency. His expertise in his field gave him a certain confidence, but he seldom talked about his work socially unless asked, and he found small talk at social gatherings a strain. He was fond of Amanda and hoped that Julia would seat her beside him at dinner. Julia always decided where their guests should sit, as she normally had a very good reason for getting them together. It would be nice to have Amanda beside him for supper, Henry told himself as he poured the drinks. She was undemanding and completely unpretentious, and he would be able to relax and not feel obliged to talk of things he either knew little or in which he wasn't interested.

They all stood drinking in the rather over-decorated drawing room. The room had doubled in size since the new extension had been built, and Julia knew it to be the largest one in the neighbourhood. It now, at last, had the same proportions as one found in large country houses. No expense had been spared on the soft furnishings. The silver frames shone with pictures of Julia in large hats at family weddings and Henry standing beside Princess Margaret at some function. There were many photographs of Rupert in his schooldays wearing either a dinner jacket or tails.

The walls were covered in expensive but obscure oil paintings that would be more valuable the day that Rupert inherited them. Julia had always encouraged Henry to collect. She found her husband didn't have enough hobbies and felt it was healthy for him to have an occupation other than his work. Instinct told her it was important for a man to have as little spare time as possible.

Julia looked round the room and decided she would give her guests time for another drink before taking them into the dining room. The judge was talking to Douglas, and the judge's wife was drinking champagne while discussing the problems of schooling with Penny Peacroft who was married to Hugo, the head of one of the largest insurance companies. Julia knew heads were rolling in Hugo Peacroft's firm. Penny had mentioned this was a stressful time for Hugo, but Julia suspected, judging by the size of their newly acquired house in Belgravia, that he probably felt very sure of his position and might even derive a certain pleasure in watching the victims of these hard times from the security of his unmortgaged house. Penny enjoyed her husband's wealth, but knew it to be unfashionable to flaunt it in the present climate. Julia had always approved of Penny and was glad she was talking to the judge's wife whom, being a new acquaintance, she was still trying to impress. People, she knew, despite whatever else they pretended, were always impressed by wealth and position.

Julia looked at Amanda and was relieved to see she had made an effort with her appearance. It was such a shame Amanda was slightly timid when Douglas was so useful at any social gathering.

At the dinner table, Hugo Peacroft asked Amanda about her children and, once he had established she lived in the suburbs and didn't work, asked whether she enjoyed gardening. This was when Amanda chose to tell him, in a loud enough voice, so that both Julia and Douglas could hear, that she had decided to get a job.

Julia heard her and, although intrigued and surprised by Amanda's news, chose to ignore it, thinking it was not an interesting enough topic for her dinner table.

Douglas looked in Amanda's direction and quickly went back to his mousse and conversation with the judge. As usual with Douglas, it was difficult to tell whether he had heard what she had said or merely acknowledged the fact she was speaking. Hugo Peacroft, in between mouthfuls of mousse managed to say, "Well done. How interesting." Penny Peacroft, experienced in dealing with her husband's disjointed efforts at conversation when talking about anything except business, came to Amanda's rescue.

"How long since your last job?"

"A very long time. I haven't worked since Kate was born. She's nineteen now."

"It's very brave of you, but a lot of women do it. Any ideas what you'll do?" She pushed her fork to one side.

"No. I used to be in advertising, but I suppose I'll have to start with something less ambitious till I adjust to working life again."

"People underestimate the skills in organisation and administration that are required to stay at home and run a family. I'm sure you'll be very useful to someone." Amanda was grateful for Penny's interest and wondered if Penny had ever wished to do something else with her life, other than being a groomed company wife.

"Have you ever heard of Jack Noel, the portrait painter?" Penny said brightly.

"No, but I am rather out of touch."

"He's very fashionable and has done portraits of a couple of the younger royals. His mother used to be a friend of ours. Sadly, she's dead now. I saw Jack a week ago at a cocktail party and he mentioned he was looking for a PA. I assume what he needs is someone to do a bit of organising for him. That is just the kind of thing you should go for. You could try him and mention us. I'll give you his telephone number before you leave. I'm sure he'd rather have someone reliable like you than a young thing."

Amanda felt encouraged by Penny and turned to talk to Hugo.

The first course was removed by the experienced staff and the conversation turned to the arts. The opinions round the dinner table on current exhibitions and plays were suspiciously close to the reviews in the Sunday papers.

Amanda's job was forgotten but to her surprise, after three elaborate courses, some cheese, port, cigars for the men and more conversation in Julia's silky drawing room, Penny Peacroft remembered to give her Jack Noel's number before she left.

They drove back in silence, Amanda secretly hoping that Douglas would ask about her intentions of finding a job. She longed to tell him how lost she felt now that her role within the family had changed, but refrained. It was difficult to discuss feelings with Douglas. He preferred facts. Douglas was too lost in thought to sense his wife's expectations of having a conversation. Since Amanda had mentioned at Julia's table her intention of looking for work, his mind had been bustling with plans and new possibilities. Fuelled by Henry's port, he assured himself of how much easier it would be to leave a wife who was independent and able to provide for herself.

*

A week after Julia's dinner party Kate had gone to Bristol and two days later Amanda had driven Mark to his boarding school. Back at home that evening, she waited for Douglas to walk through the door, with more expectation than usual. The house felt empty and the realisation it would now be empty most of the time, made her feel worse. Remembering it was one of the days Douglas played squash, Amanda had some supper on a tray. Douglas normally had something to eat at the club and didn't want any supper when he came back. After tidying the kitchen she left the light in the entrance hall on and went upstairs to run a bath.

An hour later, Douglas walked into the hall clutching a brief case, a sports bag and his squash racket. He had spent all evening with Claire who had given him an ultimatum: she no longer was prepared to fulfil the role of part-time mistress. He went upstairs slowly, pausing on the landings to give himself time and courage to prepare for what he was about to tell his wife.

Amanda sat in bed reading a light novel. When she heard Douglas coming up the stairs she picked up the diary on her bedside table and said, "Hello, darling, shouldn't we start thinking about Christmas? Pat has asked us down for Christmas Eve and Christmas Day." She didn't look up at him, hoping he would say he thought it was a good idea. She knew he preferred to spend Christmas with his sister rather than hers.

"I've been meaning to tell you..." He paused and, without looking at Amanda, said solemnly, "I won't be here for Christmas."

"For Christmas! The office has never sent you abroad for Christmas before."

"It's not the office. It's my decision. I won't be here for Christmas because I'm leaving you. I am moving out."

She looked up at him, stunned. Douglas turned his back on her and went towards the bathroom. Amanda watched him wash his hands slowly and meticulously. There was a certain finality in his gesture that frightened her. She hid her face in her hands, a gesture she so often used when she wished the present moment would vanish.

"Douglas! The children!" She heard her own voice, disbelieving and imploring.

"The children aren't children anymore." He dried his hands without looking at her.

"Douglas!" Amanda broke into a sob and, pushing the sheets to one side, got out of bed and went towards him. In her confusion and despair she became very aware of her old, discoloured night dress. "Darling, what is going on?" She stood beside him not knowing whether to touch him.

He turned round and looked at her. "Amanda, I'm afraid there is someone else and there has been for some time."

Amanda would remember later how, on hearing his words, the drabness of her nightgown suddenly became offensive to her. She took a bathrobe hanging behind the door and wrapped it round her. "Why?" she asked in a half whisper.

"Does it matter why?"

She nearly said, "It's my nightgown, isn't it?" but instead broke into tears and clung to his arm.

"I'll pack a suitcase now and come back for the rest of my things some other time when you aren't in. I can't take a scene at the moment."

Amanda sat at the end of the bed sobbing, while watching him pack. When he had finished, without any further explanation, he went downstairs. When Amanda heard the front door shut, she buried her face in Douglas's pillow and cried. The sound of her own sobs made her cry even more, stimulating the fear, pain and desolation that had taken hold of her.

The telephone rang several times but she didn't answer. There seemed to be no other reality beyond her confusion and total sense of abandonment.

★

The following morning Amanda spent all her time thinking about the past. She went over and over her life with Douglas, trying to analyse where she had gone wrong, where she had failed him. She wanted to blame herself. "There is someone else," he had said. She had always suspected Douglas might occasionally be unfaithful, but had preferred not to think too much about it. It had never occurred to her that he would leave her.

As Amanda analysed the past, she found herself thinking, not only of her adult past with Douglas, but also of what now seemed a very remote past, when she had had a mother and a father. She remembered playing with her sister in the garden of her parents' cottage in Berkshire. Faces and images from the childhood she had nearly forgotten surfaced from her subconscious, taking over her now fragile reality. She tried to control the unbidden images crowding her mind and, as she paced the room, her emotions changed with every step; one minute she felt rage, then fear, followed by rejection, till it all disintegrated into a sob of total despair.

It wasn't till she heard a loud knock at the door that she realised someone had been ringing the bell. It was Julia. When Julia saw Amanda's puffy face, she didn't ask her in her usual manner what had taken her so long, instead she said gently, "Amanda, Mark has been trying to get hold of you since yesterday. There was no reply so he rang me to ask if your telephone was out of order." Amanda burst into tears. Julia hugged her, guessing what had happened. She had always felt Douglas and Amanda had little in common and that it was only a matter of time before one of them realised it and walked away.

Julia made some tea and listened to the long string of disjointed thoughts and half-coherent notions that she knew had to work themselves out of Amanda before she could accept what had happened. Later on, when Amanda was in bed with a hot water bottle, Julia rang Mark at school to say the telephone was indeed out of order and that his mother would ring him the following day.

★

The following week Julia visited Amanda once a day. Amanda went about the household chores in a daze, still not fully accepting what had happened and secretly waiting for Douglas to walk in the door. She was dreading the moment when her children came home and she would have to tell them their father had left. She half waited, half hoped. When she went to the supermarket to buy food, Amanda found herself looking furtively round her, imagining people would notice she was shopping for one and realise her husband had left her. It was hard to come to terms with being left, substituted by someone else.

The days went by slowly. She hardly went out, afraid she would meet somebody she knew and then have to explain. A new emotion took over the pain and desolation of being alone. She felt ashamed. Surely failing was shameful.

On Sunday afternoon the doorbell rang and Amanda opened the door in her dressing-gown. Julia stood holding a piece of cake and said, "Well, are you going to let me in?"

Once inside the house, Julia took over. She rolled up her sleeves and started tidying up the messy kitchen. As she busily moved pots and pans she asked, "Are the children home next weekend?" When Amanda nodded, she said firmly, "You'd better pull yourself together. There is a life without Douglas and for all you know it might one day be a better one. You owe it to your children and to yourself to try and get on with this business of living." She paused and faced Amanda. "Henry's been unfaithful to me for years. I know I'm a bossy old bag, but it happened quite soon after our honeymoon. That's why I became such an obsessive mother and now it's the shop. You've got to pull yourself together. Love and marriage aren't the only great adventure. Amanda," Julia added firmly while vigorously drying a salad bowl, "you'd better go and see a divorce lawyer and establish what your position is."

Amanda wrapped the dressing-gown tightly round her, as though the gesture would protect her from what Julia was saying.

"Divorce?" she said in a muffled sob. "Douglas didn't mention a divorce."

"I know it's tough, but he might – and in a few months even you might – be thinking about it. Just go and see a lawyer and have a chat. It will make you feel better and at least you'll know what's what money-wise and children-wise."

"I don't know any divorce lawyers," Amanda said, hoping this would make the unpleasant prospect go away.

"I'll find out about a good one and let you know. You must be in good hands in case things get nasty. Let's hope they won't. Now, why don't you take that dressing-gown off and put some clothes on while I make some tea."

Julia's bossy and reassuring voice gave Amanda strength to go upstairs. The word "divorce" had left her feeling hollow inside. Even the pain seemed to have temporarily left her.

The following weekend Kate came home. Amanda broke the news to her daughter, hiding her own despair, conscious that Kate's feeling of loss would be different from her own. After hearing the news, Kate stormed out of the room and went upstairs, slamming the door of her bedroom.

Tears welling up in her eyes, Amanda opened the fridge. She had bought enough food at Sainsbury's that morning to last them for a month. Was she compensating for Douglas not being there by feeding her children? She would have to take a grip on herself, adjust to her new position, stop pretending it hadn't happened. Why was it so terribly shameful to be left?

She heard Kate coming down the stairs. Composing herself, she smiled and outstretched her arms saying, "It won't be that bad. You'll see Dad as much as you want and soon it will seem quite normal."

"It's your fault!" Kate hissed at her.

"He's got someone else!" Amanda felt she had to defend herself. Kate's outburst had nearly made her say something she would later regret.

"It's still your fault. You should have made yourself irreplaceable."

Amanda looked at her daughter, shocked by the remark. Is that what Kate would try and be from now on when she entered a relationship? Would she try and be irreplaceable?

"When is Mark coming home?" Kate opened the fridge and took a pot of shrimps. Taking the lid off, she started picking at it with her fingers. Amanda could tell by her daughter's tone, when she had asked after her brother, that she was sorry for having blamed her. Daughters didn't like seeing their mothers' vulnerability, specifically when it stemmed from the fact they were women, as if they sensed this weakness might one day afflict them.

As Amanda laid the table she wondered what made one replaceable or irreplaceable. Did men replace women who no longer fitted in with their fantasies or with the image they now projected to the world? Some men probably kept their wives only because they couldn't face the upheaval. She found herself reasoning that, more than out of loyalty or love, she had never expected Douglas would leave, simply because she suspected he didn't have it in him to walk off into a new life. She had been wrong. Women who were not easily replaced probably knew their men better. Perhaps Kate was right after all.

In the days that followed Amanda's life became cluttered with new experiences and emotions. At night when she went to bed she searched for an interior landscape where she could feel secure and at one with herself as a woman now alone. Every morning, as she hesitantly stretched her arm to the side of the bed where Douglas had once slept, she knew she had failed. Throughout the week the telephone rang sporadically. Friends and neighbours, she suspected, were avoiding taking sides, and when they rang Amanda felt they might be moved as much by kindness as curiosity. Julia came over to help her clear her desk and pay some bills, a job Amanda had always left to Douglas. Julia's loyalty and resolve that she be able to stand on her own two feet was touching and made Amanda suspect that Henry had never left her, despite his infidelities, because he needed her support. Despite his jokes about being bullied by his wife, he knew that the success he enjoyed might never have been possible without her.

Mark, who had come home the same weekend as Kate, had shown little emotion when given the news of his father's departure, but back at school, he had started ringing Amanda every other day asking how she was. This worried her, as she didn't want to become an emotional burden on her son, whose puberty was already making him reticent and withdrawn.

Douglas had come to collect most of his belongings one afternoon when she was out. He had left a letter saying that, because of the children, but mainly because it was a bad time to sell property, he would leave her with the house for the time eing. However, she should try and get a full-time job because he was now running two establishments. He had contacted the children and would be meeting them soon. He hoped they would be able to deal with things in an amicable way, as it would be silly to give the legal profession more money than necessary. The thought of Douglas urging her to economise on legal fees so that he might get the most advantageous arrangement and be able to spend more on his new girlfriend, made her finally aware that her marriage was truly over. For the first time, since he had left her, Amanda felt something that resembled determination stirring inside her. She rang the lawyer Julia had recommended and made an appointment for the following week. She also decided to buy an answering machine as she now felt embarrassed when her friends rang to ask how she was coping. A few husbands had taken to ringing her too, asking her if she needed a shoulder to cry on and inviting her out to quiet little suppers in which their wives were clearly not included.

Pat, her elder sister, had rung several times to say that she had never liked Douglas and that Amanda would be better off without him. Amanda wasn't sure whether she was ready to hear that she had wasted all those years with Douglas, any more than she was ready to face the ones in front of her. Pat had insisted they all come down for Christmas. Amanda knew the children liked Pat's husband, Tony. He was always so welcoming and allowed Kate and Mark to watch videos late at night. Amanda was grateful that Pat and Tony would take care of everything to give the children a family Christmas.

★

On Wednesday morning Amanda took the tube to Charing Cross station and walked down the Embankment towards the Temple. The air was fresh and the light soft and autumnal. She found herself thinking how much the light had changed since Douglas had left, the shadows longer and the sun weaker. The last few weeks had gone by without her even being aware of what season it was, so consumed had she been by the turmoil in her life.

The grounds of the Temple Court were peaceful and well tended, and the beauty of the surroundings made her feel less apprehensive. "They are one of the best," Julia had said when she had handed her a piece of paper with Fraser and Russell's address. As she sat in the chintzy waiting room that reminded her of Julia's drawing room, a well-spoken girl offered her some coffee. Amanda declined, aware that her hands would be shaking too much to be able to manoeuvre a cup and saucer.

After ten minutes, in which she tried to read the morning papers while her mind raced with half-coherent questions for the lawyer, the girl came to tell her in a hushed voice that

Mr Fraser was now ready for her. Amanda followed her down the corridor. The girl opened the door to a large room overlooking the gardens, saying, "Mrs Thompson is here to see you."

Amanda stood by the door. The room was grand but at the same time homely. The walls were lined with books, pictures and family photographs, giving it an air of someone's study rather than an office.

"Mrs Thompson, do come and sit down."

The portly, middle-aged man sitting behind the desk stood up and came towards her. She hesitated. He was now standing beside her and ushering her towards a chair by the handsome mahogany desk. In her state of apprehension Amanda found herself wondering if she would be able to afford the fees of such a smart practice. "You'd better go to someone good, in case things get nasty," Julia had stressed. Amanda sat on the chair clutching her bag on her lap and looked up at Mr Fraser, not knowing how to start.

Mr Fraser walked towards the window and, looking out at the gardens, said, "Wonderful weather we've been having lately."

When she didn't reply he added with more enthusiasm in his voice, "Let's hope it holds for the weekend. I'm shooting in Wiltshire on Saturday."

Amanda was reminded how her gynaecologist always talked to her about his gardening schemes whenever he did his probings and wondered if Mr Fraser was about to say something she wouldn't like to hear. Instead, he sat behind his desk and clasped his hands neatly together with the air of confidence so often adopted by those paid for their advice.

"Now, Mrs Thompson. How can I help you?" he said with an ingratiating smile.

Amanda, wondering if it was too late to talk about the weather, looked out at the sun-bathed gardens, and in a voice so weak it barely reached Mr Fraser at the other side of the desk, said, "My husband left a few weeks ago."

Mr Fraser leant forward, obviously straining to hear her. "Have you seen him since?"

"No."

"Have you spoken on the telephone or had any other kind of communication?"

Amanda blushed. "He left a note when he came to collect some of his belongings."

"I see. And what did the note say?"

"That it would be easier if the children and I stayed in the house for the time being as this was not a good time to sell property and that he would be contacting the children."

"Is the house in both your names?"

"No. It's in Douglas's name."

"I see." Mr Fraser jotted something down on a piece of paper. "I suggest we do something about that. It is a very simple procedure. Is the house mortgaged?"

"It used to be," said Amanda.

"But is it now? Do you know how much is outstanding?"

"I'm afraid I'm not sure."

Mr Fraser adjusted his spectacles.

"I could find out."

"I'm afraid you'll have to. All these things are very important if we are going to secure the home."

"But Douglas said there was no problem about the house." Her voice sounded alarmed.

"For the time being."

There was a long pause, in which Amanda kept her eyes on the grey carpet.

"Mrs Thompson, have either you or your husband been to a marriage counsellor?"

"No, I'm afraid it was all so sudden and unexpected. We'd never discussed", she paused, "a separation."

"Mrs Thompson, do you want a divorce?" asked Mr Fraser.

"We have children and have been together for nearly twenty years." Her voice faltered.

"Sometimes when one partner is already living with a third party and they do go to counselling, it can be a great help." He paused, and when Amanda did not respond, he continued, "Do you know how much your husband earns?"

"I'm afraid I don't know."

"Does he have a pension? Do you know what it is?"

"No, I'm afraid I don't."

"Any other assets other than the house?"

"He used to have a few stocks and shares when we were first married."

"Does he still have them?"

"I don't think so, but... I'm afraid I don't know."

Mr Fraser adjusted his glasses. Amanda noticed his slight irritation. He sat back on his chair and looked at her. He must think I'm a total fool and that Douglas had every right to leave me. She lowered her eyes, wishing she'd come more prepared or had gone to someone more low-key for advice. A woman solicitor perhaps? They were bound to exist.

"Are the children still at school?"

"Yes."

Mr Fraser smiled approvingly. Amanda wondered if it was because she had said "yes" rather than "I don't know".

"Public school or state school?"

"Mark is still at public school and Kate has started her first year at Bristol University."

"Do you know if the school fees have been paid for this term?"

"I'm afraid..." said Amanda feeling helpless, "that I don't know."

Mr Fraser adjusted his glasses again and cleared his throat. Amanda wondered whether Douglas's new girlfriend knew what he earned and whether he had paid the school fees. She most probably did.

"Do you know if he has any debts?" Mr Fraser's voice sounded flat and unenthusiastic.

"I don't think so," said Amanda defensively. She met Mr Fraser's eyes and added, "I don't know."

Mr Fraser explained in a calm and measured voice that it might take a while to find out what her position was. He gave her several forms to fill out. Amanda ran her eyes down the page and realised she wouldn't be able to answer all the questions.

When she left the building, Mr Fraser's voice was still reverberating in her ears and she felt frightened by her own ignorance. Douglas had always taken care of the family finances. It seemed natural; he was the breadwinner and older than she was. He also had a degree in accountancy. But shouldn't she have taken an interest in at least some of it? Mr Fraser hadn't even bothered to ask her if she worked, but maybe it was obvious that she didn't. Was her lack of interest in anything other than the house and the children one of the reasons why the marriage had failed?

She boarded the bus and sat up front by a window so no one would notice her tear-stained face. She thought about what the lawyer had said about counselling. She would ring Douglas and tell him she had sought legal advice and counselling had been suggested. Maybe Claire was just part of a phase in his life. Perhaps there was still a chance to save the marriage if they took advice and both tried to change. Looking out of the window, the view blurred by her tears, Amanda tried to make a mental list of all the habits she should try and change to make herself a better wife.

Back in Putney she poured herself a whisky, which she rarely drank, and dialled Douglas's office number. She recognised surprise in his secretary's voice. Amanda hadn't thought before about what Douglas's colleagues in the office might think of the situation. They were bound to know. Maybe his new girlfriend worked in the office! The thought nearly made her drop the receiver.

"Hello!" Douglas's voice sounded brisk.

Amanda took another gulp of whisky. She disliked the taste and winced as she swallowed.

"Douglas, I went to see a lawyer today. Fraser and Russell in the Temple. Julia gave me their name."

"That busybody. I can just hear her. Well, that will set us back a few thousand pounds."

"Us?"

"As I'm the only earner in the family at the moment."

"Mr Fraser suggested we see a counsellor. I'd be prepared to go along. Would you?"

"No."

There was a long pause. Amanda drank some more whisky and waited for Douglas to say more.

"Amanda, I've taken a decision and I'm not going to be talked out of it. I've made up my mind. I gave it a lot of thought. If you think it might help you, you can go along by yourself."

There was another pause.

"Mr Fraser said he would be dropping you a line about what you might expect." Amanda was surprised at the bitterness in her own voice.

"I'm sure he will. They charge per letter, didn't you know? I suppose you didn't," he added sarcastically. "Claire…" Douglas paused, to make her realise he was changing the subject, "wants to meet the children. When do you think it might be a good time?"

Amanda felt both humiliated and angry. "Have you asked yourself if your children want to meet Claire? Have you stopped to think about their emotions?"

"I have and, if anything, I think they would like to meet her out of curiosity, don't you?"

"Well, they can't. I'm sure they don't want to," Amanda stuttered. "I don't want them to anyway. Not yet." She suddenly felt threatened. She had given a lot of thought to Claire as Douglas's girlfriend, but she had never thought of her as someone anywhere near her children.

"Amanda, I'm afraid you can't dictate to them anymore about things like this."

"I know I can't. I was just thinking of what was best for them."

"Well, if you are, when do you think it would be the best time for them to meet Claire?"

"They're home in a couple of weeks. You can ring them and ask, but it's very selfish of you. It's bad enough for them to cope with all the changes as it is."

"They'll cope. They're not babies anymore."

Amanda put the phone down, put her head in her hands and cried. When she eventually stopped, it was dark outside. She went upstairs and, after rinsing her puffy, tear-stained face, fell asleep on the bed with all her clothes on.

★

The following morning Amanda woke up feeling more disoriented than usual. She remembered Julia's words: "Love and marriage aren't the only great adventure". She pondered on the meaning of the word "adventure". It implied excitement. Life was an adventure and the unexpected could also happen to those who took no risks. How did one start living an adventure? Could one just walk out of the door and embrace life with new vigour?

The day outside was cold but bright. Amanda changed into a pair of comfortable trousers and, without eating any breakfast, left the house and walked to the high street.

When she reached the end of the road, she saw a red bus approaching. It glistened invitingly in the morning light. She felt drawn to it and decided to jump on it. She would take an unscheduled journey. 'Am I going soft in the head? What a silly idea!' she thought, looking at the busy high street. The bus was now stationary a few yards away from her. Why not? Determined, she boarded the bus. She sat down by the window and wondered which bus she was on.

"Fare, please." The bus conductor was looking down at her with the authoritarian air most people assume when they are wearing a uniform.

"To the end of the line." Amanda smiled and opened her purse.

"Sorry, love?"

"I'll pay for a ticket to the end of the line," she said with a firm voice and handed him a note. The bus conductor fingered the ten pound note and raised his eyebrows.

"Next time, love, try and have the right change ready. We're not a bureau de change." The bus was empty except for a few old-age pensioners and women on their way to the West End to do some shopping.

He gave Amanda her change with an admonishing expression and made his way whistling to the back of the bus. Amanda rather than being annoyed by the man, was amused. This was all part of living in a city.

As the bus went over Putney Bridge she tried to remember the last time she had gone to an exhibition or to the theatre. Douglas had taken her to the theatre once a year. It seemed a waste not having gone more often with so much at one's doorstep. As the bus travelled slowly along the bottom end of the King's Road she wondered if her life would have been any different if she had lived in Hackney, Fulham, Hampstead or Acton. Would the days and the years have run into each other in the woolly comfort of suburbia as they did in Putney? She thought of her friend Emma who now lived in America. After school they had shared a flat where the bus had now stopped. Emma had always led a full life and she would have done so wherever she was. No opportunities were ever missed. She had used every amenity London had to offer. If the size of one's coffin was determined by the size of one's life, thought Amanda, mine would be a match box. My days running into each other in Putney are nearly identical. She imagined the days of her life all lined up and taking the shape of a fan; with a stroke of the thumb you could close it and they would all fit neatly together.

The bus filled up as they travelled through Knightsbridge and into Piccadilly, People got on and off, looking more purposeful now than they had done in Putney.

Green Park looked inviting in its autumnal colours against the grey stone of the buildings surrounding it. Amanda saw the banners of the Ritz and, soon after, those of the Royal Academy. Soon they would be going through Soho. She was happy she had jumped on a bus with such a scenic route. As they went past the Academy she told herself she should go to see the exhibition of water-colours advertised at the entrance.

As the bus turned into the Tottenham Court Road an elderly lady got up from her seat and started pacing up and down the bus looking at the floor with a distraught expression on her face. The bus jerked and she nearly fell to the floor. "My glove! I've lost my glove!" She waved the remaining one as if to emphasise what had happened. A young man got up and, after helping her regain her balance, started to look for the missing glove.

"It's so annoying when that happens," said another passenger reassuringly.

Soon several passengers had embarked on a search for the missing glove. Amanda noticed that most people were genuinely concerned. It wasn't the woman's advanced age that had moved them; the fact that a pair had been broken seemed to have touched a chord in them. The old lady kept on reminding everyone of this by waving the solitary glove and repeating, "I had them both when I got on the bus. I know I had them both."

Amanda wondered what the old woman's reaction would have been if she had lost something that didn't have a pair, such as a scarf. Would she have resigned herself sooner? Breaking a pair, after all, caused one double the pain. One not only had to come to terms with the loss but also accept that what was left behind had been rendered useless and would have to be discarded too. She wondered if the old lady would have the courage to throw away the glove she had been left with or whether she would put it in a drawer in the hope that some day she might find another partner for it.

"What's going on here?" The bus conductor joined them. To everyone's relief, the glove was found underneath someone's shopping bag. The incident left Amanda looking blankly at the busy street thinking about her life, once paired with Douglas.

They had arrived at Camden High Street. "Here we are, love. Last stop." The conductor was standing beside her with a condescending smile on his face. Wondering if he suspected that she had taken the bus with no other purpose than to get out of the house, Amanda got up. She suddenly didn't care what he thought, nor for that matter, what anyone thought.

She got off the bus and took a deep breath. North London seemed so different. She had crossed the city on an impulse to get away from her surroundings and in search of adventure. Looking at the architecture, so different from Putney, she felt excited. 'This is ridiculous', she told herself, 'that I should feel like I'm abroad'. Amanda walked away from the bus stop. She hadn't been in the area for years, not since they had been to supper there with a colleague of Douglas's. After half an hour her feet began to feel hot and swollen from walking in the wrong shoes. She looked for somewhere to sit.

Across the road she spotted a cafe called Café Algarve and sat at a clean Formica table. As she sat sipping the milky tea a smiling waitress brought her, Amanda wondered if she would be a more assertive person if she had had a career, if she had been more than just Douglas's wife. They had never discussed her going back to work after they were married; they were planning to start a family and there were lots of useful things she could do in their new home such as decorating and putting some life back into the much neglected garden. Kate had been born, then Mark. The curtains had been finished, the gardening was soon taken over by Douglas, and life had continued unquestioned in that pattern. Douglas earned enough money for all of them and, although he had nothing against women having a career, he considered this was only acceptable if they were genuinely making a financial contribution.

Amanda sat for a long time pondering on her life without Douglas and for the first time saw it as a beginning rather than an end, a life where decisions would be taken on her own and holidays would be planned round her interests and not his sporting activities. The situations that had seemed threatening weeks ago were now merely challenging. The city she had seen from the bus window was not hostile but inviting. She had never truly taken a part in it and this was the time to start.

She left the cafe feeling elated, for the first time in weeks free from fear and shame. She didn't feel like going back to Putney and took a long walk round streets she had never seen, enjoying every small encounter and every new sensation.

It was nearly dark when she took a southbound bus and decided to ring Jack Noel, the painter Penny Peacroft had mentioned at Julia's party who was looking for an assistant.

Chapter Two

On the way to Hyde Park Mansions the bus took Amanda round the edge of the park where the trees seemed ablaze in autumnal colour. This had always been her favourite season, and now she wondered if Douglas's departure would alter her feelings towards autumn.

She tried to recall what Penny Peacroft had said about Jack and Solange at Julia's dinner party and realised she never remembered what anybody said at dinner parties.

At the beginning of the week when she had apprehensively rung Jack and Solange's number, a woman with a strong French accent had answered the telephone. To Amanda's surprise she had sounded keen to see her and had insisted she come for an interview as soon as possible. Amanda tried to picture her last interview, but it had been so long ago that she couldn't even remember what her prospective employer had looked like. Reminded of how out of touch she was, her heart began to pound. She was worried about appearing ridiculous but the memory of Solange's friendly and insistent tone made her feel less ill at ease.

When the bus turned into Bayswater, Amanda jumped off. She walked slowly down the busy street and caught her reflection in one of the shop windows. She looked tense and self-conscious, like someone wearing an outfit that was too small and tight for them. She opened her bag and double-checked the address she had written in her diary, then hesitantly walked towards a smart white terrace overlooking the park. As she climbed up the stairs she wondered what qualifications or skills an artist would require from a PA. She rang the bell. Almost immediately the door opened and she found herself facing a chic and indisputably French woman. Amanda lost her composure. She felt drab and matronly wearing an old skirt and her worn loafers. Looking at the neat figure in front of her she wished she had worn the suit she had bought two years ago for Mark's confirmation.

Solange was short, but the way she held herself and the clothes she had chosen made her look svelte and sophisticated. Amanda felt Solange's eyes inspecting her from head to foot. She wanted to apologise, to invent a reason that would excuse her appearance, but couldn't think of what to say and instead felt herself blush.

"You must be Amanda." Solange smiled. "I'm so glad you've come! Do come in!" Her smile became broader and even more welcoming as she opened the door. "Jack will join us in a minute," she added, dropping her voice as though taking her into a confidence.

Solange's warm welcome made Amanda regain some of her composure. "Am I too early?"

"Not at all, but he is in 'the studio'. One never knows exactly how long he'll be when he's working and I don't like interrupting him." She lisped slightly, which emphasised her French accent.

"I could always come back later. I'm very flexible for time." Amanda was anxious to show she would fit in easily round their routine.

"Mrs Hobdon can't sit for long today." Solange shrugged her shoulders. "Jack has already done all the preliminary sketches and is now working on her skin colour. The way he works never requires his subjects to sit for too long. This has made him very popular," she said proudly. "Most of Jack's clients are very busy people who can't sit for hours, and his quick technique has helped make him so sought after. But," she paused pursing her lips in a flirtatious gesture, "they also love him because he is charming." She put one of her hands to her heart.

Solange emphasised most of her words with short and rapid movements of her hands and shoulders. What a pity, thought Amanda as she followed her into the sitting room, that the English seldom used their bodies to enhance language. When people did, one felt totally included in what they were saying or trying to express.

The reception room was light with large windows that overlooked the park. It was a happy marriage of old and new, of English and continental. The large white sofas were brought to life by ethnic cushions, and the well-polished floor boards were covered in oriental rugs. Spot lights discreetly placed on the high ceilings lit lush green plants that were reflected by a mirror-tiled wall. There was, however, despite the decor, a bohemian air to the room.

"Do sit down." Solange pointed at the white sofa. "Can I get you some coffee?"

"No, thank you." Amanda sank into the deep cushions.

Solange was glad not to have to disappear into the kitchen and appreciated Amanda's good manners – a quality she admired in the English. She looked at Amanda's tired-looking loafers and dated skirt and wondered if she would be suitable for the job. But Solange had learnt that in England the way one dressed gave very little clue as to a person's wealth, unlike in Italy or France where one could place someone immediately by what they wore. Amanda, she observed, was not only drably dressed but also had dish-pan hands. However in England, Solange reminded herself, ladies of impeccable breeding went to parties with half their flower beds under their fingernails. She looked for more clues in Amanda and decided that her slightly unkempt hair was a bad sign. English women of a certain background, despite the acceptable crumpled clothes or garden-ruined hands, kept their hair in good order, unless they were more than usually eccentric.

"Have you known Mrs Peacroft long?" Solange crossed her small but perfect legs that shimmered in the powder-grey tights.

"She is a very good friend of a friend of mine." Realising this had sounded a mouthful, Amanda added, "We met at Julia Lockhart's house at a dinner party some time ago and she mentioned you were looking for someone." She paused. "I haven't worked for many years, but I was in advertising before the children were born. This seemed like an opportunity to get started again. As I mentioned on the telephone... " She stopped, sensing she was talking too much.

Amanda heard the door to Jack's studio open and a Mozart violin concerto inundated the apartment.

Holding Mrs Hobdon's arm protectively, Jack ushered her through the doorway. Amanda, who had expected Jack to look bohemian, was startled by his conventional good looks. His stature was small but his stride was charged with energy, making his presence immediately felt. He had rich, curly, black hair that framed a fine-boned face dominated by an aquiline nose. It was a strong, handsome face one would expect to sit on the shoulders of a tall man.

"Caroline, dear, you've been as patient as ever." He kissed Mrs Hobdon's hand and led her towards Solange.

Caroline Hobdon, in contrast to Jack's dark Celtic appeal, looked rather innocuous and transparent. She reminded Amanda of many of the beauties one saw photographed in the gossip magazines: thin, fair, with a studied pallor and a pretty face one would soon forget or confuse with someone else's.

Solange got up and walked towards them, leaving Amanda feeling slightly left out. "Has Jack made an appointment for your next sitting?" she said in a solicitous tone.

"Yes, he has. He's a darling. There is only need for one more sitting and we'll be finished." Mrs Hobdon looked towards Amanda, wondering if she was Jack's next portrait.

Solange, following Caroline's gaze, added quickly, "We are interviewing for someone to help us with our correspondence."

Mrs Hobdon smiled satisfied. When she had been recommended to Jack by a friend, she had been told that not only had he portrayed the new Royal Duchess a few years ago, but also that most of his other clients were celebrities of some kind. Amanda didn't seem to fit into either of these categories. When Mrs Hobdon had left after having been escorted to the door, Jack joined them and sat beside his wife.

"I gather from Solange you know the Peacrofts." He smiled.

"I was just explaining…"

"Amanda met the Peacrofts recently through a mutual friend," Solange interrupted.

Faced by the well-groomed couple Amanda felt once more scruffy and ill at ease. She pulled her skirt down. As though sensing her unease, Jack got up and said brightly, "Come, let me show you the studio."

He took her by the arm and ushered her protectively towards the corridor in the same disarming manner he had done with Mrs Hobdon. Amanda felt herself relax walking beside him as they made their way to the studio.

"Here we are." He opened a door at the end of the long corridor. "After you."

"What a lovely room." Amanda looked up at the large skylight from where the sun was pouring in.

"I suppose it is." Jack gave her a smile.

The room smelt of turpentine and paints, but looked remarkably tidy, not at all like the messy art studios Amanda had seen when collecting Kate from her art A level lessons. A large library of neatly stacked tapes stood on a shelf by the south-facing windows and Mozart's violin concerto still poured out of the loudspeakers. A large easel with a half-finished portrait of Mrs Hobdon dominated the room. Amanda circled round it at a respectful distance.

"It still needs a lot of work done on it," said Jack.

"Solange was telling me about your technique."

"Ah, one has to adapt to suit one's clients." He sighed.

"It must be difficult to work to a deadline when one is being creative."

"It is, but at the same time it's stimulating to know someone is waiting for one's creation."

Amanda looked round the sunny music-filled room with its pungent smells and wondered if her life would have been any different if she had been born with a talent.

"Solange will join us in a minute. She must have gone to make some coffee." Jack sat on a dark green sofa at the far end of the studio.

"Tell me," he said, patting lightly the cushion beside him, "how is Penny Peacroft. I haven't seen her for years. Not since my mother died. Is Hugo still flying all over the world on business or is he finally enjoying his millions?"

"I got the impression he had retired, but I'm afraid I only met them briefly at a dinner party and when they heard I had experience in advertising and was looking for a job, they suggested I approach you."

"Is your husband involved in the same business as Hugo?"

"No." Amanda hesitated, wondering if she should tell him she had no husband. "Perhaps I should mention," she said, looking at her feet, "that I'm on my own. We are separated."

"Have you always worked in advertising?" Jack asked casually.

"No, well... Yes, I did." She felt herself blush. "Before we married, but that was a long time ago. My secretarial skills were quite good then and when Penny mentioned you were looking for someone reliable..."

"We are. Did she also mention we needed someone to concentrate on our contacts?"

Solange had joined them holding a tray.

"No. She just mentioned general PA duties. I'm sorry I hadn't realised you needed help with PR."

"Oh," said Solange, the disappointment showing on her face.

"Penny was quite right to suggest you get in touch with us." Jack got up and relieved his wife of the tray. "The most important thing for us is to find someone reliable and dependable, which I'm sure you are," he said, dropping his voice.

"Coffee?" Solange was leaning over the tray Jack had placed on a low table by the sofa.

"Yes, please."

"The trouble is…" said Jack.

"Sugar?" Solange handed her a cup. "Sorry, *chéri*." She smiled coyly at her husband.

"The trouble is," Jack continued, "we, too, have been affected by the recession, and the commissions I get now are few and far between. That's why we are really looking for someone who can help with our contacts. Word of mouth is not enough in these hard times."

"I don't have any PR experience," said Amanda, feeling her confidence plummet.

"Perhaps you know a lot of people who need their portrait painted." Solange looked at Amanda hopefully.

"To be honest, I'm afraid I don't," said Amanda. "Douglas would have been more likely to know. He was always talking of boardroom portraits he did or did not like."

"Oh! But we really do need someone who can help us with our contacts, *chéri*." Solange looked at her husband with a sullen expression. Amanda felt uncomfortable. There was nothing else she could say to give the impression she might be suitable for the job. As she was wondering whether she shouldn't make some excuse about another appointment and prepare to leave, Jack, in a tone as disarming as when he had greeted her said, "We might need someone later on if things pick up to help with the correspondence and, if you are still available, we would love to be able to get in touch with you."

"Yes, of course. You must give us your telephone number," said Solange, too eagerly to sound sincere. They exchanged pleasantries while Amanda drank her coffee hurriedly, aware the interview was over.

Out in the street Amanda walked towards the park. She felt discouraged. The mood induced by failing to get the job hung over her like a heavy mist, and it was not until she had crossed the park, as far as the Serpentine, that she was able to think rationally about the interview. Jack and Solange had been charming and, despite the shortcomings in her appearance, had made her feel welcome. They were obviously looking for someone with connections. She wondered if the interview would have been any more successful if she had mentioned more of Douglas's business contacts. Being without a husband clearly put one at a social disadvantage. She had a lot to learn. Finding a job was not going to be easy. The first thing she would have to do would be to make an effort with her appearance. People in the real world didn't go to interviews dressed like a Putney housewife. She would also have to do something about her confidence. Blushing and stammering would have to stop. 'And my age?' she asked herself as she walked away from the Serpentine. Over thirty was old nowadays. Would a visit to the hairdresser help her to look younger. Was thirty-nine really that old?

★

From the large windows of her reception room Solange watched Amanda cross the road towards the park. She could tell by the way she held herself that she was disheartened by the outcome of their meeting. For a moment she felt sorry for her, but the feeling didn't last. Instead, Solange compared her fate with Amanda's and congratulated herself on not having to go to job interviews any more. Solange had met Jack in the Seventies when she had been a ground hostess for Air France. Jack, an aspiring portrait painter, had come in to negotiate with the airline about how he could best transport one of his large canvases to Paris where he had just received a commission. Solange had immediately been attracted by his good looks and apparently exciting way of life. Solange came from Montpellier where her parents owned a small grocery shop. She had spent a year in Paris before being transferred to London where she immediately fell in love with the city and what it had to offer. Being French in England, she soon found out, gave her immediate glamour. After a few months, she even found herself telling everyone, including her French girlfriends, that she was a Parisian and had been born and brought up in the capital. Her family had a summer retreat near Montpellier where her parents were now retired. Solange liked this new image of herself and had almost started to believe it. The Parisian accent she had acquired in her year in Paris, she had accentuated, knowing the people in the circles she now moved in could tell the difference.

After a short courtship with Jack, she had moved into his Islington studio and soon started to put all her energies into furthering his career. She had soon realised that the secret of success was for them to move in the right circles, for then the right commissions would follow. She sensed her French accent and looks, together with Jack's bohemian good breeding, were assets. They were an amusing and attractive couple and made an agreeable impression at any gathering. Jack's skills as a portrait painter were poor, but Solange had observed that once you became fashionable, everyone wanted to use you regardless of your skills. She soon found, however, a skilled Romanian painter without a work permit who lived off the Portobello Road and asked him to help Jack. This, of course, was never mentioned to the clients who liked to believe that the handsome, up-and-coming artist was the sole executor of the work.

Jack, the third son of a retired colonel, had been brought up in a sleepy Dorset village. His older brothers at the age of thirteen had been sent to one of the best boarding schools in England. Jack, who suffered from dyslexia, failed his common entrance exam and ended up taking his O levels at the local school. Not being able to compete with his brothers, he tried to excel in art, a subject for which neither of them had shown any inclination. Having found his own niche gave him some confidence. Here he was able to perform better than in more academic subjects, but still he was not particularly talented. He managed to get accepted into art college and moved to London where he led a far more interesting life than his brothers now at university. When he met Solange he had just been given his second important commission that had come through friends of his parents. He recognised in Solange someone who was determined enough to help him. Once she had moved into his Islington studio and into his life, his career took off. She made sure they were seen at all the right parties of the younger society set and managed to get themselves invited to the smartest events. Gate-crashing parties, private views and restaurant openings was soon not necessary. As the affluent Eighties arrived, their enlarged social circle made sure they were asked to all the right places.

Solange left Air France and dedicated her time to procuring clients for Jack, entertaining their new acquaintances and making sure their social calendar never wavered. Jack became popular amongst the mothers of young debutantes who wanted portraits of their daughters. Thanks to Solange's relentless work, Jack also began to be known amongst the European set of London society. Jack and Solange's relationship was turbulent but at the same time successful. She had given him the self-importance he had always yearned for, and Jack had given her the opportunity to climb the social ladder.

★

Back home, Amanda hurriedly took her coat off and dropped it on a chair. It was nearly eight o'clock. She thought with annoyance of the thirty minutes she had wasted stuck in traffic on Putney Bridge. It was Friday and the children normally were home by six.

As she put her umbrella in a corner, she smelt the aroma of roast chicken. They were home! At least Kate was and she had forgotten, as usual, to put the extractor on. Why bother with the extractor! It was nice to have them home and kind of Kate to have taken over preparing supper.

"Hello. What a delicious smell." She smiled at her children sitting round the kitchen table. They both looked at her, and there was what seemed to Amanda a conspiratorial silence. She stood by the cooker where Kate was busying herself with the vegetables.

"Thank you, darling. I got delayed. Friday traffic."

"Mark was starving. There was nothing in the fridge. So I had to defrost some chicken in the micro." Kate looked round with a martyred expression.

"I hadn't realised it would take quite so long and thought I would have time to shop."

"And what took so long?" There was a hint of sarcasm in Kate's voice.

"I went to see a friend of the Peacrofts who I thought might give me a job and then went to the park."

"The park! It's freezing and nearly eight o'clock." Kate added some salt to the boiling water.

"What's this, the Spanish Inquisition?" said Amanda. It was ridiculous to have to make excuses to her own children.

"You could have rung and then we'd have known." Mark looked at her and then lowered his eyes. Amanda looked at her son's bowed head, uncertain of whose side he was on.

"This is the most ridiculous conversation. What would happen if I worked till late or if I went to night school?"

"But you don't." Kate's voice was flat.

"Mark, could you please help your sister by laying the table," said Amanda trying to change the subject.

"By the way," said Kate looking at her brother with the corner of her eye, "Dad rang." She paused and looked at her mother intently.

Amanda, aware her daughter was waiting for a reaction, tried not to show her surprise.

"He's taking us out for supper tomorrow evening with his girlfriend. He's booked a table at a restaurant in Chelsea and is picking us up at about eight. Will you be here?"

"No, I don't think so. I promised Julia I would pop in for a drink," Amanda lied.

Looking at both her children sitting at the table in front of their unfinished meals, she panicked. What if they left her too? What if they substituted Claire for her, as Douglas had. She wanted to throw her arms round them and say "I love you. Please don't leave me", but she knew any display of emotions at this stage would disturb them.

She turned towards the cooker and, while helping herself to some vegetables, said with all the composure she could muster, "How do you feel about it?"

"It'll be nice to see Dad," said Kate. "We're going to Giorgio's! I've always wanted to eat there. Two of my friends at Bristol have been and say it's great."

Amanda's heart sank. Douglas was luring them with smart restaurants. Maybe Claire was fun to be with. She must pull herself together, find a job, make a life for herself, let the children see she was not a failure.

★

Douglas let himself into the small flat he now shared with Claire off the Gloucester Road. The sitting room floor was covered with discarded shopping bags and the coffee table that dominated the room was full of magazines, video tapes and bottles of nail varnish. Douglas made an effort not to point out to Claire she was untidy, telling himself that this was only a phase. The flat was small and naturally Claire preferred to do her nails, and sometimes even put her make-up on, in the largest room in the flat rather than in their tiny bedroom at the back.

"Claire, darling, I'm back," he called, making room for his briefcase on the cluttered table.

In the small kitchen he poured himself a drink and looked at his watch. There was no time to change before collecting Mark and Kate from Putney. He would ask Claire to meet them at the restaurant. Claire would like Giorgio's. It was one of the "in" restaurants of the moment. Douglas had only spoken to the children on the telephone since he had left. It would be easier if they shared the car journey just with him. It would give him a chance to explain about Claire.

Claire walked into the kitchen. She was wearing a black miniskirt and a tight Lycra top that accentuated her figure. Claire had a small frame but her hips and breasts were full and rounded. Looking at her figure Douglas forgot about the untidiness.

"What time have you booked the restaurant for?" she asked nonchalantly, taking a sip from his glass.

He frowned. How could she be so insensitive? "For eight-thirty. I'd better leave in five minutes. It's murder crossing the bridge at this time, so I'd better allow plenty of time. You can take a taxi to the restaurant when you are ready."

"But I am ready. I thought we were going to pick them up together."

"It would be nice, but maybe not tonight, not the first time. Once they've met you it will be different."

"You mean you need the car journey to brief them," she said defensively, lighting a cigarette. Douglas refrained from rubbing his nose. He didn't smoke and the smell of tobacco bothered him but he never mentioned it to Claire.

"Darling." He came forward and kissed her neck. "Please understand. I haven't seen them since I left home. I need the car journey to break the ice."

"Okay, then. But promise not to tell them what I'm like. I want them to form their own opinions."

"Promise. Don't worry." He nuzzled her ear. "They'll love you. Who wouldn't?" He let his hand fall on her hip. "You're getting me excited. I'd better be off. I'll meet you there in about an hour. It should give you plenty of time to change and get a taxi."

"Change! I said I was ready. Why should I change? This is perfectly adequate for a smart restaurant once I've put on some jewellery and make-up."

Douglas looked at her Lycra top and tight skirt. "Oh, I know it is and you look gorgeous. It's just that... well, the children..."

"The children! They're not children. This is how I normally dress to go out. You've never objected before. They'll like me as I am. I'm sure Kate'll be dressed like this too."

"Precisely."

"It never bothered you before, my looking like your daughter," she said tartly.

"Oh, darling! Please let's not argue. We're both nervous. I was just trying to be helpful," said Douglas appealingly.

"We bought this top together in Bath, remember? When we spent that weekend in Somerset. It wasn't exactly cheap. You liked it then."

"Darling, please! This is a difficult evening for me."

Claire pouted and stubbed out her cigarette.

"I'd better be going. Here's some money for the taxi." Douglas opened his wallet and gave her a fifty pound note. He never asked Claire for the change when he gave her pocket money. Although Claire worked, she hardly contributed towards their living expenses. Douglas enjoyed spoiling her with money. He unconsciously felt that this gave him some control over their relationship.

★

When Douglas arrived in Putney and parked the car outside the house, he saw Kate looking out of the drawing room window. He felt relieved he wouldn't have to get out of the car and ring the bell. Instead, he turned the engine off and waited for the children to come out. Kate came out first wearing a black miniskirt not unlike the one Claire had been wearing. Douglas noticed she also seemed to be wearing a lot of make-up.

"Hi, Dad," she said matter-of-factly, as though she had seen him that morning. Douglas got out of the car and kissed his daughter on the cheek. He had always had a weak spot for Kate and was grateful she was making their first meeting easy for him. He had talked to her at length on the telephone and explained he was now living with someone else, so there was no need for too many explanations.

Douglas heard the front door close with a slam and looked towards the house. Mark was making his way towards them and was looking at the ground as he walked. His son's sulky expression reminded him why he had always felt more at ease with his daughter.

"Hello, Mark," he said patting his son's shoulder.

"Hi," ventured Mark, taking a step back.

They crossed Putney Bridge in silence, Kate looking very grown up sitting beside Douglas and Mark slumped in the back seat.

"Mum's gone to Julia's for a drink," said Mark flatly.

"To a drinks party!" said Kate, turning round and giving her brother a nasty look.

How stupid of Mark not to realise she was trying to make her father jealous by saying their mother was out at a party. But then, what could one expect from someone whose main interests in life were cricket and computer games.

"Claire's meeting us at the restaurant," said Douglas tentatively.

There was a silence.

"A friend of mine at Bristol said it's a great restaurant. Her parents took her for her birthday," she said pointedly.

"Claire suggested it. She thought you might enjoy it."

"Do you live near the restaurant?" asked Kate, wondering what it would be like to have a *pied à terre* just off the King's Road.

"Not very far. We're just off the Gloucester Road at the moment. The flat's very small, but when we get something bigger..." He stopped, wondering if he shouldn't discuss it with Claire before having the children round. It would be easier to assess things after tonight. He looked in his mirror at Mark's sullen expression and told himself that the best place for them at the moment was obviously school and in the company of their own friends.

When they walked into the restaurant Claire was already there. Douglas noticed the bottle of champagne in its ice bucket by the side of the table and wondered if Claire hadn't overdone the welcome. To his great relief he noticed she had changed her Lycra top for a plain white shirt.

When Claire saw them she stood up and waved. Kate, who had been walking in front of her father, stopped and adjusted her hair and, with what seemed to Douglas a forced smile, asked:

"Is that Claire?"

"Yes, darling. Come, let me introduce you."

"You must be Kate," said Claire in a loud voice and leant over to kiss her on the cheek. Kate stiffened.

Douglas was very conscious of the age difference between him and Claire, but it was only when he saw them together that he became truly aware how close Kate looked in age to Claire. He now wished Claire had dressed even more conservatively and that his daughter hadn't gone out of her way to look grown up.

Mark stood behind his sister, his sullen expression a deterrent to any form of effusive welcome.

"I'm Mark," he said gruffly, stretching out a hand.

"I got ourselves some bubbly. Thought it called for a bit of a celebration," Claire said, touching Douglas's arm.

Kate looked at Claire's youthful face and figure and then at her father and felt disgusted. She had expected Claire to be younger than her mother but it was a shock to find her only marginally older than herself. Surely, she thought, giving Claire a hostile look, her father wouldn't expect her to treat Claire like an adult or listen to her advice.

Douglas, who had noticed his daughter's tense expression, started to pour the champagne hoping that it would diffuse her mood.

"Not for me," said Mark, putting his hand on top of his glass. "I'll have a beer if it's allowed."

"Of course it is." Claire waved to a waiter. "Anything is allowed tonight."

Before taking a sip of her champagne, Claire raised her glass and said, "Well, cheers. Here we all are."

Kate didn't answer and lit a cigarette. She inhaled deeply and let the smoke out slowly and provocatively through her half-closed mouth, tilting her head backwards. Douglas, who had never allowed the children to smoke at home nor in his presence, had to refrain from saying anything.

"How long have you been at Bristol?" Claire asked Kate.

"This is my first term. I went up roughly at the same time Dad left home." She met Claire's eyes and took another long drag from her cigarette, this time exhaling the smoke in Douglas's direction.

Claire, at a loss for words, took another sip of champagne and opened the menu, trying not to react to Kate's reply. It was natural, she told herself while she ran through the starters, that Kate should be a bit unfriendly to start with. But if she didn't rise to the provocation and continued being friendly, Kate would soon relax.

"Yummy, they've got escargot, I adore them. Oh, do let's have some." She tugged at Douglas's sleeve. "I can't be the only one smelling of garlic. You'll have to have some too." She leant against him.

Douglas did not reciprocate. He could feel Kate's eyes on him and wished Claire would stop trying so hard. He was grateful she had changed into a demure shirt but it was painfully obvious, now that his girlfriend was sitting beside his daughter, that it would take more than a change of clothes to get Kate to accept someone so close to her in age.

"I'll have the quail's eggs followed by the lobster," said Kate, choosing the two most expensive things on the menu.

"I'm not hungry," said Mark. He was having to push back the tears as he thought of his mother alone at home pretending she had gone to Julia's.

"Oh, but you must eat something," said Claire, telling herself that boys were always easier to persuade than girls.

"I'm not hungry," Mark echoed with the same flat tone. He met his sister's eyes. She was smiling at him. Kate seldom approved of anything he did and he felt reassured.

"Those are lovely earrings," said Claire, offering Kate a cigarette from her packet.

"Mum gave them to me before I went to Bristol." Kate stubbed out her cigarette, took one from Claire's packet and asked Douglas for a light.

Douglas took a box of matches from the table and obliged unwillingly. The waiter came and took their order. Full of Italian enthusiasm, he tried to persuade Mark to have something to eat. The spaghetti, he assured him, was the best outside of Italy. Mark, underneath his anger towards his father, his mistrust for Claire and pity for his mother, was hungry and allowed himself to be talked into the spaghetti. Claire ordered another bottle of champagne. Not only had she changed her clothes to please Douglas but she was also going out of her way to be friendly. She felt she deserved to be rewarded.

Douglas made a mental calculation of what the bill might come to. Had it been a mistake getting the children to meet Claire so soon? Perhaps he should have waited until later when they had all grown more accustomed to the changes. But Claire, he remembered, had insisted. She wanted to be taken seriously by his family lest they thought she was just a passing fancy.

When the food arrived, it was a welcome distraction. Kate picked at her starter and lit another cigarette while the others were still eating. Claire, who had gone into raptures about her escargots, was irritating even Douglas, who wished she would be less effusive. While they were having coffee, Kate announced that it would be much easier if she and Mark took a taxi back. "It's really pointless for you to drive all the way to Putney and then back this way. I'm sure you want to go to bed," she had said provocatively. Mark, who hadn't opened his mouth all evening, suppressed a giggle.

Claire downed the rest of the champagne and ordered two packets of Marlboro giving one to Kate. Douglas added the bill and calculated they had just eaten half a week's rent.

In the taxi crossing Putney Bridge Kate asked Mark, "So, what do you think?"

Mark shrugged his shoulders.

"I think she's a cow," said Kate. "If she thinks she is going to win me over with fags, she's wrong."

"Why did you accept them then?" said Mark.

"Dad's paying for them. It's not as though it was a present from her, is it?"

"Do you think Mum will be asleep?" asked Mark looking out of the window. "What shall we tell her if she's up?"

"That Claire's a cow."

Amanda was in her bedroom and heard the children come in. She refrained from getting up to greet them. She would pretend to be asleep. If they saw her they would notice she had been crying. Amanda had left the house at about eight saying she was going to have a drink with Julia. She had even changed and put on some make-up. Mark, she suspected, knew she was pretending. Her son seemed able to see through her and Amanda would often catch him watching her. He was somehow able to read her moods more than Kate. Kate chose not to see what she didn't want to see. It was her way of coping.

Amanda had gone down to the high street and sat at the local wine bar with a salad and a glass of wine before going back home after nine, when she knew there was no danger of meeting Douglas. She had rung Julia and told her about her fears. What if the children took a liking to Claire? What if they left one day and went to live with their father? Julia reassured her this was unlikely because he had never been that close to them. Julia's sound advice had done little to lift her spirits. The thought of her children having supper with Claire and Douglas had made her burst into tears again.

★

On Monday morning Amanda went to the hairdresser in the high street. With a smarter hair-style she might stand a better chance of getting a job. It might be necessary to lie about her age. Only mid-thirties...? Could she pass for mid-thirties with some careful grooming?

At the newsagent's she bought a selection of papers. Under the hair dryer, she circled the advertisements that didn't sound too daunting. Everything in the major papers seemed out of her league. She turned to the local newspapers where, besides the advertisements for experienced masseurs and escorts, she found opportunities for well-dressed and well-spoken receptionists. One of them asked for English as a mother tongue. She realised for the first time that she might be at a small advantage. Amanda smiled at the girl who had put the colour in her hair, in the hope she would come to her rescue. The dryer had made her hot and she was aching to get on with the telephoning. She decided to ring the wine merchant's first and later the firms advertising for receptionists. It was a start and it would give her a rough idea what people expected of her.

Back home, with her hair shaped into a becoming bob, she lit a cigarette and nervously paced the room. She needed to rehearse what she was going to say. She went into the kitchen and plugged in the kettle. The thought of how many coffees she had drunk in her life in order to delay what she had to do, made her pull the plug out from the wall. She didn't need a coffee! Instead she went to the telephone and dialled the number of the wine merchant's. A young girl answered; one could tell by her voice she was young. It had never occurred to Amanda before that one's voice could give away one's age. In an apologetic tone she introduced herself. The girl's friendly manner made her feel at ease, but it soon became apparent to Amanda that she was not the first applicant of the day.

"Can I take your name first?"

"Amanda, Amanda Thompson."

"Have you worked in the wine trade before, Amanda?"

"No. But I have a clean licence and selling experience," she blurted out. Realising she had read the advertisement out aloud, she stopped and waited for the voice to say more.

"And your age, Amanda?"

"Thirty-four." Amanda touched her hair, hoping that the morning visit to the hairdresser had made what she had said nearer to the truth.

"Well, you've obviously had some experience selling and of course the clean licence is a great plus, but you must realise it's a very physical job. You would be selling to the trade and the public from our warehouse and this entails moving heavy boxes."

"Oh, I don't mind. I'm quite used to moving heavy boxes." Amanda thought of the days she went to Sainsbury's and felt pleased that loading and unloading the family shopping had come in useful.

"Wine boxes are very heavy."

Was the voice telling her that perhaps this job was not for her? She felt like asking: "Is it my age? Is it my sex?" Instead she found herself saying:

"Well, thank you for your time."

"It's been a pleasure, Amanda. Another time perhaps."

"Another time perhaps." The girl could have left it at "It's been a pleasure, Amanda." Had the girl meant her not to give up? It sounded as if the job was more suited to someone like Mark. She would keep the advertisement and show it to him. Perhaps he would ring them during the holidays and ask if they still needed someone. Trying not to feel discouraged, Amanda persuaded herself she was looking in the wrong papers and decided to wait for the *Evening Standard*. As she folded the newspaper she noticed the Nick Rubens gossip column. Another government minister had been spotted dancing the night away with a blonde who was not his wife. Amanda wondered if the minister's wife, upon reading the article that morning, would be as devastated as she had been when Douglas had told her there was someone else. Surely, their lives would be shattered on a larger scale. Because of the article, everyone they knew, and millions they didn't, would share in their humiliation.

Amanda's spirits lifted when she opened the *Evening Standard*. There were rows of small print advertisements asking for receptionists or secretaries, and estate agent's looking for sales negotiators. She decided to start ringing the companies looking for receptionists. Her typing skills after so many years were bound to be inadequate.

After an hour of ringing "city companies", "friendly small hotels" and "fashionable salons", her spirits had plummeted. The voices telling her the jobs had already been taken, or that they were looking for someone with more recent experience, were not always as friendly and encouraging as the girl at the wine merchant's. She went to the kitchen and plugged in the kettle. She was aware there was a recession on and her skills might be slightly rusty but could it be possible that no one even wanted to see her, to give her a chance to explain how reliable and hard-working she could turn out to be?

"Rome wasn't built in a day", she muttered as she stirred her sweet coffee. There was something so comforting about sugar. She remembered all the heroines in 1930s films sitting on chintzy beds nibbling chocolates. She took a chocolate-coated digestive biscuit from the tin and persuaded herself that disappointment was bound to burn as many calories as exercise. She would ring the estate agent's. After all, she had done the negotiating and all the organising the two times they had moved house.

The replies from the estate agent's, when she presented herself as an aspiring and reliable receptionist, were discouraging. When she dialled the number on the last advertisement she had circled, she did it more out of frustration than any hope of getting a different response. To her surprise, a voice told her they wanted to see her either that afternoon or the following day. Amanda looked at the paper trying to work out where the company was located. It was in W9. She couldn't envisage where it was, but it didn't sound too far away, so she found herself saying, "Yes, this afternoon will be fine. Is four-thirty any good? I'll be roughly in your area at that time." She had lied again. She had lied about her past experience, about her age, and now about her whereabouts.

★

Amanda left the house dressed in her best day suit, the one she had worn for Mark's speech days for the last two years. She had borrowed Kate's large loop earrings hoping it would give her a more youthful appearance. The suit that had seemed so appropriate for the role of Amanda, the proud parent at Mark's prize-giving day, felt dowdy. As she hurriedly dabbed some scent on her wrists, she wondered why people dressed as "parents" when they went to their children's schools.

Sitting in the car she had borrowed from Julia, Amanda studied the *A to Z* and found the Great Western Road was situated somewhere behind Notting Hill Gate, an area she seldom visited. She drove clumsily, getting in the wrong lane, annoying drivers behind her with her indecisiveness. At the Shepherd's Bush roundabout she nearly drove in a full circle and headed in the wrong direction. Past Notting Hill Tube Station she pulled to one side to consult her map. As she stretched towards the glove compartment, she caught the heel of her shoe on her tights. She could feel the mesh coming undone up her leg. Her skirt was short, and she would look untidy. First impressions were important. She wondered it her legs were tanned enough to get away with not wearing tights, but as she looked out of the window at the autumnal trees, she accepted she would have to sit through the interview with a ladder.

She drove around Notting Hill towards Chepstow Road. The houses were large and handsome with clean early Victorian lines. Some houses had been lovingly restored but others looked run down or derelict. As she tried to picture herself as an estate agent, measuring a flat in one of the houses, she took the wrong turning and had to circle the square with large double-fronted houses. They had clearly been built at the same time as Belgrave Square, but in contrast to their Knightsbridge cousins, had fifteen doorbells at each entrance instead of one.

Amanda parked the car in a narrow street where a group of children played noisily with a ball. She was early and decided to walk down the high street and look for a pair of tights. She turned down Harwood Road where she passed a fishmonger and stopped to look at the variety of fish.

"Can I help you?" A girl in large gumboots and a strong Irish accent called from inside.

"No thank you. I was just having a look. We don't have fishmongers like this any more in Putney."

"Is that a fact? What do you do for fish then?"

"Oh, there is plenty of wet fish in Sainsbury's but it somehow doesn't seem quite the same." Amanda looked at a large crab moving slowly on top of the slabs of ice. "I might get some crab on my way back." She smiled at the girl.

As she walked towards the estate agent's, Amanda reflected on how better equipped this high street was than the one in Putney. If you wanted to sit for a cup of tea you could and the local fishmonger was still in business.

When Amanda saw the bright green sign that read Plaza Estate Agents, her stomach tightened. Inside the reception room, three young men and a girl sat at their desks absorbed in their telephone conversations. Amanda stood by the door waiting for one of them to notice her. A young man in a dark suit finally looked up and smiled at her.

"Can I help you?"

"I have an appointment with Mr de Jersey at four-thirty."

"He's busy with a client. Sit down. I'll let him know you're here."

Amanda looked round the room. The walls were covered in posters, and neglected plants stood in poorly lit corners. The ficus benjamina was crying for some daylight. If she got the job, she would water it and even suggest it be moved nearer the windows. 'If they do give me the job, they will want me to sell flats, not to rescue their house plants. I must give the right impression.'

"Yes sir, that's correct. Indeed, we could get you the keys straight away." The young man was talking enthusiastically to someone on the telephone. He put the phone down and started writing furiously on a piece of paper. He can't be much older than Mark. Amanda tried to envisage her son in a boxy suit, sitting behind a desk.

"I'll tell Mr de Jersey you're here." He got up and walked round the desk.

Amanda found herself taking in his tight bottom and tried to envisage what his legs looked like underneath the baggy trousers. She blushed at the thought.

"Follow me." He stood by a door that led to the back of the building.

The office was small and had a pair of French windows that opened out into an unkempt yard. Had it not been for the large, imposing desk, the impersonal square room could have been described as dingy.

Mr de Jersey was speaking to someone on the telephone. He smiled at Amanda and pointed to a small chair at the other side of the desk. Amanda was grateful that he was busy. It would give her time to compose herself. She sat on the chair and, conscious of the great barrier the desk created between them, felt uneasy. Why did men, even young ones, need all these symbols of power? Men loved titles, medals, commemorations and other personality props such as desks, uniforms, smart briefcases and flashy cars.

Mr de Jersey was looking down at some figures on the desk. Amanda was able to take a good look at him without having to meet his eyes. He was young, younger than she. He was in shirt sleeves and a tie. The sleeves were rolled up to his elbows. She noticed his arms were strong and he looked very fit for someone with an office job. What was wrong with her today? she wondered. Normally she didn't notice men's bodies. Maybe this is what people did in a work environment, she told herself as she took another quick look at Mr de Jersey. This time she found him looking at her and thought she saw amusement in his economical smile. He placed one of his hands over the mouthpiece of the telephone and, leaning slightly forward over the desk, whispered, "I won't be a minute."

Amanda noticed his eyes rested for longer than necessary on her breasts. The lapels of her best day-suit accentuated her generous cleavage. She knew having large breasts was once again a fashionable asset but, self-conscious of her bosom in the small, airless room, wished it didn't rise and fall with every breath she took. She stopped breathing till Mr de Jersey's eyes were back on the piece of paper in front of him, busy looking at the figures. Amanda looked out at the yard. She felt trapped in the small room with its large desk.

"Sorry about all that. Clients always come first. You must be..." he looked at a list on his blotting paper... "Margaret."

"No, I'm Amanda."

"Of course. I'm sorry. I'd quite forgotten the four o'clock cancelled."

Amanda smiled, wondering if she would be remembered as the four-thirty, the one with the big boobs, or by her name.

"So, Amanda, tell me a bit about yourself. What previous experience have you had selling property?"

"I've been abroad for the past few years and haven't worked in London for a while." She felt relieved the moment she was silent again. Lying was such an effort.

"I see. That is a shame. Recent experience is quite important in this business." Mr de Jersey asked lots of other questions and explained a little about the job and its requirements. Amanda suspected he was just being polite. She could tell he had made up his mind not to take her as soon as she had mentioned she hadn't worked for a few years. She was touched by his good manners. It would have been easier for him to say "We were really looking for someone with more experience."

As he talked about the position, Amanda found herself feeling sorry for him. His face was terribly pale. It had that greyish pallor one got through lack of fresh air. He can't have had a very long summer holiday, she thought and wondered what kind of holiday a young man his age would have. She looked towards the French windows where a weak sun shone and felt like telling him to go for a walk while the weather still allowed it.

He followed her gaze. "Not a bad afternoon for the time of year. One could nearly call it an Indian summer." Amanda knew it was time for her to go. He took her telephone number and said he would give her a ring once he had finished interviewing all the other applicants.

"I feel it would be fair to mention that some people I have already interviewed have a lot more experience, though I'm sure you would be very reliable. But... "

Amanda interrupted: "I could soon learn. I really am very interested in the job." Her heart was pounding. There was nothing to lose by saying it, by half-begging to be given a chance to prove herself.

"We'll ring you in a week or so anyway." He was now standing by the door with a slight air of impatience. He had given her his time but now expected her to take the hint. Amanda left the office and walked through the reception area wishing she was invisible. The young man who had taken care of her when she came in, went to open the door for her.

The following morning Amanda went out to buy the papers, determined not to let herself be discouraged by the experience of the previous day. Back at home she sat with the papers at the kitchen table, making neat little crosses beside the advertisements that sounded promising.

By midday she had run out of telephone calls to make. No one had even suggested she came for an interview. Two people had asked her to post her CV, too polite perhaps to tell her she was unsuitable. Others had been more blunt. They were looking for someone with more experience, someone younger or they already had too many applicants. Age discrimination was used ruthlessly, as though people vented their frustration at not being able to discriminate on the basis of sex and race.

Pacing up and down the house, feeling depressed, Amanda remembered her mother. Since her death she thought about her often. Her departure from this world, although they hadn't been that close, had left her feeling lost. She remembered her parents, who had died within a year of each other, with affection, and now regretted she had never understood them better. Her father had been undemonstrative and economical with his affections. Her mother, shy and restrained, suppressed her emotions more out of respect to her father than a natural inclination to refrain. In her quiet way, her mother had always been there for her children, giving them the reassurance of her presence. It had been a quiet, undemanding love, the kind of love one assumes will never end, not turbulent enough to burn itself out. Since she had died, her absence had left a void in Amanda's life. There was no one to turn to now, when in need of comfort.

Amanda wondered if her sister, Pat, missed her as much as she did. On impulse she decided to ring Pat. She was, after all, family, and despite their differences, the only person she sometimes felt she could turn to.

*

When the telephone rang in Pat's kitchen she was adjusting a head scarf to protect her hair from the blustery wind that had been prematurely robbing the Hampshire trees of their dying leaves.

"Amanda, darling, anything wrong?" Pat looked at her watch. Her sister rarely rang before six in the evening when the cheap rates started.

"No, not really. Just ringing for a chat." Amanda wondered if it was obvious from the tone of her voice that something was amiss. Pat, who liked people enough to sense something was wrong, sat on a kitchen chair and accepted she would have to be late for her meeting. Pat was seldom home. She played bridge three times a week, was involved in most of the local charities, and spent a lot of time in her garden. She was always in good cheer, a direct result of rarely doing things she didn't enjoy. This strong sense of self-preservation was not premeditated but came to her quite naturally. She often wondered why her sister had married a man as selfish and self-centred as Douglas, when it was so obvious a man like him would never make her happy. Pat's husband, Tony who ran a successful wine bar in Winchester, never complained if she didn't make it to the supermarket before the weekend, and her children rarely pointed it out when they had been given bangers and mash for supper three nights running. Everyone knew Pat was busy, and they made allowances for her lack of interest in such things as keeping a house spotless or a larder full. But the house always looked welcoming and tidy, providing one didn't open cupboards or look under the beds. It was due to her own contentment that Pat was able to sense discontent in others. She suspected Amanda had rung because she was worried or unhappy, so she tactfully started by inquiring about the children.

"Has Kate settled in at college?"

"She's only just left but seems to enjoy it so far."

"It must get lonely without them now that..." She paused. She had only seen Amanda once since Douglas had walked out and now felt guilty at not having been more supportive.

"I've been trying to get a job," said Amanda, "but it's proving quite difficult. No one wants someone my age with so little experience."

"A job!"

"Pat, I need to get a job, now Douglas has gone. It's not only that I need the money, I can't spend the rest of my life doing nothing and being no one."

"Stop being dramatic. You don't need a job to justify your existence. You should have a hobby, it's just as time consuming! Take my bridge, for example, leaves little time for anything else."

"Pat, I need to earn some money and anyhow I don't know anyone who plays bridge."

"People play bridge all over London. You should try it. It might lead somewhere. You never know you could meet someone who could offer you a job. I'm sure you think the hours I spend playing bridge are wasted, but it's very good for the old memory and I've made many friends round the card table. When I read all those articles in the glossy magazines and Sunday papers about how beneficial counselling is for different problems one has at different stages of life, I always ask myself why people don't take up bridge! Your friends become your counsellors and not only is it cheaper but you also have a good time." Pat looked at the clock over the Aga and saw that it was getting late. She had given her sister a sound bit of advice and felt she couldn't do more.

"Why don't you all come down for Christmas Eve and Christmas Day? You bring something for the twenty-fourth and I'll take care of Christmas lunch," said Pat to appease her niggling conscience.

Pat, reflected Amanda as she put the receiver down, was exasperating in more ways than one, but she always gave just enough so that one couldn't think of her as selfish. Pat gave what a sense of duty told her was required.

Amanda sat pondering on her sister's advice. Pat obviously was not aware how badly she needed the money. She decided to ring Julia.

When the telephone rang in Julia's shop, she was up a ladder rearranging the display of bags and umbrellas that had been delivered that morning.

Her assistant, who was unpacking some earrings on the desk, answered the phone. "It's a Mrs Thompson for you. Shall I tell her you're busy?"

Julia hesitated. "No, tell her I'm coming." Julia clumsily manoeuvred her heavy frame down the steps. Had it been anybody other than Amanda, she would have asked them to ring her back later.

"You just caught me up a ladder rearranging a new delivery of Italian bags," she said panting into the receiver.

"Oh, I'm sorry. I didn't mean to interrupt."

"Well, I'm here now. What can I do for you?" Julia was brisk. She disliked wasting time.

"Julia, I've been looking for a job."

"Well done and about time too. Is that why you borrowed the car yesterday?"

"Yes. I've been trying for days, but no one seems to want to employ a woman my age with little experience. I was wondering if you knew of anyone locally who might take me on as a shop assistant." Amanda paused. "Even on a part-time basis, anything would do to start with."

"I can ask. The boutique across the road was looking for someone a few weeks ago. Mind you, I wonder if it's really suitable. The clothes aren't really up to scratch. We should be able to find you something better."

"I don't really mind. Anything will do."

"As a matter of fact," said Julia, "I've been toying with the idea of opening on Saturday afternoons, particularly now that the Christmas rush is starting. If you are prepared to work weekends, it would be a start for you, and I would be able to find out if it pays for the shop to be open."

"Julia, are you sure you want me?"

"Of course I am or I wouldn't suggest it."

"I'd love to do it. You tell me when and I'll start."

On Friday evening, when Kate walked into the kitchen, Amanda found herself saying triumphantly, "I've got a part-time job."

"Really, how nice! Well done! Pity Dad isn't here to share the good news."

Amanda stirred the soup in silence. Was there a touch of sarcasm in Kate's remark or was it pity? She sometimes wondered who Kate really blamed for Douglas's departure. Did she blame her father or did she blame her? At times Amanda even worried that Kate might be blaming herself.

"So, tell me about the job." Kate took a long gulp of orange juice straight out of the bottle. Amanda refrained from asking her to use a glass. Both children had been told enough times not to drink out of a bottle for it to be stored in their memory banks for life. They would probably stop doing it when she stopped caring about it and the decision became wholly theirs. Ignoring these small annoyances was a beginning. It would be her way of letting go of them.

"It isn't a real part-time job, it's just one afternoon a week."

"Which day of the week is this job for, then?" Kate poured the rest of the orange into a glass and threw the empty bottle in the bin.

"Saturday afternoons. I'll be taking care of Julia's shop."

"Saturday afternoons! Are you joking? That's the weekend."

"I don't mind. I'm so glad to have the opportunity to get some experience, that I wouldn't mind, even if it were on a Sunday."

"What about us? I come up from Bristol two weekends a month and Mark comes home nearly every other weekend now that he's a senior."

"Both of you are normally busy when you come home on weekends. I somehow can't see you missing me for a few hours on Saturday."

"True. But what about all the other things we do together on a Saturday?"

"Such as?" Amanda poured the soup into two bowls.

"Oh, I can't think now. Anyhow, if you've made up your mind, what's the point of talking about it."

Amanda knew the "things" Kate was referring to were their laundry and a fridge stocked up with their favourite foods.

*

Amanda spent the rest of the week looking forward to Saturday when Julia suggested she come to the shop. Every morning she still bought the papers and unsuccessfully tried to find some more work. On Thursday she eventually managed to get an interview with a Mr Stavros, who owned a small lighting company and was looking for a sales assistant. Mr Stavros had propositioned her and, when Amanda had pretended not to notice his advances, he had told her the job perhaps required someone younger with more initiative. In the bus on her way home, she decided that perhaps she ought to take her sister's advice and take up a hobby while she waited for something else to come along. The thought of the long, aimless evenings with no husband at home made the idea of taking up bridge a welcoming escape. Pat rang mid-week to suggest Maria Kovensky, an accomplished Russian bridge teacher. "I gather she's very good and not at all expensive. She lives near South Kensington. I just feel I should warn you she's quite a character and a terrible snob. I'll give you her number. Do ring back and let me know how you get on," Pat added, knowing her sister's reluctance to engage in anything new.

That evening before going to bed Amanda rang Maria Kovensky.

"Hallo." A thick voice, the kind that made one think of long cigarettes, answered the phone.

"Could I speak to Mrs Maria Kovensky?"

"Madam Maria is speaking." The tone was imperial but not unfriendly.

"Mrs Hargreaves gave me your name. Pat Hargreaves?"

"I don't know any Pat Hargreaves. Is she a friend of Virginia Hamilton-Veere?" There was expectation in her voice.

"To be quite honest, I don't know. Mrs Hargreaves is my sister and she suggested I ring you. I'm interested in learning bridge and she mentioned you take beginners."

"Maybe your sister is a friend of Virginia Hamilton-Veere's."

Amanda hesitated. Despite her shortcomings, Pat was not a name dropper and perhaps she knew Virginia Hamilton-Veere.

"So, you would be a beginner," said Maria. "In fact, Virginia Hamilton-Veere is a beginner too. She starts next week with a friend of hers. I also have the famous model, Ingrid Clark, now retired of course, starting the same day. My other lady comes from Richmond."

"Well, it sounds as though you already have enough people for your class." Amanda felt relieved. "Perhaps another time when you have another group of beginners, I'll give you my number."

"No, no, no. You must come. I need five for a beginner's group. People drop out or they don't come because of social engagements. My ladies are very busy ladies. Your name, my dear?"

Amanda suddenly wished she was the Honourable or Dame Amanda Thompson. "Amanda."

"Pretty name. I'll see you next week, my dear. Three o'clock. Kensington Square, number twenty-two." Madam Maria had put the phone down without giving Amanda time to ask how much she charged per lesson. Pat had said not expensive. She hoped the prices hadn't gone up.

*

The following week, with apprehension, Amanda crossed the leafy square that led to Maria's flat. The houses were elegant and tall and their white stucco, newly painted, shone in the low autumnal sun. The elegant Kensington façades made a welcoming change from the heavy, dark-bricked Putney houses. Number twenty-two was a large corner house, with three bells. Amanda pressed gently on the bell labelled "Kovensky". The door opened and Amanda climbed up the stairs to the fourth floor.

Maria, dressed in a red silk shirt with matching lipstick, opened the door before Amanda had time to knock. "Come in, dear." Maria looked at Amanda from head to toe. "You come from Richmond?"

"No. I rang last week. Mrs Hargreaves suggested..." Amanda paused, worried she would be asked again whether she was a friend of somebody.

"Ah, yes. Come in, dear."

Amanda was ushered into a large room overlooking the square. A card table, draped with a velvet cloth and surrounded by elegant balloon-backed chairs, was placed by the large French window. The room had an imperial elegance. Heavy Biedermeier wardrobes that had seen better days dwarfed the otherwise large, airy room. The walls were covered in icons and heavy worn-out tapestries. Tarnished silver objects adorned the tops of desks and tables, and a bad oil painting of a middle-aged man in military clothes hung on top of the unused fireplace. The Napoleonic surroundings and the slightly musty smell made Amanda feel she was somewhere on the Continent.

"This is a lovely room. You have such beautiful things," said Amanda, admiring a wood and glass cabinet full of delicate German china.

"My dear, these are the only things the *barbarians* allowed my parents to take out with them."

Amanda looked at the crude portrait. "Is that your father?"

"No. That is Count Oblensky, my uncle."

The doorbell rang. Maria opened the door and a tall, willowy, blonde woman in a long, beaded skirt of an Indian fabric walked in. She had a tight cashmere sweater tucked into the skirt and long, suede boots. Amanda guessed this was the model.

She was about to introduce herself when the doorbell rang again. Two women wearing nearly identical Chanel suits and sparkling jewellery walked into the room laughing. Amanda knew Virginia Hamilton-Veere and her friend had arrived. She was surprised, after the introductions had been made by an excited Maria, that Virginia Hamilton-Veere had an East Coast American accent.

The doorbell rang again. "I'm so sorry I'm late. I'll never try and get here on the number nine bus again!"

"Bus!" Maria had never heard of her ladies arriving to her lessons by public transport and had clearly been taken aback.

"Yes, the number nine. It seemed the most sensible thing to do from Richmond."

"Oh, dear. I'll give you some water." Maria left for the kitchen.

Amanda looked at the woman who had just arrived. Her height and weight were average, and so was everything else. She was neither good nor bad looking and was dressed in navy from top to toe. The only concession to any other colour was her large, crisp, white shirt collar.

"Thank you." She took the glass of water Maria handed her.

"Look, I'm truly sorry to be late for the first lesson." She looked round the room.

"Don't worry. Virginia has just arrived too," said Maria.

Helen drank her water and took a brand new writing pad from her large, navy blue bag. She then carefully folded the newspaper she had been holding in her left hand and placed it in the middle of the bag, closing it with a crisp click of the clasp.

"I'm ready now." She smiled at Maria, pencil and pad in hand. They sat round the card table, Virginia Hamilton-Veere facing her friend and Helen opposite the ex-model, Ingrid. Maria sat beside Amanda with her back to the window. Virginia and her friend rested their hands on the green baize of the table, allowing their diamonds, bracelets and signet rings to speak for themselves. Helen held a pencil in her hand ready to take notes, while Ingrid fiddled with the beads on her skirt and looked absent-mindedly out of the window. Amanda perched on a stool beside Maria, looked at the small group and wondered why she was there.

"Bridge is a thinking game. You need great concentration." Maria looked in Helen's direction and smiled. "You don't need to take notes now, dear. First, I will explain the small etiquettes of game."

Assuming Maria was referring to her, Helen replied, "I'm in the habit of taking notes. It's the only way I can memorise."

"I see," said Maria disapprovingly, not wanting to make an issue of it in front of Virginia Hamilton-Veere and her friend. "We'll introduce ourselves during the coffee break. But now," she said solemnly, "we'll start with the lesson."

Amanda watched Maria shuffle a pack with all the ease of a vintage card player. First she explained the value of each card. Once this was established, she explained the value of each suit. All of the women except for Virginia's friend and Amanda had played some bridge before.

"You'll all have to excuse me if I'm a bit slow on the uptake. I've never played anything other than dominoes." Amanda said awkwardly.

"We are all beginners. We'll learn together." Maria smiled, recognising the first signs of inadequacy.

As the rudiments of the bidding were explained, Virginia's friend looked very confused. Maria was not at her best with beginners. She was impatient, and her English occasionally caused confusion. It didn't take her long to realise that Virginia had a natural aptitude for cards; she had good concentration and an equally good memory. Helen's learning abilities were average but her resolve and application would get her where she wanted. Ingrid, who was clearly thinking about something else most of the time, had obviously had a few lessons before because, despite looking out of the window, she seemed to understand what was being explained. 'Maybe her husband had given her a few lessons beforehand,' Maria reasoned as she explained the same thing for the third time to Virginia's friend. This lady would definitely find it difficult to learn, Maria told herself. Ever since she had started teaching bridge to make a living, Maria had become skilled at judging the potential of her pupils. She was careful to encourage and give second cups of coffee to those who clearly had difficulties mastering the game. It was her ability to keep her pupils' confidence up that had given her the reputation of being an excellent teacher.

When the coffee and tea were served, Amanda exchanged pleasantries with the others. Virginia and her friend were young grandmothers and shared not only their grandchildren's outings but also a game of tennis once a week.

"Will you have another biscuit, Ingrid? You can afford to with your beautiful slim figure." Maria presented a plate of inviting continental biscuits.

"Thank you. They look delicious." Ingrid took one.

"How lucky you are, Ingrid, to be going to live in the Caribbean. Always sunny. We must turn you into a good bridge player before you go."

"Where in the Caribbean are you going to live?" Amanda asked, relieved that the coffee break was proving to be so long.

"We're not sure yet. My husband has retired... well, better say given up his job, and wants to run a villa or self-catering bungalows on one of the islands."

"How romantic. Leaving everything behind and making a new start on an island," said Helen, who read an average of two romantic novels a week.

"I wish I could think of it as romantic. The idea of living in a hot climate all year round and having to look after total strangers terrifies me."

"But why the bridge?" Virginia's friend was enjoying the gossip, hoping it would last well into the next hour's lesson.

"Dick plays and thinks it might be a useful thing if we both did, so that we can play with our resident guests."

Amanda noticed Maria was not only good at gauging the threshold of her pupils' patience but also their conversation, no doubt aware it was essential for the women to have time to exchange ideas and discuss trivial things. Maria was good at sensing when her pupils might have more pressing problems, such as difficult daughters or visiting mothers-in-law, and allowed them the time to unburden their worries and receive a few encouraging remarks from the rest of the group. However, she had learnt that listening to either marital or financial problems was always a mistake. As riveting as the story might be at the time, she had observed people felt embarrassed by the confidences later. Ingrid, she feared if encouraged, would end up telling them why Dick had given up his job and ask them what should be done about the imminent move to the Caribbean. No one who came to bridge lessons should be asked to give any advice on such major issues. Maria knew the women should learn to look forward to their lessons, because the couple of hours they spent at her flat should be regarded as a pleasant episode in their week, an oasis removed from the rest of their lives.

The second half of the lesson was dedicated to reinforcing the rudiments of bidding and the importance of communicating with one's partner. "I'm terribly sorry," Marjorie, Virginia's friend, sighed. "I don't think I can do this. I simply can't concentrate. I keep on worrying about poor Camilla having to cope with Jamie's measles. I suppose bridge just isn't the right thing for a worrier like me."

"Are you sure you don't want to persevere, honey?" Virginia tried to encourage her friend.

"I simply can't do it. My mind goes blank and my heart isn't in it."

Maria was secretly pleased. She had learnt in her years of teaching that nothing was worse in a small group than one person slowing down the pace.

"I feel I'm letting you all down. I suppose you could find a replacement?" She looked hopefully at Maria.

"Not to worry. So many ladies want to join these classes. We'll find someone else soon. Of course, if you have a friend, it is better." She looked round the table, hoping one of them would have a suggestion.

When the lesson was over, Virginia's friend left quickly, wanting to give the impression she had more pressing things to do than playing cards. Maria handed out neatly typed notes of what had been covered in their first session and urged them all to revise before they met again the following week.

Out in the street by the square they saw a man sitting in a shabby Lancia convertible. "Oh, there's Dick," Ingrid cried. "See you all next week." She ran towards the car, her beaded skirt wrapping itself round her long, booted legs.

Dick was wearing a pair of dark glasses and had the collar of his jacket turned up so it was difficult to see him properly. He never turned round to look at them, nor at Ingrid. There was something about his appearance that told Amanda, even from a distance, that Dick, like his car, was a tribute to better days.

"I'll try the number eleven bus this time. See you all next week." Helen walked resolutely towards the bus stop.

Virginia suddenly remembered she had left her Hermes scarf in Maria's flat. Amanda suspected this was an excuse to have a private chat with Maria about her friend, whose interest in learning bridge she had so clearly misjudged.

★

Amanda crossed the square. There were still enough leaves left on the trees to make one think of the season as autumn. She walked slowly, her face tightening as a cold wind brought more leaves gliding down on to the damp ground. She was feeling tired and slightly disoriented. Entering Maria's world had been like a trip to a foreign country and the contact with the women she had never met before and hearing snippets about their lives had been a novel experience too. Concentrating on the cards and trying to memorise everything Maria had said, had been taxing, but she had for two hours forgotten about her own life and worries. She dragged her feet, allowing the blackened leaves to cling to her shoes, wishing there was somewhere else to go other than to an empty house.

Someone called her name. It was Virginia. She had stopped her car at the end of the square and was waving. When Amanda joined her she asked, "Can I give you a lift?"

"I live in Putney, which is rather out of the way, but thank you for offering."

"I have to collect some fabric for new drapes from the Designer's Guild and then I'm going home for a strong cup of English tea. All that concentrating has left me quite exhausted. Would you like to join me? I live near the King's Road. You could catch a bus or the subway from there."

"Tea sounds wonderful!" Amanda got into the car.

They drove down the leafy Kensington streets across the Boltons and into the King's Road. Amanda noticed the detailed perfection of Virginia's clothes. Her shimmering tights were the right shade of green to complement the olive weave of her Chanel suit, and her expensive shoes were the latest vogue. Looking at Virginia's profile she noticed that her skin was smooth and almost flawless. There were no broken capillaries or deep wrinkles. It was a cared-for indoor face, the kind that made you wonder if she had never had a bad night's sleep or too much gin. But, despite its perfection, Virginia's face had a friendly and eager expression. As Virginia changed gears, Amanda noticed the manicured hands and, without looking at her, remembered the perfect teeth that made her smile so attractive. Amanda ran her hand through her hair wishing she had washed it the night before. Virginia was the kind of woman who made one wish one had gone to the hairdresser's.

As they walked into the Designer's Guild they were greeted by the manager. Amanda wondered if Virginia would mind being seen with a friend who had worn-down loafers and was wearing a bright fuchsia jacket, a colour that had ceased to be fashionable two years ago. When Virginia turned round and introduced her warmly to the manager referring to her as "my girlfriend", Amanda understood that Virginia wasn't threatened or embarrassed by lack of glamour in her female friends. To outshine her, however, might be a mistake.

Virginia's house stood in one of those quiet Chelsea streets that run between the King's Road and the Embankment. It was a tall handsome house with a large drawing room on the first floor, from where one could see the river. The house was spotless and had been as professionally adorned and decorated as its owner. The colours were pale and peaceful. The antique furniture had been restored to such a standard that all traces of any past use had been erased. The rows of books sitting on the study shelves also looked pristine and in remarkably good condition. A few had been left scattered casually on the edge of the shelves. The interior designer had no doubt advised her that a slightly more informal look was appropriate for the library.

When Virginia went into the kitchen to prepare some tea, Amanda walked round the room, looking at the faces smiling at her out of beautifully polished silver and rosewood frames. There were several of Virginia looking younger with two good-looking children beside her. There was one of a serious, slight-looking man who, despite the weak chin and receding hair-line, looked rather distinguished.

"That's Percy," said Virginia, entering the room with a tray laden with fine china cups, a silver teapot and mouth-watering pastries. "Do you take milk?"

"Yes, please." Amanda couldn't resist picking up a frame with a picture of three girls in long graduation robes. "Are you the one in the middle?"

"Sure, that's little me a very long time ago at Smith College in Massachusetts."

Amanda was surprised by this new academic image. "Where did you meet?"

"I was doing a postgraduate course at Cambridge. I met him there. Happy days," she said wistfully. "Those were happy days."

Was she implying that these days were not? Amanda put the frame back on the shelf and sat by the coffee table, from where Virginia was now pouring tea. Virginia's English was nearly faultless; she had dropped Americanisms such as "highway" and "refrigerator", but she had kept a soft and measured East Coast accent that enabled everyone to consider her foreign enough not to be expected wholly to conform. Long country walks and joining Percy for shooting parties, she could still avoid after twenty-five years of marriage by saying playfully, "I'm sorry. I need the sidewalks." However, she did help run the family estate in Dorset with great efficiency. The Hamilton-Veere's also had a house in the South of France that Virginia loved and escaped to whenever she had a chance.

"Do you have kids at home?" Virginia handed Amanda the sugar bowl.

There was nothing easier than asking a woman where her children were, in order to establish at what stage of her life she was.

"No, they are both away except for odd weekends. The eldest has just started university and Mark has gone to boarding school for his A levels." Amanda stirred her tea.

"The bridge will help." Virginia smiled.

"I work on Saturdays and I'm still looking for something part-time during the week," Amanda said, wanting to make it clear that bridge would never be a way of life. Looking at the wealth around her, Amanda guessed that Virginia would never need to do a day's work, but she knew American women were more career-oriented than English ones and somehow hoped Virginia might give her some advice.

"Is your husband away a lot on business?" Virginia poured some milk.

Amanda could tell that Virginia, without sounding too prying, was trying to establish whether she wanted to work because they needed the money or because, with the children gone, she didn't have enough to do.

The phone rang in the study.

"Help yourself to more tea. I'll take the call next door where I have my diary."

While they had been talking, Amanda had noticed a large portrait of Virginia at the far end of the drawing room. She got up and stood in front of it. Virginia looked very regal: family tiara, jewelled hands folded over a full ball gown. The portrait, however, was a good one. Behind the society lady's image that he had been commissioned to portray, the artist had skilfully managed to retain something of Virginia's determined expression.

The door opened and Virginia walked into the room with a worried expression. "Oh, dear me," she sighed as she sat heavily on the sofa. "Our treasurer at the charity is expecting a baby! I'm thrilled for her, of course, but she will be leaving us next week, which is a small disaster. She's terribly efficient. The poor woman had a terrible pregnancy last time and is taking no chances. Can't blame her, but we'll have to find someone to replace her. She types like a demon and is so reliable." Virginia poured herself more tea.

"Could I help? I can type and, since my husband left a month ago, I have been looking for something to do."

"Sure you can, but it's voluntary work, I'm afraid. You'd only get your expenses paid, and the hours are long. Surely you need something more substantial." Virginia looked at Amanda, surprised.

"I need to start somewhere. I've been trying to get a job for weeks now. It isn't easy after so many years. This would be a start. I could help out till she has the baby. It would be a wonderful opportunity for me."

"I can't see why you shouldn't be able to help us out." Virginia gave her an encouraging smile. "I'll give you Lady Ashcombe's telephone number. Have a word with her and say I suggested you got in touch with her to replace Cathy. Say you're a friend of mine."

"I'm so grateful for the opportunity." Amanda blushed. Feeling she might have imposed on Virginia's hospitality and surprised at her own persistence, Amanda changed the subject.

"It's a lovely portrait." She stood up and walked towards the mantelpiece.

"I was hoping my grandchildren would be able to sit for the same artist. He portrayed three generations: my father-in-law, then Percy, and our children, but as perhaps you know, he died last month. Terrible loss. Did you see the obituary in *The Times*?"

"I'm afraid I've hardly read anything other than the vacancies section of the papers for the last two weeks." Amanda thought it better not to pretend she knew who the artist was.

"He was a favourite with the royal family, you know. A great loss. One somehow expected him to be there for another twenty years. I'll have to think of someone else for the grandchildren. Percy is so thrilled our daughter-in-law has produced a son and heir. He'll want a portrait of his first grandson the minute he is old enough to sit still."

Looking at the portrait and listening to Virginia talking about her husband's heritage, Amanda hoped this hadn't been the allure of the man whose photograph she had seen.

"I'll show you the portraits he has done of the children. They're next door in the library. They say the best one is the one he did of my father-in-law in his regimental uniform. That one, of course, is in Dorset in the Hall."

Amanda suddenly thought of Jack. He was quite well known. She would mention him. It would be nice to make an introduction for him.

"Have you heard of Jack Noel?" Amanda's voice was timid.

"Yes. Funnily enough he has just finished a portrait of my god-daughter, a debutante. He seems to be quite a favourite at the moment with the younger set. Do you know his work?"

"In fact, I saw him and his wife at their studio a few weeks ago."

Virginia looked at Amanda with renewed interest.

"Maybe I could try him on the grandchildren. Let me show you the portraits in the study."

After admiring the portraits in the study, Amanda felt it was time to leave. Clutching the card with Lady Ashcombe's telephone number, and after reminding Virginia once more about Jack Noel, she walked out into the dark evening air with renewed confidence.

Chapter Three

On Amanda's first morning as a shopkeeper, Julia came in early to explain how one should deal with credit card payments. She had also hurriedly demonstrated how to wrap purchases that were destined to become presents.

"We are a gift shop. The wrapping is very important, if customers request it. I hope you don't have two left thumbs." She had stared at Amanda's hands with an admonishing expression.

Amanda had watched with relief as Julia clumsily folded a sheet of wrapping paper over a silver picture frame, reassured that her own ability as a packer, if nothing else, would satisfy her boss. Julia's impatient hands had left the square frame looking like an amorphous object strapped together by unnecessarily long strips of sellotape. Before leaving, Julia had given Amanda a list of things to do in case the shop was quiet.

"It normally picks up at lunchtime. Don't look so worried. I'm sure you will cope. If in doubt about anything, just take the customer's telephone number and we can always deal with it later." She hurried out of the shop with her usual urgency.

When Julia was gone, Amanda went round the shop trying to get acquainted with the displays of silver objects, scarves, leather goods and kilim cushions that cramped the room, giving it the appearance of an Aladdin's cave. She looked out of the shop window at the busy high street and felt excited. She had never been responsible for anything other than the house and the children since she had married. Selling a few knick-knacks might not be a great challenge, but it was a start.

Worried she might not hear the front door open while she went down to the stockroom in the basement, Amanda turned off the classical background music Julia had left playing on the tape recorder. Downstairs, unpacking a new delivery of leather-bound diaries and address books, she concentrated on the noises in the shop. In contrast to the sometimes oppressive silence of her house, the shop was full of sounds coming from the high street. She was diverted by the different noises made by cars, lorries and taxis. She could hear footsteps on the small skylight on the pavement, some were heavy and slow, some light and hesitant and others quick and determined. The sounds kept her company and gave her confidence.

When the doorbell rang it startled her. She rushed upstairs and said awkwardly, "Can I help?" to the two women who were now standing in the shop.

A tall, well-groomed woman addressed Amanda. "We're looking for a present for my husband. It's not a big birthday, but still I was hoping to find something special."

"Look at these!" Her friend's voice filled the shop. "Aren't they adorable." She held in her hand a silk tie with small motifs of birds.

"Yes, they are fun, aren't they. We also have them with bears, tortoises and cats," Amanda said feeling helpful.

"You must get one of these even if you buy him something else. You've always called each other 'bird'." The woman holding the tie looked in Amanda's direction and winked.

Feeling included gave Amanda a surge of confidence.

"We have some lovely Italian belts that came in last week and, if you are feeling generous, we also have a small selection of cashmere cardigans for men. The navy blue ones are on special offer." Amanda was amazed she had managed to remember what Julia had told her.

"A cashmere cardigan and a tie would make a lovely birthday present," the friend enthused.

"I always shop with her for company and end up spending a fortune," the tall woman confided in Amanda.

"I'll get one of the cardigans to show you. They are excellent quality. I gave my husband one for Christmas and it was a great success. Have a browse. I won't be a minute." Amanda went down to the stockroom for the cashmeres.

As she went down the stairs she wondered why she had mentioned Douglas. Why had she wanted to mention having a husband? It was true she had given Douglas a cashmere cardigan from Julia's shop two years ago when it had first opened. She remembered saving for it from the housekeeping and economising on her hairdressing allowance. But why had she mentioned it now? Was it all part of her newly acquired salesmanship or a desire to show the women that, like them, she bought presents for a husband.

She found the cardigans behind the door. Julia had obviously not bothered to stack them by sizes. Pulling them hurriedly out of the shelves, she looked for a size forty-six and couldn't find one. Soon they were scattered all over the floor and she began to panic. Her first customer and it was all going wrong. She began to pull them all out of their bags to double-check their sizes. Sitting on the floor, surrounded by unwrapped cashmeres, she finally found one the right size.

The doorbell rang and she rushed upstairs taking two steps at a time. What if the women had left? Or, even worse, taken something with them? Why should they steal anything or leave the shop for that matter? She had only been in the stockroom for a few minutes. But she remembered Julia had talked at length about kleptomania and how it made no race or age distinctions. She disliked mistrusting people and wished Julia had not sown the seeds of suspicion. Upstairs she found the women were still looking at the belts and, to her surprise, found one of her neighbours standing in front of the pine table that doubled as a counter, waiting to be helped.

"Mrs Stewart, how lovely to see you!" Amanda felt herself blush. Since Douglas had left she found it awkward meeting with neighbours.

"I met Geraldine Blackstone at the grocer's yesterday and she mentioned you would be working in Julia's shop. I'm visiting my sister next weekend and need to take a present. Rather than going to one of the stores, I thought I'd come and support you. You poor thing! It can't be easy for you."

Amanda looked in the direction of the two women, hoping they weren't listening.

"What do you think your sister would like as a present?" Amanda was eager to change the subject.

"No idea. I'll have a browse and see what you've got. But first, I'd like you to know that if you ever need anything you can feel free to call. I know what it's like to be alone. I've been widowed for years."

The two women turned, looked in Mrs Stewart's direction and then looked at each other.

"In my day one could expect more loyalty from men." Mrs Stewart continued, oblivious of their looks. "Family values were different. Chaps got killed in service but they didn't walk out on their wives and children." Her voice filled the shop.

Amanda knew there was little she could do now to stop her neighbour's small speech. She looked in the direction of the women. They were still looking at the belts but Amanda knew they were also riveted by the tale of her misfortune.

"...Mind you," continued Mrs Stewart, "it could just be a mid-life crisis. They say men get them too. They never did in my day, but then everything has changed."

Amanda's face flushed with embarrassment and she wished Mrs Stewart would notice and stop talking. With all the composure she could muster, she said, "Do you think your sister might like a flower pot? We have some beautiful hand-painted ones that come in three different colours. Let me show you."

"What a good idea! She loves her plants, more than her children, I sometimes suspect."

"Have a look by the front door. We have two of them displayed. They also come in red," said Amanda.

The women walked towards Amanda, holding a tie and a belt.

"Would you like to see the cardigans?" Amanda avoided their eyes, all her confidence gone.

"Could we exchange it if it doesn't fit? Hugo is a forty-six but one never knows till one tries things on."

"Of course you can, providing it's the same colour. Remember the blue ones are on special offer. This particular make is quite generous in size. Douglas is a forty-six and I remember getting him a forty-four." Amanda took a deep breath and met the women's eyes. She felt better the minute she had said it. She was not a widow. Douglas had left her but he was still alive and wore a forty-six size jumper. She wrapped the cardigan in the shiny, red paper Julia kept for presents and attached a festive bow.

"Doesn't that look lovely?" The tall woman looked at the wrapping and then smiled at Amanda. Her smile was full of sympathy. When they were gone she turned towards Mrs Stewart, who was looking at the selection of silver frames displayed on a small table.

"Found anything suitable?"

"I can't make up my mind whether I should give her the pot you suggested or a picture frame."

"If she loves plants, the pot might be a better present."

"You're right. I'll take the green pot."

"Shall I wrap it as a present? There's no extra charge."

"Oh, yes please. I'm a clumsy wrapper and..." she paused, looking round the shop, "don't forget what I said about calling." She watched Amanda while she folded the red wrapping paper.

"Thank you. That's so kind of you, Mrs Stewart, but I'm really quite busy nowadays one way or another."

"Good. It's good to be busy, make them see they are not the only thing in one's life. He might come back, you know. It does happen," she half whispered.

Amanda looked at her. "I don't think he will and, if he did, I'm not sure I would want him back."

Mrs Stewart looked shocked. "How are the children?"

"Fine. We are all fine," said Amanda firmly as she secured the bow.

Her irritation was wasted on Mrs Stewart who sighed and added, "That's men for you."

When Mrs Stewart had gone, Amanda busied herself in the stockroom. The thought of Geraldine Blackstone and Hilda Stewart discussing her misfortunes and her future, at the grocer's, filled her with anger. But why shouldn't they? All she had been to the neighbourhood to this day was Douglas's wife or Kate and Mark's mother.

*

As Julia had predicted, the afternoon in the shop was busy. Amanda spent her time serving customers and wrapping their purchases. Whenever there was a quiet moment she returned to the stockroom to unpack the delivery of leather goods. She reflected on how much easier it was to look at her life objectively from under the umbrella of shopkeeper. Her fears since Douglas had left didn't only stem from the fact she was unloved and unable to love in return but also from her shattered identity. Douglas's wife no longer, who should she be? A shopkeeper was better than nothing. Anything felt better than being just a piece of a broken pattern.

Later, when Amanda was wrapping a china cat, a customer handed her an umbrella.

"Someone must have left this behind. It was in that corner by the flower pots."

Amanda immediately recognised Mrs Stewart's umbrella.

"Thank you very much. Fortunately I can remember exactly who left it behind. A neighbour in fact. I'll drop it in on my way home." She smiled at the customer.

She was glad the umbrella would give her an excuse to see Mrs Stewart again. She felt she had been short with her when she had inquired after the children. Hilda might be a nosy old thing but she meant well.

At six o'clock, as Amanda was about to turn the lights off, the front door opened. She was ready to welcome a new customer and say she was in no rush to go home, when she saw it was Kate.

"Hi Mum. How has it been? Have you sold much?" Kate stood firmly in her Doc Martin shoes on the front door mat.

"Do shut the door, darling, or the bell will keep on ringing."

"Dad's coming. He's just parking the car. We've been shopping. He got me a second-hand word processor to take to Bristol." Kate spoke hurriedly, wanting to get it all in before Douglas appeared.

Amanda heard herself saying, "How nice." She hadn't seen Douglas since he had walked out. She felt Kate watching her closely, wanting to see her reaction. Guessing her daughter had carefully planned bringing her father into the shop, she tried to hide her anxiety. Douglas walked in and automatically closed the door behind him. The bell stopped ringing to Amanda's relief.

"Julia isn't in," she said in the form of a greeting.

"The shop looks very nice." Douglas looked round him, clearly uncomfortable.

"There are always lots of new things being delivered. Julia has a good eye for buying." Amanda was relieved she could talk about the shop.

"Kate tells me you're only here on Saturdays but that you are trying for something else during the week."

"Yes, I am. But it isn't easy."

"I suppose not. Your typing skills must be rusty by now." He avoided her eyes and looked at the display of picture frames. "They have good refresher courses nowadays," he added.

"I'm not looking for secretarial work," she said defensively. How dare he send her back to school now that he needed her skills as a wife no longer.

"Oh, I see. What are you looking for?"

"Something I can build on."

"I'm afraid one can't be too fussy these days." With his hands in the pockets of his navy blue overcoat he looked down at the floor.

"Amanda, I really think you should..." He was interrupted by the front door opening. Mrs Stewart walked in. When she saw Douglas she looked taken aback.

"Mrs Stewart, how lovely to see you." Douglas was suddenly all charm.

Before Mrs Stewart could start acting as a marriage counsellor, Amanda rushed forward and said, "Here's your umbrella. I was going to drop it on my way home." Reminded why she had come into the shop, she thanked Amanda and, after telling Kate how much she had grown, picked up her umbrella and prepared to leave. Amanda saw her to the door. Mrs Stewart gave her a knowing look which she pretended not to notice.

"Silly old boot. I haven't grown a single inch for the last four years," said Kate as soon as she was out of earshot.

"She was only trying to be friendly." Douglas thumbed for his keys in his coat pocket. He looked at Kate. "We'd better be going. Good luck with your job hunting," he said uneasily without looking at Amanda. "I hope you find something soon." He put his arm round Kate and ushered her out of the shop.

As she locked up, Amanda watched them get into the car. She felt in no state to greet any more customers and put the closed sign up on the door. She went downstairs into the stockroom where, clutching one of Julia's Italian bags, she burst into tears. She tried to reconstruct the encounter in the shop, hoping, that if she dwelt on it for long enough, she would find some overlooked expression that might tell her something new about Douglas. He had looked exactly the same. But then why should he have changed? Just because her life had been turned upside down and she no longer knew who she was didn't mean he should be any different or feel any differently. He had probably stopped loving her long before he had left. He had, in fact, left her long before the day he had walked out of her life.

*

On Monday morning Amanda took the bus to the Cancer Research Centre where the charity Care Campaign had an office. She was directed through a large Victorian hospital to a small alley at the back where a square, grey, Sixties-style building, resembling a concrete and glass box had been erected in what once must have been a garden. When Amanda pulled at the door after reading the sign that read "push" she knew she was in a state of anxiety. At reception she asked for Lady Ashcombe and was directed to a small office at the bottom of the corridor.

"She won't be long. She normally gets here by ten." The receptionist tried to smile while taking a call. Amanda stood in the room that obviously doubled as a storeroom judging by the boxes labelled "Care Campaign London". A table with two chairs took most of what was left of the floor space and a fluorescent neon strip illuminated the room. She sat on one of the chairs and waited anxiously. Although this was not strictly a job interview as the work was voluntary, she still worried about being rejected. She might be labelled too old or too inexperienced to help. Meeting Douglas on Saturday at the shop had left her drained of confidence.

After waiting for ten minutes the door opened and a smart middle-aged woman walked in bringing with her the smell of fresh air. Amanda, who had so far been interviewed by people either younger than herself or male, felt herself relax a little.

"I sometimes wish I had a helicopter and could just drop myself into London. The traffic is a nightmare." Lady

Ashcombe smiled at her as she unbuttoned her overcoat. "Did you have far to travel?"

Amanda wondered if this was the first question of the interview. How long it took one to get into work must be important.

"I live in Putney." Amanda's voice trailed as she wondered if this would be considered too far.

"You are lucky. On Mondays and Fridays I commute from Worcestershire and the rest of the week from Smith Square, which is convenient for John for the *House*, but ghastly otherwise. The Embankment is always jammed. Silly isn't it, with life so short, that a simple exercise like getting home should be a source of anxiety."

Amanda looked up at Lady Ashcombe and smiled with relief. Despite her rather grand manner, Lady Ashcombe was friendly and informal.

"Coffee?" Belinda looked behind the door up the corridor. "Being part of the hospital, tea and coffee are always available. Someone will be round soon." She sat on the chair opposite Amanda. "Difficult to get started without coffee. Now," she gave a deep sigh, "you must be Amanda. Virginia mentioned that you might help us with some typing."

The door opened and a woman with a determined stride walked in.

"Lady Ashcombe, thank goodness you're here. We're having all sorts of problems with the arrangements for the bridge lunch in St John's Wood." She paused and looked at Amanda.

"Lydia, let me introduce Amanda, a friend of Virginia Hamilton-Veere's. I haven't had a chance to talk to her but we hope she might be helping us with some typing."

Lydia looked down at Amanda suspiciously and, after giving her a dismissive smile, said to Belinda, "When you are free, could we have a few minutes?" She fiddled impatiently with a dog's lead she held in her hand.

"I'm here all morning. As soon as I'm finished with Amanda I'll come and find you. Oh, Lydia, if you see Clara at reception, could you be awfully kind and ask her for two coffees?" Lydia looked at Amanda with a reproachful expression before turning towards Lady Ashcombe with her best smile. The role of tea lady was obviously not the one for which Lydia had joined the charity. As though reading her thoughts, Belinda Ashcombe waited for Lydia to leave the room and said, "Lydia has been with us for a long time and has fixed ideas on how things should be run." She laughed. "But she's a tower of strength – an indefatigable worker.

"Now," Lady Ashcombe gave another sigh, "Virginia tells me you play bridge together and that you might have some spare time to give to Care Campaign."

Amanda found herself explaining for the first time at an interview why she really needed to work.

"I work for a friend only once a week and I'm hoping I will find some more work. It isn't easy after all these years of being just a mother."

Belinda's sympathetic smile encouraged her to continue.

"I'd love to be a part of Care Campaign and feel useful. At the moment I've too much time on my hands." Amanda paused.

"Can you type?"

"Yes. I haven't done it for a while but I used to be quite competent when I was younger."

"You don't look as if you're over the hill yet and one doesn't forget typing skills. Would you be able to come in twice a week and occasionally three if we have a crisis?"

"I'd love to. The children are away most of the time and with no Douglas…"

"Splendid! Could you start next week?"

"Yes!"

Amanda looked round the cluttered office wondering how it would feel to belong there.

"Lydia is organising a couple of bridge lunches at the moment to raise money for a dialysis machine, one in London and one in Hampshire. She seems to be having problems with the London venue. We never do terribly well out of it, but it's become a kind of tradition. Perhaps you could give them a hand with the organising. It would be a good way for you to meet some of the others. As for myself," she added brightly, "I'm going to use you for all my correspondence on Monday mornings, if that is a good day for you."

"Mondays are fine." Amanda thought with expectation about how nice it would be for the days of her week to have a structure again. Since Douglas had left, the days merged into each other leaving behind few memories.

"Let me take you to our other little office down the corridor and introduce you to some of the team." She stood up. "We never got that coffee. Clara must be busy."

Amanda followed Belinda down the long corridor. The shiny, freshly washed linoleum floors smelt of disinfectant. She inhaled the medicated air and felt excited. Lady Ashcombe had not judged her too old or too inexperienced to be useful to Care Campaign. Age and inexperience were a contradiction, but they seemed to have been the main reasons for her failure to find a job so far. Without knocking, Belinda opened one of the doors. Amanda hesitantly followed her. Inside the room, only marginally larger than the one used by Lady Ashcombe, three women sat round a table scattered with papers. Two of them looked up and smiled in their direction, the third one had her back to the door. Amanda recognised Lydia's red jerseyed back and the dog lead hanging from her chair.

"Good morning. Let me introduce Amanda who will be joining us on Monday," said Belinda cheerfully, while Amanda smiled self-consciously.

"Lady Ashcombe, I'm so sorry you never got that coffee. I couldn't find Clara anywhere. She must be having a coffee break herself," Lydia said without turning round.

"Thank you for trying. I'm sure she will reappear soon. Come on in," Belinda said to Amanda, who stood awkwardly by the door.

"On Monday mornings Amanda will deal with my correspondence and any other typing that is needed. She has kindly volunteered to help us twice a week, so I suggested she help the special events committee. I know you're having difficulties with one of your fund-raisers and perhaps some extra help will come in useful." Belinda looked towards the corridor at a girl pushing a tea trolley. "Ah! There's Clara. I'd better run after her and get my coffee. See you on Monday." She smiled in Amanda's direction and left the room.

"Isn't Cathy coming back to do the typing after her baby is born?" Lydia looked at her colleagues, ignoring Amanda.

"She might, but you never know how you'll feel after your first baby. Specially in her case, after losing one in the third month. I was in a state of panic for the first fourteen months after my first one was born. Never left my baby's side. I hardly slept, worried she might stop breathing. Maybe Cathy will be more relaxed about it. But in the meantime it'll be wonderful to have someone to help with the typing. Come and sit down." The woman patted the chair beside her and smiled to Amanda.

"Not having children myself, I wouldn't know, but Cathy seems pretty competent. I'm sure she'll be back." Lydia looked in Amanda's direction for the first time since she had entered the room. "It is kind of Lady Ashcombe to suggest you help with the special events, but I can't think what you could do. At the moment, all we are doing is organising two bridge lunches and, thanks to our kind hostesses, everything seems to be pretty much under control."

"Are you still having the London venue at Mrs Maxwell's?" asked one of the women.

"Very much so," said Lydia emphatically. "This is the third year Bernice has kindly put her house at our disposal. We are very fortunate because her drawing room is, for London standards, vast. We can always fit at least twenty tables."

"And the one in the country?"

"Good Lord! Susan, you are out of touch! Didn't you read the minutes of our meeting? We're having it near Newbury at the Countess of Avercorn's, a future neighbour of ours once we move to the country. I gather she's an excellent bridge player. We had a little lunch last week at Bernice's to finalise the arrangements. Bernice was so pleased to meet the Countess as they themselves are planning to buy a country retreat near Newbury," Lydia said with satisfaction.

"I thought you were having trouble with the caterers for the London venue."

"Yes, it's so tedious. The small catering company who had volunteered to sponsor the lunch is closing down. You don't know anyone in catering who would be willing to help, do you?" Lydia looked at Amanda.

"I'm afraid I don't." Amanda was sorry to miss her chance to endear herself to Lydia, who obviously saw her as an unwelcome intrusion.

"I'm sure something will come up, but they'll have to be very professional. I can't run the risk of poisoning people or have some bunch of hooligans in Bernice's kitchen." Lydia looked at the clock above the door and said, "Is that the time?" and then looked reproachfully towards Amanda. "With all the interruptions this morning I've achieved nothing, and poor Snuffy locked up in the car all this time." She felt for the lead behind the chair. "I must take him for a walk." And without saying goodbye, she left the room.

"She doesn't have children and her life revolves round Care Campaign, bridge and Snuffy," said the second woman who had been silent until then.

"She's moving to Hampshire at the end of the month. Her husband is retiring and I think they have a lot of friends in that part of the world." Susan opened a packet of digestives.

"She seemed keen to add the Countess to her list of acquaintances." Her friend took a biscuit.

"Anyhow, don't worry if she is a bit offhand. She does it to everyone new at Care Campaign. She's a bit possessive about her patch." Susan laughed good-naturedly.

"Did you hear she upset Mrs Karalambos the other day by making a remark about foreigners. Rather silly, if you ask me, when Mrs Karalambos is indisputably not English."

"Have you done much charity work before?" Susan offered Amanda the packet of biscuits.

"None really. I've been busy with the children till now and somehow have done little else other than look after them."

"Nothing to be ashamed of. I'm sure your children as a result are beautifully behaved."

Amanda didn't want to disappoint Susan by telling her that they were not, and smiled instead.

"I met Virginia Hamilton-Veere a few days ago and when I mentioned I had some spare time she suggested I approach Lady Ashcombe about the typing." Both women looked up approvingly. Virginia obviously ranked high in the Care Campaign pecking order.

"Don't let me keep you from your work," said Amanda, getting up.

"We come in once a week and deal with the general queries, so I dare say you'll be getting some typing from us." Susan took another biscuit.

"Oh, yes. Anything I can do to help," Amanda said eagerly.

At the bus stop outside the hospital, Amanda reflected that Lydia's offhand manner was a small cross to bear weighed against the satisfaction of having something purposeful to do. She would continue looking for a full-time job, but in the meantime, in between Julia, Care Campaign and the bridge lessons, the days would seem less daunting. She remembered what one of the women had said about Lydia. "Care Campaign, bridge and Snuffy are her life". Amanda thought of her children and how sporadically they needed her now. Was she that different to Lydia after all?

★

One month after joining Care Campaign, Amanda waited in the small cramped office for Belinda to arrive. Judging by the time, she might have been caught in traffic on the Embankment. Having already dealt with Belinda's correspondence over the past few weeks, Amanda didn't feel as apprehensive as she had done at first. To her surprise, her typing skills weren't too rusty and her shorthand was still good enough to scribble down at a competent speed what Belinda dictated. Belinda had warned her that this morning would be very busy as there was still a backlog of old correspondence. To save time, Amanda started clearing the desk and took out of the cupboard the old manual typewriter she had now become familiar with. As she tidied files, bills, lists and memos into Belinda's in-tray, Amanda was reminded of the efficiency and commitment of most of the women who helped with the charity.

At Care Campaign, in only a few weeks, Amanda had met women with ambition, vision, stamina, creativity, imagination and a relentless desire to succeed. Some were obviously doing it for their own gain but others were truly committed to the cause and worked long hours for no other reward than the knowledge that they were doing something worthwhile. Many, like herself, had started working at the charity because they needed the company and the stimulation, only to discover later that they had other abilities. Amanda wondered what a mainly female Cabinet would be like. Would there be more back-stabbing? Would the debates be shorter or longer? Would they be less interrupted by bad jokes? And would the decisions taken be any different?

Working only with women was a new experience. Despite the inevitable drawbacks Amanda knew she was gaining valuable experience. Lydia was one of the drawbacks. She was curt and unfriendly whenever they met. As Susan had pointed out the day of her interview, Lydia disliked newcomers, particularly if they spent more time than she did with the chairman of the charity. At ten-thirty Amanda decided to go to the main reception in the hospital to see if there was a message from Belinda. She was normally very punctual, and the delay could mean something had gone wrong. Perhaps she had been clamped and been unable to get to a telephone. At the far end of the corridor, just as she was about to cross into the main building, Amanda met Belinda and Lydia.

"Amanda, I'm sorry about the delay. Lydia wanted a word. I won't be long." Belinda's usually cheerful face looked strained.

Lydia looked at Amanda over the rim of her glasses and raised her thin pencilled eyebrows. She was annoyed by the encounter, as it gave Lady Ashcombe an excuse to hurry to her office leaving the matter in hand open for further discussion. Sensing Lydia didn't want her to join them, Amanda said she was on her way to the Ladies and went back to the office where she waited for Belinda. Ten minutes later the door opened.

"Amanda, I'm truly sorry. Would you mind awfully staying an extra hour today? I'm afraid my impromptu meeting with Lydia has taken the best part of our morning." She gave a short sigh as she dropped her rain coat on the chair.

"I'd be happy to stay on till we're finished with the typing. Anything wrong?"

"Lydia is insisting on having the bridge lunch in London catered professionally. She feels this way one could charge more for the tickets. She believes the combination of Mrs Maxwell's posh North London home, plus a three course lunch, would make it easier to sell more tickets. I think she's wrong. Besides, she seems unable to find a caterer to sponsor the lunch." Belinda ran a hand through her hair, a gesture Amanda had noticed she only used when she was worried or concentrating.

"Are we having the one in Hampshire catered?" Amanda asked.

"No, and it will be delicious I'm sure, as it always is. We have excellent cooks amongst our committee members. When I suggested that we should have a different type of venue in London, Lydia didn't seem too pleased. She feels we have put

Bernice Maxwell through so much trouble already we can't change our plans now. I can't see why. All she's done to date is offer the use of her house. Still, I'm afraid you'll have to get used to all this charity politics." Belinda sighed and continued. "The bridge party, as I mentioned before, is never too successful financially and it's also old hat. It would be difficult to say that to Lydia. She's done it for years and perhaps this is the right time for a change. She's moving to Hampshire soon and it might be an idea if she only concentrates on that venue."

"If you're considering new ideas, perhaps a second-hand designer show might be something different. I went to a fashion show organised by one of our small charities in Putney. It was very successful. In fact, I got this Jaeger blazer there."

Belinda looked up at Amanda with interest.

"Well, a second-hand designer show in London, if it was well targeted, could be a very successful fund-raiser. Without wanting to put down your lovely Jaeger jacket, the cast-offs one could collect from some of our committee members and their friends would make any show look worthy of a Paris fashion week." Her face brightened as she looked towards Amanda and picked up her correspondence.

"We better get started. A lot of these have to be answered today." She paused. "I'll think about the fashion show."

"Oh, but you don't have to. I only said it because it suddenly crossed my mind."

"Ideas are what we want for special events."

The thought of overshadowing anything Lydia did with one of her own ideas worried Amanda.

"I'd hate to suggest anything that might upset anybody."

"You must leave that aspect of things to me. Our main concern is to raise more funds. In the event of the fashion show coming to fruition, would you be prepared to put in longer hours and be part of the special events committee? You don't have to answer now. Think about it and let me know next week. It would mean longer hours and an extra day a week at least!"

★

On Monday morning Amanda woke up early. Since she had started helping at the charity, she looked forward to the beginning of the week. Monday was no longer the day assigned to doing the laundry and tidying the house. The children came home on alternate weekends and, with no husband to cook Sunday lunch for or garden with, the weekends were often silent and lonely. Mondays spent in Belinda's small office were something to look forward to. The drawing room that on past Mondays had been full of Douglas's presence, scattered Sunday papers and crumpled cushions, was now always tidy. Amanda avoided sitting there on Sundays and spent most of her time in the kitchen or in the small family room overlooking the garden.

This Monday morning she dressed carefully and put on some make-up. She enjoyed her "office look" of sensible skirt and navy blue blazer. It made her feel confident to be dressed for the part. Men, no doubt, felt the same in their overalls, pin-striped suits and uniforms.

Downstairs before going into the kitchen, she crossed the hall and picked up the post and the morning paper. Her mail looked dull; two brown envelopes, no doubt bills, a bank statement and a rectangular white envelope with the logo of a local estate agent's. Since joining Care Campaign, Amanda hadn't given up her search for a proper job and every morning she read the vacancies section. She had been to most of the estate agent's in the area. The letter in the white envelope was from a small company in Richmond she had been to a couple of weeks ago. She opened the envelope unhurriedly, expecting another polite letter saying that they didn't need anybody at the moment. Her eyes skimmed the page, not taking in what it said till they fell on the bottom line that read: "please contact us if you are interested". They were offering part-time work; four mornings a week and a modest basic salary plus commission if she brought them any business.

Amanda stood in the hall waiting to feel elated and triumphant. Wasn't this what she had been looking for? She would at last have a small income apart from her alimony. Her children would be proud of her and her days would be busy and purposeful. Why was she not excited?

Holding the letter in her hand, she walked into the kitchen and plugged in the kettle. While she waited for the familiar sound of water boiling, she tried to analyse her reaction to the good news and soon understood that what was dampening her spirits was the thought of having to give up her work at Care Campaign. She had grown fond of Belinda and some of the other women and wondered if she would still be able to fit it in.

In the bus crossing Putney Bridge, Amanda rehearsed what she would tell Belinda. She needed the job. Quite simply, she needed the money and wondered if, once she started with the estate agent's, she wouldn't miss Care Campaign so much.

*

"Good morning," said Belinda brightly when Amanda walked into the office. "I managed to get here early. The Embankment was miraculously uncongested. Dreadful word, uncongested. Makes me think of blocked sinuses more than of a traffic jam. Not so good for you, my getting in early though." She smiled mischievously. "I've managed to scribble half a dozen letters you'll have to type now." Belinda looked over the rim of her reading glasses at Amanda who was hanging her raincoat behind the door. Noticing she hadn't responded to her light-hearted chatter, she said, "Anything wrong? You look very pensive for a Monday morning."

"I've been offered a job. Nothing too exciting. Four mornings a week at a local estate agent's." Amanda paused. "I really need the money. I'm afraid this means I won't be able to come in and help as much, but I could still fit in some evenings or afternoons, if that's convenient for you."

"Have you accepted already?"

"No, not yet. I only got the job offer this morning. To tell you the truth, it came as a real surprise. I'd given up hope of ever being offered anything."

"Someone else was clever enough to spot a hard worker," said Belinda. "In fact, I was thinking about you over the weekend. You have been very responsive and reliable since you joined and you also seem to have good ideas. Take the fashion show. I've made some inquiries. There is a chance if we went ahead with it, we could use Mosimann's as our venue and many of our members, such as Mrs Karalambos and Virginia, would be willing to give us some of their designer cast-offs. It could, with some thought and a lot of work, become quite an event. What I'm getting at is that we could also employ you." Belinda looked up. "For a very modest salary of course! Your predecessor got paid for doing the typing and helping with some of the accounts. As I said, you wouldn't get paid much but you would also get some of your expenses covered. What I had in mind was to keep you for my correspondence and all that, but... also to put you in charge of the special events and get you to work on your idea of a show. Would you like to think about it?"

Amanda wondered if she was being offered a job or whether Belinda was trying to say something else in her usual chatty disjointed manner?

She heard herself say, "But what about Lydia? Her bridge lunches?"

"I had a long talk with Lydia on Friday." Belinda folded her hands on the desk. "I told her I felt the London venue should be changed and asked her to concentrate on the Hampshire lunch. She was upset, admittedly, but I think mainly because she didn't want to disappoint Mrs Maxwell, who seems to enjoy hosting our events. There must be a reason for it that I'm not aware of." She rolled her eyes. "Still..." she sighed, "the end result is what one must focus on. I also explained to Lydia that I felt now that she was moving to Hampshire it made more sense for her to concentrate on the venue there. I can't believe once she is in the country all week she'll want to come into the office in London as often as she does now."

When Amanda left the hospital it was already dark. She was about to open her umbrella when she saw the bus hurtling by. She rushed towards the bus stop ignoring the rain, the umbrella still in its sleeve under her arm. The traffic lights changed to green and she watched, out of breath, the bus disappear into the traffic. She stopped running and smiled at her bad luck. Nothing could dampen her spirits that evening. She had been offered a job for the second time in one day.

On Tuesday morning Amanda sat in the office she now shared with Belinda, who only came in three times a week and who had left her in charge of setting up the fashion show. After her conversation with Belinda, Amanda had rung the estate agent's and told them she was unable to take the job at the moment but she might be available some time later. She still found it hard to believe she had a full-time job at the charity. Determined her new project should be a success, she threw herself into her work. The first step was to procure the designer clothes. She rang Julia with the news. Julia immediately volunteered to ask amongst the well-dressed women in her circle.

When she rang Virginia Hamilton-Veere she found she not only knew all about her new position at Care Campaign, but she had also already put aside some designer cast-offs for her. Her first reaction was to feel uneasy. Up to last week, if she had gone missing, only Julia and the children would have noticed and now suddenly everyone seemed to know what she was doing.

"Belinda thinks you are a gem and is so grateful I put you in touch with her. So, please keep it up." Virginia had joked but the expectation in her voice was not wasted on Amanda.

"Let me give you the names of some of our members who I'm sure will be able to help with clothes."

The addresses that accompanied the names Virginia gave her were all very smart: Kensington, Belgravia and Hampstead. Some were outside London, either in the home counties or in secluded areas of rhododendron-sheltered Surrey. Amanda worried that collecting all these fine garments was going to present a problem, since Douglas had taken the family car. She would have to approach other members of the charity to ask who could volunteer to collect the clothes.

Her days were becoming full but arriving home in the evenings the emptiness of the house would embrace her, reminding her she was alone. On the answer machine she would still find messages from curious acquaintances wondering how she was coping and occasionally the voice of a stray husband. Amanda would pour herself a drink and while she ate a pre-cooked meal, would review the lists of names she had typed in the office till it was time to go to bed. At times, when she could forget the humiliation of having been left, she was overcome by a new sense of freedom. The hurt caused by Douglas's departure was now overshadowed by her new-found desire to succeed.

Chapter Four

Amanda got off the bus at Ebury Street and walked towards the smart houses that surround Chester Square. As she stood in front of the large, white, stucco house with tall windows she noticed that the houses either side had two bells, but this one had only one. She rang the bell and, while she waited for someone to open the door, found herself remembering the houses she had seen on her way to her interview with Mr de Jersey, the estate agent. Those houses had been built at the same time and the proportions were the same, but they now had fifteen bells cluttered beside the door.

A small dark woman in a black and white uniform opened the door.

"I've come to see Mrs Karalambos. She's expecting me. I'm from the charity Care Campaign." Small electronic eyes followed her down the hall and into a large room where she was asked to wait. Amanda wondered if she should be carrying some sort of identification to enter such a well-guarded mansion. The elegant proportions of the room had been obscured by the effect of mirrored tiles. The walls were covered in rich silk panels from where gilt-framed pictures had been lit with such accuracy one was forced to look at them. A marble slab supported by four stone lions served as a coffee table and was covered with every glossy magazine that had been printed in the last two months.

Amanda had just settled down to *Harpers & Queen* when a second uniformed woman appeared to conduct her into the conservatory. As they went down the hall, Amanda caught a glimpse of the other reception rooms laden with wealth. The conservatory was several degrees warmer than the rest of the house and full of exotic plants. The combination of the temperature and the foliage made the atmosphere soporific. A fountain played at the head of an indoor swimming pool that was surrounded by wicker and rattan chairs. Mrs Karalambos, wrapped in a towelled gown, was reclining in one of the chairs. When she saw Amanda she stood up and walked towards her. "I hope you don't mind my greeting you like this." She gestured at the space around her.

Amanda, who had never been greeted in such opulence, pretended she was quite used to this sort of welcome. "Not at all. It's so generous of you to have volunteered to give some of your dresses for the fashion show. But am I interrupting your swimming?"

"No. I've just finished my fifteen laps. I'm exhausted." She laughed. "What can I offer you to drink? I'm going to have a Turkish coffee. Would you like one?"

"That would be lovely." Amanda remembered the thick black coffee she had drunk on holiday with her sister before she was married. The Turkish coffee arrived with an array of small sweet pastries. Amanda sipped slowly. Her heart began to thump and she wondered if it wouldn't have been wiser to have asked for tea.

"Are you a personal friend of Lady Ashcombe's?" Tina Karalambos looked at Amanda taking in her appearance. Amanda was touched Tina hadn't scrutinised her clothes before making her feel welcome. Nonetheless, she was glad she had dressed carefully, her new Russell and Bromley shoes still constricting her toes.

"I share an office with Lady Ashcombe. You could say I'm her secretary, but I see more of her friend Virginia Hamilton-Veere. We play bridge together."

Mrs Karalambos smiled approvingly, as to a child who had done well at school. "Oh yes! Virginia Hamilton-Veere. I met her at a party. Her father-in-law has the most beautiful estate. Constantine was a guest there at a shooting party. I hear

Mrs Hamilton-Veere's husband will inherit the title and the estate some day soon. Lord Hamilton-Veere isn't too well."

Tina sipped her coffee. "My husband is always encouraging me to play bridge. He says I'll enjoy it and that I'll make more friends. Constantine went to school here and he has a lot of friends. I was brought up in Athens, but went to school in Switzerland. Most of my girlfriends are Greek or American. I have just taken up tennis though." She paused as if waiting for Amanda's approval.

"Tennis is a nice game as one can normally play it well into one's seventies," said Amanda, not knowing quite what to say. She took a sip of water from the glass that had been brought to her with the coffee.

"Do you play? Perhaps you would like to join us sometime at the club."

"I used to play regularly when I was younger but I'm probably pretty unfit now."

"We are not very competitive." Tina Karalambos laughed. "I once played with someone at the charity who is. Do you know Lydia Cosgrave?"

"Yes. Is she a good player?"

"Very competitive. She got quite uppity with me for not being a good enough partner and said something about foreigners not learning sports at school. As you can imagine, I haven't played with her again." The smile left Tina's face. "I also hear she will be moving to Hampshire soon and that her bridge lunch in London is cancelled and you are doing the fashion show instead." Amanda was left wondering if Tina's hospitality and forthcoming generosity had anything to do with her dislike for Lydia. The thought that some people might see her as the person who had replaced or pushed Lydia aside worried her.

As Tina led the way up to her bedroom, Amanda found herself taking in her shape and size. It was important to have dresses of an average size for the fashion show, as more women would be able to fit them. Tina, she observed with relief, was about a size twelve. Under her robe one could see her breasts were full and her hips rounded; it seemed she kept her naturally voluptuous figure under control with rigorous dieting and exercise. Her jet black hair had been expertly streaked to give one the impression she was a brunette, but her best feature was undoubtedly her smooth, olive skin. Money had given her the opportunity to exploit the good features she possessed and had also enabled her to conceal or curb the less attractive ones. Tina's bedroom was as opulent as the rest of the house. The room was dominated by a four-poster bed which was covered in discarded garments, as was the chaise-longue by the bathroom, where a sunken bath and Jacuzzi could be seen reflected in the mirror-tiled walls.

"I've been putting some things out for you." Tina pointed at the clothes on the bed. "I'm sure we can find a few more if we look properly." She pressed a button and the cupboard door opened, revealing rows of dresses, jackets and shirts neatly hanging from matching hangers.

Amanda felt as if she was standing in one of the departments of Harvey Nichols. She couldn't believe one woman could have so many clothes. Ungaro dresses, Chanel suits and Armani trousers were unceremoniously piled on the bed.

"It's such a relief to do this. It's so much easier to choose from the new collections when one's cupboard is uncluttered." Tina picked a black crepe and satin evening dress and, looking at it hesitantly, said to Amanda. "You must be roughly my size, but you are taller. This dress..." She turned to look at her, "was always too long in the sleeves for me. If you let the hem down, it should fit you. It doesn't look much on the hanger, but it is very sexy. Why don't you take it? Let's put it to one side so we don't mix it up with the rest."

"Oh, but I couldn't!" Amanda was taken aback by this unexpected gesture. "It is very kind but... but it should either stay here or go to the charity."

"I would like to make you a present," Tina insisted. Amanda knew in some cultures refusing gifts could offend. Not wanting to upset Tina she found herself thanking her and at the same time wondering what she would look like in the dress.

"Would you like any bags or belts?" Another cupboard was electronically opened. Amanda tried not to show her amazement at this new display of wealth. "No, thank you. We're just doing designer clothes this time."

Amanda looked at all the garments on the bed and started to panic. It would be difficult to take it all back home on a bus. The last batch she had collected from someone in Kensington the day before had only been a few dresses, and that had proved difficult enough to manoeuvre on and off the bus. At the last Care Campaign meeting she had mentioned that she would need help collecting dresses. There had been little enthusiasm amongst the women who, Amanda suspected, were busy with Christmas shopping, school carol services and office parties. Two women had volunteered but both lived in the country and Amanda hadn't wanted to leave it till after Christmas. The sooner the clothes were collected, the easier it would be to organise the models, the prices and the theme of the show.

She worried about the expense of a taxi from Tina's to Putney. She hadn't discussed expenses with Belinda. Perhaps she should take half the dresses back in the bus that evening and come to collect the rest another day. Amanda felt she was panicking. She must control herself and take decisions without fussing. It was silly to flap about how to get a few dresses home. Douglas had always said she fussed. "Stop flapping", she could hear him now. It had all started after the children had been born. Little things like being late, running out of milk or petrol had become a reason for panic.

She looked at the pile of clothes on the bed and took a deep breath. She would take a taxi, keep the receipt and then talk to Belinda about the difficulty she was having with collecting the garments. No need to flap. This was all part of learning to cope alone.

★

Amanda was standing in the hall with Tina when the front door opened and two men walked in. One was small and dark, the other broad shouldered.

"Good evening." The dark man smiled at them and, handing his briefcase to the athletic looking one, kissed Tina lightly on the cheek. Amanda wondered if the aide now holding the briefcase was a secretary, chauffeur or a body guard.

"Thank you, Peter." The man was dismissed.

"Constantine, this is Amanda Thompson. She is from the charity I was telling you about yesterday."

"Of course. I was reading one of your reports last night. I noticed Lady Ashcombe, the wife of the Minister of State at the Department of Trade and Industry, is your chairman. I gather she has supported the charity ever since her mother died of cancer."

Amanda was surprised at how well informed he was.

"Did Tina find anything to give you? She always tells me she has nothing to wear." He smiled affectionately at his wife. "Was there anything you could use for your fashion show?"

"Mrs Karalambos has been terribly generous. I was only expecting a couple of dresses." Amanda felt ill at ease. Perhaps she shouldn't have accepted quite so much from Tina. Maybe Mr Karalambos, who most likely paid for all the designer dresses, wouldn't find her generosity so amusing.

Amanda's fears were immediately allayed by Constantine who said in the same measured tone, "I'm delighted she is backing such a good cause."

Feeling some form of appreciation would be appropriate, Amanda found herself saying: "I was just telling Tina that she must come to the fashion show and bring some of her friends. We, of course, won't charge an entrance fee to any of the ladies who have so kindly given their clothes. In fact, we've been considering the idea of having a small buffet after the show for the committee members and all those who help put the show together. We still haven't got round to thinking where we

118

should have it. We're hoping to stage the show at the Mosimann's, in which case I suppose the most practical thing would be to have it there." Amanda paused, realising she was talking too much.

"I'm sure Tina would love to hostess your buffet here. You don't need to incur expenses when you are trying to raise money." Amanda noticed Tina looked just as surprised as she was by Constantine's suggestion.

"We are conveniently located. Your guests could walk over after the show," he continued.

"What a wonderful idea, Constantine. Why can't I think as cleverly as you? Of course, it would be a pleasure to help." Tina looked at her husband with admiration.

"If Lady Ashcombe came to the buffet Tina, darling, maybe you should ask Alfred and Patsy Halford. I'm sure Alfred and Lord Ashcombe would have a lot in common." Amanda wondered who Alfred Halford was and why Constantine wanted him to meet the minister.

The maids packed all the dresses Tina had put aside and the chauffeur was told to drive Amanda home in the family Bentley. Amanda realised she had a lot to learn about what people expected from charity work. Who was she to judge? Had she not started to help at Care Campaign out of loneliness and to fill her aimless days? Why shouldn't Constantine take part in charity work to further his business. After all, his contribution at the end of the year was bound to be in proportion to the business he did with his new found contacts.

On the way home, as the Bentley stopped at the red traffic lights on Sydney Street, Amanda noticed the couple in the next car were looking at her. How easily people responded to status symbols. She instinctively patted her hair. How easily one responded to admiration.

★

In the weeks that followed, Amanda worked long hours for Care Campaign, helped Julia at the shop over the weekend and also kept up with her bridge lessons where Tina had now replaced Virginia's faint-hearted friend. She was glad she had suggested Tina should join the class. She felt Constantine would approve and was happy to be able to do something in return for his offer of hosting the buffet at their house.

Amanda was aware that her new-found energy and need to be occupied was fired by a fear of being alone. In the evenings she would sit at home longing for someone to walk through the door. The silence in the house depressed her. It was in the evenings when she had nothing to do that she would start to analyse her marriage, her life and her evident failure as a wife. Sometimes she would sit and relive a certain episode of her life with Douglas. She would reconstruct a conversation, wishing she had said something else or had behaved in a different way. Her regrets would sometimes make the room close in on her. Familiar surroundings became threatening. She would double lock the doors and check the windows. She knew she was afraid of her loneliness and not a burglar, but the instinct to cower away and hide was sometimes too strong. Only when she was busy was she able to forget, only then the small problems that in her mind became large and insuperable, resolved themselves or disappeared.

One evening, as she was hanging the dresses she had collected that morning from a friend of Virginia's, she looked round the spare room which now had the semblance of a boutique and decided that as soon as Christmas was over she would talk to Belinda about her travelling expenses and the possibility of finding a temporary store for the gowns.

The doorbell rang. She rushed downstairs, undid the various locks on the door and there in front of her stood a group of small children, who began to sing a Christmas carol. Their solemn faces, flushed by the chill in the air, looked angelic. She let them finish singing "Away in the Manger" and went into the house in search of her purse. Overcome with emotion, she gave them some money and saw them make their way to the house next door.

Why was it, that the Christmas season made her remember happier days, underlining her loneliness? She must stop this self-pity. What positive measures had she taken about Christmas so far? There were only ten days left before Christmas Eve when they would go down to Pat's and she hadn't even thought of presents. The children would be home that weekend and there was no Christmas tree up. There were plenty of things to rejoice about if she stopped being negative. The children, her job, her new friends.

She opened the cupboard where the Christmas decorations were kept and started resolutely to sort them, when the telephone rang.

"Amanda, it's Solange. I am ringing to thank you for suggesting Jack to Virginia Hamilton-Veere. He will be painting her grandchild in the new year. They met today. Jack thought she was 'charmante'. And Amanda, Jack wants me to thank you from him too." Solange paused. "We would like to give you something for the introduction; a small commission. We hear from Virginia you are now doing a lot of charity work and... Well, who knows, some other ladies might need a portrait painted. Virginia says you work very hard now. It would be good if you could make a little more money."

"Oh, please, I don't want to hear about it. It was a pleasure to put Virginia in touch with Jack. You don't owe me anything."

Solange, sensing this wasn't the time to be insistent, did not pursue the subject. She had mentioned it. Amanda had naturally refused, but she would no doubt think about it.

"Are you staying in London for Christmas?" Solange changed the subject.

"No, we're going to my sister's."

"After Christmas," continued Solange in her purring voice, "you must come and join us for dinner. We would love to see you and hear about your charity work." After putting the phone down Amanda decided that if Solange did ring, she would accept the invitation to dinner. She had grown used to people asking her because they knew she was alone. At first there had been something humiliating about people's hospitality, conscious they were doing it out of pity, curiosity or duty but now she welcomed an evening in company.

Amanda went back to the decorations scattered on the drawing room floor and, after sorting them out, went to her desk and started writing the Christmas cards she had so much dreaded doing. What could she write? "Douglas and I have parted. Totally desolate. Hope you are all well, love, Amanda".

At one in the morning, when she had finished the cards, not mentioning their separation and signing only her name and the children's, she went up to bed and slept deeply and soundly for the first time in weeks.

★

Half an hour at a cocktail party had always felt like an eternity to Amanda. Making small talk on her feet with strangers was something she had never been good at but she was determined to make a big effort this evening and concentrating on her appearance would be a good start. Looking at her reflection in the mirror, she found herself wishing Douglas was there. This was her first party without a husband and she knew that no amount of grooming would hide her apprehension. Her hostess, one of the committee members, had been insistent when she had tried to decline the invitation with some feeble excuse.

"Amanda, you must come! I've especially asked Clive Grey, the young designer, who will be showing part of his collection at our show. He won't know many people there and I'm counting on you to look after him and find out if it's a good idea for him to join our fund-raising efforts. He came recommended by a friend and a Christmas party seemed a perfect opportunity for you to meet, without having to commit ourselves too much if we don't think either he or his clothes suitable."

Amanda knew that having a designer show part of his collection at their second-hand fashion show would add glamour to the event and was looking forward to discussing the possibilities with him. She just wished the introduction could have been made somewhere other than at a cocktail party. But, on the other hand, having a concrete reason for going and the certainty that at least one person at the gathering would be looking forward to meeting her, made her feel better. The thought gave her confidence. She applied her make-up meticulously, rather than with her usual haste. Amanda was aware her pent-up impatience was responsible for many of her failings. Impatience made her a bad driver. Impatience also made her a poor cook, not taking the time to thicken a sauce, or chopping things instead of grating them. Impatience also made her apply make-up hurriedly, only concentrating on the areas she saw. The result was often satisfactory from the front, but in profile the neck was often white and the temples lighter than the cheek bones.

As she carefully thickened her lashes with mascara she remembered how at ease Douglas had always been at cocktail parties. He would circulate from one group to another, asking amusing questions and always managing to sound confident and in good cheer. When they had first married, she had possessed the gregariousness that so often is only a part of youth. With age she had become less extrovert and being at home all day with the children had made her conscious that she had little to say or add that might be of interest to anybody. Douglas had been irritated by her social reticence and had often muttered to her in a crowded room "Don't look so glum" or "please make an effort".

Amanda took Tina's black crepe and satin dress from the cupboard and laid it on the bed. The dress was exquisite in its simplicity and deserved good quality tights. She opened the packet she had bought the day before and, eager to try them out, did so hurriedly. This resulted in one of her nails making a small hole above the knee.

"Damn it!" she shouted to the empty room. Tina's dress was quite short and the damage couldn't be disguised. Amanda rushed into Kate's room, hoping she would find a pair of suitable black tights. In Kate's top drawer amongst letters, used cinema tickets and unopened biscuit packets, she found a pair of black tights. They were Lycra and thicker than the evening ones she had just ruined. Back in her bedroom Amanda slipped the tights on. She looked at her legs in the mirror and thought they looked very shapely. Hurriedly she put on Tina's cocktail dress and, to her surprise, it worked. Kate's tights gave the outfit a continental chic. Her old evening shoes, however, stood out: tired, dated and out of place with the expensive looking dress and the modish tights. She ran down to Kate's room and, in the cupboard underneath a discarded guernsey, found a pair of black suede shoes. They had a thick heel and a two inch platform. Amanda looked at them suspiciously. Perhaps her old evening shoes would be safer. Up in her bedroom, with something that resembled excitement, she tried her daughter's accessories. The heavy earrings made a youthful frame for her face. The platform shoes accentuated her long legs and made her feel daring.

She stood back and gazed at her reflection in wonder. 'I look younger,' she thought. Something inside her came alive with this realisation. For a moment she was looking forward to the party, to the adventure of looking young and being alone. 'Is the thrill of looking young again born from the hope we might have more time left to enjoy ourselves,' she wondered as she applied some scent to her neck. The bottle was nearly empty. Douglas had always given her a bottle of her favourite scent for Christmas. She would have to buy some more herself, unless her sister Pat gave her some. She knew this was unlikely. Pat wasn't a scent giver, an oven glove was more in her line of presents. She would have to replace the bottle herself and be reminded that she had joined that group of women who buy their own flowers and chocolates. As Amanda put the bottle back on the dressing-table, she felt annoyed by her self-pity.

With a last approving glance at her reflection, she went downstairs. The platform shoes made her walk with hesitation. Looking at the address on the invitation card, she decided she would go by underground. It was too far to take the bus. As she tried to memorise the address, she realised it was very familiar. Her hostess lived a few doors down from Jack and Solange.

*

Outside Bayswater Tube Station it was raining. Amanda looked up at the dark sky trying to judge whether the downpour was temporary and soon decided it was a well-settled December drizzle. She looked at Kate's platform shoes. Walking fast with them required practice and skill. Not wanting to spoil her daughter's shoes she hailed a taxi.

At the front door of the house a couple standing under an umbrella seemed to be having an argument. Amanda heard the woman saying in a reproachful voice, "You could have parked nearer".

"It might have been easier to park if you hadn't kept me waiting for half an hour. I had plenty to do at the office."

Not wanting to intrude Amanda stayed on the pavement wishing someone would open the door quickly before Kate's shoes were completely ruined. She remembered how easy it was to argue with one's husband on the way to a party. One of them was always in a rush and irritated by the other's lack of cooperation. The front door opened and they were greeted by a woman in a black and white uniform who offered to relieve them of their coats, and a waiter who hovered towards them with a tray full of drinks. Amanda, although longing for a drink, declined one and followed the uniformed woman up the stairs where she hoped to find a bathroom where she could tidy her damp hair.

Most of the first floor was taken up by a large bedroom with an elaborate four-poster bed. The bed was covered with the furs of most animals that could be used for either warmth or decoration. Once her serviceable wool coat was placed between a sober camel and a lush red fox she felt reassured that, despite the amount of coats on the bed, there was no danger of anyone walking out with hers by mistake.

As Amanda told herself that the owners of the coats had most probably never come across an animal rights campaigner lurking in the safe pockets of SW1, two women walked into the room. One had a fur-lined cape wrapped round her and her companion was enveloped in a mink coat.

"Haven't seen you in ages!" the cape said to the mink.

"I know. Julian is so busy lately we hardly entertain."

"That's a beauty. New?" The woman in the cape stroked her friend's coat.

"Yes. But I can assure you I've earned it."

As both women were relieved of their wraps by the maid, Amanda considered what one had to do to "earn" a mink coat. Brushing her hair, she wondered if their husbands were also unfaithful and whether excess money helped them cope with the humiliations of deceit.

Amanda went down the stairs ahead of the two women, hoping she would find her hostess. The rooms either side of the hall were full of people, their voices high and full of the merriment reserved for pre-Christmas celebrations. Two men waited at the bottom of the stairs. Amanda guessed they were the husbands of the two women behind her and wondered which of the two overweight, tired-looking men was married to the wife who had "earned" her mink.

Amanda looked towards the crowded drawing room and wondered if there was still time to sneak upstairs and leave unnoticed. When she reached the bottom of the stairs she found the waiter with a tray of drinks. She took a glass of champagne and, holding it at a distance so that it wouldn't spill over Tina's dress, she walked into the crowded room, looking for a pocket where she could stand unnoticed till the champagne warmed her enough and gave her the courage to start circulating. She recognised Lydia, who stood talking to a committee member and a man in a dark suit. Her first reaction was to disappear in the opposite direction but, realising Lydia had seen her, instinct told her that avoiding her would be a mistake as it could easily be misinterpreted.

She took a gulp of champagne and walked resolutely towards her. Since she had joined Care Campaign, Lydia had been frosty and they had hardly exchanged a word. Meeting her now would be a good opportunity to have an informal talk and hopefully clear the air.

"Quite a gathering." Amanda squeezed past a woman holding a tray of canapés and stood by Lydia.

Lydia looked at her blankly. Amanda hoped the couple would come to her rescue and include her in their small talk. The woman seemed engrossed in the story the dark-suited man was recounting and neither of them seemed to notice she had joined them.

Lydia's expression had changed from lack of recognition to measured civility.

Amanda tried again to make conversation.

"Pre-Christmas parties are always special," she said, trailing her words, giving Lydia a chance to join in and approve or even disapprove; anything was better than the unwelcoming silence.

"You're quite right. They are always fun and full of surprises." The dark-suited man had unwittingly come to her rescue.

Lydia, who obviously didn't want to make the couple uncomfortable, said, "Let me introduce Amanda. She works with us at the charity. It's all still new to her, isn't it?" She looked at Amanda with a patronising air.

"Enjoying it?" said the dark suit.

"Yes, very much." Amanda smiled at the man who, out of natural good manners, was putting her at ease.

"She's been very adventurous. She has embarked on a new project which is quite experimental. We're all rather worried for her, of course."

"When one is aiming high, there's always an element of risk," the man said pompously.

"I suppose that is all very well for high finance but in our charity projects we have to be conservative," said Lydia.

The man smiled at them with the benign smile so many men reserve for women, children and pets.

"What does this risky project involve?" he said.

"It's a second-hand designer fashion show."

"Well, that doesn't sound too risky. Unless you're renting the Savoy," he laughed.

"You're planning to stage it at Mosimann's, aren't you?" Lydia said reprovingly.

"Lady Ashcombe has made some inquiries through a friend and it seems we might be able to stage it there." Amanda hoped the mention of Belinda's involvement would make Lydia less reproachful. But it was apparent by looking at Lydia's tight jaw that mentioning the chairman's patronage had been a mistake.

"Any relation to Lord Ashcombe?" The man sounded interested.

"Yes, his wife. She chairs our charity," said Lydia, "which reminds me, I've got to talk to her about our Hampshire fund-raiser. I thought I saw her near the window a minute ago."

"Is Lord Ashcombe here too?" The man looked eagerly round the room.

"He doesn't always accompany her. He's a busy man, you know," said Lydia. With the conversation having turned to the Ashcombes, Amanda took the opportunity to leave.

"I must go upstairs," she said weakly and moved away. She was about to be squashed in between two bejewelled ladies, when she saw her hostess making her way towards her.

"Amanda, how lovely to see you. You look stunning. Isn't that a lovely dress." She sounded surprised.

Amanda felt she should explain it wasn't really hers. "It's Tina Karalambos's. Well, I suppose it's mine now. She gave it to me when I went to collect some clothes from her house."

"Very nice." Her hostess's mouth tightened and she looked at the dress in more detail. "Nice perk. Wish we volunteers got some too. My husband sometimes thinks I'm mad slaving away at good causes. But then men are selfish but practical. Let me introduce you to a wicked male. I'm afraid our designer hasn't arrived yet." Amanda followed her hostess into the centre of the room till she abruptly stopped in front of a tall man.

"Amanda, let me introduce you to Rupert Swindon-Smith. Rupert let me introduce Amanda Thompson." Amanda looked up at a large man in a pin-striped suit. His full and flushed face was framed by damp curls.

"Amanda runs several projects in our charity. She works day and night. I don't know where we'd be without her. A treasure." Her hostess patted her on the shoulder and was gone, swallowed by fragrant bodies in party dresses.

"And what has your husband to say about these long hours you work?" Rupert looked down at her. His confident manner, wide lips smiling at her, his dark, damp curls over the collar of the expensive-looking shirt, provoked her into saying:

"I actually don't have a husband to check up on me."

He looked at her with a mixture of amusement and curiosity. Amanda started shifting her weight from one foot to the other as she always did when she felt she had said the wrong thing. He'll think I'm a widow, which she had secretly told herself would have been easier to come to terms with. Maybe he'll think I'm a spinster or a career woman, who chose something other than marriage.

She looked up at him. There was something very irritating about his posture. He exuded self-confidence, yet didn't try to put one at ease.

"In fact," she found herself saying, "we separated a few months ago. He left me for a younger woman."

"How unwise. Will you have one of these?" He pointed at a plate with small canapés. "They're delicious." Without waiting for Amanda to help herself, he picked one up with his wide fingers and dropped it in his mouth, his full lips closing up for the first time. "Apart from working so hard, how do you occupy your time?" he asked as he chewed.

She hesitated. "Caring for the children when they are at home and doing the shopping."

"My wife only has time for the horses," he laughed. "Can't even get her up to London for a good party like this one." His eyes were now resting on her cleavage. "Don't think this will be quite enough, do you?" He dropped another piece of brown bread and smoked salmon into his mouth. "Maybe you would like to join me for supper." He was getting closer to her than was necessary.

"I'm already expected to supper with a girlfriend. Oh, there she is." Amanda left him dropping another piece of bread and salmon into his mouth, and walked purposefully into the middle of the room. She was about to join a group of three women when she bumped into the waiter who offered her another drink. She smiled gratefully as he refilled her glass, hoping Rupert wasn't looking in her direction and planning to join her for a refill. She downed the champagne in a gulp. Holding her glass, Amanda searched the room for a familiar face, the faces all flushed by champagne and conversation seemed very similar. The back of a small, dark woman surrounded by three dark-suited men stood out. The most striking thing about her was her vivacity. Her hands moved busily as she talked and her head gestured from one man to the other with the quick movements of a bird.

Amanda recognised Solange, who was clearly enjoying the attention she was receiving. She was tempted to join her to avoid Rupert's advances but the memory of their last telephone conversation, in which Solange had offered her a commission for introducing them to wealthy members of the charity, made her hesitate. She took another sip of her champagne and, after checking if Rupert was out of sight, started to circle the room. She recognised one of the committee members and was about to go over and say hello, when someone put a hand on her shoulder. Amanda froze. The thought of Rupert's wet, heavy lips made her turn round ready to tell him to leave her alone. But she found herself facing a man much smaller than Rupert.

"Fancy meeting you here. You look smashing." Jack met her defensive expression. Amanda, happy to see him instead of Rupert, greeted him warmly.

"What brings you to this neck of the woods? I thought you were a Putney dweller," he said smiling at her.

"I do get around since I started work. Our hostess is a member of our charity and we are raising funds for a new Care Campaign project." Amanda found it strange that Jack should imply he didn't know she worked for Care Campaign when Solange had only rung her about it recently.

"Really, how interesting. It can't be easy to raise funds in these lean times."

"That's what I thought when I was put in charge of special events but I've been amazed by people's generosity."

"Isn't that good to hear. Tell me about the events you're planning to put on."

Jack's eyes moved quickly round the room as he talked to Amanda. She noticed he gave a smile of recognition to a couple beside them but turned his attention back to her. Touched by his interest in what she was doing and feeling more relaxed after a second glass of champagne, she told him about the fashion show and Constantine Karalambos's kind offer to host the buffet dinner. Jack's small stature became more apparent in a crowded room, where he was marginally shorter than most of the men and many of the women. He made up for this with his charm and manner. Amanda was aware several people had recognised him while they were talking and yet he made no attempts to leave her side or try to disengage himself from her by introducing her to someone else. She was flattered, aware she was talking to a popular guest. Every so often Jack looked in Solange's direction where she was still surrounded by men.

"Amanda, darling, Clive Grey has arrived. As hard as it is to leave Jack's side, I feel I ought to drag you away and introduce you. He looks a bit lost." Their hostess had joined them, her face flushed by the success of her party.

"Amanda and I are old friends. Solange will be mortified if I don't take her over for a few minutes. I'll bring her back to you soon, I promise." He took Amanda by the elbow and guided her in Solange's direction. The room was now packed like a bus in rush hour but Jack led the way with the determination so often adopted by men of small stature.

"Solange, look who I found." Jack stood by his wife, his arm over Amanda's shoulder. Solange met her husband's eyes.

"Amanda's been very busy raising money since we saw her last." He smiled at the men, letting them know there was no need to break up the group. Solange introduced Jack and Amanda. There was a moment's silence in which everyone searched for the appropriate thing to say.

"Are you an artist too?" The tall man in the blue suit looked down at Amanda.

"I'm afraid not. Jack's the portrait painter."

"We know that. We were just discussing with Solange the possibility of persuading my wife to sit again. The last portrait she had done five years ago by a German artist was not a favourite with the family and it sits in the attic rather than hanging over the mantelpiece as intended."

"Jack doesn't keep his ladies sitting for too long. *C'est vrai, chéri*?" Solange purred.

Amanda looked in admiration at how Solange flirted both with the blue suit and her husband, her eyes sparkling, her busy hands occasionally brushing the sleeves of their jackets. The tall, blue suit asked Jack about his work and Solange turned towards Amanda.

"So, tell me how you raise all this money in these hard times." Amanda told Solange what she had told Jack, sensing she would be impressed. She was telling her about the wonderful dresses that were being donated, when she saw her hostess walking in their direction.

"I must go. There's a young designer here we are planning to use for our show. I haven't said hello yet."

"We'll be in touch. We'd love to support your show. Let us know when it's on." Solange kissed her affectionately on both cheeks.

Amanda followed her hostess past a group of people discussing their Christmas plans. "I've got wonderful news." Her hostess stopped by the Christmas tree in front of the window, her face still flushed. "A friend of our vice chairman, who is a member of Mosimann's, has just confirmed that we can hold the show there. Far more glamorous than an impersonal hotel. You might mention it to our young designer. It would be very good for his reputation to show at such an exclusive club. The last designer who had a show there was Bruce Oldfield." Amanda didn't know where Mosimann's was but felt excited. The fashion show, which had started as a modest event, was turning into a glamorous production.

"There's our designer looking a bit lost. Let me know how you get on. Just remember he came through Sarah Selby; he designed her daughter's wedding dress. He's up-and-coming, Sarah says." She left, balancing on her evening shoes.

Amanda looked at the young man standing by the Christmas tree and wondered how best to introduce herself. He was wearing a black silk shirt under a loose jacket and didn't seem to have noticed her presence. Just as she had decided to say, "Hello, I'm Amanda", he walked away towards the mantelpiece and stood with his back to the crowded room examining a water-colour above the chimney breast, his hands clasped behind him knotting and unknotting into a tight fist, giving away his unease. He's probably bored and wishes he wasn't here, Amanda told herself. Aware that she had felt the same way half an hour ago made it easier for her to walk up to him and introduce herself.

"I've been looking for you. I'm Amanda Thompson of Care Campaign. Our hostess might have mentioned me?"

He turned round and looked down at her with an amused expression. "I had given up hope of ever meeting you. It's very clever of you to find me in such a crowded room. On the other hand I must stick out, being the only one without a tie."

"I don't think anyone minds. You did the wedding dress for Mrs Selby's daughter. I hear it was a big wedding."

"Yes, I was lucky. The bride and the dress were photographed in most of the glossy magazines, so we both ended up with good write-ups." He grinned and shrugged his shoulders.

"Mrs Selby mentioned you mainly design ball gowns and wedding dresses. We don't have any ball gowns for our show. It would add a lot of glamour to the event if we had some. As you know, we are showing second-hand designer day wear and we have a few important cocktail dresses by major designers, but all second-hand. Could you help us with the show?"

"Beggars can't be choosers." He looked round the room. "I suppose you're likely to have a lot of these people at the show. It'd give me good exposure and we all need that."

"I've just heard we might be allowed to have the show at Mosimann's." Amanda looked up, wondering if it would mean more to him than it had to her.

"Really!" His face lit up. "Bruce Oldfield showed his winter collection there a few months ago."

"I'll have to confess. I've just been given the news about Mosimann's and I'm sure it is a lovely place but I don't know where it is. My life revolves round Putney. I only cross the river because of the work I do for the charity."

He looked at her with renewed interest. "Putney! I used to live there before I moved to Fulham. I thought you were a Belgravia lady."

"It's this smart dress I've inherited from one of our benefactresses that is deceiving." She smiled, feeling more relaxed.

"Your shoes are the latest fashion, I see. I like the combination of high street shoes and top of the range dress."

"I hope not everyone in this room is as observant as you are. The shoes belong to my daughter. They were the only decent evening shoes I could find."

"You don't look old enough to have a daughter who wears platforms."

Amanda felt herself blush. He is being polite, she told herself, and wished there was something she could say to make him feel more at ease; he obviously didn't feel at home in the crowded room.

"Could I come with one of our committee members to see some of your dresses?"

"Sure. Any day will do. I'll give you my card. I suppose you can't commit yourself before you see the kind of things I do. They might be a bit too grungy for you or even worse, cheap looking," he said defensively.

"I'm sure they are neither or you wouldn't have been recommended so highly. It's just that I like to involve the women on the committee before taking a decision." The waiter stood beside them with a tray of drinks. Clive pointed towards the tray and looked at Amanda.

"Not for me, thank you."

"I'll have one for the road." He took a glass of champagne. "I shouldn't keep you. I'm sure there are plenty of people in this room you need to talk to. You've got my card." He emptied his glass.

"I was thinking of leaving myself. I don't really know many people here either, other than the committee members. I only came because I knew you would be here and I would be able to talk to you about the show."

"I feel flattered," he said awkwardly, looking towards the window. "I hope your car is parked near and that you have an umbrella. It's pouring out there. If you stand near the window you'll be able to hear it coming down. More like a monsoon than a December downpour."

"I had to take a taxi from the tube station, not to ruin Kate's shoes. I don't think I've got enough money to do it again," Amanda muttered to herself, looking down at the suede shoes.

"The tube!"

"I don't have a car. We were a one-car family. Douglas hardly ever used it during the week, but it was a company car so I'm afraid when he left he took it with him."

"Was Douglas your husband?"

Amanda felt herself blush.

"Yes. I'm sorry. I always seem to presume everyone knows."

"Don't worry about it. Look, shall I give you a lift home? It really isn't out of my way. I'm off the Fulham Palace Road."

"Are you sure? It would save me having to buy Kate a new pair of shoes."

"It's no trouble. I'm ready when you are." He put his glass down by the window sill.

As Clive ushered her under his umbrella to the car, she felt protected. How easy it was to be stirred by the presence of a man, she thought as she walked beside him. They were sharing his umbrella and she could smell his aftershave. 'I'm constantly around women. I'd forgotten about the smell of men.' The thought surprised her. The smell had excited her and she didn't know what to do with the sensation. 'I've obviously had too much to drink on an empty stomach,' she silently reprimanded herself. When she stopped in front of a large puddle Clive said, "Are you all right?" He was holding the umbrella over to her side.

"Yes, thank you. Trying to save Kate's shoes."

"We're nearly there. I'm parked round the corner."

"This is very kind of you. I really hope I'm not making you late for something else."

"The only thing you are making me late for is going to the pub for a couple of drinks and a quick meal."

"Oh, I'm sorry. Are you hungry?"

"Yes, but I'll survive. What about you?"

"I was just thinking. I skipped lunch and shouldn't have had all that champagne."

"Shall we have a quick bite on the way back? There's a nice little pub on the bottom end of the King's Road run by an Irishman that has excellent food. Want to try it?" He opened the car door.

The pub was small and friendly. Most of the people were clearly local. Clive left Amanda at a round table by the door and went to the bar. She watched him walk back towards her, his eyebrows knotted into a frown. He was lithe and had an angular face and close cropped hair. She wondered how old he was and guessed in his thirties. She smiled up at him.

"We're too late for food. He's willing to make us some sandwiches though." He stood in front of her waiting for her approval.

"Anything will do. I'm not fussy."

"I can see that. What would you like to drink?"

Amanda hesitated, wondering if she should drink anything at all, but sensing he would like some company, said she would like some white wine. He was soon making his way towards their table, this time holding a glass of white wine in each hand and a packet of crisps clasped between his front teeth.

"Cheers! To the success of your show." He pressed his glass against hers.

The publican brought them some sandwiches. They ate while Clive talked about his ambitions to become a successful designer once the recession was over and women started to spend more money on their clothes again. Amanda told him about her fears and the new life she was having to build for herself now she was alone. Clive listened. There was something reassuring about the way he listened. He seemed to understand. She felt touched by his concern for her and his obvious desire to please her.

"Are you still hungry?"

"A little."

"We could go home to bacon and eggs or there is a pizza place round the corner." He waited for her reply.

Amanda, conscious it had been left for her to take the initiative and not wanting to be the one to spoil the moment answered, "Whatever is easier."

"We'll go home then. It will be quicker and cosier."

They drove in silence. The festive streets with the Christmas decorations made her think of the children, of Pat and even of Douglas. 'What am I doing?' she asked herself looking at Clive with the corner of her eye. 'I'm not really drunk,' she told herself, wrapping his overcoat round her. The smell of him once more took her by surprise. 'I am lonely. I'm behaving like a fool, an irresponsible fool, because I am so lonely. Isn't this desire for a man's body and for his protection the most basic of all instincts?'

As though reading her thoughts, he said, "There is nothing to worry about, but if you've changed your mind, it's okay. I'll take you home." When they reached the end of his street, he parked the car, leant towards her and kissed her lightly.

Inside the small first floor flat of a two-storey terrace house off the Fulham Palace Road they made love, first guardedly, then freely. There was a harmony in the pleasure they found together that only joint experience could give. Strange, thought Amanda as she lay in his arms looking through the gap in the curtains, that pleasure could be so simple. She thought of how restrained she had been with Douglas, letting the routine and demands of everyday life detract from the moments that could have been so pleasurable to share. Something long dormant or diverted by motherhood and the routine of marriage had been pushed aside and now, once again, she had experienced the relief of physical fulfilment.

They ate scrambled eggs and listened to music as they chatted about inconsequential matters.

Clive drove her back over the bridge to Putney. Before she got out of the car, he bent over to kiss her again. Amanda looked round nervously in case a neighbour might see them.

"You're adorable. I'd love to see you again. If you want to see me, that is."

"You know I'd love to see you, but it's wrong. You are younger and..."

"Different background, perhaps?" he added wryly.

"Don't be silly. What difference does that make?"

"None to me, but you've just admitted there was one."

"Please don't spoil it. I liked being with you so much, but I'm not ready for any kind of commitment. I really should have taken the tube home after all."

"I'm glad you didn't. Anyhow, see you soon. I'll be expecting your committee members too."

She got out of the car and watched him drive away, the rain falling on her head. As he drove away, the memory of passion ran through her like an electric current. Amanda stood in the rain waiting for the feeling to be washed away. She wanted to feel guilty and to be cleansed, but she felt only the memory of pleasure as the soft rain seeped into her clothes.

Chapter Five

The morning of Christmas Eve, Amanda drove to Pat's in Julia's car. She hadn't been out of London since the summer and the beauty of the countryside overwhelmed her. Even on a cold December day, with nature asleep, the ploughed fields and the neat villages made a welcoming change from the noisy city streets. Before reaching their junction, Amanda slowed down. She was driving very cautiously. Julia's Mercedes had a powerful engine and she hadn't done much driving since Douglas had left taking the car. Once more, she was touched by Julia's generosity. Driving down to Pat's with the children instead of taking the train gave them more time together as a family. Kate was listening to her Walkman in the back of the car and Mark sat beside her in silence, his face wearing the sombre expression he had adopted since Douglas had left home. Amanda turned the radio on hoping some music or a news item might stir him into saying something.

As they approached Pat's village, Amanda found herself wondering if life was easier in the country for a woman alone; she compared Pat's life with hers. Pat's telephone constantly rang. Friends and acquaintances would ring to ask her if she could join them for tennis or bridge, or whether she could bake some cakes for the food stalls at the hunter trials. Pat was involved in most of the local charities and also helped with the village magazine. Her life seemed full of activities she shared with other women, and no one had ever suggested her life was either aimless or frivolous. It was as though all these activities were expected of women in rural surroundings and work, unless a financial necessity, was not a means for fulfilment.

Amanda remembered when the children were young how she had once suggested to Douglas they move to the country. He had refused even to discuss it saying commuting was not for him. He couldn't understand men who spent one quarter of their waking hours on trains just so that the family could enjoy some fresh air and more space. She wondered what life would have been like if they had lived in the country. Would she have grown more independent of Douglas and the children? Like Pat, would she have made a life for herself?

As they left the dual carriageway she found herself thinking about Clive, but Mark's voice brought her back to the Hampshire village they were driving through.

"Mum, are we nearly there?"

"Nearly. Another ten minutes. Are you looking forward to seeing your aunt?" Mark shrugged his shoulders.

It suddenly dawned on Amanda that her worries and her struggle to make a life for herself made her self-absorbed at times. She loved her children, they were all that really mattered to her and she wanted to protect them. But since she had become so busy with her new commitments, she felt that she rather overlooked their needs. Looking at Mark, nearly a man, she felt ashamed of herself. What would a son think of his mother behaving as she had the other night? The thought made her slip the clutch.

"Are you getting tired, Mum? Next summer we should be able to share the driving," said Mark.

Touched by her son's protective tone, she felt a new pang of guilt.

"We must do something about some more lessons during the half-term or the Easter holidays." Amanda looked at her son. Douglas, who had on weekends in the past taken Mark for a drive, had stopped doing so since he had moved out.

"About half-term," said Mark looking at her with the corner of his eye. "I've been asked to go skiing," he paused and then quickly added: "Skiing is expensive. There's the air ticket, ski pass, ski hire, and spending money. I could try and find some work after Christmas till I go back to school and save up, but I don't think it will be enough. Do you think Dad would help out as an early birthday present?"

Looking at Mark's anxious face, Amanda thought how good it would be for him to have an active holiday with people his own age in a happy family environment.

"I'll write to Dad straight after Christmas. I'm sure if we all contribute we'll sort something out." Mark half smiled in anticipation and Amanda felt her own worries, compared to her children's, meant little. Pain in one's children was hard to bear. One felt guilt, a sense of failure and total helplessness.

Kate turned off her Walkman and, reclining on the back of Mark's seat, pulling a face worthy of a five year old, said, "It's all right for some. Skiing holidays! Driving lessons!"

"Kate, come on! You could have done something about your driving test ages ago but you keep postponing it." Amanda knew her daughter wasn't as interested in driving as Mark and only remembered when her brother mentioned it.

"Anyhow, you couldn't drive this one, not even with L-plates because it doesn't belong to Mum. It's really kind of Julia to lend you this car for Christmas. I always thought of her as being a stuffy old boot but she has been rather nice lately. Or better said since..."

"Mark, can you kill that music. It's awful," Kate interrupted. Mark ignored her.

The sight of Pat's house diffused what Amanda feared would be the start of a pointless argument.

Pat's house rested on the edge of a village and from the outside lacked any attractive features. The barn at the back that was used as a den for the children was old but had been restored. The house itself which Pat always referred to as "Victorian" had been mainly built between the wars when the emphasis had been on practicality rather than beauty, but inside, the house was warm and welcoming and they immediately felt at home.

Soon Mark and Kate were sprawled on the sofa in the study, their legs intertwined, the nearest they would ever get to an embrace. The cat sat with them purring at the new-found joy of two warm bodies and the Labrador, stretched out on the rug, knew he wouldn't be asked to leave while the children were there. To ensure a permanent place in this temporary haven, he would regularly lick Kate's hands and put his paws on the sofa. Amanda looked at them and, closing the door behind her, was grateful to her sister for having asked them all down. She was glad she had brought the smoked salmon and champagne left over from the Christmas party at the hospital. Belinda had suggested she take home the leftovers which had amounted to two bottles of champagne and enough smoked salmon to make a starter for the family on Christmas Eve.

Pat and Tony's children were older than Mark and Kate and they now both lived and worked in London. Peter, the elder, had gone abroad with his girlfriend and Sophie would be arriving that evening with her boyfriend. Kate liked Sophie, whom she saw as grown up and sophisticated. They were all staying till Boxing Day. It would be a proper family Christmas, Amanda thought with relief as she made her way to the back of the house.

In the kitchen Amanda found Pat wrapping some stocking presents.

"They seem to have settled down nicely." Pat looked at her over the rim of her glasses.

"It's so wonderful to see them curled up and contented as they used to be when they were children. Thank you, Pat. You'll make this Christmas seem almost normal."

"You don't thank your sister for Christmas. You must stop being so grateful to everyone whenever they do something for you. I've noticed you do it a lot since... Anyhow... What is *he* doing for Christmas? Is he going to see the children at all?"

"He's gone abroad with his girlfriend till New Year. He knew we were coming here." Amanda found herself defending Douglas out of habit. Pat had never hidden her dislike for him and she had grown accustomed to championing his cause when in her company.

"Selfish pig! Never mind." Pat put some sellotape on the badly wrapped box.

Amanda, who had been longing to unburden the guilt about her night with Clive, looked at Pat and wondered if it was wise to take her into her confidence. She knew her elder sister had always considered her impractical and, she suspected, also naive. Perhaps, as in Kate's case, this was instinctive in an elder sister. Amanda had always wanted to impress Pat, if not with her capability, then with her daring.

She watched her sister's busy hands.

"Pat, I've had an affair," she blurted out, pressing her own hands against the warm Aga.

"Already? Good. I thought it might take you longer." She didn't look up, clearly not giving too much importance to what Amanda had said.

"It wasn't exactly an affair, more of a one-night stand. He's younger."

"Suitable?" Pat looked up at her. Amanda thought she recognised excitement in her sister's voice.

"What does suitable mean? Anyhow, he's a fashion designer. He's charming, really sweet. But younger, which maybe makes him unsuitable."

"You better be careful. Hope you took the right precautions." She cleared her throat. "Nonetheless, it's a start. Better than..."

The kitchen door opened. Kate walked in and asked for some orange juice. Amanda looked at her daughter's face wondering if she could tell by her expression whether she had overheard their conversation. Kate's face betrayed little, but Amanda knew that, like her father, she was able to conceal her feelings.

Kate opened the fridge. "Oh! Smoked salmon and champagne!"

"Your mother is spoiling us all. She brought it down with her," said Pat.

"It was a present from the charity." Amanda wanted to be above suspicion when it came to any claims of extravagance.

"Mummy gets lots of presents nowadays. You should see her new designer dress."

"There seem to be quite a few perks in this charity business. It makes up for the pay," Amanda said defensively.

"Hum!" Kate gave them both a knowing look and left the kitchen.

"Ignore it. It's 'the age'." Pat went to the sink.

"Do you think she heard us?" Amanda feared that disgruntled and suspicious teenagers tended to eavesdrop.

"Not unless she was hanging around outside the door."

Pat squirted some washing up liquid. "Douglas has got a girlfriend and you've had your first little fling. A bit unsuitable maybe, but quite understandable. So stop worrying!"

Amanda was grateful to Pat for making light of the situation.

"I must have a lie down before Sophie gets here with her boyfriend. We've only met him briefly once in London. A nice enough boy but he seemed rather shy. I'm glad you are all here. It'll make it less daunting for him. Right," said Pat impatiently pushing a saucepan onto the draining board. "I'm off for my kip. We had a very late night and I'm feeling sluggish already and Christmas hasn't started."

"Let me put things away. You go upstairs," said Amanda, leaving the warmth of the Aga and making her way towards the sink. "Should I lay the table?"

"That would be a great help. I'm afraid for Christmas Tony likes the full works, silver candelabra, best china... Do you think you can manage? It's all in the corner cupboard in the dining room."

"I'll find it. Don't worry." Amanda was glad she could be useful and at the same time do something for Tony who was always so kind to her children and rarely indulged by his wife.

"You'd better put your feet up too when you're finished. We're having a few people round for drinks tonight and we won't be eating till late."

"Oh, I didn't know you were expecting anyone else."

"Just a few friends and neighbours," said Pat leaving the kitchen.

After tidying the sink, Amanda went into the dining room. Pat had decorated it with streamers that hung festively from the ceiling lights. A large bowl of fruit and nuts adorned the centre of the table, and stems of shiny, deep green holly had been placed behind the pictures. 'It smells of Christmas!' thought Amanda as she went past the sideboard where a large Stilton, surrounded by figs and dates, let out a pungent aroma. Amanda stood at the head of the table and, looking out at the wintry garden, was suddenly overwhelmed by grief. Her first Christmas without a husband, the children's first Christmas without a father. Why should it hurt more today? Standing in Pat's festive dining room, the memories of previous Christmases flooded her mind. She tried to push back the unbidden images of Douglas and the children together in their dining room in Putney, but they kept on re-emerging, vivid and persistent. Pushing back the tears she went towards the corner cupboard and carefully took the crystal glasses and the china and placed them on a tray. She lay the table slowly and meticulously as the tears began to pour down her cheeks. Amanda sat in a corner and sobbed as she remembered Christmases past.

Christmas with her parents when she and Douglas were newly-weds had been full of wonder and she had always felt like a child. Whether this was because, at the time, the children had still believed in Father Christmas or because of her mother's reassuring presence, she did not know. Since her parents had died, when Kate was six, Christmases had been spent mainly in Putney. Pat and Douglas had never got on, and Douglas had preferred having his elder sister, Penny, over to them for Christmas Day. Penny was undemonstrative and slightly pompous, like Douglas. She was a lawyer and worked in a small practice in Cambridge where her husband was a don. Douglas had liked to refer to his sister as an "intellectual" and Penny was obviously flattered by her younger brother's admiration which surpassed that of her husband, who had a less romantic view of her capabilities. When they had come to them for Christmas, Penny had rarely lifted a finger, encouraged by Douglas's comments of: "Penny, now you leave all that to us, you work hard enough as it is". "Us" had always meant Amanda, as Douglas hardly knew where the coffee cups were kept. Penny would talk to the men about politics and current affairs, only occasionally addressing Amanda to say, "Well done, Amanda. Such a lovely lunch". Amanda had always felt depressed when Penny left, wishing she had been more forceful and had insisted on having her own family for Christmas.

Amanda heard a car coming up the drive and looked out of the window. It was Sophie with her boyfriend. She went to the front door to greet them.

"Auntie! How lovely to see you." Sophie hugged her. "I'm so glad you could come. This is Paul," she said, motioning to the shy-looking young man beside her.

To put Paul at ease Amanda gave them some tea in the kitchen before going up to change for the evening.

*

Later in her room, Amanda wondered if Douglas's girlfriend looked as young as Sophie. Sophie was now nearly twenty-four. Kate had said, "Claire's a cow and only a little bit older than me". What could a girl like Sophie offer a man of Douglas's age other than her youth, Amanda wondered, examining the lines round her eyes. She tried to think of her youth, her twenties and what she had done with them, other than being with the children. She had done little else and now it seemed she was being punished for it.

The door opened and Kate walked in. She threw herself heavily on the bed and said with a sulky expression, "Sophie isn't like she used to be. She's all lovey-dovey with Paul and the only time she's bothered to talk to me, she said how sorry she was to hear about Dad leaving. I hate people feeling sorry for me," she muttered into the pillow.

"She was only trying to show you she cares for you. And it's only natural she's giving Paul extra attention. He isn't part of the family and doesn't know anybody. I'm sure once he feels more at home, Sophie will have more time for the rest of us."

Kate started pulling at a piece of thread on the side of her shirt. As she pulled Amanda could see the seam unstitching but refrained from telling her to stop.

"I hate Christmas."

"Oh, darling." Amanda came and put her arms round Kate.

Kate wriggled out of her mother's embrace. "Dad said he'd ring from France on Christmas Eve... He could have offered to take us. I bet *she* didn't want us there, the cow," she murmured under her breath.

"Maybe next Christmas he'll stay in England," said Amanda in the form of consolation.

"Maybe next Christmas I won't be here. If Sebastian and I are still together we might do something by ourselves," she said angrily.

Kate hadn't mentioned having a boyfriend before.

"Oh, did you meet in Bristol?" asked Amanda casually as, after all, it would be good for Kate to have a boyfriend to confide in and unburden her worries.

"I don't want you being nosy. I wish I hadn't told you." Kate buried her face in the pillows again.

"I won't mention it again unless you do," said Amanda stroking her daughter's head. This time Kate didn't wriggle away and allowed herself to be caressed.

"Welcome! Welcome! May I come in?" Tony's friendly voice was accompanied by a knock on the door.

Amanda opened the door and kissed her brother-in-law on both cheeks. Tony's eyes fell on Kate's slumped figure on the bed.

"Hi, Kate," he said cheerfully, winking at Amanda. "Have you passed your driving test yet?"

"No. It's pointless anyhow. We are a car-less family now. Well, Dad has a car, but we don't see him that often."

"You've got your provisional though, haven't you?"

"Yep."

"Mark is driving me into the village. I've got to get some more drink for tonight. Would you like to come and drive us all back?"

There was a pause.

"All right. I need to buy some cigarettes so I might as well come."

Tony smiled at Amanda and rested his hand reassuringly on her shoulder. Amanda wanted to fling herself into his arms and thank him and at the same time beg him to help her. If only the children had a father like him. It was so difficult to cope on her own. The marriage counsellor she had visited a couple of times for advice had said it was natural for teenagers to put the blame on the parent left behind and vent their anger on them, but knowing it was common did not make it any easier to cope with.

When Kate and Tony had left the room, Amanda thought of Douglas and Claire getting ready for Christmas Eve in some hotel in the South of France, oblivious of the children's unsettled feelings. Full of anger and indignation she sat at the dressing-table and wrote Douglas a short note asking him if he could finance Mark's skiing holiday. She stressed how much their son would benefit from the experience, particularly under the circumstances.

Later, when Amanda heard voices in the drawing room she went downstairs and met Pat in the hall. Pat had curled her hair and was wearing a festive red dress. Her sister had looked more attractive that afternoon in a guernsey and jeans with her hair windswept, but that was so often the case with outdoor women, thought Amanda. They always looked slightly out of place when they dressed up for an occasion.

Pat's drawing room was full of friendly faces. They were red country faces, different from the ones in the London charity circuit. The women wore either very bright dresses to mark the festive season or dark skirts covered in dog hair. The atmosphere was friendly and relaxed, friends and neighbours had gathered to celebrate. It was a world apart from the Christmas party at which she had met Clive, where people seemed mainly to have gathered either to impress or to be seen.

The children and Tony were back from the village. Kate had changed into her black miniskirt and tight Lycra top. She looked precocious and provocative beside the neighbours' daughters in their Laura Ashley skirts.

Sophie was introducing Paul to a couple who had just arrived and Tony was pouring drinks, but when he saw Amanda walk in he immediately came towards her.

"Our little trip to the village was a great success," he whispered in her ear having made sure Kate was out of earshot. "She enjoyed driving and was actually smiling by the time we got back."

"Oh, thank you, Tony. It's sometimes so hard to know what to do to cheer them up."

"Amanda, darling, it's the least I can do. I wish we could do more."

Amanda knew Tony meant what he said and that it wasn't only Christmas spirit. Tony was the kind of person who thought of others all year round, not only when the calendar dictated it.

"Have some bubbly," he said handing her a glass. "Come, I'll introduce you to Mrs Fairbanks. She does a lot of charity work locally. I gather from Pat she was impressed to hear you worked for Care Campaign in London."

Amanda followed Tony across the room. Pat intercepted them.

"I was just going to introduce Amanda to Mrs Fairbanks," said Tony.

"She can talk to Mrs Fairbanks later. I'm sure she'll have much more in common with Colonel Hunter." Pat gave Tony a meaningful look. Tony didn't want to disagree with his wife, although he was sure that Amanda would have more in common with Mrs Fairbanks. After twenty-five years of marriage Tony had learned it was not worth disagreeing with Pat when she put on her bossy voice. On the whole, he found that his life was easier if he kept his opinions to himself.

Amanda was deposited by Pat in front of a tall middle-aged man who seemed painfully shy. She soon found out he was a widower and had two children of similar ages to Mark and Kate. One of the prim-looking girls in a Laura Ashley skirt was the colonel's daughter. Amanda felt sorry for the girl who had lost her mother at such an early age. The sad figure of Colonel Hunter also aroused her sympathy. While they talked and exchanged pleasantries on the weather and local Christmas activities, Amanda found herself wondering if death was really harder to come to terms with than desertion. The Hunter children had lost their mother, but they were sure of her love for them, whereas Kate and Mark felt not only abandoned but also rejected by their father. No wonder they were aggressive and difficult.

As she answered Colonel Hunter's hesitant and predictable questions, Amanda wondered if she would, from now on, be paired by everyone with respectable widowers. She suppressed a smile. Pat had always been practical. Perhaps it was just what she needed. It was very hard to be a single parent. She looked at Colonel Hunter's pinched face and then thought of Clive and realised that perhaps Pat was, after all, right in thinking the widower and she had a lot in common. Suddenly the image of Clive and their love-making came into her mind and made her blush. She was watching Colonel Hunter's thin lips move but his words didn't reach her. The memory of her impulsive indiscretion with a younger man filled her with shame.

She smiled at the colonel and mumbled something about having to keep an eye on how things were progressing in the kitchen. As she was about to leave the room she heard the telephone ring. Tony, who was standing near it while pouring drinks, picked it up. Amanda saw him call Kate and knew it must be Douglas. Kate left the room, obviously wanting to talk to her father in the privacy of the kitchen. Before leaving the room she gestured towards Mark who followed her.

Amanda felt angry with Douglas for ringing. It no doubt made him feel less guilty to ring on Christmas Eve and, although the children would have been upset if he hadn't, she wondered if the call would have an adverse effect on them. They had both looked so much happier and settled since Tony had taken them for a drive and made them feel part of the family. Later, while she talked with Mrs Fairbanks, Amanda's fears that Douglas's phone call had been disruptive were confirmed. Kate looked tipsy and was flirting with a man twice her age and Mark sat sullenly in a corner. Tony, who was now busy with a room full of thirsty guests, had asked Mark to help him with the drinks but this hadn't help to change Mark's mood. He would join the clusters of guests with a bottle of champagne and pour it into their glasses without meeting their eyes and, if spoken to, would give a monosyllabic grunt as a reply.

When the guests were gone, the family sat round the crystal and silver laden table. Kate, who was now slurring her words, sat beside Paul. Mark sat beside Pat declaring he wasn't hungry. To everyone's surprise the shy-looking Paul kept them amused throughout dinner, never allowing the conversation to waver and even getting Mark to smile as he recounted the adventures of his trip to the Far East. 'Sophie has chosen a kind man just like her father,' thought Amanda as she watched Paul including a tipsy Kate in his conversation. 'Where have I gone wrong? Should I have been bossier, like Pat, asserting myself more within the family?'

On Christmas Day Amanda woke as the first crack of light filtered through her bedroom window. She jumped out of bed with a child-like excitement. She drew the curtains and saw what she had always hoped to see every Christmas past. It was snowing! The fields and trees were covered in a soft, white blanket. She turned round instinctively wanting to share it with someone.

'I'm alone!' she said to herself. 'And, it's a white Christmas!'

Overwhelmed by memories and the reminder that she was on her own to deal with the difficulties of life, she realised she was also alone to experience life's joys. The tears poured down her cheeks. Drying her eyes, she took the stocking presents she had prepared for the children out of her suitcase and tiptoed into their bedroom. They were both asleep, their expressions angelic. She placed the stockings at the end of their bed and went downstairs to make herself some tea. As she walked past the Christmas tree in the hall she saw two large parcels wrapped in bright metallic paper. She bent down and looked at the label. "With all my love, from Claire" it said. Kate had obviously put them under the tree at the last minute. Angry at the intrusion of Claire into her family's Christmas, Amanda realised that there were many things she would still have to come to terms with. Feeling depressed at Christmas time and birthdays was one of them, and strangers buying her children expensive presents was another.

She put on the kettle and stood against the Aga. She felt the warmth filtering through her dressing-gown. Her New Year's resolution, she told herself, was to be more positive. The children were healthy, they were still in their house in Putney, she had a job and it was a white Christmas!

★

Back in London after New Year, Amanda threw herself into her work. The invitations for the fashion show had to be designed and printed, models had to be hired, and special "At

Home" cards had to be written out with Tina's address for the buffet supper.

Mark had taken a job as a packer at the local Sainsbury's. Amanda was relieved that the skiing holiday had given him something to look forward to and work for. He now jumped out of bed in the mornings and occasionally even made his bed, instead of lying in a heap under his duvet with the curtains drawn watching television, as he had done at the beginning of the holiday. She still hadn't heard from Douglas but decided to give him a few more days to reply to her letter before ringing him at the office.

Kate had gone back to Bristol early, implying she would have a better time there. "Maybe you should ask the charity to pay for another telephone line? If they refuse, ask Mrs Karalambos. She's the one who rings most of the time anyhow. Doesn't it drive you crackers?" These had been Kate's parting words, and Amanda knew her daughter had every right to complain. Tina had taken to ringing an average of twice a day. She would run over the menu of what she was planning to serve at the buffet supper and even discussed the wines. The menu would change daily and it was always described in great detail.

Amanda sometimes wondered if it wouldn't have been easier to have the party at a hotel or at someone else's home. But when she thought of the contribution Care Campaign might receive from Constantine, she knew she had taken the right decision.

Tina, Amanda discovered, had two sides to her nature and lived in a woman's world she herself had never encountered. It was not like Pat's country woman's world of bazaars, summer fetes and tennis tournaments. Tina dressed and entertained so that she could compete with her girlfriends. Her reception rooms were redecorated, dragged, distressed, and chintzed to comply with the latest fads promulgated by the decorating houses. Tina was disconcerted if anyone in her circle outshone her by having better clothes, more lavish decorations or better parties. When she had heard Virginia mention to Amanda that she was very pleased with the progress Jack was making with the portrait of the children, she had immediately enquired who Jack was. Constantine, she added, would love a portrait of her in the main reception room. If Virginia Hamilton-Veere was using him, he was bound to be a good painter. She wanted to be the first within her circle to be portrayed by an English society painter.

One evening, as Amanda was making a list of her travelling expenses, the telephone rang. It was past ten o'clock and she immediately worried it might be the school saying something had happened to Mark. For once, she was relieved to hear Tina's voice.

"Constantine just rang from New York. I mentioned the idea of a portrait and he approves. There is a portrait of both of us in the library that was done by an artist in Athens just after we were married. I find the style a bit dated now. I would like to meet this artist of yours, Jack. Virginia seems to be happy with him and she tells me you know him."

"Yes, I've met him and his wife a couple of times. Let me give you their number and I'll let them know you'll be ringing. By the way, I spoke to Lady Ashcombe and she mentioned Lord Ashcombe will be able to join her at your party after the show."

There was a silence born out of delight on the other side of the phone.

"Constantine will be pleased. I'll ring Patsy Halford immediately. I'll also ask Patsy if she would like to give you that St Laurent dress she tells me she can't wear any more. I'll ring you back tomorrow."

When she put the phone down, Amanda realised Tina had until now held back from procuring the couture dress for her. She had saved it as a reward if she managed to persuade Lord and Lady Ashcombe to join them. Tina's world, she was learning, was full of rewards or slights for favours that had, or had not, been granted.

*

The following day Amanda prepared to leave the office early to go to the supermarket. When she peered out of the window to see if it had stopped raining, she saw a familiar figure standing on the corner of the Fulham Road. Her office window looked out onto a mews, but also gave her a good view of the main road. The familiar figure was Jack. She recognised him the minute he turned round. He looked pensive as he paced up and down the pavement and Amanda wondered if he was waiting for someone to leave the hospital. She went back to her desk and made a list of what she had to discuss with Belinda the following morning. When she got up and peered out of the window she saw Jack was still there. He was bound to see her if she left the hospital through the front door. She hesitated. If she bumped into him she might find out if he had got her message about Tina being interested in a portrait. Out in the street she looked in the direction where Jack had been standing, but he was gone. She made her way towards the bus stop and was about to cross the road, when she heard someone call her name.

"Well, what a lovely surprise! Fancy meeting you here. I've just this minute jumped out of that taxi." He pointed in the direction of a cab that had just sped by.

"Are you going into the hospital?" she asked.

"No, I was on my way back from a meeting and decided to jump off here to buy a couple of cinema tickets."

Amanda wondered why he was lying. She had seen him there half an hour ago. Perhaps he had been to visit someone who was ill in hospital and wanted to keep it a secret.

"You look well. In fact, as stunning as you did at the party before Christmas. Obviously all this hard work agrees with you."

Amanda smiled at the compliment.

"Are you rushing anywhere?" he asked.

"Well, in fact, I was on my way to the supermarket."

"Come and have a drink at the wine bar on the corner." He looked at his watch. "It's past six."

"I really shouldn't. I must do some shopping. I don't think there is as much as half a pound of sugar left in my kitchen cupboards."

"You've got a lifetime to shop and how often do you bump into a friend at the end of the day who offers you a drink." He grinned. Amanda was tired, but she felt like a drink and was also intrigued by Jack's behaviour. He had been hanging around for half an hour before she had left the hospital and yet was eager to point out they had met by chance.

In the wine bar on the corner of the Fulham Road, they sat at a table by the window overlooking the street. The noise of the traffic outside was drowned by the loud music inside. She made an effort to hear what the waitress was saying, her voice struggling against a fashionable tune. When the waitress had left with their order, Jack, leaning over the table so that his voice would reach her, said, "Thank you for putting Tina Karalambos in touch with me. We met earlier today and I should be able to start on her portrait as soon as I'm finished with Mrs Hamilton-Veere's grandchildren."

"I'm glad it's all worked out," Amanda shouted across the table.

"This is the second commission I've got through you. We are grateful, you know." The waitress arrived and put a chilled bottle of an expensive-looking wine in the centre of the table. Jack poured the wine. "Amanda, tell me, how many of you are there on the committee?"

Amanda hesitated. "About twenty-five. But some people are more involved than others."

"Of course, it's always the case, particularly with voluntary work," he said knowingly. "Have you made many friends? Tina sounds very fond of you. You obviously see quite a lot of each other."

"I suppose because of the bridge, I tend to see Tina more than the other charity members."

"Bridge?" asked Jack.

"Yes, I play once a week. Or rather, take lessons."

"You must have made some new friends through your bridge too. It's a very sociable game." He lit a cigarette and inhaled, looking at her with interest.

"In fact, it's through the bridge lessons that I met Virginia Hamilton-Veere who put me in touch with the charity."

"Interesting," said Jack, inhaling deeply, "how one thing leads to another." He poured some more wine and, after a pause, said, "Amanda, I wish you'd allow us to give you a small commission for the contacts you give us. It would be helpful if we were introduced to more Tinas and Virginias."

"Jack, I'm delighted to recommend you. Please, I won't hear any more about this business of commissions." Jack didn't pursue the subject and instead inquired about Tina's background and then talked about the opulence of her house he had clearly enjoyed visiting that morning.

When they left the noisy wine bar, Amanda felt exhausted. She had drunk more wine than she had intended and couldn't face the prospect of spending an hour in a busy supermarket. She would have to shop another day. As she boarded the bus that took her to Putney, she thought about Jack's behaviour. The meeting outside the hospital had been deliberate. He had obviously wanted to tell her about Tina so that he could bring up the possibility of more commissions. It must be humiliating for an artist having to procure clients this way. Looking at the grey river, she found herself feeling sorry for Jack.

★

Soon after dawn Amanda got up. She'd rather be up early than lie in bed tormented by the after-taste of her dreams. She had a shower and washed her hair. Wetting her head always made her feel better and invigorated. Since she was a child, she had enjoyed diving into the sea head first. Wetting her head represented a new start and she often wondered if it related to her baptism. With her head wet, she felt as she must have done the day when, wrapped in her christening robes, she had been given the chance to be saved. Amanda was not religious but she liked moral messages and the romantic notion that opportunities to be saved were put in front of us to take or to pass by.

She listened to Radio Four. Someone was talking about dreams, but he was suddenly dismissed to make room for the news. She went downstairs and made herself some coffee. When she poured some milk she realised too late it had gone off. There was no bread in the bread box and the cereal in the half-finished boxes Mark had left behind had lost their crispness. It was time to go to Sainsbury's and also time to look in the sales for some new clothes. Her daily life had now become full of meetings, visits to smart homes and lunches. While sipping a mug of black coffee, she heard the postman drop some mail in the hall. She walked slowly towards the door, anticipating it would only be more bills. Julia had taught her the art of paying them at the last minute, so reminders were constantly being dropped through the letter box. Amongst the brown envelopes she saw a white, crisp one with the name of Douglas's firm printed on the outside. She opened it quickly and with trepidation. She knew it would be about Mark.

I'm glad you all had a good Christmas at Pat's. She's at her best at celebrations.

The dislike between Douglas and Pat was mutual.

Regarding Mark's holiday that you mentioned would be good for him, I personally feel it might be more beneficial if he worked for some money over the half-term and saved for Easter. You always have indulged him.

"But his friends are going out at half-term. Not at Easter! You ass!" Amanda shouted at the empty room.

On the other hand Kate tells me you are doing very well at your job and I'm delighted to hear you have a boyfriend who keeps you in smoked salmon and champagne.

The first thought to cross Amanda's mind was that Kate had overheard her conversation with Pat and knew about Clive. The thought made her shudder. How could she have allowed this to happen? Amanda's next reaction was to feel anger towards her daughter for spying on her and telling stories to her father. She knew Kate was probably doing all this to make Douglas jealous, hoping for a reconciliation between her parents. Confused and angry, she decided to ring Julia and ask her advice. Being a single parent wasn't getting easier.

While the telephone rang unanswered in Julia's house, Amanda found herself thinking of Jack and Solange and their suggestion that she accept a commission for introductions she gave them. By the time she had put the receiver down, Amanda had made up her mind to ring Solange. It was, after all, quite harmless accepting money from them, and she needn't do it on a regular basis. Perhaps she could accept a commission for Virginia and Tina's portraits only. Accepting money a couple of times to pay for Mark's holiday and replace the boiler seemed a perfectly acceptable thing to do. After all, some people made a living out of taking commissions for far less worthy jobs than finding work for an artist.

Amanda dialled Jack and Solange's number.

Trying to sound matter of fact and concealing her unease, she said, "I've been thinking about your suggestion of a commission... perhaps we could meet and talk about it."

"I knew you would change your mind, *chérie*. Let's meet at the Royal Academy next week. We could have a look at the Impressionists and then have something to eat. The restaurants in English institutions seem to have pulled their socks up lately. I'm looking forward to our little chat."

★

The traffic moved slowly down Piccadilly. From her window seat Amanda could see the banners of the Royal Academy and her natural impatience urged her to jump off the bus and walk the rest of the way. The traffic lights at the Ritz had gone red and she knew it would take at least five minutes before they reached Burlington House. She checked her watch and realised she was early. Solange had said one o'clock, so there was no need to hurry.

Looking at the passers-by, their heads bowed to protect them from the rain, she was reminded she had no umbrella and opted for staying on the slow-moving bus. Amanda started for the umpteenth time to rehearse what she would tell Solange. Like the rain, Solange had been persistent and had tempted her into accepting her offer. Instinct told her it would be wise not to get too involved with Jack and Solange. She would have to make it clear over lunch that she was only prepared to take a commission from them just this once to help with Mark's holiday.

The bus jerked. The traffic lights had turned green. Amanda got up and made her way to the back. She met the eyes of a few passengers, their tired winter faces looking sad and resigned. Spring was a long way off and Christmas had most likely left them feeling poorer. The bus came to a halt outside the Palladian grandeur of Burlington House. Amanda ran towards the arches that surrounded the courtyard to shelter from the heavy rain. She looked round the courtyard, taking in the proportions of the house and remembered reading that the land Burlington House stood on had been given to a supporter of Charles II, who had remained loyal to the King while he was in exile. A commission for loyalty, Amanda thought. This shrewd royalist had built himself a house on the land. The prevailing style at the time was a mixture of classical and Dutch architecture. This modest brick manor house was remodelled at the beginning of the eighteenth century in the Palladian style by the Third Lord Burlington. Looking at the imposing façade, Amanda reflected on the obvious expense. It had been during his grand tour that Lord Burlington had purchased copies of the architectural books written by Palladio and, when arriving back in England, had remodelled his house into what was commonly known as the "grand style". Looking at the statue of Reynolds that dominated the courtyard, Amanda found herself smiling at the memory of how long it had taken her to get a new garden fence out of Douglas and wondered, if in the eighteenth century had she been Lady Burlington, she would have had just the same problem.

A tall woman with a sharp, intelligent face asked if Amanda wanted to shelter under her umbrella to cross the courtyard.

"Thank you. It was silly of me to leave the house without an umbrella." Amanda smiled in gratitude – a thoughtful gesture in the busy London streets.

"Are you here for the Impressionists?" The tall woman hurried across the courtyard, making sure her umbrella was giving Amanda the right protection.

"I'm meeting someone for lunch but I'm planning to walk round the exhibition after that."

"I do hope you enjoy it." They were now standing under the centre arch of the façade out of the rain and the woman was shaking her umbrella.

As soon as Amanda walked through the doors of Burlington House, she felt herself relax. There was something about grandiose public places, museums and churches, that made her feel uplifted and at ease. There was a soporific element in these surroundings that transported her to a different reality. She felt suspended in time and unfettered by the constraints and worries outside.

After leaving her coat in the cloak room, she picked up a small booklet by the entrance and decided to make her way towards the restaurant on the lower ground floor. She admired the frescoes on the ceiling of the hall and, with something resembling pride, she read that the very handsome painted panels on the sides were the work of a woman called Angelica Kauffman, who had been one of the Academy's first founder members. She read on:

There were two women amongst the thirty-four founder members; Mary Moser and Angelica Kauffman. After them more than one hundred years went by before there were other women accepted in the Royal Academy.

"Well done, ladies," Amanda muttered under her breath.

She followed the signs to the restaurant and walked past the staircase with its handsome wrought-iron balustrade. There were small, round tables dotted around the bottom of the stairwell where people sat eating unhurriedly. The tamed voices seemed to fit in with the surroundings. Amanda noticed the average age seemed over fifty. Time for contemplation of beauty was clearly a luxury one could not afford till later in life.

Inside the restaurant dishes of colourful salads, roulades, pies and mouth-watering puddings were displayed. Amanda looked for Solange amongst the tables at the back. As her eyes moved from one table to another, she noticed the wonderful bird-like English faces. These were not the flushed, wide faces found round sport fields or in yacht marinas. As Amanda reflected on how one's pursuits could shape one's anatomy, she spotted Solange sitting under the large fresco by Rosoman. Solange looked urbane and affluent, the detail of her clothes made her stand out. She was wearing a neat city suit with a colourful scarf tied loosely round her neck. Surrounded by women in blue cardigans and dark tweeds she looked unmistakably French.

Amanda walked towards Solange who saw her and got up. "Lovely to see you, *chérie*." Solange kissed Amanda on both cheeks.

"I was silly enough to leave without an umbrella."

Solange laughed. "I don't know how you English would break the ice if you didn't have the weather to talk about."

"You're so right, but you'll pick up the habit eventually if you live here much longer."

Solange tossed her head. "Some things you never pick up or get used to. The weather is one of them, particularly if you've spent your childhood in the South of France."

"I'm embarrassed to admit I hardly know the South. I was near Nice with my parents once as a child, but I remember very little."

"It's not what it used to be. You have to go inland nowadays to find any peaceful spots, and even there it is now full of English. Living in this country one begins to believe that foreign is something the English can never be. I'm sorry." She giggled. "I love to tease the English. Jack is always so rude about the French, I have to defend myself. But this I love!" She gestured round her. "I love English institutions. They have much more character than French ones. Jack, of course, comes here a lot. He is a Friend of the RA and never misses a single exhibition. I'm afraid I don't have the same love for the visual arts as he, but I try to help him in other ways. Artists aren't very practical people, they are too preoccupied with their art. Anyhow, why don't we go and get some food and then talk a bit more about practical things." Solange looked at Amanda meaningfully and got up, adjusting her scarf.

Back at their table and picking at her salmon, Solange said, "Jack is nearly finished with the portrait of Virginia's grandchildren. He should be able to get Tina Karalambos to sit for him soon."

"It's wonderful how quick he is. It must make him very popular."

"He's so talented. He's skilled and quick, not an easy combination."

"Solange..." Amanda fiddled with her cauliflower cheese. "I know I mentioned on the phone that I had reconsidered the possibility of taking a commission from you. Actually," she lowered her voice, "I desperately need the money at the moment because, as you know, I'm in the first stages of a divorce and, well, there isn't enough money for everything."

Solange listened attentively giving Amanda time to find the appropriate words.

"My son, our son... well," Amanda continued, "he has been badly affected by his father leaving home. He's been invited to go skiing and I feel it would do him a world of good to get away with his friends on a holiday." Amanda pushed her cauliflower round the plate, aware she hadn't said what she had been rehearsing all morning. She took a deep breath and looked up from her plate. "Solange, the point I'm really trying to make is that... I really don't like accepting a commission when the people concerned are friends. I only met Tina recently, but she's been very helpful with the fund-raising and it somehow feels wrong."

"But, *chérie*, you must not be so hard on yourself. They will never know and anyhow it is quite normal. If we had got the commission through a gallery, they would have taken a percentage."

"Yes, but I'm not a gallery and these ladies are well... kind of friends."

"I understand in these two cases it is a bit close to home but in the circles you move in nowadays, because of your work, you are bound to come across other ladies who might like their portraits painted. We would like you so much to recommend Jack, and..." she said pointedly, "make some money for yourself."

"Oh, I would be delighted to put more people in touch with Jack, but," Amanda took a sip of water, "Solange, what I'm really trying to say is that I only need the money at the moment because of Mark's holiday, so let's say that it would just be this once. It really is an exception and I'd rather not think of it as a commission for putting you in touch with my friends."

"You think too much." Solange leant across the table and patted Amanda's hand. "Look, there's Jack with Mrs Hobdon." Her face lit up. "He's been showing her round the exhibition. He's so knowledgeable and loves doing things for his clients."

"Had a good lunch?" Jack rested a hand on Amanda's shoulder.

"Will you join us, Mrs Hobdon?" Solange got up.

"No thank you." Mrs Hobdon smiled at Amanda in the way of a greeting. "I must collect something from Ralph Lauren round the corner. I feel most enlightened after the guided tour Jack has given me. I never realised there were so many hidden messages in paintings. Fascinating."

When Mrs Hobdon was gone Jack sat beside Solange facing Amanda. Amanda felt intimidated. The two of them sitting opposite her, so groomed and composed, gave her the feeling of being interviewed.

"So, did you girls manage to have a good chat?" Jack looked at his wife and then at Amanda.

"I was just explaining to Solange that I find the whole arrangement very awkward."

Jack's face creased into a frown.

Solange interrupted. "Don't worry, *chéri*. We have sorted it all out. Amanda will help us on a temporary basis."

"Good. I'm delighted to hear it. The date for your fashion show must be approaching. You must be very busy." Jack looked at her with renewed interest.

"Two more weeks," said Amanda with a sigh. "We are in the midst of cataloguing all the dresses. Now that we know for certain it's being held at Mosimann's we must be as professional as possible."

"At Mosimann's! But *chérie* you never said!" Solange's voice rose a level.

"It's very exciting but also daunting. Some of the press have already made enquiries. It'll give the charity a lot of exposure, but it's nonetheless nerve racking."

"Tina mentioned she is hostessing a party after the show." Jack took a sip of Solange's white wine.

"Yes, it's for the committee members to thank them for all their hard work." Amanda was anxious to make it clear it was a small private affair for the volunteers.

"Of course. Such a nice gesture. Anyhow, I'm sure Solange will support your efforts and come to the show." He smiled at his wife.

"Absolutely. Might even be tempted into buying something. I hear you have a St Laurent dress that is practically new. Is it a small size?"

"The owner is Patsy Halford. I hear she's thin but quite tall."

"Halford? Any relation of Alfred Halford? His wife, I presume?"

"Yes." Amanda felt she was being asked too many questions and was frustrated by her inability to change the subject.

"I must say, you do have a very glamorous group of people supporting you. No wonder the press have approached you wanting to cover the event."

"It was so kind of Mrs Halford to let us have the dress, which reminds me, I have to collect a few suits from the cleaners. Not everything arrives in immaculate condition, but one can't complain." Amanda got up quickly not wanting to waste her chance to leave.

"Solange will be writing to you to formalise our little arrangement." Jack rose to his feet.

"Oh. But there's no need for that." Amanda protested.

Jack ignored her comment and, coming towards her, said, "Tina is starting to sit for me next week. She'll no doubt keep me informed on the progress of the preparations for the show. Women who sit for me love talking about their week. I encourage it because it's better when they forget they're posing. Don't work too hard and good luck with it all." Jack waited for Amanda to be out of sight before he sat down again beside Solange.

★

On her way up to the gallery where the Impressionists were exhibited, Amanda felt ill at ease. The prospect of a budding friendship between Tina and Jack made her feel like a conspirator in a not very honourable affair.

Holding on to the railing of the glass lift, Amanda could see the original back wall of Burlington House with its Palladian style windows and doors. On the opposite side, only twenty feet apart, stood the wall of the building that housed the exhibition halls and the schools. The journey in between these two buildings distracted her and, by the time she arrived on the top floor, she was looking forward to the Pissaro exhibition. With a pair of headphones, she started to tour the rooms where serial paintings of Paris, Rouen and Dieppe soon transported her away from Jack and Solange. She stood for a long time in front of the paintings of the urban streets that captured the weak light of a winter's morning in Paris. As she heard the voice on the tape explain how Pissaro had discovered the city very late in life, she realised this had also happened to her. She had spent her childhood in the country and the first twenty years of her married life in Putney. From this suburban backwater she had never really got to know the city she lived in. The school run, her weekly trips to Sainsbury's and her long walks in the park had always kept her south of the river. She had never perceived, in her short and isolated trips to other parts of London, that there was another side to the city. Since Douglas had left her, she had been forced to go to other areas, but was she even now only seeing London, like Pissaro saw Paris, from a narrow window?

The voice on the tape brought her back to the bustle of the Paris streets teeming with people. When Amanda took her earphones off she felt refreshed and invigorated. Looking at life through a narrow window needn't be limiting; the perspectives were endless and, as the artist had written in a letter to his son, "every glance is a new sensation".

In the gift shop Amanda bought some cards and a colourful calendar for Kate's room at college. She was about to turn the corner and go down the central staircase when she overheard raised voices. She immediately recognised Solange's husky accent. Her first reaction was to hide. She didn't want them to see her. Amanda stood very still pretending to read the catalogue of the exhibition she had seen upstairs.

"Of course she understands what we expect of her," Solange snapped as they turned towards the stairs.

"I still think you left things too open. We've got Tina and Virginia but the whole idea is for her to promote me amongst the other wives."

"She understands that very well. I think it's a good thing she is not 'pushy', chéri. Remember she's not done this before. Give her some time."

"Did you ring Jose?" asked Jack impatiently. "He'd better be quick. There's a lot of touching up to do on Virginia's grandchildren. She's not too happy with the skin tones."

"Couldn't you sort out that side of things yourself? I can't do everything." Solange's voice rose. "I spent most of yesterday getting quotes for Mrs Hobdon's frame. We won't make much profit out of that either." She sighed.

"Bad luck. You won't be able to do the Bond Street sales." Jack's voice was sarcastic. There was a silence and Amanda heard Solange's sharp voice say something in French as they moved away and their voices were submerged in the general hum of the crowd.

Amanda went downstairs cautiously, making sure Jack and Solange were not there before crossing the hall to collect her coat from the cloakroom. Outside the rain had stopped but the clouds sat heavily and low on top of the courtyard, blocking the weak afternoon light. It was oppressive, as though a metal canopy were suspended from the cornices of the main entrance across to the gates on Piccadilly.

Waiting for the bus, Amanda wondered who Jose was and what he had to do with Jack's paintings. They had never mentioned him before. She felt uneasy and resented being involved with them. The unpleasant exchange she had overheard had left a bad taste in her mouth. Surely Penny Peacroft wouldn't have recommended Jack unless she considered him to be respectable and above suspicion. Maybe it was only Solange's insistent manner that made things seem so sinister.

Looking out of the bus window, Amanda tried to assure herself that she had done the right thing. She needed the extra money for Mark's holiday and Jack and Solange had presented a solution.

Chapter Six

When Amanda drew the curtains, she found a solid, silent blanket of mist outside her window. Her immediate reaction was to panic. She had a busy day ahead and worried the traffic might be affected. She was expected at Mrs Halford's in Regent's Park by mid-morning, from where she was planning to collect the St Laurent dress that promised to be the highlight of the fashion show.

"The mist should lift by midday." The monotonous voice on the radio became the bearer of good news. Amanda felt relieved. The prospect of looking smart and at the same time dressed for the weather seemed daunting. Today she would have to make an effort with her appearance as Mrs Halford was bound to be immaculately groomed like most of the other women in the charity circle.

She took a pair of black boots from the cupboard. They looked scuffed and in need of a good clean. In an old plastic bag she found some dried-up black polish and applied it generously. After rubbing the boots vigorously with a cloth, they looked revitalised enough to tread the smart carpets of Mrs Halford's apartment. She found some thick tights and, after putting them on, she slipped into a long grey skirt. It was loose around the waist. Since Douglas had left she had lost weight. Amanda was aware it suited her and realised that after all there were some benefits brought on by his departure. She secured the skirt with one of Kate's fashionable belts and tucked her old cashmere sweater into the skirt so it wouldn't hang so loose around the hips. Amanda looked at her reflection in the mirror. She looked neat but plain. From her top drawer she took the Kenzo scarf Pat and Tony had given her for Christmas. The bright colours and the ethnic pattern gave some style to her otherwise severe appearance. Her spirits, uplifted by the result, motivated her to put on some make-up. She looked at her watch. The whole operation had taken just over twenty minutes. She wondered how long it took other women to dress in the morning.

Amanda rang the bell of Mrs Halford's first floor apartment. A maid showed her the way to a large modern drawing room with windows that overlooked Regent's Park. The mist, as the voice on the radio had predicted, was lifting and through the dissipating clouds she could just see the outline of the black branches on the trees. Amanda stood in front of the window trying to conjure the view that would unfold once the mist had lifted.

"It's ever such a lovely view. Let's hope it clears before you go."

Amanda turned round. A young woman in her late twenties wearing a pair of jeans, a tight top and no shoes was smiling at her. Her face was heavily made up and she wore a lot of jewellery. None of these adornments seemed necessary, thought Amanda, on one so beautiful. Judging by the rows of gold chains hanging from her neck this could not be a domestic help. It must be Mrs Halford's daughter.

Amanda smiled back. "I've come to see Mrs Halford. She is expecting me. I'm afraid I'm a bit early. The traffic, despite the weather, wasn't too bad. The bus hurtled straight up Park Lane..." She paused, aware she was giving too many unnecessary details. She still found it hard to overcome her shyness. Amanda sometimes wished she had the flair of Belinda, whom she had heard ask for donations with a tone of voice that made the person approached feel they were honoured to be given the chance to contribute.

"I'm Mrs Halford," the girl smiled at her. "You came by bus? You poor love, you must be frozen! Let's have some coffee." With her foot she pressed a bell under the coffee table and the maid re-entered the room.

"Two coffees please, Rosita."

A toddler with a mass of blond hair came crawling into the room, followed by a nanny in a blue and white uniform.

"Damian! You leave mummy alone! She's busy," said the girl in the protective manner often adopted by over-paid staff.

"Hello, poppet." Young Mrs Halford had gone down on her knees and was crawling towards a delighted Damian. "You can leave him, Jane. He's no bother. It's only a friend. I thought it was going to be one of the old dragons."

"He'll get spoilt and you'll never have any peace." The nanny looked reproachfully towards Damian.

"It won't spoil him. It'll make him sociable. Won't it, poppet?" She crawled towards him. "Let me introduce you to…" She looked up at Amanda. "Do you know, I've forgotten your name."

"It's Amanda. Amanda Thompson." She smiled at the sight of Mrs Halford and her son sitting on the floor.

The nanny left the room and the maid placed a tray with coffee and biscuits on the table. Damian immediately crawled with tremendous speed towards the biscuits.

"You're as greedy as your father." Patsy Halford patted his nappy-padded bottom.

"Is he the youngest?"

"Not only that, but the only boy. Alfred would kill for him."

"How old are his sisters?" Amanda assumed the girls must be at school.

"Oh," Patsy giggled. "Much older. Only a bit younger than me. From a previous marriage, you see. I've always had a weakness for older men, particularly when they're generous." Patsy winked and, leaving Damian on the floor eating a biscuit, she got up and sat beside Amanda. Amanda smiled back not quite knowing what to reply. It had been said so candidly.

"He can be quite terrifying, Alfred, if you don't know him, that is. But deep down, he's a big teddy bear. I do love him, you know," she added. "D'you take milk with your coffee?" Patsy was pouring a second cup.

"Have you known Tina for long?" Amanda said, trying to steer the conversation away from Alfred.

"Only since we've been married. Constantine and Alfred do a lot of business together. Alfred is ever so pleased I'm getting involved in this charity fashion show and Tina's party. He's always trying to get me involved in charitable works and lunches with the posh wives of his business friends. To be quite honest I'm much happier at home with Damian."

"This is lovely coffee," said Amanda trying to digest these revelations. Patsy obviously said whatever first came into her mind, but she seemed to be devoid of any malice or pretension. "We're very grateful for your contribution. It's a designer fashion show but yours is the only couture cocktail dress. All the other ones are off the peg."

"I'll show it to you as soon as we finish our coffee. It's really gorgeous. Alfred got it for me after Damian was born. He wanted me to look my best for some big business dinner. I know I shouldn't say this, but he paid £12,000 for it."

"Are you sure you want to part with it?" Amanda hadn't realised that couture dresses came to quite that much. "You perhaps should keep it as a…" She was about to say investment or family heirloom but was interrupted by Patsy.

"I can't wear it again. Everyone has seen it several times. I asked Alfred last week and he said to give it to Tina's charity. Don't look so worried," she laughed. "I'll get another one just as nice."

"The models will be fighting over it. I can just see it. They'll all want to be the one who shows it," said Amanda.

"I used to be a model before Alfred." Patsy took a sip of her coffee.

"Really? Would you like to model your own dress? I have a friend who plays bridge with me who is an ex-model too. She's volunteered."

"I'd love to. It'd be such fun to be under the spotlight again. Mind you, I mostly did photographic work but used to have at least one catwalk assignment per season. Right then. I volunteer! I'm sure Alfred won't mind if it's for the charity. I've got to be a bit careful though. He's rather possessive. He doesn't even like me talking about my modelling days." She lowered her voice. "Since Damian was born he's become ever so conscious of my image. I suppose he wants me to go up in the world. Fat chance!" She giggled. "I'll go and get the dress. I'm talking too much again, I know. It happens when you spend a lot of time at home with a toddler. You miss company so much it turns you into a chatter-box. Alfred doesn't approve of my old girlfriends too much either, so it gets a bit lonely sometimes with my mum and sister up in Nottingham."

As Patsy walked out of the room, Amanda wondered if it wouldn't have been better for Patsy to have stayed in her own environment, doing whatever it took, rather than to be cooped up in this gold cage pleasing Alfred. Amanda looked out of the window and saw the mist had lifted completely and the park now glimmered in the winter sunshine. She decided to ring for a mini cab as she felt that taking thousands of pounds worth of couture on public transport verged on the irresponsible.

★

Back in the office at the hospital, Amanda found Belinda sitting beside a blue-suited man. Eager to share her good news, she only acknowledged his presence with a quick smile and, looking at Belinda, said:

"Look at this!" She presented Belinda with the dress Patsy had given her. She had it draped over her arms and manoeuvred it with the care one would a newborn baby. "I don't know if we'll be able to sell it, not even second-hand. It seems unaffordable to me but anyhow, it should add a lot of glamour to the show just having it as part of the collection. And Patsy Halford, the owner, has offered to model it at the show!

Patsy's very young and..." She stopped to draw breath and her eyes fell on the man sitting beside Belinda, who was looking at her with amusement. "I'm sorry, I didn't see you. Well, I did, but I think I'm just over-excited about the dress."

"Your enthusiasm gets a lot done round here. Let me introduce Simon Banks." Belinda helped Amanda drape the dress over a chair in the corner of the room.

Before sitting beside Simon, Amanda took a last glance at the dress, making sure it was safe.

"Simon is a friend of Virginia's," Belinda continued. "He's in between jobs at the moment and has very kindly offered to help us with the administration. Next summer's fund-raiser will be a ball at the Savoy, which will take a lot of organising. Your fashion show is becoming quite an event too, so it looks as though we'll need someone to help with the accounts, and so on."

At the word accounts, Amanda thought of her taxi fares and whether they would find it excessive.

"We were just looking at some of your expenses for the show so far. The travelling seems to be..."

Amanda interrupted Belinda. "I'm terribly sorry. I've taken the bus whenever I could. I did mention at the last two meetings that I badly needed more help with collecting the dresses. The problem is most people were busy with Christmas shopping and school holidays. I don't have a car and sometimes I'm given so many things or, like today, such expensive things that public transport becomes..."

"Amanda, we were about to point out how well you had coped without a car." Amanda felt herself blush. She had done it again, gone into a long string of unnecessary explanations out of nerves.

Belinda smiled. "You've been so noble! All these journeys with dresses to boot. I think, that if you're going to be running around for us, you might need a car. The charity could advance you the money to buy one and, at the end of the year, we could deduct some of it off your wages. Nothing racy, of course, just something small to get you round town."

Amanda looked both at Belinda and Simon and realised her mouth was open. "Are you sure? Once the fashion show is over it won't be so bad."

"It will. There is always something. For the summer ball you'll spend your time running up and down to the Savoy, having to sort out something or other. If you had a car I would feel less guilty whenever I ask you to do the odd errand." Belinda started tying a Hermes scarf round her neck. "By the way we're having difficulty finding a sponsor for next year's summer ball. If you have any ideas or new contacts, let us know. You did very well getting Mr Karalambos to host the party. I'm starting to believe you're a natural at all this." Belinda got up. "Simon, I've got to run. If you need to see any more of the paperwork, Amanda will show you where to find it."

When Belinda had gone, Amanda looked for the first time at the man sitting beside her. He wore a dark navy suit and no tie, as though stressing that his business with the charity was not only temporary but also unofficial. His hair was abundant and slightly too long at the back and sides, as so often worn by men after a long holiday. He had good looks and, despite his casual air, it was apparent he had spent some time on his appearance. His striped shirt with thick cuffs looked professionally pressed and the shade of blue in the stripe blended perfectly with his navy suit. He wore glasses, which he constantly adjusted as he spoke, his eyebrows joining in a puzzled knot each time the glasses were readjusted on his nose.

His expression was devoid of the self-importance so often adopted by successful men. His eyes looked rather sad and the way his shoulders stooped made Amanda think that perhaps he was feeling ill at ease in his new role at the charity.

"Has Belinda explained where the bills are kept?" She tried to make him feel welcome.

"Sort of, in her breezy way. She said most bills were kept in those two blue files." He pointed at the bookshelf behind the desk.

"Let me know if there's anything you need or can't find. We are a bit chaotic in here, but somehow we get there in the end."

"Do you mind if I use Belinda's desk for an hour or so and go through the files?"

"Not at all. I normally work on that table anyhow. It's a bit cramped, I'm afraid." Amanda started tidying Belinda's desk.

"Don't worry. Just leave things as they are. I'm sure you've got work to do." He smiled at her.

Amanda sat at the table behind the door that served as her desk making a list of the dresses they had collected so far. Simon seemed immersed in sorting through the files of unpaid bills.

Amanda looked at him with the corner of her eye. He looked vulnerable. His gentle expression didn't match his large frame. She could sense youth was still trapped inside him, despite the greying temples and thickening waist.

★

The following evening Amanda perched on the table that was also laden with files, boxes and garments for the fashion show. Despite the lack of space, she preferred working at the office rather than at home. Since the charity had given her a salary, the attitude of some of the volunteers towards her had changed. Some of the women had made cutting remarks about the small perks that came her way and they had also taken to commenting in front of her about how hard they worked. Instinct told her it was wiser to work where everyone could see her, suspecting that if she worked from home someone might imply she was not doing enough.

She was drawing a seating plan on a large piece of paper when someone opened the door. She put her pencil down and turned round expecting to find one of the volunteers.

"Sorry, have I startled you?" Simon stood by the door, briefcase in one hand and two large files in the other.

"No, not at all. Your raincoat looks drenched. I can't believe it's still pouring out there." She smiled back.

"I'm afraid it is. They say it won't change all weekend. I hope you have a good book to curl up with."

"No time for reading. There are so many last minute hitches with the show, I'll probably spend the weekend in here."

Simon hung his raincoat behind the door. "I hear you got offered Mosimann's for the evening and a lot of press will be turning up."

"So many of the ladies who have donated clothes are regularly in the limelight, that it's attracted the press. I'm delighted as it will give Care Campaign terrific exposure. We need it in the present climate. It's become quite difficult to raise money."

"Belinda tells me you're a great asset to the charity." Simon placed the files on the overloaded desk.

"It's kind of her to say so but it's all thanks to the hard-working team around me." Amanda wished the two women who were being hostile could hear her.

"How many invitations have you sent out?" Simon sat on a stool beside her.

"About a thousand, which reminds me, here's one for your wife. I meant to get your address from Virginia but she's been away in Paris."

Simon looked down at the carpet. His expression reminded her of Mark when he was in need of encouragement.

"I don't think Sue would come up to London for the day, particularly if she knows I'm indirectly involved in the event. We're in the midst of a separation."

"I'm sorry, I didn't know." She paused. "I can understand how you feel. My husband and I parted five months ago and I still find it difficult to adjust to all the changes." For the first time she didn't volunteer the information that Douglas had left her, just in case Simon had been the one to walk out of his marriage.

He looked up at her with his puzzled, boyish expression. "I assumed you knew. Virginia is a family friend and…" The door opened and two cleaning ladies carrying a vacuum cleaner and some dusters walked in.

"Is it six-thirty already? We'll be out of here in a minute. Would you mind doing the office next door first?"

"No problem. We will come back in ten minutes." They left some bin-liners and went next door.

"I'd better start packing." Amanda got up and started to sort out the clothes on the table.

"Are you taking those away with you?" Simon stood up.

"I'm afraid so. It always pours when I'm carrying expensive dresses around London."

"Of course, now I remember. You don't have a car. Let me give you a lift back. You can't manage all that on your own."

"Are you sure? I'm in Putney. We'll catch all the traffic over the bridge."

"If you're not in a rush, we could go and have a drink somewhere till the rush hour is over and then I'll drive you home."

"That would be very kind." She looked up at him and smiled. "I might take advantage of you giving me a lift and take these home too." Amanda pointed at two boxes. "Someone has given us a lot of designer leather wear. I haven't had the time to look at it yet." She bent to lift one of the boxes.

"I'll do that. You take care of the dresses." He knelt beside her at the same time as the cleaners came in to reclaim the room.

Simon followed the slow-moving traffic down the Fulham Road and when they reached The Chelsea Hospital he turned right into Hollywood Road. Changing into second gear, he looked at her and said hesitantly, "There's a small wine bar on the right that has good food. Are you hungry?"

"I suppose I could manage something light." She looked out of the window at the new flats with large 'for sale' signs.

"Good. You can keep me company. I'm starving. I don't think I'm too good at looking after myself. I skip meals and then when I suddenly feel ravenous all the shops are shut. They all know me at the midnight deli near the flat. They must think I keep odd hours."

"I also went through a stage when I didn't make an effort with food. It's all part of not being able to do things just for yourself."

"I suppose you're right. I never thought about it that way. I always put it down to being a hopeless male, not cut out to be a bachelor."

How much better "bachelor" sounded than "spinster". There was an enigmatic glamour that accompanied an unattached man of middle years. There was nothing but unspoken failure that accompanied the label of "spinster", as though women were rendered incomplete if they were unattached. Amanda's train of thought was interrupted by someone hooting at Simon as he tried to reverse into a parking space.

At a small table overlooking a neat walled garden, Simon told Amanda how his wife had left him soon after he had been made redundant from the firm he had been with for fifteen years.

"I wasn't the only one to go. Although I was assured that it wasn't a reflection on either my character or performance, my wife, Susan, still felt I had let them all down." He smiled ruefully. His soft blue eyes with their boyish, half-puzzled expression looked sad as he talked. He picked at his food sparingly. Remembering he had said he was starving, Amanda felt sorry for him, sensing that talking about his situation had made him lose his appetite.

With their coffee Simon lit a cigarette. "Susan's family have always been very well off. When I married her I knew her father was worried I might not be able to keep her in the manner to which she was accustomed. I went straight into the City and admittedly did very well, not only because of my hard work but also because of some of my in-laws' connections. Whenever we had an argument Susan brought this up." He stopped, took another sip of wine and looked towards Amanda. "I'm sorry. Am I boring you?"

"Not at all. It's good to talk sometimes." She encouraged him, sensing he needed to clarify things in his own mind. Sometimes strangers were easier to talk to than friends or relations.

"We lived on her father's estate because that's what she wanted. A large farmhouse beautifully converted. Of course my father-in-law gave it to us for very little. But this, too, although it wasn't my choice, was constantly rubbed in. I've paid for all the restoration, the various extensions, swimming pool and tennis court, but she still feels her father gave it to us. Anyhow, when I lost the job, we rented it out to pay for the school fees and moved back to the Hall with her parents."

Amanda suspected his story might be one-sided, but nonetheless he wanted reassurance and she felt sorry for him. His perplexed expression asking for sympathy was difficult to ignore.

"Right now, I'm looking for a job along with hundreds of other over-qualified, over forty males." He looked out towards the wintry garden.

Later, crossing Putney Bridge where the river graciously turned past Bishops Palace towards Barnes, Amanda was delighted at how festive this familiar route looked today. The bridge lamps reflecting against the wet windscreen and the soft sound of the traffic on the wet road seemed to awaken new sensations.

"Have you lived in Putney long?" Simon filtered towards the right.

"A lifetime." She sighed involuntarily.

"Sounds bad." He stopped at the traffic lights.

"Not all bad, but too long when you look back. I've been here since I married and at times it feels as though, apart from my childhood, all I've had is Putney!"

"Would you move out if you had a chance? The traffic over the bridge at the wrong time of the day must be dreadful."

"Douglas travelled to work by underground and I didn't often cross the river. When I did, if I got caught in the traffic on the bridge, it only made me more aware that I was at the Gates of Putney."

"You make it sound like a concentration camp."

"It was, in a way. Like all confined spaces when you try and leave them, it isn't easy. Everything outside feels so different and threatening."

"Should I turn left at the next traffic lights?"

"Yes. Sorry, I wasn't concentrating."

They drove in silence down the dark suburban streets.

"Next left." Amanda broke the companionable silence. "I'm the second on the right. The lights are on. Kate must be home. She mentioned she might be coming home sometime this week for a party."

"Is Kate your daughter?"

"Yes. She's at Bristol University." She opened the car door.

"You carry the dresses and I'll take care of the boxes," said Simon.

In the hall Kate was listening to music with her hair wrapped in a towel.

"How lovely to see you, darling." Amanda walked over to kiss her daughter after dropping the dresses on a chair. She noticed Kate was looking past her at Simon. "Sorry, I forgot to introduce you. Kate, this is Simon Banks. He also works at the charity."

"Hello, Kate." Simon put the boxes on the floor. "I'd better be off." He looked at his watch, clearly embarrassed. "Good luck with the preparations. Hope to see you at the show," he said addressing Kate and backing out the door.

When he was gone, Kate said, "He's quite nice. I thought you only worked with women!"

"Simon only helps with the accounts. He's doing it on a temporary basis while he looks for a new job."

"I see." Kate raised her eyebrows. "What's in the boxes?"

"Designer leather wear." She tried to ignore Kate's inquisitive tone.

Amanda had supper with Kate and later, as she lay in a hot bath, wondered what her daughter would have thought if the man helping her with the boxes had been Clive's age instead of reassuringly middle-aged like Simon.

★

Climbing the stairs to Maria's flat, Amanda stopped to draw breath. She had spent the morning tying up the loose ends for the impending show. She had never anticipated, when she had first suggested the show to Belinda, that she would have lighting experts, dressers and photographers to contend with. Although she enjoyed the challenge, she worried about overlooking details that could undermine the success of the event.

"My dear, you're late today." Maria's thick voice reprimanded her.

"I know. I'm sorry. I'm terribly busy at work." Amanda took her coat off.

"Bridge is a very difficult and a serious game, my dear. If you don't give yourself to it, you will never learn."

Amanda walked into Maria's drawing room to find Virginia and Tina wearing identical jackets. Helen, who sat opposite Ingrid, raised her eyebrows and looked at her watch. "We waited for ten minutes and then assumed you weren't coming."

"I thought the whole idea of being five rather than four was that if one of us was late or unable to come, there would still be a foursome and... I'm sorry I'm late, but I am simply rushed off my feet," she blurted out, surprised at the irritation in her own voice.

"Come and sit beside me and relax, you poor love. You look exhausted." Ingrid patted the cushion beside her.

"Perhaps I should stop coming for a month or so. I really don't think I can spare the time at the moment." Amanda sat heavily on the small sofa.

They all looked up at her with shocked expressions.

"But you can't!" Tina's dark eyes fixed on her. "What will we do when I go skiing for a week next month and when Virginia is away for the half-term with her grandchildren?"

"I don't want to let anyone down but perhaps bridge isn't something I can afford to do at the moment."

"The rush is only temporary because of the show. It's good for you to have other interests." Virginia's voice was cautioning.

"We are all helping you with your project as much as we can. It seems unfair you should walk out on us." Helen sounded like a schoolmistress, reasonable but at the same time inflexible.

"I think I will make some coffee." Maria left for the kitchen, aware it was better if she didn't interfere at this point.

Virginia looked at Amanda over the rim of her glasses. "I heard that Nick Rubens might be covering the fashion show." She fixed her eyes on her, waiting for a reaction.

"Nick Rubens! But it's only a small event."

"Not so small any more. The guest list seems to have mushroomed and the fact that the Duchess is planning to come has no doubt attracted his attention."

Tina listened with interest. Perhaps this famous social columnist would write something about her buffet dinner and mention that Lord and Lady Ashcombe had been her guests.

"I'd be rather worried about him turning up. He must have upset more marriages and careers than the financial crash," said Helen.

"He's not always dangerous." Virginia eyed Helen who, she knew on principle, would dislike anyone who made a living out of social gossip. "If he were to give us a good write up..." she continued, "it would be very good for the charity. I won't go as far as to say he'd put us on the map, because we are established, but it would certainly make us a 'fashionable charity', which we are not at present."

"Fashionable charity! Honestly, what next? Will certain illnesses become fashionable too!" Helen retorted.

"Belinda never mentioned Rubens," said Amanda still surprised by the news.

"She probably doesn't know yet," said Virginia smugly.

Amanda looked at the women sitting round the table. To them, meeting once a week at the same time and sharing a small corner of their lives, was a true commitment. She had only started to play bridge out of a desire to be distracted and a need for company. She knew all these women were fundamentally playing for the same reason.

Looking at Virginia's immaculately made-up face, Amanda was reminded that had it not been for her encouragement and introduction she might never have started at Care Campaign. Ingrid had volunteered to model at the show. Helen had addressed most of the invitations in her beautiful rounded handwriting and Tina was helping her in more ways than one. They were all supporting her efforts.

"All right. I'll stay," said Amanda. "But you'll have to be patient if I'm not the best of partners and if my mind keeps drifting." She smiled brightly at the small group.

"Sure, we all have commitments. The whole idea is being able to disengage and give oneself to the game." Virginia's drawling voice was cautioning her again.

After an hour of being dealt very bad cards, and Helen repeatedly pointing out her errors, Amanda was about to resign again.

"I think it's time to stop for coffee." Maria left for the kitchen when the last rubber had been scored.

While Virginia and Tina discussed intensely which tricks had been lost unnecessarily, Amanda turned to Ingrid and remarked on how much weight she had lost.

"I'm glad you noticed. I'm determined to be a size ten for the show."

"Oh, please. I don't want you wasting away. It is good enough of you to spare us the time to model."

"I'm looking forward to it. It brings back the old days." She sighed.

Amanda looked at Ingrid's wide-eyed face, a face of the Sixties, and tried to imagine her in her twenties rather than her forties. With the skin pulled tight over her wide cheek bones, her straight blonde hair and her lips fresh and full, she must have been stunning. She still had the long legs and shapely figure of a model but her face, that had once been trained to light up as a response to admiration, looked tired and devoid of expression. Ageing was hard. One was never ready to fully accept it, especially in Ingrid's case, as her beauty had been her greatest achievement.

Tina looked at her watch. "I must rush. Derek is coming to do my hair in half an hour."

"Going anywhere tonight?" Virginia asked out of politeness.

"To the opera at Covent Garden. We're entertaining the Selbys. You know, the racehorse breeder. Constantine is doing some business with them."

"Is it *Othello* that's on? I haven't read any of the reviews yet." Helen, who normally queued for her opera tickets, thought seats in the stalls would be wasted on Tina.

Tina pretended not to hear the question. "I must dash. Amanda, why don't you drop in later on and collect that Versace jacket I mentioned was too small." Tina wrapped her cashmere cape round her and, leaving Helen's question unanswered, said goodbye and left the room.

"I bet she doesn't even know what she's going to see," Helen muttered to herself, loud enough for everyone to hear.

"They do go out an awful lot and maybe Constantine arranged it all." Virginia felt she had to defend Tina.

"Maybe she'll read about it while she's having her hair done." Ingrid was upset by any form of friction and always agreed with everyone.

"Maybe Derek, her hairdresser, is musical." Helen got up and tidied the pleats of her navy blue skirt.

Amanda, who found Helen's remarks at times very irritating, felt a certain admiration for her. Although there was a dryness in her manner that spoke of unfulfilled emotions, she had the firm, decisive demeanour of someone who was not afraid of her own company.

*

Outside Maria's flat, Amanda hailed a taxi. Mark would be arriving at Victoria coach station in half an hour and she wanted to be there to greet him. Casually meeting him off the Winchester coach would give them some time together. Amanda had observed that it was easier to talk to Mark when they were doing something together, whether it was tidying the back garden or simply walking to the bus stop. Usually, inside the house, Mark withdrew to his room and his own world, rarely communicating his plans, opinions or feelings.

Since Amanda had written to Mark at school letting him know she would be able to finance his skiing holiday, he had sounded cheerful and full of expectation.

Amanda made her way round the coach station, taking in its drabness. As she walked past the fast food shops where people in dark anoraks queued with unsmiling faces, she wondered if Tina had ever been to a coach station. Waiting for the doors to their coaches to open, young and old with their grey, tired, winter faces, huddled together on the long benches. When she went to survey the cheap literature kiosk, Amanda thought it was not surprising that people read mainly for escapism.

A group of young people in heavy boots and thick anoraks sat on their rucksacks and smoked mechanically, staring blankly at the empty bus park. Was Mark as unhappy as they looked? She could hear Douglas's voice reprimanding her whenever she had tried to protect him: "He's got to toughen up. Life is not easy and the sooner he realises that the better."

When Mark's bus arrived Amanda was overwhelmed by a mixture of joy and excitement, and when she saw him come off the bus, tall and serious, she was full of pride, her apprehension gone.

"Hello, Mum." Mark came to her, rucksack over his shoulder. She wanted to kiss him, but felt he wouldn't approve, not in a crowded station.

"Did you have a good journey?" she said instead, the gesture of love wasted.

"Yep. What are you doing here anyhow?"

"Oh, I'm on my way to Tina's house up in Belgravia. I had half an hour to spare and thought it would be nice to see you, in case you're out when I get back home. Do you have any plans for the weekend?" They walked slowly towards the door.

"I thought I might look for some ski gloves. Stephen is lending me an anorak. I'll pick it up from his house in Richmond this weekend." His face brightened as he talked about the holiday. "Two more weeks and it'll be time to leave. I'm really looking forward to it." He looked down at her. "Thanks for helping out with the money, Mum."

"It seemed silly to waste the opportunity." She tried to make light of his gratitude.

"I think I'll take the tube home. How are you getting to Belgravia?"

"I'll walk. It's only a few minutes down the road."

"When are you buying your little car?"

"Some time at the end of the month. I just want to get the fashion show out of the way before I start visiting second-hand car dealers."

"Oh yes, I'd forgotten about your show. It's soon after I'm back. Are you all set?"

"Nearly." Amanda smiled, wondering how Mark could forget about it when his home had looked like a Turkish bazaar ever since she had started collecting the dresses.

"See you later then." He walked towards the escalator.

Amanda made her way towards Tina's house, feeling reassured that her trip to the bus terminal had been worth it. She had shown her affection and Mark had responded.

★

Outside Tina's house, waiting for the maid to open the door, Amanda realised she was becoming annoyed by Tina's power games. She knew the Versace jacket had been held back as a reward both to her and the charity. A few days ago Belinda had rung Tina to confirm she would be able to come to her buffet party after the show.

Lord Ashcombe would be collecting her and joining them for coffee at the end of the evening. Tina already had been spreading the news amongst her friends that the Ashcombes were attending her party. When Amanda had first met Tina she had thought of her as a devoted wife who entertained only to please her husband. Although Constantine expected her to perform her duties as an industrialist's wife, Tina did this not only to please him, but to impress their circle of acquaintances.

The maid opened the door and took Amanda's coat. "Mrs Karalambos is waiting for you in her dressing room. She is having her hair done."

Amanda followed the woman to the first floor of the house where, to the left of the master bedroom in a room full of cupboards with a large dressing-table, she found Tina wrapped in a silk dressing-gown. Behind her stood a lean, handsome, young man.

"Amanda, darling, I have wonderful news for you. I have persuaded Derek to do the girls' hair and make-up for the show. He's doing it to please his favourite client, aren't you?" Tina looked at Derek's reflection in the mirror.

"I can't deny Tina anything! And it's also such a good cause. I'd be delighted to help." Derek, who knew the show would be a great social event, was happy it would give him exposure.

"It's wonderful news. A stylist and make-up artist of your reputation will make a big difference. The girls will be thrilled!"

Amanda watched how Derek, with expert hands, was applying blusher to Tina's rounded cheeks, making her face look more angular.

"What colour is your dress?" Derek looked at Tina's reflection.

"Burgundy."

"Ah! Stay still then for another five seconds. We can afford to make the eyes look a little more mysterious with a darker shadow."

Amanda watched the young man at work. He was wearing tight-fitting trousers tucked inside heavy boots. His movements were quick and lithe and, as he applied more eye shadow on Tina's lids, he teased and stroked her hair with the gentleness of a lover.

"Doesn't she look wonderful in these colours? So fresh." He adjusted the fringe.

Amanda looked at Tina's face that, with Derek's subtle shading, looked softer and younger. Watching Derek at work, Amanda wondered if he was aware of what he gave to women. The illusion of recaptured youth and the confidence with which they left him, no one else but a lover could give.

"Tina, darling," he half stroked her head, "is it all right if, while you get changed, I rearrange your friend's hair. Her parting is all wrong for the shape of her face."

"Of course you can." Tina smiled at Amanda. "He is an artist, Amanda, so let him do what he wants. You won't regret it."

Amanda left Tina's house feeling five years younger. On her way home she stopped at the printers to see if there was still time to put Derek's name on the programme. She knew it would not only please him, but also add glamour to the event. As she stood at the counter waiting for the assistant to come back, she caught her reflection in the window. For a second she didn't recognise herself with her new hairstyle.

★

Back home, Amanda ran up the stairs to her bedroom and inspected her reflection in the mirror. Derek had reshaped her eyebrows, making her eyes look larger. He had also tinted her pale eyelashes and rearranged her hair, making it fall to one side. She was amazed at how these small details had transformed her face. She looked more sophisticated and her eyes stood out, becoming the main feature of her otherwise neat face. She was wondering if anybody else would notice the change when suddenly the telephone rang.

"Hello," she called into the receiver.

"Amanda, are you busy? You sound in a rush. It's Simon."

"No. I've just come in from the printers but I've been rushing all day. It must show in my voice. I'm sorry." She sat on the bed.

"Funny you should mention the printers. I was going through the expenses today and I pointed out to Belinda how much cheaper your printers are compared to the ones the charity used before. She was delighted."

"It's nice to give local people business. I saw Mrs Karalambos today and she gave me another designer jacket."

"Hasn't she run out yet?"

They both laughed in unison. "She's persuaded Derek Ballantine, one of the top hair and make-up artists in London to do up our models."

"That's wonderful. I was, in fact, ringing to see if there was anything I could do to help. I know you're not planning to look for a car till after the show is over. Do you need any last minute chauffeuring? I'd be only too glad to help."

"I might well do on the day of the show." Amanda patted her hair, unaccustomed to the new way it framed her face.

"Just give me a call if you need anything. If you like, I can look in the *Exchange & Mart* for a car."

"That would be kind. Everyone, including my children, seem more keen on my having a car than I am."

"I know Belinda wants you to get one soon. She mentioned it today."

"Mum, is that you on the phone?" Kate's voice came up the stairs.

"Simon, I must go. Kate's home and I think she needs the phone. Thanks for offering to help. I'll certainly let you know if I do need anything."

When Amanda went into Kate's bedroom she found her curled up on her bed, crying into the pillow.

"What's wrong, darling?" She knelt down beside the bed and put an arm around Kate's shoulder. Kate sobbed without replying. Amanda stroked her head. "Darling, has anything happened at college?"

"No. College is great. It's when I come home that it all goes wrong. Dad promised to collect me from the train station tonight and he never turned up! No doubt too busy with Claire. I hate her."

"Maybe something happened to his car." Amanda found herself defending Douglas for Kate's sake.

"I doubt it. He just couldn't be bothered. He doesn't really care about me." Kate hid her face in her pillow and started to sob again.

"I'll soon have a car and be able to pick you up from the station like I used to," said Amanda, stroking Kate's head. "Now why don't you have a nice long bath and I'll get some supper ready."

"I'm not very hungry."

"Just some soup. I've got mushroom, your favourite."

Kate blew her nose noisily. "All right. Some soup."

Amanda was stirring the soup in the kitchen when the telephone rang. She picked it up hurriedly and said with an impatient tone, "Hello", anticipating it might be Tina expecting her to listen to another lengthy discourse on the progress of her preparations for the party.

"Hello, Amanda. Is that you?" It was Douglas.

"Oh." Amanda was taken aback.

"Anything wrong? You sound annoyed." Douglas's voice had a trace of concern.

"I am annoyed."

"Look, I'm terribly sorry about not meeting Kate off the train. Is she back?"

"Yes. She's upstairs crying."

"It couldn't be helped. Something came up at the last minute and I was unable to leave on time."

"Haven't you upset your children enough? Do you have to let them down too?"

"Stop being melodramatic!"

Kate's tears had stirred her anger and for once she was not going to hide it.

"Melodramatic! Have you any idea of how the children are reacting to all this? You aren't here to see what a state they're in."

"Can I talk to her?" said Douglas.

"Yes. And when you do, could you say something that will make her feel better. Could you perhaps lie and say you were clamped, rather than your business meeting was more important than seeing her."

Douglas didn't answer and waited for Kate to come to the phone.

Amanda went up the stairs. Each time she spoke to Douglas it seemed easier to vent her anger. She had always spoken to him with a degree of respect, the respect that came from being

younger and subservient. His selfish behaviour towards the
children shocked her. Douglas had always, if nothing else,
inspired respect but she now saw him in a different light.

She opened Kate's door. Kate was still slumped on her bed,
her face buried amongst the pillows.

"Kate, darling," she said softly. "It's Dad for you on the
telephone."

Kate sprang up and sat on the bed, her face suddenly looking
alert and nearly cheerful. Seeing Kate's reaction made Amanda
bridle. Douglas always rang the children either at school or, in
Kate's case, at her digs in Bristol. Ringing the house was
something new. She left the room and went back to the
kitchen, venting her irritation on the soup, which she stirred
with unnecessary vigour.

"Hi, Dad." Kate's voice was barely audible, letting her father
know she had been crying.

"Kate, I'm so sorry. I wasn't anywhere near the station when
it happened or I would have come in a taxi. I'm afraid I got
clamped and by the time I dealt with it, well, it was too late."

"I waited for ages," she sniffed.

"Oh, you poor love. I'm awfully sorry, darling. I could pick
you up on Sunday and take you to Paddington. How about
that?"

"Okay," answered Kate unenthusiastically.

"If I came slightly earlier, let's say six o'clock, we could have
something to eat on the way," said Douglas, dreading the
moment he would have to tell Claire he would not be there on
Sunday evening.

*

When Douglas put the phone down, he felt guilty. Kate had
obviously been very upset. It hadn't occurred to him it would
upset her that much. Maybe the separation had indeed made
the children more sensitive to things they wouldn't have
minded about before. He lit a cigarette. He rarely smoked,

except for the odd cigar on special occasions. He looked round for an ashtray. The coffee table was still littered with magazines, make-up and bottles of nail polish. The carpet was wet. He remembered that, before storming out of the flat, Claire had thrown a glass of whisky at him. He got up to look for an ashtray in the kitchen. The sink was filled with the dishes and pans from the night before. Underneath a smelly cloth, he found an ashtray full of Claire's half-smoked cigarettes. She had rung him in the office that afternoon to say she had tickets for the seven o'clock performance at the local cinema and that she would be picking him up at six-thirty. When Douglas had replied he had promised to pick up Kate from the station, Claire had sounded disgruntled.

"We could go tomorrow instead," he had said encouragingly.

"Tomorrow we're going away for the weekend, if you remember, to Jane and Keith's." Douglas had indeed forgotten about the arrangement. It had only been mentioned casually at a party two weeks ago. Claire had started to cry, saying he never remembered anything about their life together. She was fed up and wanted to leave him. He had come home to calm her down.

In the flat they had a terrible row. Claire had called him a boring old man with a bad back, whose only interest was his work.

"And what do I get out of it?" she had shouted, throwing the whisky at him. "All the money seems to go on school fees or legal fees. So much for the fun time we were going to have once we had our little pad. This dingy hole was only going to be temporary. I know I'm untidy but a girl needs a little more space than this, you know." She had kicked the chair so hard, it had knocked over the lamp on the table. "Go and collect Kate, if you want," Claire had shouted as she slammed the door.

This had reminded Douglas of what the time was. It was too late to collect Kate. Her train had arrived ten minutes ago. Leaning back on the sofa, exhaling slowly, Douglas felt sorry for himself. It wasn't easy to keep a young girl happy. Admittedly, there were some insuperable problems, such as Claire's friends. The main reason why he had forgotten about the weekend was because unconsciously, he was hoping Claire had forgotten as well. She hadn't brought it up since the party at which they had met Keith and Jane. Her friends were, on the whole, too young for him and had other interests. She had a lot of friends, but he was bored in their company. Claire, on the other hand, seemed to like being with his colleagues, although he seldom took her out with his old acquaintances as he suspected most of them would still be loyal to Amanda.

His thoughts returned to Claire. It was true he had made Claire promises he was now finding difficult to meet but, nonetheless, he paid for most of her expenses and was always giving her lavish presents and took her away on weekends. The thought often preyed on his mind that he might have made a mistake moving in with Claire so soon. They should have kept separate flats, but then she had insisted.

He poured himself another whisky and decided to go and find Claire. He knew he would probably find her in the wine bar across the road. She usually went there whenever they had a row. He would take her away next weekend to Paris or Amsterdam. He was bound to find some reasonable two night package. It was still cheaper than moving flats. He didn't want to move. The flat was small, but central and had all that was needed. Claire was very untidy. That was the problem, he told himself.

*

Amanda was still stirring the soup when Kate came into the kitchen. Her expression was nearly cheerful and she had brushed her tangled hair.

"Well, I suppose it wasn't entirely his fault if he did get clamped," she said sitting at the table.

Pouring the soup into two bowls Amanda realised Douglas had taken her advice and had lied to Kate about the clamp. She felt a certain satisfaction that he had done as she had asked him to.

"They're having a real blitz lately," she said placing the steaming bowls on the table. "Julia very nearly got clamped last week outside the shop."

"He's picking me up on Sunday to take me to supper on the way to Paddington Station. Will you be here?" Kate asked looking over her spoon.

"I'm afraid not. I'll have to pop into the office to meet Simon. We're pricing some of the dresses."

"On a Sunday?" Kate looked at her suspiciously.

"The show is next week and we're miles behind with everything."

"Hum. This Simon chap sounds very helpful."

"He's a great help to me at the moment. There's still so much to do," said Amanda casually.

"I don't think Dad knows the show is at Mosimann's." Kate looked at her mother.

"I suppose he doesn't." Amanda thought it better not to mention to Kate she would rather Douglas knew as little about what she did as possible.

"I might bring a friend next time I come home," said Kate, out of the blue.

"Is this Sebastian?" Kate hadn't mentioned him since Christmas.

"No. We're not seeing each other at the moment." She tossed her hair. "It's a girlfriend. I stayed with her parents last weekend."

"Oh, Sita Anderson?"

"Yes." Kate was impressed her mother remembered as she had only mentioned Sita once.

Amanda cleared the dishes, wondering if Kate was having problems with her boyfriend and if this was adding to her unsettled and increasingly difficult moods.

Chapter Seven

At five o'clock Amanda collapsed on a balloon-backed gilt chair and surveyed the ground floor of Mosimann's. The electricians and sound experts were still at work, but the catwalk had been finally erected and the chairs were all in place. There was only an hour left for all the last minute preparations to be carried out before the guests arrived. Since the morning the place had been buzzing with people trying to do their jobs. It hadn't taken Amanda long to realise that everyone considered their contributions to be the most important. It was difficult to please everyone and inevitably there had been arguments amongst the participants. The five models supplied by the agencies, plus Ingrid and Patsy, had managed one rehearsal, but the top model who was supposed to show part of Clive's collection hadn't arrived. Derek, who had been with them all morning, kept on assuring Amanda that the girl would turn up eventually.

"It's quite common for top models to arrive late for charity shows. She's a nice girl. I've worked with her before. Don't worry, she'll turn up," he had said reassuringly.

Amanda looked at Simon, who was talking to one of the electricians and wondered what she would have done without him. Not only had he collected the champagne donated by a friend of the Halfords, and made sure it was properly chilled, but he had also helped her with the seating arrangements which had proved to be a major problem. The people who had given generously, like the Karalamboses and the Halfords, would expect to be seated in the front. There was also the press to think of and, as Simon had pointed out, it was important to have the faces that attracted the press on the front rows too. Amanda suspected that the women, who had given their favourite designer cast-offs, would feel left out at having to watch the show from the gallery on the top floor. Keeping everyone happy was her job, but she realised it would be very difficult to succeed in doing so.

At five-thirty, Amanda started worrying the top model would never arrive. If she didn't, Patsy or one of the juniors would have to replace her. As she wondered how the preparations were progressing on the third floor, she found herself feeling sorry for Clive, who had been working so hard. She knew that opportunities to show a collection in front of the best-dressed women in London didn't come to a young designer often. Whenever Amanda saw Clive, she felt guilty. Looking back at the evening they had spent together, she knew she shouldn't have allowed it to happen. His success this evening would appease the nagging guilt she felt whenever she saw him. Clive, who was polite and solicitous whenever they met, was also clearly uneasy in her company.

Amanda was about to ask Simon where he had put the programmes, when a striking girl with long legs walked in. Her face was beautiful, despite the unflattering hairstyle. Amanda hurried towards her. "You must be Bianca. I'm so glad you're here. We were getting a bit worried you might be late. It's so kind of you to do this for us. Derek is upstairs doing the girls' hair." She looked hopefully at Bianca's aggressive hairstyle, no doubt left over from her last assignment.

"I don't think even Derek will have time to change my hair now. I'm exhausted. I've had two gruelling photographic sessions today." She sighed. "What I need is a bath and a glass of champagne."

"I think the bathrooms upstairs have showers."

"Welcome! Here is your champagne." Simon was standing beside them. He simultaneously placed a glass in Bianca's hand and in Amanda's.

"Cheers." The girl emptied her glass in a gulp. "Nothing like a warm welcome when one's had a long day."

Amanda took a long sip of the chilled champagne and looked gratefully at Simon who, with his six foot stature, was only marginally taller than the girl.

"Why don't you take Bianca upstairs?" He put his hand reassuringly on Amanda's shoulder. "I'll finish sorting out the seating arrangements and put out the programmes."

The third floor of Mosimann's was a hive of activity. Members of the committee, acting as dressers, rushed in and out of the different rooms carrying garments, shoes and pieces of costume jewellery. Some of the models sat round a table sipping the champagne Simon had sent up, while others concentrated on their make-up. Derek was styling Patsy's hair and Ingrid was helping one of the younger girls with her eye shadow when Amanda walked in followed by the beautiful Bianca. When they reached the centre of the room everyone stopped talking. The silence was hostile and Amanda instinctively walked in Derek's direction.

Derek, who, in his years as a make-up artist, had diffused as many arguments before a show as he had styled heads, acted as though nothing was amiss.

"Hello, love, had a busy day?" His eyes fell on Bianca's "space age" hairstyle. "I'll do something different, softer, that will complement Clive's romantic dresses." He winked at Amanda. "Don't worry about a thing."

"This is the third time today I've had to change my hair. Can't I just stay like this!" Bianca pouted.

"It's the first time today *I* will be doing it." He looked at her teasingly. "And that's the only one that counts."

"Derek, sweety, you win." Bianca smiled.

"It's all right for some. They miss the rehearsal and when they decide to swan in, everyone is at their beck and call." The girl standing by Ingrid hissed loud enough for half the room to hear.

"Ignore it. There are always prima donnas around. The fashion world was full of them even in my day," Ingrid whispered, trying to avoid any more animosity for Amanda's sake.

Clive, who had heard Bianca had finally arrived, came into the room and walked towards her with a big smile. Amanda suspected that what he really felt like saying was, 'You selfish cow. You could have ruined the show'. But instead she watched him take her hands and whisper, "When Derek is finished with you, I'll show you what you'll be modelling. It's a new collection. Floaty and dreamy. Hope you'll like it, Bianca."

Bianca was clearly flattered by his approach. She normally was treated like a clothes-horse by the more established designers. She preferred the catwalk to photographic sessions and being included in this way obviously appealed to her.

"Derek, love, will you be long? Clive here would like me to get a feel of his collection," Bianca said full of self-importance.

Amanda gave a sigh of relief. Bianca was going to give her best. She looked at Clive and noticed that the frown he had been wearing all day had vanished. She was both relieved and happy for him.

"I'll come to touch up your make-up and hair when I'm finished with the girls," Derek whispered to Amanda as she passed him on her way to the door.

Amanda rushed down the stairs wondering if the electricians had gone. There were only forty minutes left before the first guests arrived.

"There you are! I've been looking for you everywhere." Julia, wearing a red dress, stood panting in front of her holding a cardboard box.

"You don't mind my dotting cards around in the obvious places like the bar and the loo, do you? It'll give the shop great exposure. I'm sure most of the people here tonight wouldn't buy their presents and knick-knacks in Putney, but now that we do mail order it's good publicity." She paused to draw breath. "We miss not having you at the shop on Saturdays.

Hope you'll come and help again when all this is over. And..."
she dropped her voice, "you won't forget to introduce me to
Jack and Solange. They sound so cosmopolitan. I'd also love to
be introduced to Lady Ashcombe. Henry, you know, was
introduced to Lord Ashcombe at a business dinner a couple of
years ago and says he's simply charming."

Amanda wished Julia would stop talking so she could get on
with the last minute arrangements.

"Of course, you can put the cards wherever you want, and I
promise I won't forget to introduce you." Amanda looked at
her watch. "But I must fly. There's so much to do."

"I'm really proud of you." Julia met her eyes. "You've come
a long way since... well, you know. Goes to show one can
manage quite well, if not better, without them."

"You were a brick at the beginning, Julia. I wouldn't be here
without you."

"Off you go then." Julia pushed her gently.

Rushing down the stairs, Amanda felt ashamed at her
annoyance when Julia had first mentioned the cards. Had Julia
not given her all her support and the job at her shop, she would
never have got her confidence back. It was easy to forget a good
turn when one's life was busy. The thought of Julia bustling
about Mosimann's in her crimson dress, advertising her shop,
suddenly filled her with joy.

Downstairs Amanda found the electricians were gone, the
flowers were in place and a programme rested on the velvet seat
of each chair. Some photographers had already arrived and
were standing by the door in case anyone worth photographing
came early. Simon, who was checking that the cards with the
guests' names had been placed on the right chairs, saw Amanda
and came towards her.

"Things under control upstairs?"

"They are now. For a moment I thought the girls were
going to upset Bianca. Luckily Derek took over and made light
of the situation. He's priceless. He seems to be able to handle a
room full of egos like a seasoned psychiatrist."

"Talking about hair, your new style, all swept to one side, is very becoming."

"Thank you." Amanda felt herself blush. "It was Derek's idea."

A tall, blonde woman wearing a lot of jewellery was making her way towards them.

"That's Annabel Partridge. She's lent us the costume jewellery. She's a great talker and, if I'm still with her after five minutes, will you please come and rescue me? I'll never get away otherwise."

"Leave it to me." Simon smiled as he watched Amanda go towards Annabel.

"I thought I'd better come early," Annabel's fingers played busily with the gold chains round her neck, "just in case there was something else you might need. I have a large assortment of earrings and bracelets in the back of the car."

"I think we've got enough, but it's very efficient of you, nonetheless, to bring some more."

"It's a good cause and I'm delighted to help. It also gives me a chance to show my latest range. It was so sweet of you to mention me in the programme." Annabel looked around her. "You've worked very hard. It promises to be quite an event. In fact, no different to the big designer shows one goes to at the beginning of the season."

Amanda saw one of the committee members coming towards her and was relieved. It would make it easier to get away.

Annabel took a box out of her evening bag and handed it to Amanda. "I'd like you to have these as a present. Hope you'll wear them tonight."

Gillian Berman, a charity member acting as a dresser, was now standing beside them looking at the box.

"Aren't you going to open it?" said Annabel. "I suppose I should have asked what you'd be wearing, but the good thing about these earrings is they go with everything."

Amanda could do nothing but open the box.

"Aren't they gorgeous! She's so lucky with all her perks. Are you wearing that gorgeous dress of Tina's tonight?" The innuendo in Gillian's voice was not wasted on Amanda.

"I will if I ever get round to changing." Amanda tried to ignore the taunt.

"Please wear them tonight. It's good publicity for me. If you give them away as a tombola present after that, I'll quite understand," said Annabel.

"I'll tell you if we need anything else at the last minute. Does it look as though we might be short of jewellery for the models?" Amanda looked towards Gillian.

"Not jewellery, but shoes! One of the girls is a size eight. We don't have many shoes that size. She's upset and making a fuss."

"I'll come up." Amanda put the earrings in her pocket.

"Amanda, someone is asking for you at the door." Simon was standing beside her.

Not sure whether Simon's remark was genuine or part of the rescue plan, she hesitated. "If you could deal with it, I'd be grateful. There's a small crisis upstairs."

When Amanda walked into the section of the third floor being used as one of the dressing rooms, she heard the girl complaining.

"Had I known, I would have brought my own shoes. I was told by the agency it was a very high profile charity and that everything would be provided."

"We were given a list of sizes by the different agencies. I'm sorry, someone must have made a mistake," one of the helpers said apologetically.

"What size are you?" Patsy had walked into the room at the same time as Amanda.

"I'm an eight," the girl replied sulkily.

"I'm that size too. I brought my own shoes just in case. Always had trouble with my size in the old days. You can borrow mine."

"What about you?"

"I'm only showing the St Laurent dress. I can squeeze into a smaller size. You'll be showing most of the day wear, you need to be comfortable."

"You sure?" The girl looked relieved.

"Yeah. No problem."

"Thank you, Patsy. That's so kind. But are you sure you're only showing the St Laurent dress?" Amanda asked anxiously. "I thought you were modelling some of Clive's as well."

"Yeah, so did I. I'm afraid Alfred's put his foot down. He doesn't mind me modelling my own dress, but he'd hate me showing anything else. It's beneath me now, he thinks. That's men for you. They want a tart before the wedding bells and then a nun." She shrugged her shoulders and laughed.

"Derek's looking for you, Amanda. He wants to tidy your hair before the guests arrive," one of the girls called.

Amanda looked in the direction of the committee member who had remarked on her perks. She was busy trying Patsy's shoes on the model. She remembered the earrings and took them out of her pocket. She would wear them tonight and keep them. She felt she deserved them.

★

At seven o'clock, fifteen minutes past the scheduled time, the lights were dimmed and the spotlights came on, their stark light directed solely at the platform. From a corner by the front door Amanda watched the guests. The sound of a familiar Sixties tune and the champagne that had flowed freely for the last half hour, had softened their expressions. The space round the catwalk was packed and not a single chair remained empty. On the first floor people stood round the banisters of the gallery, pressing against each other in order to get a better view. On the first row reserved for the press, Amanda saw Nick Rubens. She recognised the face always pictured at the top of his gossip column. He specialised in exposing skeletons in cupboards. Although an established charity, Amanda worried that Rubens could easily find dishonour somewhere amongst the members of Care Campaign if he wanted to. She also worried about Clive. This evening was a great opportunity for him but unfavourable comments from Rubens about his collection could ruin it.

On the second row Amanda saw the Karalamboses. Constantine looked relaxed, as though he had sat in first rows all his life. Tina was dressed in all her regalia and had the air of someone who assumes they are the centre of attention. Alfred Halford sat to the left of Tina. He looked distinctively masculine and nearly out of place on the seat of the gilt chair. Amanda, who had never met Alfred, strained her eyes in the darkened room to get a better view of the man Patsy seemed to fear and care for. Alfred was definitely past sixty, but his obvious virility somehow made his age unimportant. His face was weighed down by thick, unruly eyebrows and a large nose. Amanda could tell by the length of his arms and legs that his stature was small, but this too seemed unimportant. Belinda Ashcombe sat to the right of Constantine. Amanda observed how Constantine talked and laughed with Belinda and wondered what he had in mind to propose to Lord Ashcombe that evening. On the second row, amongst friends of the Halfords and the Karalamboses, to her surprise she saw Jack and Solange. Amanda, who had checked and double-checked the seating plan with Simon, knew they were not supposed to be there. They were in the seats reserved for Tina's sister-in-law and her husband who, Amanda guessed, looking up towards the first floor gallery, were now standing, crushed amongst the crowd upstairs. Jack and Solange looked totally at home smiling at the guests either side of them. Amanda wondered what had gone wrong. There was always a chance Tina's sister-in-law had decided not to come at the last minute. But why would Jack and Solange be sitting in their seats when all the seats were clearly labelled?

Beside Jack sat Bernice Maxwell and she was clearly enjoying his company. Lydia had insisted Bernice was placed in one of the front rows, stressing how disappointed Mrs Maxwell still was at not being able to hostess the London bridge lunch which, she took every opportunity to remind Amanda, had been replaced by the fashion show. Watching Bernice laughing flirtatiously, no doubt affected by Jack's charm, Amanda reassured herself that perhaps Jack being in the wrong seat was a fortuitous mistake. She only hoped that Tina's sister-in-law wasn't in the crush upstairs.

When Amanda looked up to see if she could recognise them amongst the faces in the gallery, she saw her own sister and brother-in-law. She had to control her desire to wave at them. Pat and Tony were spending the night with her in Putney and were planning to take Kate out to a restaurant with them while she was at Tina's party. Pat had been looking forward to the show since Amanda had first mentioned it at Christmas. They didn't often come up to London and, when they did, they usually ended up watching a play they either didn't enjoy or understand, just to justify their visit. Amanda knew her sister would spend the next day in the West End stores and come back exhausted in the evening laden with parcels, asking her how she could bear to live in London. "So noisy and dirty." Pat would then go back to Hampshire feeling jet-lagged by the visit and tell all her friends what a wonderful time she had had. Tonight, judging by her sister's excited expression, the outing to Mosimann's would be a topic of conversations for several weeks.

Amanda looked for Kate, but couldn't find her and, wondering whether she might be standing at the back, circled the room. There were a few minutes left before the first model came out and she wanted to say hello to her daughter before the show began. In the dim light she saw Lydia walking towards her. Lydia, unlike the other members of the Special Events Committee, had not been assigned a specific job. Amanda had planned to use her as an usher, which she was sure Lydia would have enjoyed, as there were plenty of famous people attending. Lydia had been stand-offish and had said she wasn't sure whether she would arrive in time from the country and therefore would rather not be involved.

"Oh, there you are!" Lydia was now standing beside her. "I had difficulty parking. I'm sure I wasn't the only one." She looked up at Amanda, obviously glad she could give her bad news.

"Have you seen Bernice?" Her voice sounded alarmed.

"Yes. She's sitting in the third row behind Lady Ashcombe and Mr Halford."

"Haven't you put Lady Ashcombe on the first row? My dear girl, you should know better…"

"It was her suggestion that we keep the first row for the press. We weren't expecting much coverage but things seem to have mushroomed. I think the Duchess being here tonight has a lot to do with it."

Lydia's mouth tightened as she said, "It might have, but most Care Campaign functions get coverage because it's a good cause. However, the one who might not give the event such good coverage is Nick Rubens. I gather he's here tonight." Her eyes searched the room. "I wonder if he'd like to join Bernice's little gathering round the corner after the show?"

"Is Mrs Maxwell entertaining this evening?"

"We've organised a last minute informal buffet party on the top of the Carlton Towers for 'old hands' of the charity," she said smugly. "Mr Maxwell is a director of the Carlton Group and has kindly put one of the small reception rooms at our disposal."

Amanda was horrified, realising that Lydia had schemed with Bernice Maxwell to jeopardise the Ashcombes attending the Karalamboses' party.

"Are Belinda and Lord Ashcombe expected at this gathering?" she asked, trying to conceal her anxiety.

"Of course they'll come. She is, after all, our chairman. I'm sorry we didn't include you but we assumed you'd be too busy."

Amanda wondered whether she should confront Lydia and ask her bluntly whether she was deliberately trying to upset Tina. The thought of the Ashcombes not turning up at the Karalamboses' party made her feel cold with apprehension. Not only had Tina spent hours on the preparations and told everyone she knew that the Ashcombes were coming, but Constantine had only sanctioned the evening in the hope Lord Ashcombe would be his guest.

The lights became dimmer. Amanda knew this meant the models were about to come out. She turned towards Lydia and said, "Tina will be very upset if the Ashcombes don't come."

"I'm sure everyone will enjoy her party with or without the Ashcombes," Lydia said primly.

Realising it was pointless to pursue the matter further, Amanda walked away from Lydia and stood by the door where she had a better view of the catwalk, her heart pounding after Lydia's revelations. The music was, this time, a familiar Seventies tune. The first model appeared wearing a day suit. She walked in time to the music, stopping occasionally to look at the audience. The music quickened and a second girl came out. Amanda recognised her as the model who had borrowed Patsy's shoes. Both girls were now walking side by side and there was applause as they walked away. Two more girls appeared; the clapping had obviously given them confidence. Their step quickened in time to the music as they swirled their jackets to reveal the garments underneath, clearly excited by the reaction of the audience. Like peacocks spreading their plumage, the girls swept down the catwalk with confidence and ease. Amanda watched the faces of the guests partially obscured by the dim lights. Their expressions were alert. Some were tapping their feet to the beat of the music.

Nick Rubens was taking notes. Amanda noticed his hand moved swiftly across the piece of paper that rested on his programme. She strained her eyes, trying to read his expression, wondering if it would give her a clue as to what he was writing. He didn't look bored, and Amanda wondered if

210

this was a good sign. When she saw Belinda sitting in the row behind him, her heart sank. Nick Rubens was bound to talk to her and enquire after Lord Ashcombe. If Belinda mentioned her husband would be joining her at the Karalamboses', and that was put in print, Constantine's expenses and Tina's hard work would be rewarded, but if Lord Ashcombe went to Bernice's gathering instead, the success of the evening would be ruined. Why hadn't Belinda mentioned Lydia's gathering for "old hands" at the Carlton Towers, Amanda wondered.

Trying to concentrate on the show, she turned her attention to the catwalk, where the last of the day wear was being shown.

The music softened and Patsy came in alone wearing the St Laurent evening gown. She moved with all the expertise of a professional but with the more demure air of someone who no longer relies on modelling for a living. As she approached the side where the press sat, one photographer called out, "Look this way, Patsy." Clearly someone had recognised her from the old days. All the photographers were now clicking their cameras. Amanda looked in Alfred's direction. He was clearly not amused by the man's familiarity with his wife. There was a round of applause as she left, but Alfred didn't clap.

The music changed and there was a pause. Guests looked at their programmes, remembering there was a young designer showing his evening wear. Bianca came out wearing one of Clive's ball gowns. When Amanda saw her gliding down the catwalk like a swan, her head high and her limbs loose, she understood why she had been worth waiting for. If the clothes had looked beautiful or sexy on Patsy and the other girls, the dress came alive on Bianca. She gently lifted the full organza skirt and trailed it alluringly behind her as she walked away, making the fabric look rich and desirable. One of the younger models, followed by Ingrid, came in showing two more of Clive's ball gowns, and then Bianca was on again, this time wearing a tight-fitting black gown with a plunging back. The atmosphere was electric. As the music changed and Bianca half-walked and half-danced, her long legs appearing and disappearing from behind the slit at the back of the skirt, the photographers came forward, their cameras clicking. When Bianca and the black dress left, there was loud applause and some cheers from the gallery.

The music changed and the models came and went, their clothes glittering and sparkling. With the last round of applause Clive and the production assistant joined the girls on the stage. Amanda heard someone call her name and then saw Simon come towards her. He gently pushed her towards the platform. As she stood there with the girls and Clive, dazzled by the lights and the applause, she longed for something familiar to centre herself on and then, amongst the figures at the back of the crowd, she saw Julia's red dress. She was clapping and waving and Kate stood beside her.

Belinda came to join them on the stage and gave a small speech in which she thanked everyone for coming and contributing so generously. Amanda heard her give a special thanks to the Karalamboses for their "tremendous support" and then Belinda mentioned her name and all her hard work that had made the evening possible.

It felt like a very long time before they all left the platform. The audience was still clapping when a waiter came towards them with a tray of champagne.

"Well done, Amanda!" Belinda said, her cheeks still flushed from her speech.

Amanda wondered if this was the right moment to ask whether she and Lord Ashcombe were still planning to join the Karalamboses after the show.

"Amanda, Kate's looking for you." Simon joined them.

"We'd better circulate," said Belinda. "But before you disappear and join Kate, let me introduce you to the Duchess." She took a sip of champagne before easing her way to the centre of the room where the Duchess stood surrounded by admirers.

Amanda followed Belinda. She felt full of energy and the confidence that comes from success. People smiled at her as she walked past them. Being recognised and appreciated made her feel self-conscious but at the same time excited and, to her surprise, important.

The Duchess was talking to an elderly gentleman, who was introduced as Major Fleming. Belinda obviously knew him because they kissed lightly on the cheek. Amanda waited to be introduced. The Duchess congratulated both Amanda and Belinda on the success of the evening. Her voice was low and her diction full of studied pauses. The role of patron that accompanied her newly acquired title was something she still clearly enjoyed.

Major Fleming, who nodded his head in an affirmative gesture each time the Duchess spoke, looked at Amanda's cleavage. She met his eyes and he smiled. To her surprise, she felt touched rather than indignant by his prying stare, happy for him that he should still take an interest in the shape of a woman. He must be in his eighties, she calculated. Standing behind the Major, Amanda saw Julia's red dress and, hoping Kate was still with her, excused herself and left Belinda and the Duchess who had now been joined by two guests.

"Well done, Mum," Kate pecked her on the cheek. "You look great! I like the earrings and the dress. A bit short, but I suppose you can just get away with it in the evening." Kate lifted the skirt of Amanda's dress playfully and gave it hard tug before letting it drop again.

Amanda adjusted the dress at the waist line. "I'm so glad you made it in time from Bristol, darling."

"So am I. I wasn't expecting anything like this," she said, looking towards the Duchess. "I'm very impressed. I was just telling Julia I never thought you had it in you to be such a little business lady."

There had been an undercurrent of sarcasm in Kate's congratulations, imperceptible perhaps, even to her, but not lost on Julia.

"I always knew you had it in you, given half the chance." Julia patted Amanda on the shoulder.

"Have you seen your Aunt Pat?" Amanda was keen not to be the topic of conversation.

"There she is. They're coming in this direction." Kate took a glass of champagne from a tray behind her.

"There you are. Well done." Pat kissed her on both cheeks. "I was just telling Tony that it's wonderful to see you so involved in something you enjoy. We always used to worry about you in London with no hobbies, just the house and the children. One is always so busy in the country," Pat went on. "Village life makes it so easy to have access to all this sort of thing." She gestured at the room.

"Not a fashion show at Mosimann's with royalty present, surely." Julia couldn't control herself. Living in Putney and having a shop in the local high street made her feel a staunch Londoner.

"Not literally, of course. We tend to do things at the church hall. But it's wonderful to see Amanda doing so much, and so busy." She looked at Julia reprovingly.

"Where are you taking me to supper this evening?" Kate put on her little girl's voice as she addressed her aunt, letting her know she was on her side.

"I left it to Tony. Where are you taking us, darling?" She turned towards her husband, turning her back on Julia.

"A new Italian restaurant just off the Fulham Road. You're sure you won't join us, Amanda?"

"I'd love to, but Tina has organised a buffet supper for the committee members at her house."

"Is Simon a committee member?" Kate asked pointedly.

"No, he's not. But he is one of the organisers," Amanda answered awkwardly, wondering when Kate would outgrow this phase of being provocative. "I must go and say hello to Jack and Solange. I'll be back later."

"Will you introduce me to them?" Julia whispered. Amanda sensed Pat had taken an instant dislike to Julia and decided it would be better if she came with her. They made their way across the room to where Jack and Solange were talking to Tina and Constantine. When Tina saw Amanda, she waved emphatically, more like one does across a crowded railway station than at a cocktail party.

"Amanda, it was all lovely except this terrible mistake." Tina frowned. "Constantine's sister had to watch the show from the gallery upstairs."

Amanda looked in Jack's direction, wondering what explanation he had for having taken their seats.

"I was just telling Tina this kind of thing always happens, even in the most organised events. Solange and I feel mortified. Someone must have put our names on their seats by mistake."

Amanda, who had double-checked the seating arrangements at the last minute with Simon, knew Jack was lying but was relieved, for Tina's sake, that he should be doing it with such flair. She was certain Jack and Solange hadn't been allotted those seats.

"I remember you said Maria and Ari would be in the row behind us," Tina went on disapprovingly.

"Like Jack said, my dear, mistakes do happen." Constantine smiled, patting his wife's hand. "Maria and Ari, I'm sure, don't mind as much as you do. It was a lovely show and Lady Ashcombe's speech was so appropriate. We are so much looking forward to meeting Lord Ashcombe this evening."

Tina, suddenly reminded by her husband of the true objective of the evening, said in a forgiving tone, "It was a lovely show."

"Bernice Maxwell, who was sitting beside us, mentioned Lord Ashcombe would drop in at the Carlton Towers to collect his wife after the show," Solange said, looking at Amanda questioningly.

"The Carlton Towers!" Tina raised her voice in alarm.

Amanda felt Constantine's eyes on her.

"Did she? It must be a misunderstanding." She looked in Constantine's direction, inwardly praying he wouldn't notice her unease. But Constantine did.

"Maybe you should have a word with Mrs Maxwell yourself and clarify the situation," he said dryly.

"Yes," said Amanda. "Of course it must be a misunderstanding."

Julia coughed. Amanda, who had completely forgotten about her, was grateful she could change the subject by introducing her. Amanda tried to get away. She had to talk to Belinda. The Karalamboses' evening was in jeopardy.

"We will see you all later." Tina looked towards Jack and Solange as Constantine walked her towards the door, where photographers waited.

Amanda had to control herself not to confront Jack about the seats and wondered if he guessed how annoyed she was. She could hear Solange trying skilfully to disengage herself from Julia and failing, leaving her with no other option than to listen to her anecdotes about the shop. When Amanda saw Annabel Partridge coming towards them, it suddenly became apparent to her which would be the best way to punish Jack.

"Jack, let me introduce you to the lady who is responsible for all the wonderful jewellery the models were wearing this evening."

Jack, who would have preferred to have been introduced to the Halfords or the Karalamboses' friends, gave Mrs Partridge his best smile. When he politely inquired about her jewellery, Annabel Partridge started telling him how she had started the business and then proceeded to give him a chronological history of her company. Amanda left both Jack and Solange with the two most talkative women in the room and, as she saw them looking around in the hope someone would come and rescue them, she felt partly vindicated over Maria and Ari's seats.

Amanda looked round the room for Belinda. She would have to ask her, even beg her, to go to Tina's and not to the Carlton Towers. The thought that Lord Ashcombe might have already been given instructions of where to go made her feel faint. She looked for Belinda amongst the guests, the triumph of her evening forgotten.

"Are you all right? You look harassed." Simon bumped into her.

"Have you seen Belinda? There's a crisis."

"Can I help?" He sounded concerned.

"At the moment all you can do is help me find Belinda."

"I saw her a minute ago, talking to Bernice Maxwell near the door."

"Oh no."

"Amanda, what's wrong?"

Amanda made her way towards the door, ignoring a couple of people who called her name. Belinda stood talking to Major Fleming.

"Oh, there you are. Have you been upstairs with the models? Anything wrong?" Belinda looked at her questioningly.

"Are you going to Bernice Maxwell's party at the Carlton Towers?" Amanda asked apprehensively.

"Well, I didn't know anything about it until a minute ago. The internal politics of a charity! It seems this time my husband is the prize. But don't worry." She sighed. "I told Bernice that we're already expected at the Karalamboses', so..." She looked up at Amanda and winked. "We'd better go straight there as soon as you are ready."

Amanda's fears had turned into elation. The evening would be a success after all. She took a glass of champagne from a tray left on a side table, when she heard someone call her name.

"Mrs Thompson. Could I ask you a few questions?"

She turned around and saw Nick Rubens. He was inhaling his cigarette and smiling at her at the same time. Despite his tie and dark jacket, he had a dishevelled air, as though he had dressed in a hurry. He was thin and his eyes, that dominated his pinched face, were alert and constantly moving.

"I gather you and Lady Ashcombe are responsible for the success of this evening," he said, while the smoke filtered out of his mouth and nose.

"Not entirely. A lot of Care Campaign members have worked very hard to make this evening possible," she said stiffly.

"Of course," Rubens smiled. "I hadn't realised till tonight that the Duchess was the patron." He inhaled again.

"It was very kind of her to support us tonight. We all know how busy she is." Amanda wondered if she was irritating Rubens with her safe replies but continued, "Mrs Constantine Karalambos is very kindly hostessing a dinner for our members at her home this evening. Lord Ashcombe will be joining Lady Ashcombe there later on." Amanda wondered if it was obvious she wanted him to know.

"Constantine Karalambos? Ah yes, he used to be in shipping. Is he containers now?"

"I'm afraid I don't know," said Amanda.

"They live somewhere off Chester Square, I believe."

"Yes."

"Nick, there you are. You have to be careful what you tell him," a tall man joked as he joined them. Amanda took advantage of the interruption and made her way towards the stairs.

*

Upstairs, the models were changing and drinking champagne with Derek and the production assistant. Everyone was in high spirits. The show had clearly been a success and they would all get more press coverage than they had ever anticipated. When Amanda joined them to thank them for their hard work, she noticed that Patsy, who always had a smile on her face, looked worried and withdrawn.

"Anything wrong?" Amanda sat on a chair beside her. Patsy, who was wriggling into a cocktail dress to wear at Tina's, looked at her and shrugged her shoulders.

"Alfred's mad because that photographer chap recognised me and was ever so friendly. If Constantine wasn't a business mate of Alfred's, I'm sure he'd march me home with no supper. He's terribly possessive and can't handle anything about my past life. It's a drag and it makes things such a pain sometimes."

"Maybe after a couple of glasses of champagne at Tina's he'll cheer up and forget about it." Amanda tried to sound encouraging.

"It takes more than two glasses of champagne to cheer Alfred. I'll have to swing from the chandeliers for a week now, and maybe even that won't help. It used to in the old days, but since Damian's birth it's become ridiculous. He wants me to be the perfect posh little middle-class wife. I was a model when he fell for me. It's not fair."

"It's a lovely dress." Amanda tried to change the subject.

"Alfred chose it." Patsy looked at Amanda and suddenly her face broke into a smile again. "I suppose I knew he was a difficult old man when I married him. Oh! I did enjoy the catwalk tonight." She sighed. "It's been a great night. I hear from one of the other girls in charge of sales, that we've sold a lot already and there've been lots of enquiries. Have you heard Clive's already sold two of his dresses to friends of Tina?"

Amanda, who had been busy circulating and had left the sales to other women on the committee, was delighted by the news. She was particularly happy for Clive, but secretly wished, now that the show was over, they wouldn't have to meet again. His success this evening, she hoped, was a happy ending to something she felt should never have happened.

"Do you need a lift to Tina's? It'd be great if you joined us. Alfred won't nag and bring the photographer bloke incident up again in the car if you're with us."

"I'd love too, but I've already told Simon and Lady Ashcombe I'll go with them."

"Never mind. See you later." Patsy left, balancing on her high heels.

As Amanda watched Patsy leave, she wondered if she shouldn't have accepted her offer after all. She was planning to approach Alfred Halford's group to find out if they would consider sponsoring the charity's summer ball. The ride in the car would have been an informal way of getting acquainted. 'Has my mind started to work like Solange and Jack's? I'd better be careful,' she reprimanded herself and then smiled at the thought of them still trapped downstairs listening to Annabel's life story and Julia's rendition of Richmond's Peerage.

★

After saying goodbye to Kate, Pat and Tony, Amanda left Mosimann's. Simon and Belinda came with her and, once outside, they decided to take a taxi. Tina's house would have been walking distance on a balmy summer's evening, but the persistent February drizzle had made it an unpleasant distance to bridge on foot. Amanda stood shivering under her umbrella, her head bowed to protect her from the wind. Tina's short organza dress and the thin wrap across her shoulders weren't designed for blustery weather. With her eyes fixed on the pavement, hoping a taxi would soon come along, she suddenly saw, a few feet away from her, a pair of familiar legs. Amanda knew immediately, without looking up, they belonged to Douglas. She looked up, and their eyes met. She had stopped breathing, as though the lack of air in her lungs would help arrest her emotions.

"You've changed your hairstyle." He looked at her with a mixture of surprise and admiration.

"Yes, so I have. It's been a while since I've done it. I'm not conscious of it any more."

"It suits you," he said, as though letting her know he approved.

The thought that Douglas might still think she needed his approval made her feel angry. How dare he suddenly appear and talk to her as if nothing had changed.

She took a deep breath. "What a coincidence to find you here," she said hurriedly with the tone one reserves for impending goodbyes. When she heard a taxi stop nearby Amanda looked hopefully in Simon and Belinda's direction.

"No coincidence at all." Douglas ignored the fact she might be trying to leave. "Kate asked me to collect her tonight."

"Kate! But she's having supper at a restaurant with Pat and Tony; at least that's what she said earlier on." She shrugged her shoulders and one side of her wrap came undone, disclosing the pretty black dress Tina had given her. Douglas's eyes moved unceremoniously from her face down the rest of her body. Amanda felt naked, aware he knew every contour of her. The way in which he was looking at her, as though she still belonged to him, annoyed her.

"Kate tells me," his eyes moved slowly back to her face, "that you keep yourself, or are kept, in smoked salmon and champagne these days. Mind you, it agrees with you." His eyes went to her body once again.

"Amanda, are you coming?" Simon's voice was accompanied by the clicking of the taxi's meter.

"The job with the charity gets me occasional perks. As we usually raise money through social events, the perks I get are inevitably things like the champagne that's left over." She had blurted the explanation out too fast and now wished she hadn't. Why should she justify any of her actions to this man, who had decided to walk out of a life they had promised to share, for better or worse. At the sight of him now, looking at her with the same expression he had always worn whenever he was hoping to make love to her, she realised she no longer wanted him back and that she had finally left him behind.

"You'll find Kate inside," she said as a goodbye and left him standing on the pavement, aware he was still watching her as she got into the taxi.

"He didn't seem to want to let you go. Anyone we know?" said Simon as the taxi turned into Belgrave Square.

"That was Douglas, my ex-husband. He's come to collect our daughter," she said matter-of-factly as though she and Douglas were the best of friends. There was a moment's silence and then Belinda, still excited by the success of the evening and her short speech, started talking animatedly about the evening's events.

Amanda looked out of the window and tried to put some order into her emotions. She had been shaken by the unexpected encounter with Douglas, but something else inside her had precipitated the melancholy that now dampened her high spirits. When she remembered the feeling of repulsion at the thought of physical contact with Douglas, she understood that the emptiness she felt stemmed from the realisation that she didn't love him any more. All these past months she had secretly hoped for a reconciliation, believing that contentment could only lie in married life. All that was gone, finished: the man, the life, the emotions and the dreams. She didn't want them back. Amanda thought of Kate. She had obviously been trying to get them together, fabricating stories to make Douglas jealous. She would have to talk to her daughter, ask her to stop, and explain she no longer was prepared to share her life with her father. She looked away from the window as the taxi stopped outside Tina's house. She met Simon's eyes and smiled at him, thinking he probably understood, going through a divorce himself.

★

As soon as Amanda walked into Tina's large and sumptuous drawing room she felt herself relax. The rest of the evening and its outcome were no longer her responsibility, for this was

Tina's party and Lord Ashcombe would be attending after all, despite Lydia and Bernice's attempts to sabotage it.

Tina had planned and gone over every tiny detail assiduously. She had changed her instructions to the florist and caterers each time she changed her mind about what to wear that evening. Everything had been colour coordinated. Tina's dress blended in with the soft furnishings of the room and the sumptuous buffet was also predominantly pink, with lobsters, langoustines, pink meats and tropical fruits decorating the large table in the adjoining dining room. The guests had been as carefully chosen as the wines. Minor politicians, fashionable surgeons, elegant socialites, industrialists and television personalities mingled in the spacious rooms. As Amanda made her way across the room towards the fireplace, she could overhear snippets of conversations from the different groups. Everyone seemed to be either talking about the success of the show or about Lord Ashcombe's imminent arrival. Most people talked about him as though they knew him, or they had some anecdote to recount, in which a friend of theirs and Lord Ashcombe played the central role. They either knew his brother, or had a friend that had been at school with him, or knew of someone who played golf at the same club. Lord Ashcombe was discussed with great interest and familiarity by the different clusters of guests. But everyone agreed that Belinda, his wife for the past ten years, was a wonderful woman and had been a pillar of strength to him as well as a good mother to his already grown-up children.

Tina moved briskly from guest to guest, happy they were all there, each one carefully chosen to fulfil his or her own role, which more often than not was to impress or amuse the others. For the last month Tina had been visiting an acupuncturist. Her sleep pattern had been badly affected by the build up to the party. She would lie in bed thinking about the guest list, the menu, the flowers and she had sudden panic attacks each time she thought of the possibility of Lord Ashcombe being taken ill or having to suddenly go abroad on unforeseen affairs of State.

The evening had finally arrived and everything had gone according to plan: Lord Ashcombe was in good health and after listening to the debate in the House of Lords, would be joining them.

Tina was satisfied that she had performed a service none of Constantine's cheap girlfriends could perform. Even the more expensive one, she knew he kept in a flat off South Kensington, wouldn't have access to the guests here this evening. Tina punished Constantine for his infidelities by spending his money voraciously. She was too proud to discuss her husband's other women with her girlfriends and often, when she bought herself a new piece of jewellery, would insinuate that her husband had given it to her as a reward – a reward for what? Her friends were left to wonder what she had done to earn the gift.

"Amanda, let me introduce you to Pia Perreira. She is married to the attaché to the Brazilian Embassy."

Pia Perreira was small and dark. She could never have been described as beautiful but was so striking that it was difficult not to stare at her. All the beauty seemed to spring from the way she moved both her body and head. Even small movements, such as sipping her champagne, were performed with a degree of eroticism.

"Such a lovely show. I loved the ball gowns." She stretched her words making them last and cling to her wide lips. "I bought the black one. Irresistible and so reasonable. New designers are so often better than the established ones."

Amanda was happy for Clive as she envisaged Pia turning heads at embassy functions in the clingy black dress Bianca had modelled.

"Tina tells me you organised the whole show. So much organisation. You must be an expert at social events."

"Not at all. I just do it for the charity. It's my job."

"Oh! Luis and I have a yacht we keep in the Mediterranean. We were thinking of giving a party on board for his birthday. Life is so hectic with the embassy, we were looking for someone who could perhaps organise the event for us. So much to do, chartering a small plane and all that." She looked at Amanda questioningly. "Would you be interested?"

Amanda was taken by surprise. She had never thought of herself as a "party planner". "I couldn't possibly do it. I only work for the charity, you see. I'd be no good, but if I can think of anyone, I'll let you know."

"Maybe you could do it in your spare time. We'd pay all the expenses. Taxis, telephone calls."

"I don't really have the time, much as I would like to."

"Don't worry. No trouble. Maybe one day."

Someone came and took Pia away in the direction of the dining room. Amanda was left standing in the middle of the crowded room reflecting on the different propositions she had received lately. She eased her way towards the adjoining reception room and was about to put her empty glass on a tray held by a waiter, when she saw Jack waving at her. He was standing by the large fireplace at the end of the room. He blew her a kiss, flamboyantly but graciously. Unable to ignore his gesture, she demurely waved back. As she crossed the room towards him, she saw on top of the fireplace the completed portrait of Tina. She knew he had started working on it soon after he had finished with Virginia's grandchildren. The cheque she had received a few weeks ago, specifying it was her commission for procuring a client, still made her feel uncomfortable and an accomplice in something dishonest. Mark had rung her from the Alps two days before the show. He had sounded happy and was clearly enjoying his holiday. The memory of her son's cheerful voice somehow allayed her guilt.

"Hello, darling." Jack pecked her familiarly on the cheek. "We expect you to be more selective in your introductions. One couldn't paint a portrait of the likes of Annabel Partridge for all the tea in China. The perpetual vibration of her voice would upset the setting of the paint."

Amanda couldn't suppress a small laugh. "She's very well connected," she joked.

"Not well enough. Not well enough," he said, looking round the room with satisfaction.

"I didn't know you were planning on finishing Tina's portrait so quickly," she said looking up at Tina's regal figure.

"Ah! Caught the bug, I see. Wondering when your next commission is coming up?" He looked at her mockingly.

"Not at all." Amanda blushed. "Not at all. It never crossed my mind. As I said, I don't want any more commissions. I just didn't expect Tina's portrait to be finished. Tina never mentioned it was nearly done."

"She wanted to surprise Constantine with it this evening. What do you think of it?"

"I'm no expert, but it is a true likeness and very flattering at the same time." She looked at the gentler and softer looking Tina.

"I like to portray my subjects at their best. Expressions can change and distort a face. That's why I like them to sit for short periods, listening to music and relaxing. I capture the best and portray that moment when they are at peace with themselves. There's beauty in everyone and it is the artist's task to reveal it."

Amanda tried to disengage herself from Jack, who ignored her weak attempts to leave by talking with increasing enthusiasm about his technique and the people he had painted. He recounted his favourite anecdote about what had once happened while he had been working on the portrait of one of the young royals. As he talked, including her in his monologue by asking at regular intervals, "Don't you agree?" she was once more lulled by his charm. His voice was soft and his eyes never left her face. Whenever someone brushed passed them he would protectively put an arm round her. When Jack asked her how well she knew the Halfords, Amanda knew she was about to be pressured into an introduction and tried to change the subject. Jack's eyes moved round the room. He was clearly excited by the wealth around him. Tina's home was now full of mini celebrities, dethroned royalty from obscure kingdoms, and money that had survived the recession. When Amanda saw Helen standing alone in one corner, she seized the opportunity to leave Jack and went to join her. She had not expected to see Helen amongst Tina's hand-picked guests.

"This is the kind of decor that makes one feel like becoming a socialist again." Helen greeted Amanda with an economical smile.

"Yes, it is rather over the top, I suppose. Still, it's a lovely party and superb food."

"I haven't been in to the dining room yet. I'm trying to adjust to one room at a time. I can't stay long. I'm not used to late nights, but Tina insisted I come, which was very nice of her, I suppose." Helen looked primly round the room.

"You're her favourite bridge partner," Amanda said, realising why Tina had asked Helen.

"Funny, never expected her to be that loyal but there you are. Human nature is unpredictable. They say Goering was a dedicated father."

The voices in both rooms suddenly became subdued and there was a feeling of anticipation amongst the guests. Amanda, who was standing by the door, saw Constantine greeting Lord Ashcombe with a beaming Tina beside him. Lord Ashcombe was taken round by his host, who introduced him to the guests in order of importance. He seemed a jovial, friendly man who appeared totally unaware of the importance some people attributed to his presence. As Amanda watched him circulate round the room, she gave an involuntary sigh of relief. Her mission was completed. She felt suddenly tired, aware of her aching feet. Worry and excitement had fuelled her with energy all evening. Now, released of tension, she was exhausted and felt like going to bed.

Patsy, who was standing by her husband near the hall, gestured in her direction. Amanda made her way towards the Halfords and, as she moved past the clusters of guests, she overheard half-finished conversations on finance, Lord

Ashcombe, and the snow conditions on the Continent. When Amanda shook Alfred's hand, she sensed that this was a man with strong likes and dislikes. He seemed genuinely pleased to be introduced to her and made her feel comfortable by saying, "The evening was a great success. I hear Patsy's dress was sold straight after the show."

"It was so generous of Mrs Halford, both to donate the dress and to model it. She didn't want to do it, but I'm afraid we forced her. We felt no one would show it off better."

Alfred smiled, pleased to hear that Patsy had been persuaded to model to help out.

"We're planning our ball for next summer and aim to raise enough funds to buy a new scanning machine. We are hoping Patsy will be on the committee. I know she's busy with Damian but we won't take too much of her time."

"It's for Patsy to decide. She always has my support when she is involved in purposeful projects." Alfred looked at his wife.

"Amanda, darling, I've been looking for you." She recognised Jack's voice behind her. He had obviously been watching her and waiting for the moment when she spoke to the Halfords to join her and force an introduction. Jack had just turned towards Patsy and given her his most disarming smile, when they were all interrupted by Constantine and Tina who, accompanied by Lord Ashcombe, had joined their group so that Alfred could finally be introduced to the minister.

The Halfords and the Karalamboses moved to the dining room and Jack joined Solange, who was talking to the Brazilian beauty. Amanda looked round the room, wondering if it was too early for her to leave. The events of the evening – Lydia, Bernice, Lord Ashcombe, Douglas and Kate – had left her feeling drained. She looked round the room for Simon. She would let him know she was ready to leave. The party was now in full swing and it was unlikely that anyone would miss her at this point in the proceedings. The mouth-watering buffet had now taken centre stage.

Chapter Eight

A week after the fashion show, Amanda sat in the office writing thank you letters to those who had supported the evening. Simon sat opposite adding up how much money they had raised, while Belinda, perched on the edge of the desk, was talking on the telephone. Her strident voice, punctuated by her laughter, made it difficult for them to concentrate.

"We must go out and buy *The Standard*. Apparently Nick Rubens has featured the fashion show and the Karalamboses' party in his diary, and very favourably too!" Belinda mouthed in their direction, putting her hand over the receiver. "Thank you for ringing. Yes, yes of course, we'll go and buy a copy now. Isn't that wonderful!" she said, putting the telephone down and looking at Simon. "I'll buy a copy of *The Standard* on my way out. I'm meeting someone for lunch just off the Fulham Road in ten minutes. We haven't had any publicity in a long time." Her voice was full of excitement. "Well done, Amanda." She circled the desk and squeezed Amanda's shoulder. "It was a wonderful idea, and you worked so hard at it."

Amanda, who had felt in low spirits since the night of the show, welcomed Belinda's praise. After months of working to a deadline and worrying about the preparations, the success of the evening had left her feeling surprisingly drained.

"Wouldn't it be easier to type a general thank you letter and then sign it by hand?" said Simon when Belinda left.

"Oh, no! That's too impersonal. People have worked so hard. Writing by hand is the least I can do."

"You are good," he said, picking up the phone.

"Care Campaign research. Can I help you? Yes, she's here. Whom should I say is calling? It's Lydia." Simon stretched across the desk and handed Amanda the receiver.

"Hello, Lydia," said Amanda with hesitation. They hadn't spoken nor seen each other since the evening at Mosimann's.

"Nice little write-up in Ruben's diary. Have you seen it yet?" Lydia's voice was unusually friendly.

"No, I haven't. Belinda has gone out to buy a copy."

There was a short pause and then Lydia said:

"Amanda, we were wondering if you could come to our rescue. We're desperately trying to find a fourth for one of the tables at our bridge lunch on Thursday and were wondering if you could come down?"

"But I'm only a beginner. I'd love to help but I don't think I'm good enough to enter a tournament."

"We need someone for a beginners table. I have asked everyone I can think of locally, but most of them are advanced players or are already playing at other tables."

Amanda hesitated. There were still a lot of letters to write, she hadn't done any housework for days and she wanted to get things organised before the children came home that weekend. Driving all the way to Hampshire to play bridge was the last thing she wanted to do.

"Yes, of course I'll come if you are really stuck. But I must remind you, I am a beginner."

"So are the other women at your table. We're all meeting for coffee at ten. Lunch will be at twelve-thirty, so I wouldn't plan on being back in London till late afternoon," said Lydia.

"See you on Thursday then." Amanda gave the receiver back to Simon and looked at the pile of letters on her desk.

"Taking the day off on Thursday?" asked Simon.

"I couldn't refuse. Not after all the bad feeling since the bridge tournament in London was cancelled. It's a bore though. I had planned on finishing with the thank you letters by the end of the week and I need to do a big shop before the children come home this weekend. I'm afraid I've rather neglected the house lately."

"A bit odd, Lydia asking you. I can't believe she can't rustle up someone local. How are you getting down there?"

"Haven't thought that far yet. The train from Paddington, I suppose." She sighed.

"Now the show is over, you must really do something about looking for a little car. Belinda asked me this morning, when we were looking at the accounts, to encourage you to get one."

"Yes, I suppose I should. I'm afraid cars were very much Douglas's department. We always had a company car. The thought of buying a second-hand car makes me rather nervous as I wouldn't be able to tell if half the engine was missing."

"We'll get an *Exchange and Mart* next week and, if you want, I'll help you look."

"That's so sweet of you, but I'm sure you've got better things to do. Aren't the auditors coming in next week?"

"Yes they are, but things are pretty much in order." He got up. "I'm driving to Swindon to see an old client on Thursday. I could drop you on my way. Isn't the bridge party somewhere near Newbury?"

"Are you sure?" Amanda's face brightened.

She had never told Simon about Lydia's plan to sabotage the Ashcombes attending the Karalamboses' party. Being driven there by Simon made the whole prospect of meeting her again and playing bridge less daunting. Amanda watched Simon bend over the filing cabinet. His sloping shoulders and slow movements were so unlike Douglas's confident exterior. Simon was unassuming and it was his undemanding, and at times hesitant, approach that encouraged her to take the initiative when with him. Why would a woman want to leave a man like that? Her thoughts drifted to her own failed marriage. Did their acquaintances discuss why Douglas had left her? She was younger than he, a good mother and had been a faithful wife. Where were the flaws in her that others saw? Perhaps there were no flaws and it was only a matter of erroneous expectations. We sometimes expect our partners to be someone they cannot be. What should Simon have been to Sue other than the unassuming man he was?

*

On Thursday morning Simon rang Amanda's doorbell. Amanda was wearing her best day suit, the one she had always worn to the children's school plays and speech days. As they drove through Barnes Common, Amanda was studying her Acol bridge manual.

Simon looked at her with the corner of his eye and said, "Green suits you."

"You're just trying to cheer me up."

"I suppose I am. You do look terrified, as if you were reading your death sentence! But it doesn't change the fact that green does suit you."

Amanda smiled and looked out at the river. The tide was high and the waters grey, reflecting the sky above. How sensitive of him, she thought, to realise she was in need of reassurance. Since Douglas had left, her only encouragement had mainly come from her women friends. Had they sympathised because she was now a woman alone or because this might happen to them one day too? Was Simon only concerned about her because he too had been left? As though reading her thoughts, he said, "Funny how long it takes to get used to doing simple things without one's other half, even something as mundane as sharing a car journey."

"Yes. It's the changes in everyday life that are the hardest to adapt to. I find eating alone and never having enough laundry to do a full load difficult to get used to, yet the bigger things seem to be easier to overcome."

"For example?"

"Being on my own. Now I lead my own life. It's a lonely life, but it's my own."

"I suppose it's different for me. I miss the company and the children. Not having a job and not living in my own house doesn't help. I wish I could say that being on my own is new and exciting, but it isn't."

"Was it a good marriage?" asked Amanda.

"And what is a good marriage?" said Simon filtering on to the motorway.

"Don't ask me. I wasn't too successful at it. I still think it would have been better if I'd worked, though. I think, if it was easier for women to raise children and work, there would be more good marriages."

"Sue never felt the slightest inclination to work. She's always been content taking care of the children and keeping up with country life."

They drove out to the countryside in companionable silence. A few miles off the M3 they crossed through an orderly Hampshire village. At the top of a steep hill Simon swung into the Countess of Avercorn's drive and stopped the car at a respectful distance from the front door. Amanda now wished she had done some more revision and, clutching her Acol bridge manual, looked apprehensively towards the imposing front door where two women stood talking. She tried to memorise the conventions Maria had taught them at their last lesson and failed.

She turned towards Simon. "I really shouldn't have come. I can't even remember the bidding."

"Of course you can." He patted her hand. "Once you start playing, it will all come back. You'll surprise yourself." He turned the engine off so that Amanda didn't feel she had to jump out. "I'm not sure how long I'll be in Swindon. My client mentioned lunch and, if I remember correctly, he enjoys his food. Let me give you the telephone number of where I'll be and if I'm still there when you're finished, I'll come and collect you. You might even have developed a taste for the game by then."

"I doubt it," Amanda said, pulling a face.

Simon scribbled a number on the back of a card and put Amanda's bridge manual in the glove compartment. "You'd better leave this in the car. You'll just have to bluff a little."

Amanda walked towards the house. The outside was dark and foreboding and was surrounded by funereal cypresses that stole most of the light from the north-facing windows. Once in the hall, she joined a group of women standing in front of a notice board pinned to the wall. Most of them looked as if they had just been to the hairdresser and Amanda was relieved she had decided at the last minute to wear her best suit. It was too late to worry about her hair, which was pulled back casually with a couple of combs. She looked amongst the women for a familiar face and couldn't find one. Most participants had clearly been recruited from the neighbouring countryside.

Amanda was standing in front of the notice board reading a list of names with table numbers printed on the side, when she heard Lydia's voice.

"There you are! Found it all right? Actually, how did you come down? You don't drive, do you?"

"Simon Banks gave me a lift. He was meeting a client not far from here."

"I see. How convenient." Lydia raised her thinly pencilled eyebrows. "I suppose you don't know many people here. Let me introduce you to your table. I think they've all arrived."

Amanda followed Lydia into a large reception room that had been cleared of most of its furniture, where two dozen bridge tables had been laid.

"What an enormous room!" said Amanda.

"We've managed to fit twenty tables. Mind you, we could have done the same at Bernice Maxwell's. She has a huge reception room too."

Would Lydia ever allow her to forget Bernice's disappointment, wondered Amanda as they eased their way amongst the tables and chairs.

Lydia stopped in front of a small group. "Let me introduce you to Amanda, who volunteered to come all the way from London to make a foursome."

The women smiled. "Jolly good of you to drive all this way! Mind you, it is fun to play with different groups. I must say, I so enjoy my yearly tournaments up at the Lansdowne Club," said one of them.

Amanda looked in Lydia's direction but she was now talking to a group of women behind them. She wondered if Lydia had made a mistake. Surely beginners, even in the country, didn't go to tournaments at the Lansdowne. Another woman joined them. They were introduced and Amanda recognised the name typed beside hers on the notice board. Hilary McLean was her partner. They stood exchanging pleasantries about the weather and sipping their coffee till it was eleven o'clock and the Countess of Avercorn welcomed everyone and said it was time to get started. Amanda followed Mrs McLean to table number eleven and, while anxiously trying to remember the different conventions, all she could think of was number eleven. She had married Douglas on the 11th of September, and had, since the break up of their marriage, made up her mind that this was an unlucky number. Hilary McLean, she noticed as she followed her across the room, had a determined stride; there was a schoolmistressy air about her and Amanda couldn't decide if this was a good or a bad sign.

Hilary stopped in front of a table by the window. "If you don't mind, I'll go this end. There's more light and my eyes aren't what they used to be."

Amanda sat opposite her. Their opponents were making their way towards their table. They obviously knew most of the other participants.

"Do you play regularly?" Amanda ventured.

"Mondays and Thursdays and occasionally on weekends. I'm a widow and this gives me a wonderful opportunity to get out and meet other people." She gestured towards two packs of cards neatly prepared in the centre of the table.

"Here we are." The two other players sat down. Amanda smiled at them and wondered, as her stomach tightened into a knot, how many times a week they played.

She was tempted to say, "Lydia said we were all beginners", but suspected at this stage it was pointless to bring it up.

"Do you play high or low 'no trumps' when you play up in London?" one of her opponents asked.

"Low," said Amanda in a half whisper, reminded that, as a Londoner she was an outsider.

The voices round the room started to die out and soon there was, what seemed to Amanda, a tense silence. The cards were dealt. Amanda watched the expert hands of her partner and her opponents nimbly sorting their cards. As she cautiously sorted her own hand, she tried to add up her points without moving her lips. At Maria's, she would normally count the points under her breath, but she felt this would be frowned upon here. She sensed all eyes were on her. Everyone else was clearly ready to start bidding. Noticing she had placed one of her hearts with the diamonds, she hurriedly tried to move the card. In the process she dropped one of them on the silent baize table. She didn't look up; she could feel they were all still looking at her. The card had fallen face up and it was the ace of diamonds.

"I'm so sorry." Amanda picked up the card and looked towards her partner.

The fingers of Mrs McLean's right hand were tapping lightly and soundlessly on the edge of the table. She was sucking her lips inwards and, as a result, her mouth had become a very thin line. She met Amanda's eyes without smiling, her tight mouth unmoving.

"I suppose you'll just have to leave it on the table and the first time that suit comes up you'll have to play it." One of her opponents was addressing her.

"Oh, I'm so sorry." Amanda laid the offending ace face up, a reminder of her clumsiness.

Mrs McLean cleared her throat, clearly not amused.

"Are we ready?" The one whose turn it was to open the bidding looked at Amanda.

Amanda nodded.

"One spade."

"Double," said Mrs McLean.

"Pass," was the quick reply of the other opponent sitting beside her.

Amanda looked at her cards. She had no points except for the ace that now lay exposed, face up on the table. She hesitated and vaguely remembered, in her state of nerves, that she was obliged to bid if her partner bid double. She looked at her hand again, unable to decide on what to bid. The woman beside her pushed her chair back slightly and Mrs McLean loudly cleared her throat again. They were letting her know she was taking too long.

Amanda decided that saying "no bid" couldn't really get her into that much trouble.

"No bid," she said timorously, looking at her partner.

She knew immediately that she had said the wrong thing. Mrs McLean's lips had now been totally sucked in. She looked at Amanda over the rim of her thick glasses. She said nothing and, after a few seconds of reproving silence, her eyes went back to her cards.

"I suppose," she said, addressing her opponents, "that we'll just have to play one spade doubled."

Amanda felt not only humiliated but also totally excluded. Her stomach felt tight and had started to rumble. The thought of everyone in the room hearing the sounds of her nervous stomach made it worse. She looked furtively round the room, wondering if anyone else looked as miserable as she did.

"If you don't concentrate, things will continue to go wrong." Mrs McLean's voice was icy.

Amanda knew she should concentrate on the game but all she could do was think of Lydia and how she must have engineered this for some specific reason or just to humiliate her. When she followed her partner's moves, she noticed how skilfully she was making the best of a difficult situation. They continued playing for over an hour, Amanda constantly aware she made mistakes the others would never have made. Her stomach rumbling, her mind drifting, she thought of the shopping she needed to do and the letters she had left unanswered on her desk at the office.

Eventually it was time to stop for lunch. Amanda toyed with the idea of saying she had developed a migraine but knew this would give Lydia great satisfaction. As she made her way towards a table where a large buffet had been laid, she told herself resolutely that some food would no doubt stop her stomach from rumbling, and a glass of wine might improve her memory. She piled her plate with food and perched on the edge of a deep window seat, too embarrassed to make an effort to talk with other participants. The room was soon full of voices and laughter. A group of three women perched beside her. Amanda ate heartily, hoping they wouldn't include her in their conversation.

While she ate her salad she overheard one of them saying: "Gorgeous food."

"The food's always very good, but I don't think it's that well organised otherwise; apparently Hilary McLean has been stranded with a partner who can barely bid," said one of them.

"I never saw Hilary. There are so many tables," said her friend.

"I haven't seen her either, but anyhow, that's what I heard Rosemary say when we were waiting for the wine."

Amanda continued to eat her salad, grateful that one of the bridge conventions wasn't to have your partner's name pinned to your lapel. She got up and went for some coffee. As she crossed the room she noticed some of the women looking at her. Some must know she was Hilary McLean's partner. In the hall where coffee had been laid she bumped into Lydia.

"Having a good time?" Lydia walked hurriedly past her, holding a large cake.

"Lydia, there you are." The Countess of Avercorn walked into the hall.

Lydia stopped and looked back at her hostess.

"Would you be kind and see if you can find someone to volunteer with the washing up after the tournament. Otherwise, my housekeeper will be here till midnight," said the Countess.

"Amanda here would love to do it, I'm sure," said Lydia. "She's one of our indefatigable London members."

"I presume you are Amanda," the Countess smiled, looking round the otherwise empty hall.

"Yes," said Amanda feebly as Lydia's footsteps disappeared down the hall.

*

When lunch was cleared they returned to their tables to resume their game. The rooms, that had been full of laughter and light chatter during the break, became quiet once again, except for the low voices calling their bids. Amanda sat opposite Mrs McLean who, after some food and wine, didn't look any happier to have her as a partner. Intimidated by her unfriendly manner, Amanda started to wonder once more why she was there. I should get up and go, say I'm sick, after all it is true I am sick with humiliation.

The next two hours went by painfully slowly and Amanda found herself longing to do the washing up.

At three o'clock it was finally over. They had lost all three rubbers but, nonetheless, Mrs McLean was congratulated by their opponents for her tremendous effort. Amanda looked round the room where players still sat at their tables concentrating on their cards and wondered where she would find the Countess.

In the hall she looked for a telephone. She would try and get hold of Simon. Maybe there was still time for him to pick her up.

"Ah, Mrs Thompson. There you are. So kind of you to volunteer with the washing up. Poor old Mary isn't as quick as she used to be, but she still enjoys helping after parties. Are you sure we're not making you late? It shouldn't take that long. It really is awfully kind of you..." The Countess had taken her by the arm and was gently ushering her towards the kitchen. "I'm afraid as much as I'd like to help Mary, I feel I should stay out here to see everyone off. Did you enjoy your table? I noticed you were playing against Mrs Russell-Baker, who chairs one of your sister charities. I gather from Lydia, you might be co-funding one of the summer balls next year. A good idea, if you ask me, joining efforts. After all, the cause is the same and it keeps the expenses down."

They were now walking down a narrow corridor at the back of the house. "Anyhow, I'm glad you met Mrs Russell-Baker because I gather from Lydia she's in charge of special events and," she paused to draw breath in front of a door, "I gather so are you. Here we are." She pushed the door open and they walked into a dark Fifties-style kitchen painted in pale green gloss.

"Mary, this is Mrs Thompson, who works for our charity in London and she has kindly volunteered to give you a hand." She turned towards Amanda. "Is your car parked up front? It might be a good idea to bring it round the back."

"I don't have a car," said Amanda.

"Oh Lord! How are you getting back? Is someone giving you a lift?"

"If I could use your telephone, I could arrange for a friend to pick me up."

"Wonderful! Now Mary, don't make her work too hard. I'll see you later." The Countess and her strident voice left the kitchen.

"There's a phone on that table, dear. Now what would you rather do? Wash up or dry and put away?" Mary said in a heavy Scottish lilt.

"I don't know where things are kept, so I suppose it might be better if I wash up."

"Very good then." Mary started peeling off her rubber gloves. "Would you like a wee cup of tea?"

"Thank you," said Amanda. "I'd love one. Two sugars please."

"That's unusual nowadays."

"Concentrating on the cards has left me feeling quite weak."

"Never mind. Standing at the sink will soon make you feel better." Mary's eyes twinkled behind her thick glasses. Amanda went to the table where the telephone stood and dialled the number Simon had given her.

"Amanda! How was it?" He sounded happy to hear from her.

"Dreadful." Amanda's voice broke.

"Are you all right? It can't have been that bad surely." When there was no reply, from her, he asked, "Would you like me to come and pick you up?"

"I won't be finished for another hour." Her voice was subdued.

"You're still playing?"

"No. I've been asked to do the washing up."

"I see. Well, don't worry. I still have some things to go over with my client, so I'll pick you up at about five."

"Here's your tea, dear." Mary had lit a cigarette and was sitting at the kitchen table with two mugs of tea, clearly looking forward to a chat.

"So, you're involved in the cancer charity up in London, are you? Haven't been to London for years now."

"If you don't mind," said Amanda, "I'll sip my tea as I wash up. Someone is picking me up in an hour and I don't want to keep them waiting."

"Well, the sink's all yours."

Amanda put her hands in the greasy water. It had gone cold. "I'll put in some more hot water if that's all right. Shall I do these pots?"

"Yes, please. All the things piled on that wee corner won't go in the dishwasher."

Amanda watched the greasy water disappear down the sink and thought about what the Countess had said about Mrs Russell-Baker. Lydia had clearly planned it very carefully. Belinda and she were meeting the chairman of one of their sister charities next week to find out if they could join forces for next year's summer ball. Care Campaign were having difficulty finding a major sponsor and Belinda felt a joint effort could be an alternative. Amanda filled the sink with hot water and squirted more washing up liquid than was necessary. She needed to do something to vent her anger. Pressing the plastic container made her feel better.

She would have to tell Belinda what had happened this morning. If she went to the meeting, and Mrs Russell-Baker was there, it would be very embarrassing. She would be the woman who had driven from London to play in an advanced bridge tournament, who hardly knew the basic rudiments of bidding. As Amanda scrubbed the fat off a Tupperware dish she could feel the steam from the soapy water making her hair frizz. She should never have come, but she had. As she mechanically washed the pots and pans, Amanda half listened to Mary's chatter. Mary had been with the Countess for twenty-five years. She came from Aberdeen and was a widow. She loved her visits to London and clearly was disappointed Amanda didn't have more exciting stories to tell her about her life in the big city.

Half an hour later, when Amanda was helping Mary put things away, the Countess put her head round the door.

"Are you all right? I'm afraid I have to dash into Newbury. You said someone was collecting you, didn't you?"

"Yes, they should be here in ten minutes."

"Good. Well, thank you so much for helping Mary." She paused. "I'm sorry to hear Mrs McLean lost her sense of proportion."

242

The word had indeed gone round and, not knowing what the Countess had exactly heard about her, Amanda added, "I suppose she had every right to be annoyed. It can't be fun for someone of her standard to play with a beginner."

"Don't you worry about it. It's only a game. People really shouldn't take it so seriously. I'll go and see they're putting back the furniture properly," the Countess continued in the same breath and left the kitchen.

★

At five o'clock Simon arrived. As he turned out of the drive, Amanda covered her face with her hands and suppressed a sob.

"Come on, it's only a game. I never thought you'd get upset so easily."

"I was made to look like a fool, who had asked to play with advanced players. One of the women on my table is going to meet with Belinda next week about a joint fund-raising event. I can't go with her now. It would be too embarrassing. Lydia planned the whole thing. Her revenge, I suppose, because of the fashion show. I won't be able to work on the project as this woman will be running it."

"You mustn't let this kind of thing upset you so much. It's women. They're always sniping at each other. Sorry, I didn't mean to sound sexist. It must have been a nightmare for you, playing cards once you knew what had happened."

On their way back to London Simon tried to distract Amanda by talking about his day. She could tell he was embellishing it with funny anecdotes about his client just to make her laugh. Amanda felt comforted and reassured by his presence and, when they arrived in London and he suggested they had a drink in his flat, she accepted.

Simon's flat overlooked the river. The lights of Albert Bridge twinkled in the dark. They were bright and nearly circus-like in contrast to the austere lamps that flanked Putney Bridge. Sitting in Simon's drawing room she suddenly felt very tired and drained by the day's events and yet, when he took her in his arms, she did not resist. As he held her she felt cocooned in the protection of his embrace. How kind he was. She turned towards him and kissed him.

★

On Sunday morning Amanda was in the kitchen chopping vegetables for lunch while the children were still asleep upstairs. The house was silent, but the silence wasn't oppressive as it so often was during the week when she was alone. It was a homely silence, an interval to be enjoyed before the crashing of their feet down the stairs and the blast from their stereos inundated the peace of the house. Kate had brought a friend home for the weekend, and Amanda hoped Sita's presence would shame Kate into being more civil. The telephone rang. Anticipating it would be, as usual, for one of the children, she picked up the receiver with a smile, but the sudden thought it might be Tina instead made the smile vanish from her face as she said, "Hello," hesitantly.

"You sound very distant this morning." It was Simon.

Amanda was glad to hear his voice, and yet it didn't seem to fit into the tableau of a Sunday morning at home with the children. Since they had spent the night together after the bridge tournament, Simon would often collect her after work and they would go for long walks in Battersea Park, enjoying the lighter evenings. As it got dark, they would cross the bridge and have some supper near his flat off the Embankment.

"I'm missing you," he said in a whisper. "Sundays are depressing as it is, but I've been spoiled this last week. Could we meet later on? I could pick you up and we could go to Richmond Park for a change. Spring is in the air. It's a gorgeous day!"

"Simon, I'd love to, but the children are home."

There was a short pause. "Would they like to come too or would you rather they didn't see me?" He sounded hurt.

"Of course I don't mind them seeing you," she replied cheerfully, although wary of the children meeting him. "It's just that they aren't home very often and Kate has brought a friend for the weekend. I was just preparing a proper Sunday lunch for them and I don't think we'll be finished before two-thirty. They haven't even got up yet!"

There was another pause. "What about this afternoon when they are gone?"

"They don't go back till this evening. Oh, I'm sorry, didn't you say you normally played tennis and had lunch with your friend on Sundays."

"I usually do, but he's spending the weekend away."

Amanda felt sorry for Simon, spending Sunday alone in his rented flat. She was touched he should miss her and want to be with her. She had nearly forgotten what it felt like, being wanted and needed by a man. Had the children not been there, she'd be missing him too.

"Would you like to join us for lunch?"

"Are you sure? I don't want to impose."

"I'm quite sure," she said with enthusiasm, reassuring herself as well as Simon. "I've got a leg of lamb and plenty of potatoes. Kate's met you before and she knows you work for the charity," she muttered as an afterthought.

"Amanda, if you're worried about the children meeting me, I quite understand." Simon didn't sound very convincing.

"No, of course I'm not worried. It's just that they've had to adjust to so many changes lately. I'd rather they didn't notice... well... that there is anything between us. I'll mention that you're bringing over some charity paperwork and that I've asked you to join us for lunch."

"I understand. I'll behave, I promise."

Back in the kitchen, Amanda was peeling the potatoes when she heard Mark's unmistakable footsteps coming down the stairs, taking two steps at a time and dropping all his weight as he landed.

"Did you have a good sleep? Would you like some cereal?" Amanda looked up at her son's sleepy face.

"No, I'll wait. Smells good. What is it?" He opened the oven door. The sudden blast of heat made his head recoil.

"Ooff. Hot!" He wiped his face. "Great! Lamb! We never get any decent meat at school."

"A colleague from the charity will be dropping in with some paperwork. I've asked him to join us for lunch. I hope you don't mind."

Mark shrugged his shoulders and poured himself a glass of milk. "Why should I mind?"

Perhaps I'm giving too much importance to Simon coming over for lunch, Amanda reassured herself while putting the potatoes on to boil. Why would the children mind her having a colleague from work?

Sita and Kate came down the stairs. Kate was wrapped in a towelling robe. Without saying good morning to Amanda, she opened the fridge and, after looking inside it with great concentration, she turned towards Sita and asked, "What would you prefer? Some orange juice or some pineapple juice?"

"Good morning, Mrs Thompson." Sita smiled at Amanda from behind Kate and then replied, "Some pineapple juice, please. What a treat! We never get pineapple juice at home."

"Do you like lamb?" asked Amanda, pleased by Sita's appreciation.

"I love it. We don't often have it either. Mum prefers to cook her own dishes. They're very nice, but it does get a bit repetitive. Always rice or noodles."

Sita looked Eurasian. Amanda wanted to ask where her mother came from but didn't, in case Kate didn't approve. Kate had reached the age when she felt she should criticise all her mother's questions and often even insinuated that Amanda's interests were boring or banal. Amanda went to the dining room and started laying the table, while the girls sat in the kitchen with their fruit juice discussing the party they had been to the night before.

"Why are we eating in the dining room?" asked Kate, when she saw Amanda piling the plates on a tray to take next door.

"I thought we might be a bit squashed in the kitchen."

"Sita doesn't take up that much room, and she is not a guest of honour either." Both the girls giggled.

"A colleague from the charity is joining us for lunch too, so we'll be five," she said, hurrying out with the tray before Kate had time to ask another question.

When Amanda came back into the kitchen for some glasses, Kate was pouting.

"What a drag, someone else coming. I was planning to have lunch in my dressing-gown. All my clothes are in the washing machine. Hope your girlfriend won't mind if I don't change."

"It's not a girlfriend. It's Simon Banks. I think you met him one evening when he dropped me back with some of the dresses. I'm sure he won't mind if you're still in your dressing-gown." Amanda thought it better not to antagonise Kate by asking her to change.

"I also met him at the fashion show, remember?" Kate pulled a face. "Why is he coming over on a Sunday?" She sounded annoyed.

"He's bringing some paperwork I need and, as he's driving all the way here, I thought I ought to ask him to join us for lunch." She tried to sound casual.

"He's very helpful for an accountant!"

Amanda turned towards the corner cupboard to get the salt cellars and, giving her back to Kate and Sita, said, "It's a very small charity and there is an awful lot to do. We're still tying up the loose ends from the fashion show."

"Is that the fashion show at Mosimann's Kate was telling me about? The one with the Duchess?" asked Sita. "Kate said it was great fun."

"Yes, it was," said Amanda, relieved Sita had turned the conversation away from Simon.

"You can borrow a pair of my leggings," said Sita, looking at Kate.

"I suppose I'll have to wear Sita's leggings and one of your jumpers." Kate got up and went upstairs, muttering something about not being able to relax in her own home. Sita, clearly embarrassed by Kate's behaviour, asked Amanda if she could help by laying the table. When the doorbell rang, Amanda was already worrying about the outcome of lunch. Kate was having one of her bad days. Hopefully, Sita's presence would make her less aggressive and argumentative. Had she acted on impulse when she had asked Simon to join them? Had it been selfish of her to expect her children not to mind? But why shouldn't she have friends to lunch? Amanda opened the door. Simon stood holding a bottle of wine. Their eyes met and although they didn't kiss, it felt as if they had.

"Come in." She blushed and, as she hung his Barbour in the hall, whispered, "I'm afraid Kate is in one of her moods."

"Don't worry. I've come to see you. I can handle it."

Simon was wearing jeans and a red cashmere sweater. The colour suited him. Amanda had never seen him informally dressed. During the week, he always wore a suit or a jacket. His jeans were pressed and his shoes polished. He clearly paid a lot of attention to his appearance. Simon had probably led a very social and glamorous life during his marriage, thought Amanda, wishing she had done something more about her own appearance. She had come down for breakfast with a pair of leggings and an old sweater and never managed to get back to her bedroom to change. She hoped he wouldn't think she was too sloppy.

"What can I get you to drink?" she asked in the kitchen. "I'm afraid I don't have any white wine that's cold."

"I'll have some red. Just tell me where to find a corkscrew and I'll do it." He looked behind him, making sure no one was around. "You look lovely with your cheeks slightly flushed from cooking," he whispered.

Amanda was reassured by his appreciation but wished he wouldn't say such things in the house. She felt uncomfortable, knowing the children were upstairs.

In the dining room, Simon carved the lamb. Amanda watched him with something that resembled pride. He was a very skilful carver. Since Douglas had left, carving a piece of meat was one of the many things she had had to learn to do by herself, but she still wasn't very good at it. Mark stood beside Simon holding the plates and watched him carve. When Kate and Sita walked in, Simon put the knife down and, after greeting Kate, introduced himself to Sita.

Kate looked towards the sideboard at the half-carved leg of lamb and volunteered, "A bit underdone, isn't it?"

"It looks fine to me. The French always prepare it this way." Simon smiled as he sharpened the knife.

"Well, maybe the French don't like their lamb well cooked, but I do. What veg are we having, Mum?" She turned towards Amanda, who was standing by the door with a jug of water.

"I'm afraid there were no Brussels in the supermarket. They must be over. We're having courgettes and carrots."

"I love courgettes," said Sita.

"I prefer Brussels," said Kate. "Still, as long as we don't have peas. I hate peas."

"I love peas," said Mark.

"I know you do. That's why we have them, silly. Nobody else likes them. Neither did Dad."

"What's so wrong about liking peas?" Mark's voice rose in irritation.

Mark knew his sister's was once more getting at him and talking about his personal habits to others to annoy him. She had always enjoyed doing it ever since he could remember.

"A boring vegetable," said Kate, winking at Sita and slumping on a chair.

"Come on. You're not going to have an argument because of some peas?" said Simon cheerfully.

There was a long silence. Forgetting their differences, Mark and Kate looked at each other conspiratorially. Amanda understood the undercurrents in the silence, but Simon didn't seem to have noticed the hostility and continued to deal with the joint. The presence of a man in the house, particularly over Sunday lunch, doing mundane things their father had done such as carving, was felt as an intrusion by the children. Particularly by Kate. Mark, who had initially seemed happy to help Simon, had become defensive when Simon had voiced his opinion on the matter of the peas. Obviously, one thing was to carve, but another was telling them not to argue.

"I shouldn't have said that," Simon whispered a few minutes later to Amanda in the kitchen. "They're older than my children and obviously don't want to be told what to do. Can I help with anything else?"

"No thanks. Just the gravy to do and we're ready." She turned and looked up at him. "I'm sorry Kate is so prickly. She's still very upset by the separation and it's a difficult age anyhow."

"I understand. I shouldn't have interfered on the subject of the peas." He laughed.

So he had noticed! She looked up at him, glad he was there and suddenly felt it was easier to cope with Kate's moods and Mark's sulks. She felt protected by Simon's presence. If anything, it was an assurance that she was not being unreasonable with the children. Sometimes, when they were difficult, she wondered if it wasn't something she did that instigated their moods. But today, she thought as she took the gravy into the dining room, they were reacting to Simon's presence.

Over lunch the children discussed the latest films they had seen at the cinema. Whenever Simon tried to join in the conversation Kate was offhand and barely acknowledged his questions, but fortunately Sita made sure he was included. Mark was silent. He hadn't made up his mind whether he should back up his sister or form his own opinion on their guest, to whom he had taken an initial liking. As they were clearing the plates, Sita knocked the gravy bowl over and some of it spilled over the sleeve of Simon's cashmere sweater. He sprung to his feet and dabbed at it with his napkin. Sita looked distraught, but Simon didn't seem to notice her discomfort. He was clearly too upset by the incident and was now frowning.

"I'd better put some hot water on it straight away." He looked in Amanda's direction as though asking for help. He looks like a boy who has broken his favourite toy, thought Amanda. She found his reaction endearing, but wished he would say something to poor Sita. She was wiping the gravy off the table with her napkin and kept on repeating, "I'm sorry. I'm so sorry."

As though reading Amanda's thoughts, before leaving for the kitchen, Simon put his hand on Sita's shoulder and said, "Don't worry about it. It's just an old sweater."

"Rather fussy about his clothes, isn't he?" said Kate when he had gone into the kitchen.

Mark and Sita giggled. Kate looked at Amanda with the corner of her eye. She had never considered the possibility of her mother having a suitor or a boyfriend. She presumed Simon was just a friend. Her mother couldn't possibly be attracted to him. Simon seemed a bit precious and so unlike her father, who was so manly and commanding. While she waited for the pudding to arrive, Kate wondered if her father would get jealous if she mentioned casually that their mother had a suitor who looked quite rich and now came to Sunday lunch.

"I've got an urgent phone call to make. I won't have any pudding," she said abruptly and left the table.

Upstairs, she rang Sebastian. They had argued on Friday just before she had left for London. If she told him what a wonderful time she'd had with Sita at the party and how late they had arrived back home, maybe she would succeed in making him jealous too.

*

After lunch Simon suggested they went to the park.

"It's a nice day for kicking a ball around," he had said, looking in Mark's direction. Mark's eyes had brightened. He liked any sport and got bored sitting in his room, avoiding his sister, listening to music on his own. Kate and Sita said they had lots of phone calls to make and wanted to keep an eye on their laundry in the washing machine. They would stay behind.

Later, as they made their way down the avenue of trees that led towards the lake, Amanda became aware of the other couples in the park. She wondered how many, like herself, were sharing their afternoon walk with someone else's husband. After all, neither Simon nor she were divorced yet. She watched each passing couple, wondering if there was a gesture or a sign that might give away how long they had been together. Some held hands and leant gently against each other as they strolled. Some looked so in love. Were these married couples or lovers? Others walked alone, their hands in their pockets, their expressions pensive and their heads bent. The lone figures looked sad. Was loneliness something to be ashamed of? She had never thought of her life in terms of being on her own. She had often felt lonely within her marriage with Douglas but that was different to being completely alone. Watching Simon kicking the ball to Mark, the thought of entering a new relationship made her shudder. Was she afraid? Douglas's desertion had left her wondering what love really meant. Maybe love wasn't really an emotion but just a choice, a way of life. Then she thought of the unconditional love she felt towards the children, the same love she had once believed she had felt for Douglas.

She heard Mark calling to Simon, "Here! Here!" and watched him jumping up in the air to catch the ball. Watching them playing and laughing together made her think of how good it would be for Mark to have a father figure. Douglas had always had a weak spot for Kate. She was wittier and brighter than Mark. Douglas had been hard on his son, always highlighting his weaknesses. Simon wasn't an overpowering personality, and someone like him would be a good companion for a boy like Mark.

Amanda lay back on the grass and felt the warm sun filtering through her clothes. It was, at long last, the end of winter. She would never forget her first winter alone, and this in itself made the arrival of spring more significant. Looking up at the blue sky she searched for a clarity of feeling. Could she experience love again? Were Simon and she just testing if they were ready for love? She had married young and, after leaving her parents' home she had only lived for a few years as an independent woman. After that, she had only known life as part of a couple. Shouldn't she wait before entering another relationship?

"Mum! Come and join us!" cried Mark, throwing the ball in her direction.

"Yes, come on," cried Simon. "We're getting exhausted and it's time you started to work off that huge lunch!"

'More than Douglas's desertion,' she thought as she rose to her feet, 'more than his walking out on us, I won't forgive his refusal to give our marriage another chance.' But would she herself, now if he came back, give it another chance? She was unsure. She looked in Simon's direction and felt emotions that encircled love. They were tentative emotions, a stepping-stone for a new start. Simon was kind, appreciative and seemed concerned for her. He needed someone to look after him. Love, in this season of her life, was no longer a sparkle. It had also to be a choice.

*

On Wednesday afternoon, as she left the office, Amanda remembered Simon had said he was going to be out of London for a couple of days. He had mentioned some consultancy work near Bristol and Amanda knew that on his way back he was going to drive through Wiltshire and visit his wife. He always referred to Sue as "my ex-wife" although little had been done about a legal separation. Simon and Amanda often spoke about their past lives and failed marriages, and Amanda felt she had got to know Sue only too well. He would often say how much easier it was to love her than it had been to love Sue. Amanda sometimes wished he wouldn't make comparisons as this created an unnecessary rivalry. As she got ready to leave, she reflected on how effortlessly and naturally their relationship had developed. She was aware that, with Simon, she was the stronger. Amanda liked this new role as, having been married to an older man for twenty years, she had always waited for his approval and, sometimes even, permission for the most mundane decisions. Simon, on the other hand, wanted her to take the initiative. Having always played the role of the stronger one in his own marriage, Simon now enjoyed having a partner from whom he needn't conceal the weaker side of his nature. He allowed himself to be taken care of by Amanda.

Sue, Amanda learned, being the only child of elderly parents, was capricious and used to getting her way. It appeared that Simon, who had had to prove himself worthy of Sue, had always pretended to cope and had grown into the habit of never discussing his fears and insecurities with his wife. When he had lost his job, he had not only lost an income but also his self-esteem. Sue had felt disappointed by Simon whom she had expected to be a provider. She resented having an unemployed husband. Caring for a man who needed her support was a new and stimulating experience for Amanda. She felt that being needed by Simon not only made her a competent lover but also filled her life with purpose.

In the street Amanda found the signs of early spring were everywhere. The air was fresh and window boxes and gardens had been tended with renewed energy, which manifested itself in colourful bulbs and bright flowers. When she saw her car, Amanda felt a child-like pride. Simon had helped her choose the little Renault. He had looked in the trade catalogues and gone with her to several second-hand dealers. It was doing these small mundane things together that had brought them close. Driving down the King's Road towards Putney, Amanda felt tired and was looking forward to a long bath. Having recovered from the fashion show, the charity was now busy planning its annual summer dance which was the main fund-raiser for the year. Amanda, who was in charge of special events, was responsible for the outcome. At the bridge lunch, Lydia had successfully poisoned any relationship Amanda might have had with Mrs Russell-Baker, the chairman of the charity with which they hoped to co-fund next year's summer ball. Despite Belinda's encouragement, Amanda often felt intimidated by the Ball Committee which was composed of women who had been with the charity for much longer than she. Amanda was reminded that despite her position as Head of Special Events, she was nonetheless a newcomer, who didn't really know how things should be done. Since the success of the show, she had felt a lot of animosity from some of the volunteers who had previously been friendly. When Belinda had pointed out at a meeting how well the charity had done with the show and how grateful they were to Amanda for all her hard work, she had felt the resentment in the room. "Wouldn't you have a lot of initiative if you were given all those perks and now a car!" she overheard a committee member say as they broke up for lunch.

As she crossed Putney Bridge, Amanda gave a sigh of relief. A few months ago she had felt trapped by her suburban life, but today she secretly welcomed its cosy familiarity. Sometimes she felt out of place in the new life she had carved out for herself. Jack and Solange, Tina and Constantine, the titled ladies of the charity committees, were unable to reach her once she was back in Putney. Inside the house, Amanda picked up the post that was scattered on the mat in the front hall. Without taking her coat off, she sat in the kitchen with the two letters in the white envelopes. One was postmarked Winchester, so she knew it was from Mark. The other letter was from Pat; her sister's round handwriting was unmistakable.

Mark's letter was a long stream of complaints. He had had an argument with his housemaster, he had been put in detention and wouldn't be coming home next weekend. She might also get a phone call from the school. Amanda decided to ring the school straight away and find out exactly what had happened. Since Douglas had left, her children's worries weighed heavily on her shoulders. Had she not done enough? She probably would never have got involved with Jack and Solange if she hadn't thought that Mark's holiday would help him get over the separation. She sometimes wondered, nonetheless, if Mark wouldn't have been just as difficult and uncooperative if Douglas were still at home. She dialled the school number. A secretary answered and, after what seemed like a very long wait, she heard the headmaster's solemn voice.

"Ah, Mrs Thompson. I'm so glad you rang." He paused. "We tried to contact Mr Thompson, but we only have his office number." There was another pause. "We felt it would be better if you both came together so we wrote you a letter to that effect which, no doubt, you'll be receiving in the next few days."

"What's happened?" Amanda said with alarm.

"It's a delicate matter. Could you and Mr Thompson drive down to see me as soon as possible?"

"Yes, of course. Tomorrow?"

"Let me have a look at my diary. After lunch, at about two o'clock? Could you manage that?"

"Yes, I'll be there. I'll ring Mark's father straight away."

"It would help if you were both here." His tone was admonishing.

When Amanda put the receiver down her hands were shaking. What could have happened? Mark hadn't mentioned anything being wrong last weekend. She pictured him playing in the park with Simon. Mark had seemed so happy. Could Simon's presence have upset him? Had he misbehaved as a result of seeing her with another man? She dialled Douglas's office number. When Douglas came to the phone, without stopping to say hello she blurted out, "Mark's school rang and they want us both to go down tomorrow afternoon. He's done something, but I don't know what."

"I'm afraid tomorrow is impossible. I have a meeting which will carry through till mid-afternoon. I can't change it."

"But Douglas! I spoke with the headmaster. It's obviously very important. He made it sound as though... well that they might be considering asking Mark to leave."

"You'll have to go alone and find out what's happened. I'm sure it's not as serious as you make it sound."

"You don't want it to be serious because you can't make the time to come." She raised her voice.

"I'm sure both of us being there won't alter the outcome. Now, I'm afraid I've got to go. Give me a ring tomorrow afternoon and let me know how you got on. I can always go down to the school later in the week."

Amanda went back to the kitchen and plugged in the kettle. Her hands were still shaking. The indignation she felt towards Douglas was only marginally less than the anxiety she felt about Mark. She sat at the kitchen table and opened Pat's letter. It was cheerful and full of local news. She hoped they would all come down to see her over the Easter break. Amanda remembered Simon had mentioned going away with her for a couple of days during Easter. She crumpled the letter and threw it in the bin. She couldn't think ahead, not till she found out what had happened with Mark.

★

The following day Amanda arrived at Mark's school half an hour late. She had allowed plenty of time, but there had been an accident on the M4 and two lanes had been closed. When she was shown into the headmaster's office, she was breathless and longing for a cup of tea. While she waited in the traffic jam she had become increasingly anxious about Mark.

"Mrs Thompson to see you," the secretary said as she opened the door.

The headmaster got up slowly from behind his desk. "Mrs Thompson, do come in."

"I'm terribly sorry I'm late. There was an accident and..."

"Do come and sit down," he continued, gesturing at the chair opposite his desk. His voice was reassuring, but his eyes looked furtively at the clock above the door.

Amanda could sense his disapproval at her late arrival and suspected he didn't believe her story about an accident.

"Is Mr Thompson joining us?" He raised his heavy eyebrows inquiringly.

"I'm afraid not. He had a meeting he couldn't cancel. I did ring him yesterday. As you probably know," she paused, "Mark's father and I have separated."

"I see." The headmaster picked up a pen and looked at it intently. "Mrs Thompson," he said putting down the pen and adjusting his spectacles, "we are worried about Mark. We feel that perhaps the separation might have something to do with his behaviour. That's why we were hoping to talk to you both. After all, he is a teenager, which is difficult enough anyway and, well... it can't be the same for a boy without a father. I gather both the children live with you?"

Amanda was annoyed by the condescension in his voice. Was he telling her she couldn't do a good job on her own?

"What has happened with Mark?"

"He was seen smoking." He paused, leant back on his chair, crossed his hands over his lap and, looking at her, said solemnly, "Smoking cannabis."

Amanda looked at him speechless. It had crossed her mind that Mark had been found drinking, but not smoking pot.

"It was not in the school grounds. Just outside the village. A prefect saw him and... smelt it, of course." He cleared his throat. "Had it been in the grounds, as you know, it would have been immediate expulsion. Those are the rules. But because it was not in the school and, bearing in mind the matter of Mark's unsettled home life, we are prepared to give him another chance."

"Thank you," said Amanda.

He gave her a little smile. "We do, however, feel that there should be more communication between the school and the parents. We appreciate it must be difficult for you to implant a certain discipline perhaps and…"

Amanda interrupted him. "When did this happen?"

"Three weeks ago, but it was not reported to me till this week. The prefect obviously didn't want to get Mark and his friend in trouble and spent an agonising fortnight deciding whether to cover up for them or report them."

Amanda felt relieved. It had not happened straight after Sunday lunch with Simon.

"We have another boy in the school whose parents are divorced," the headmaster continued, putting his fingertips together and leaning forward as if to take her into his confidence. "The mother finds it very difficult to cope and often rings to ask our advice on matters that normally, had there been a man in the house, would have been easier to resolve."

Amanda was irritated by his assumption that, as a single woman, she would be unable to cope.

"We want you to know that we are here if you need us."

"Thank you. I will talk to Mark and I'm sure his father will talk to him too," she said crisply. "How is he getting on with his work?"

"Very well, I'm glad to say. He's a good pupil and a good sportsman. A credit to the school in many ways." He looked at his watch and rose to his feet. "I'm afraid I'll have to leave you now. But before you go, any chance you could have a quick word with the bursar since Mr Thompson isn't here. Apparently," he lowered his voice, "this term's fees haven't been paid." He circled the desk and stood beside her. "I dare say, you'd like to see Mark. I think he'll be practising at the pavilion." As he shook Amanda's hand she caught a whiff of gin on his breath.

After seeing the bursar and reassuring him Douglas would be paying the fees, Amanda made her way towards the pavilion in search of Mark. When she saw him in his games clothes, he looked so much younger and her heart went out to him.

Mark saw her and ran towards her. "Mum! I'm sorry!" He put both arms round her.

"Oh, darling!" Amanda suppressed a sob.

"Please don't worry, Mum. I don't do it all the time. It was a one-off. We had this joint, we thought it would be fun. It won't happen again." He looked behind her. "Where's Dad?"

"I'm afraid he couldn't make it."

"Busy, I suppose." His voice was full of disappointment.

Mark walked Amanda to the car, his arm protectively over her shoulder.

"I'll be home in a fortnight." He kissed her on the cheek.

Amanda looked up at him and, as she opened her mouth, he interrupted her, saying gently, "I know. I promise. Never again."

★

Driving back to London, Amanda felt weary. Mark smoking pot! It was not a hard drug and she knew most young people smoked cannabis at some point and never had any problem with addiction later, but Mark was a withdrawn boy who was clearly not happy with himself at the moment. She worried that one thing might lead to another. Mark spent much too much time alone in his room. She must find something purposeful for him to do during the summer holidays. Some volunteer work abroad might be beneficial. She would find out what the possibilities were. Her brother-in-law, Tony, might help. His boy had gone to help in a camp after his A levels. Underneath her anxiety, Amanda could feel the pulse of her anger, but her anger was not directed at Mark, but at Douglas. Why hadn't he made the time to go to the school? Was any meeting more important than Mark's well-being and future?

She saw the signs to a Little Chef and filtered towards the exit. She couldn't wait to get back to London to ring Douglas.

She would ring him straightaway. From a telephone box outside the ladies toilets she dialled Douglas's office number. His secretary answered and said he was tied up in a meeting.

"I'm afraid it's important." Her voice was shaking with indignation.

"Mrs Thompson, I'm afraid he's in a very important meeting. I have instructions not to interrupt him, but I would be very glad to take a message."

"I'm afraid," said Amanda, emphasising each word, "you'll have to get him out of the meeting. What I have to tell him is more important. It concerns his son and it can't wait."

"I'll see what I can do." Amanda was put on hold.

"Amanda," Douglas came on the phone. "What's going on? I can't be dragged out of meetings like this."

"You can't be dragged out of meetings! You can't go to the school." Her voice rose. "What can you do for your children? In fact, were you ever there for them? Playing golf on weekends or squash or whatever you said it was in the evenings." She stopped to draw breath.

"And you had me called out to tell me this? What's come over you?"

"Your son was caught smoking pot. That's why the headmaster wanted to see us. It was important to the school to see both of us."

There was a long silence.

"When is Mark out next? I'll talk to him," said Douglas with authority.

"And what are you going to tell him? That he's been a naughty boy? Have you ever stopped to think that your son might be unhappy?"

"I've got to go back to the boardroom. Are you going to tell me when he's next home or shall I ring the school?"

"I'm sure the school would love to hear from you. The fees apparently have not been paid."

"We'll have to talk about that, at some point too. Next year, if you want to stay in Putney you might have to take in a lodger to help with your expenses. Look, I've got to go. I'll ring the school and see Mark on his next weekend out." Douglas's voice sounded somewhat subdued.

Amanda put the phone down and rang Simon's number. He suggested they go to the cinema that evening to distract her, but she declined saying she wasn't up to it. The day's events and her outburst with Douglas had left her feeling shaken. In all her years of marriage she had never spoken to him in such strong terms. Simon persuaded her to come over for a meal, and she felt reassured by his gentle and concerned voice.

★

When Douglas put the phone down he didn't go into the boardroom but sat in his office, remembering the time when he had been let down by his own father. It had happened on speech day of his first year as a senior. His parents hadn't arrived on time to see him get his prize for swimming. He had been the only boy without his parents present; even the ones that lived abroad seemed to have managed to attend. Douglas could still feel anguish when he remembered that day. He recalled his friend had tried to cheer him up, but this had only highlighted the feeling of abandonment. When his parents had finally arrived they had made light of the situation, saying they had been delayed. In the back of the car on their way home he had pretended to be asleep and had overheard them talk about the wedding they had attended that afternoon that had clearly meant more to them than seeing him claim his prize. The memory of his parents' desertion, still vivid in his mind, filled him with sadness and a wave of self-pity overtook him. He felt a lump in his throat. Had he hurt Mark as much with his absences?

In need of some reassurance, he dialled Claire's number. She worked in the floor below and, although she always finished work before he did, she was bound to still be there. When Claire answered the telephone she was short. That morning they had had another argument about money. She still felt the flat was small and claustrophobic. Douglas had, at one point, considered agreeing with her and moving to something larger. He was now longing to confide in her about his worries, but her tone made it clear that today he would get no sympathy. Had he really ever got any sympathy from her? Would Claire have understood his feelings anyhow, even if he had bought a new apartment and showered her with presents? He suspected she would not.

Back in London, Amanda drove straight to Simon's flat. She felt tired from the long drive back. She was also drained by the anxiety and anger that had consumed her all day. She decided to ring Tony, her brother-in-law, in the morning when, after a night's sleep, she would feel less agitated and see things in a different light. Tony was bound to have some good suggestions about what to do with Mark over the summer holiday while he waited for his A level results. Her instinct told her the best thing for Mark was to be busy and not have time to ruminate. When she parked her car near Simon's flat it was still light. It was summer time at last! The clocks had gone forward during the weekend. She took a deep breath and walked towards the river. The tide was high and the river sparkled in the evening sun. It's always the same river, she reflected, and yet some days it shimmers full of promise and others it's grey and foreboding. She looked up at the trees that formed a canopy over the Embankment and saw the small buds bursting with new life.

Inside the flat, Simon was waiting for her. He had laid the table in the kitchen and decorated it with spring flowers. Amanda felt touched by this small gesture of affection.

"You look exhausted!" he said, taking her coat off. "Let me get you a drink and then you can tell me exactly what's happened."

Amanda curled up on the sofa by the window and told him what the headmaster had said, but refrained from telling him about her outburst with Douglas. She still felt that whatever happened between her and Douglas was not to be shared with

Simon. Simon was a good listener and knew how to encourage her to talk. By the time she had finished recounting, stroke by stroke, what had happened at the school, she felt less anxious. Simon reassured her that a lot of young people smoked pot out of curiosity or just to prove to themselves they could do it, but it didn't mean they would end up in a rehabilitation centre and, anyhow, there was even talk of legalising it.

When Simon went into the kitchen to check on the supper, Amanda was reminded how comforting it was to share one's worries. She found the hardest part of being alone was having no one in the evening to talk to. She had stopped sharing her days with Douglas long before he left. The first years of their married life, he seemed to have enjoyed the evenings when she would recount small trivial episodes of her day. But gradually his interest had waned, and she had felt the moorings of their relationship coming loose. The distance between them grew, but the small things of every day life kept them together. Hearing Simon preparing the supper in the kitchen, made her wish she could share the small things of life again. The telephone rang. Simon took the call in the hall, although there was a telephone where she was sitting. Amanda wondered whether he wanted the privacy or simply didn't want to disturb her with his conversation. The flat was small and she couldn't help overhearing him.

"Oh, hello John. Yes everything's fine. A few letters, that's all. No, no messages. Next Thursday's fine. Yes, I should be in."

She guessed he was talking to John Blunt, the owner of the flat. John Blunt was a mutual friend of Simon and Virginia's who had lent him the flat on a temporary basis after the divorce. Amanda knew he came in occasionally and collected his post. On the occasions that she had spent a night in Simon's flat, she had felt apprehensive in case he should walk in unannounced.

"Oh, and John!" Simon's voice became hushed. "About the loan. Would it be all right if I repaid it a bit later than promised? The firm I did some consultancy work for last week hasn't paid me yet. I've just covered the school fees and… "

An aeroplane flew over them and muffled the rest of the conversation. Amanda felt sorry for Simon. It must be humiliating having to borrow from friends. He seemed to have been well off before he had lost his job and he was now trying very hard to make sure his wife and children's lifestyle didn't change too much. So unlike Douglas, who was putting his lifestyle before that of his children.

During supper Simon suggested they went away for the weekend. A friend, who had a cottage in Cumbria, had offered it to him while he was abroad.

"I know it's a long drive, but if you took Friday off and we had three full days, it would be well worth it. Are Mark and Kate home for the weekend?"

"No." Amanda helped herself to some more vegetables.

"Would you like to think about it?"

Amanda hesitated. She ought to refuse, but it would do her good to get away. She hadn't left London since Christmas. The thought of Simon's company and some peace and quiet made her say:

"I don't need to think about it. I've already made up my mind."

Chapter Nine

On Friday morning, as they drove out of London, Amanda leant back in the seat of the car with expectation. She was looking forward to the weekend in Cumbria. An early spring sun was dispersing the clouds and it promised to be a nice weekend.

"I can't wait," she sighed. "Long walks and fresh air." She clasped her hands in a gesture of delight. Simon stole a glance at her before changing gears and rested his hand on her knee.

"Not only good walks, good food too! I love cooking in the country. One can always find some local delicacy."

Amanda sat up abruptly. "I hadn't thought about food. Should we have brought something with us?"

Simon's lips curved into a smile. One of the endearing things about Amanda, he thought, was that she was sensitive and yet also a trifle impractical, so unlike Sue whose days were so organised that little time was left for pleasure or fancy. With someone like Amanda life, if less organised, was more spontaneous. Since he had lost his job he enjoyed taking last minute decisions and sometimes even unnecessary risks, as though emphasising that he now had the time and freedom to take chances. He had always had to conform, keep others happy, impress, please, listen and oblige. His parents-in-law had always made him feel he was a lucky man to have entered their family and Sue allowed them to have this attitude. He accelerated. Small, childish things like driving fast and having his hair slightly longer or arriving late, had become small triumphs.

"We'll do all our shopping up there," said Simon. "If I remember correctly, the nearest town has a wonderful old covered market."

"I hadn't realised you had been there before."

"Yes. We were all up about two years ago. We had good weather then. Let's hope we'll be lucky this time too."

Amanda felt a pang of jealousy or was it fear? Were these small flutters of insecurity whenever Simon mentioned his past with Sue, a sign that her feelings towards him were becoming stronger?

As they were approaching the motorway, Simon pulled into a petrol station.

"I'd better fill up now," he said, looking at the flashing light on the petrol gauge.

After filling the tank and checking the oil, he touched the inside pocket of his jacket and gestured. He looked worried.

"Anything wrong?" she asked.

"You won't believe it. I left my wallet behind with all my cards. I don't have any cash either. It was all in the wallet."

"Oh, don't worry. I've brought some cash and my cheque book."

"Are you sure? We could drive back."

They had just spent forty minutes crossing London.

"Oh, don't be silly," She handed him a fifty pound note. "It's all I have in cash, I'm afraid, but I've got my cheque book."

"Have you got a card? They might not take a cheque without a card in Cumbria, as no one knows us locally."

Amanda checked her purse. "Yes," she said, remembering that she hadn't paid her last Barclaycard statement.

★

Seven miles west of Kendal Simon turned off the lane into a bumpy drive. The jerking of the car woke Amanda, who had been asleep for nearly an hour. Disoriented, she opened her eyes and looked at Simon.

"Where are we?"

"We've arrived. It's the cottage at the end of the drive," he said, pointing.

Amanda looked ahead. Behind the stone cottage stood a range of barren hills. Everything else round her seemed to be heather, rock and sky. The silence and the rugged beauty of the country overwhelmed her as she continued to stare out of the window in amazement. Simon looked at her with the corner of his eye.

"I told you it was isolated."

"It's beautiful! So peaceful." Her voice was hushed, as though not to disturb the silence outside.

"I wouldn't call it beautiful, but it's certainly imposing. I personally prefer the gentle undulation of Wiltshire," said Simon.

"I don't think I do."

Simon smiled. "The cottage is very comfortable inside. Anthony's wife is an interior decorator, amongst other things. She also writes books on cookery and how to entertain – that kind of thing. They don't seem to use the cottage very much at all. They like letting it to friends who can keep an eye on it and report back. I think she has some family up north and when they got it she saw it as a bolt hole to hide in and do her writing."

Once inside the cottage, Amanda said in an eager tone, "Let's go for a walk!"

"Already?"

"Yes, I can't wait."

"You go. I've got to make a couple of phone calls."

Amanda changed into a pair of walking shoes and, as she was about to slip out the back door, Simon caught her by the arm.

"You won't be too long, will you? I'll miss you and, besides, we'd better go and do some shopping before everything shuts. Lunch was a long time ago and I'm quite looking forward to some tea."

"I won't be too long," she said, looking out of the door with anticipation.

Outside, the air was fresh and the wind swept her hair. She headed towards the hills. She wouldn't have time to reach them as Simon wanted her back early, but maybe tomorrow she would. She felt drawn by the rugged hills in front of her and, as though being pulled by a foreign force, she strode forward, enjoying the feel of the rocky ground under her feet. The solitude and total silence filled her with joy. In the city, crowded with people, she so often felt terribly lonely. At the foot of the majestic hills she felt small and insignificant, alone but not lonely.

Amanda sat on a rock and raised her face to the wind. She looked round her, wanting to embrace it all, but it was too great. 'If I had been born in a place of such stirring beauty,' she thought, 'I would love it fiercely. I would want to immortalise it either in rhyme or song. That failing, I would want to climb the hills and feel a part of the stone. Everything in my life has always been so bland and passive.'

She thought of the undemonstrative, undemanding love of her parents, the gentle beauty of the home counties where she had been raised and the security of her middle-class life in Putney. Were these the reasons for her acceptance, for her marriage to Douglas and her unadventurous life? After being left, the pain had brought her close to the edge. She had nearly seen herself fall but, instead, she had found herself. The night she had spent with Clive had been a warning. Would she from now on snatch small moments of intimacy just to feel loved? But Simon was different; there was room to build. As she made her way back towards the cottage she could feel the strength of the rock-encrusted hills behind her. Like life, the barren hills were hard to climb, and yet when one reached the summit, so rewarding.

In the cottage she found Simon impatiently pacing the kitchen.

"I thought you said just a short walk." He was sulking and it reminded her of Mark.

"I'm sorry. Out there, time seems to stand still."

"Let's go to the village first. If we don't find what we need there, there's still time to go into Kendal." He looked at his watch.

In the village they drove past a Co-op and a small grocer's.

"We can probably get most things at the Co-op," said Amanda. "At least what we need for tonight and breakfast tomorrow."

"We can do better than that," said Simon, speeding past the shops. "Let's go to Kendal. If I remember correctly, it has a good covered market and also a good wine merchant's."

Their first stop was the wine merchant's where Simon chose half a dozen bottles of very expensive wine.

As Amanda was wondering whether to pay by cheque or Barclaycard, Simon turned over towards her and asked, "Would you prefer some gin or some vodka. I've noticed you drink both."

"I'm quite happy with some wine."

"Oh, come on. We must have something different before supper."

Not wanting to make it too obvious that she was counting the pennies, Amanda said, "A little gin."

"We'll have a bottle of gin and one of whisky and some lager." Simon turned to face the attendant behind the counter. Amanda wrote out the cheque, reminding herself she was lucky to be in such a beautiful spot and in such a comfortable cottage.

"Let's go to the market," said Simon cheerfully after he had loaded the box into the boot of the car. As they strolled down the market they stopped to buy their groceries at different stalls, and Amanda paid for their shopping with the cash she had left over from the petrol. When Simon spotted a stall that sold local crafts and thick hand-knitted Aran sweaters, he turned to Amanda and said, "Look! Aren't these lovely!" His face lit up as he picked out a large Aran and put it against his chest. "You won't mind if I buy one, will you? I'll pay you back in London. I've only packed a couple of thin sweaters. Forgot it's always cooler up here."

"Will they take a cheque? I don't have much cash left."

"I'm sure they will, but you'd better cash a cheque tomorrow morning. We don't want to be caught with no cash on Sunday."

The crafts stall, amongst pots of honey and hand-made jewellery, also sold shaped candles. "We must have a couple of those candles, too. Don't you think they are original? It would be a nice present to leave as a thank you for Anthony and Gillian." His tone was full of excitement and Amanda found herself agreeing with him.

On their way back to the cottage, Amanda made a mental note of what they had spent so far. With the petrol, it came to over two hundred pounds. She reassured herself that Simon would remember to pay her back once they were in London. She would insist on covering some of the food expenses and the petrol. She was tempted to give him the sweater as a present for giving her such a nice weekend, but she knew she couldn't afford it. Worrying about money reminded her of Jack and Solange. Once again she regretted being involved with them. Looking at the rugged countryside in the soft evening light she wondered why she had done it. Up here, away from the bustle of London, it seemed unnecessary and even degrading to have accepted money from them. She sighed. Had Mark really benefited from the skiing holiday after all? She thought of the commission on Tina's portrait and how it had covered the repair on the boiler. In the summer she would have to take in a lodger to help pay the bills, but to have done it before would have been hard on the children. They had had to adjust to so many changes and having a total stranger in the house straight after Douglas had left would have been an added strain. She didn't think she would have coped with it too well herself either, but now she felt more ready for it.

"What was that deep sigh for?" Simon rested a hand on her knee.

"Oh, just thinking about the children and..." She stopped.

"I brought you up here to relax and switch off. Mark gave you his word it wouldn't happen again. He seems like a sensible boy."

"I hope you're right. Sensible unhappy boys sometimes do silly things too."

"You worry too much abut them and anyhow if he smokes a bit of pot now he won't end up buying a motorbike when he's fifty."

Amanda smiled. "Did you smoke pot at Mark's age?"

"Not enough, can't you tell?"

"Neither did I. Do you think that's what's wrong with us?"

"Maybe." Simon laughed. "But seriously you shouldn't worry so much about the children. I'm sure you do because you are on your own. Mark will be fine, you'll see."

Amanda felt reassured and was again conscious of how much easier it was to share one's worries with someone else, particularly when it related to the children. She looked at Simon and was tempted to confide in him about Jack, but Simon was a friend of Virginia's and that made it awkward. Anyhow, she reassured herself, soon Jack would be something she wouldn't have to worry about.

That evening as they sat having supper, the telephone rang. Amanda was startled by the intrusive sound that seemed so out of place in the peaceful surroundings. Simon rose quickly to his feet as though he had been expecting the call.

"Ah, Alistair. You got my message. Thanks for ringing back. No nothing yet, still looking." There was a long pause.

"Are you sure it's all right if I don't repay you till later." He dropped his voice. "It's very kind of you. The rent on the flat is quite steep, but I have to be up in London while job-hunting."

Amanda was surprised to hear him say this because she remembered Simon telling her the week before that John Blunt had let him have the flat for a peppercorn rent providing he covered all the expenses. Simon was obviously having more financial difficulties than she had realised. She knew he was very generous with Sue and the children. As she took a sip of the expensive wine she was reminded that he also had very expensive tastes. It must be hard to give up things one nearly took for granted like good wine.

★

The following morning when Amanda woke up she felt disoriented. She had dreamt she was in the room she had shared as a child with Pat in her parent's home in the West Country. She sat up in bed with a start and rubbed her eyes. The wallpaper had a busy white and pink pattern and was very similar to the one in her dreams. Simon lay beside her still fast asleep.

She got out of bed and looked out of the window towards the hills. They looked dark under the cloudy sky. Suddenly she felt something that resembled homesickness. The few times she had woken up in Simon's flat in London she had known Putney was just up the river. Home, the children, her working life and the man lying beside her had all been a part of the same tableau. Here, surrounded by the hills, away from it all, the commitment of a new relationship seemed more daunting. With Simon, Amanda shared so many things she had never shared with Douglas; small, mundane things like shopping and working together. Simon was also more dependent on her. He always wanted to know where she was and how long she'd be. This flattered her and made her feel wanted but, at the same time, worried her. She took her clothes downstairs and dressed in the hall so that she wouldn't disturb Simon, who hadn't stirred since she had got out of bed. Without having any breakfast, she left through the kitchen door and started walking towards the hills. Soon she could feel the weight of her body as the ground became steeper. The same feeling of well-being and communion with her surroundings that she had felt the previous day took a hold of her. Climbing the hill, she suddenly understood that this lightness of spirit came from the realisation she no longer was afraid of being alone. As the ground became steeper and her thoughts clearer, she felt light and free.

When she got back to the cottage, her cheeks flushed from the walk, she found Simon making himself some coffee.

"You've deserted me again, and this time first thing in the morning," he joked, his expression sullen, obviously not sure himself of how he felt.

"I'm sorry. You were fast asleep. It seemed the perfect time to try and climb the hill. Which means I won't have to abandon you again for the rest of the day if you don't want me to."

"Good! Have you had any breakfast?"

"No, not yet, but I have certainly built up an appetite." Amanda hung her jacket on the back of the chair.

"Splendid. I don't like eating by myself, but with company it's another matter. How about the works? Mushrooms, eggs, bacon." He opened the fridge door and started to pull things out. Amanda started laying the table while Simon beat the eggs.

"We'll go into town so you can get some more cash and then how about a drive towards the lake district? I heard the news while you were out and apparently it's going to clear up."

Amanda had to refrain from saying that they seemed to have enough food and drink to last them a week, but she knew Simon wanted the money to do some more shopping in the market. After all he had mentioned something about presents for his children.

★

On Sunday afternoon, as they drove back to London, Amanda felt rested and invigorated. The sun had shone for most of the weekend, and they had toured round the Lake District. In the evenings, after eating gourmet meals, they had read their books by the fire. Now, driving back, it felt as though she had been away for a week rather than just three days. She was looking forward to being back in London in case there was any news from the children. When they were in the outskirts of North London Simon asked, "Would you like to stop at the flat?"

"I think I'd better go straight home in case there are any messages from the children."

"You must stop worrying so much. They are, after all, of an age when it's probably beneficial for them to sort out some of their own problems."

"I know, but without Douglas there, I feel so responsible in case they need me."

"Surely they would ring their father in an emergency if you weren't there."

"They probably would, but somehow I feel I should be there."

Simon didn't answer and instead patted her knee in a reassuring gesture.

Back in Putney, he was helping Amanda with her case, when Kate opened the door.

"Kate, darling! I wasn't expecting you home this weekend."

"I changed my mind at the last minute because Sebastian decided to go home to his parents." She stressed the word *his*. "Not much fun though, to arrive to an empty house with an empty fridge." Kate looked in Simon's direction with a reproachful expression. "Where have you been?" Her eyes fell on the suitcase Simon was carrying.

"To visit some friends of Simon's up north." Amanda felt uneasy. She didn't want Kate to know that they had spent the weekend alone.

"I suppose I'd better be going," said Simon, sensing Kate's hostility.

As he made his way towards the car, Amanda couldn't stop thinking about the box filled with leftovers in the back of the car.

As soon as Amanda shut the front door behind her Kate said, "You could have said you were going away."

"I'm sorry. I didn't think it was necessary. You said you weren't coming home this weekend."

"Great! But, if I do change my mind and decide to come home, no one's here and I have to starve, too."

At the thought of how much money had been spent on food for Simon over the weekend, Amanda felt a twinge of guilt.

"Let me take you to the wine bar in the high street. We'll have a meal together and then we can go to the late night shop and stock up."

"There's no point. I'm going back in an hour. I rang Julia to see if she knew where you were and she sounded very surprised you weren't here," said Kate pointedly. "Mum, what is going on? Are you going to leave us too?" There was aggression in Kate's voice but Amanda could tell she was also frightened.

"Of course not. Oh, darling!" She flung her arms round her daughter. "You know I would never ever leave you!"

Kate clung to her. 'Do I have a right to the companionship and love of a man if it's going to cause my children such anguish,' she wondered as she pressed Kate's head against her shoulder. Maybe it was all a matter of timing. It was all too much and too soon. Douglas, Claire and now her. She would have to be more discreet, and not have Simon round till the children were more settled. Amanda gave Kate a lift to Paddington Station. Kate seemed more cheerful and was now talking about two black tie parties she had been asked to.

"Mum," she said, putting on her little girl's voice. "I need a new dress. I've asked Dad and he said he'll be giving me some money, but I don't think it will be enough for the dress I've fallen in love with. Maybe I could do some babysitting next time I'm home and earn a little extra. Do you know anyone local with tiny brats that need babysitting."

Amanda immediately thought of Patsy. When they had spoken last on the telephone, Patsy had been in a panic because she had just sacked her nanny, whom she had caught spanking Damian.

"I can't think of anyone local, but I have a girlfriend I met through the charity who lives in North London who may well welcome some help with babysitting. I'll ask her and let you know when you are next home."

"You do get around, don't you? Young friends in North London. Who is she anyhow? Anyone I've heard of?"

"Yes, Patsy. Do you remember she modelled the Ungaro dress at the show."

"Oh, her. I'd love to work for her. She looked well... the kind of person in whose house I could relax and chill out."

After dropping Kate at Paddington Station, Amanda went back to Putney and found three messages on the answering machine. There was one from Tina asking her to ring back, one from Julia saying Kate had rung wondering where she was, and a third from Virginia Hamilton-Veere asking to be contacted as soon as possible. Rewinding the tape, Amanda decided not to return Tina's call till the following day anticipating it was not urgent.

She dialled Julia's number but there was no reply. So she rang Virginia. The telephone had barely rung twice before Amanda heard Virginia's drawling, "Hello" into the receiver.

"Virginia, it's Amanda. You left a message." She paused.

"Thank you for ringing back. I'm afraid the matter is rather delicate and I'd rather not discuss it on the phone." Virginia was curt. "Could you come and see me tomorrow afternoon?"

"I won't be leaving the office till six o'clock. Is that too late?"

"Not at all. I just thought you might be busy in the evening. That's why I suggested the afternoon." Virginia's unusually abrupt tone made Amanda feel uneasy.

"Anything wrong?"

"That, of course, might be a matter of opinion. We'll talk about it tomorrow."

When Amanda put the phone down she could feel her pulse racing. What had gone wrong? Maybe someone had again complained about her perks or the fact that she had been advanced some money to buy the car.

As she carried her suitcase up the stairs she felt uneasy. All the joy and confidence she had felt climbing the hills in Cumbria seemed to have vanished. Kate's confrontation, and now Virginia's warning tone, made it seem as though she had never been away at all. All that was left of the weekend was the mud on the soles of her walking shoes.

★

The following day when the housekeeper left Amanda in Virginia's first floor drawing room, she noticed the room looked different. On top of the fireplace in a gilt frame hung the new portrait of the Hamilton-Veere grandchildren painted by Jack. The children, dressed in pale blue reclining on a white sofa, looked angelic. Amanda stood in front of the painting that had earned her the commission to pay for Mark's holiday and wondered what Virginia had done with her old portrait. As she looked around the room, she noticed that not only the wall-hangings had been changed, but also some of the furniture and the curtains. The room looked more sober and less fussy than it had six months ago. A lot of people had lost their money in the recession, and the rich now talked about "the good old days" and looked down on those who hadn't lost as much money as they had. Showing excessive wealth was now out of fashion. The Hamilton-Veeres hadn't lost their money in recent years, but Virginia knew that most of her husband's friends had, so she had changed her decor, taking into account the mood of this more austere decade, in which she hoped finally to become Lady Hamilton-Veere. Titles required sobriety.

Looking out of the window at the blossoming square in the fading light, Amanda reflected on how it felt more like a millennium than six months since she had last been in this house. Part of her life had come to an end and a new episode had started in the same time it had taken Virginia to change her curtains.

"Sorry I kept you waiting. Percy just rang from Hong Kong. Can I get you a drink?" Virginia's voice sounded friendlier than it had earlier.

Encouraged by this, Amanda replied, "Only if you're having one. This room looks lovely. It's so restful in the darker colours."

"I chose everything myself this time. These days I find rooms done up by decorators always a trifle cold and impersonal. Besides, understatement is back in vogue." She paused. "I'm having a glass of white wine. Same for you?"

"Yes, please." She watched Virginia leave the room.

"Here we are." Virginia was back with two glasses of chilled white wine. Amanda noticed Virginia's hair was shorter and the strands of grey were no longer totally concealed.

"Amanda, the best thing is if we get straight to the point. I need to discuss what's going on between you and Simon. You must understand, I feel responsible. Remember that both Simon and Sue are old friends of ours and it was me who suggested Belinda take him on to help with the charity's accounts. We could tell he was feeling depressed and needed something to do after being made redundant."

Amanda felt herself blush. She knew not only her face, but most probably her neck too, was red. She adjusted the silk scarf that hung loosely on the inside of her shirt.

"I can't understand why you should feel responsible. He is a grown man and I..."

Virginia interrupted. "He happens to be married to a very old friend of mine and I expected some degree of loyalty from you. After all, it was me who suggested you join the charity." Her voice rose slightly.

"They're planning to get a divorce. Sue doesn't want him at home any more. Don't you think you're overreacting? I understand your loyalty to her..."

"Is that what he's been telling you?" Virginia took a sip of her wine.

"It is common knowledge that they're planning to get a divorce," Amanda said defensively.

"Well, it's certainly not common knowledge amongst their friends. We're all hoping for a reconciliation and, according to Sue, so is Simon."

Amanda felt breathless. She could think of nothing to say to Virginia; that is, nothing Virginia wanted to hear. The unspoken words filled her head: 'Simon says he loves me, that he always felt inadequate with Sue, that they were ill matched. I've given him back his self-esteem. We're happy together and care for each other.' The silent words churned in her head while she waited for Virginia to say more.

"I've had my suspicions for a while. Since the show, in fact. Simon never seemed to leave your side. I'm sure I was not the only one to notice. Funny, I always thought of you as someone discreet."

Amanda bit her lip. She had to stop herself interrupting.

"I was hoping it wouldn't last; after all Simon has always had a bit of a roaming eye, and I felt that perhaps after Douglas left you, you might benefit from a bit of male adulation," she drawled. "But when John Blunt told me that whenever he pops back to his flat to collect his mail, he finds some of your belongings there... Well, I felt it was time to mention it."

Amanda got up. Not only were her face and neck red, but she was aware her breathing had become irregular. She was, she knew, on the verge of tears: tears of indignation, confusion and anger.

"Virginia," she said with all the composure she could muster, "I am most grateful for your concern. Both Simon and I are adults and can resolve our relationship. As for the divorce... Simon says he is getting a divorce!"

Virginia felt she had said enough. Amanda was bound to confront Simon and the truth would come out. She felt sorry for Amanda and yet loyalty towards Sue. What Virginia was unaware of, was the undercurrent of jealousy she felt at the thought that Amanda might have found love at this stage of life.

"Well... who knows, these things are always complicated and have more than one side to them. Anyhow, I'm so glad you came and we had this little chat."

Virginia got up and straightened her skirt. She crossed the room and in front of a mirror adjusted a strand of hair.

"Amanda," she said, in a surprisingly friendly tone, "as you know, I'm planning a bridge weekend in the South of France for our little group at the end of April. It would be too bad if I felt I had to pretend I didn't know."

Virginia walked Amanda to the front door and before saying goodbye, added, "Sue is such a good person and they have such sweet kids."

Out in the street Amanda drove round the square in the dark till she felt more in control of her emotions. Later she drove to Simon's flat and left him a note saying she would be there the following day at six as something had cropped up. When she left his flat she drove straight home, longing for the familiar streets of Putney.

At five o'clock the next day Amanda started tidying her desk. It would only take her fifteen minutes, at the most, to drive to Simon's flat – to John Blunt's flat, she reminded herself as she put some papers in the bottom drawer of the desk. It was too early to leave. She had mentioned in her note to Simon that she would be arriving at six, but she felt she needed time to get ready, to brace herself for the confrontation to come. All day she'd been rehearsing what she was going to say: "You've misled me. You've lied to me. You said that you had left Sue, and it isn't true." But she knew Simon had never promised her anything. He had only wished, planned, and she had accepted him unquestioningly. They had never talked about the future in concrete terms but alluded to it as somewhere they would be together. Amanda put on her coat. The office now felt airless. She would go for a walk and try to put her thoughts into some kind of order. She knew Simon had met Sue for lunch earlier in the day. He had said they needed to discuss the possibility of changing Timmy's school. Amanda parked the car near the

Embankment and walked towards the Thames. The sky was grey and the river at low tide looked drab. The trees were still bare and, if it wasn't for a few scant daffodils in the square, there seemed to be little hope for a new beginning. After an aimless walk, all she had achieved was to get her hair damp and frizzy. She let herself into Simon's mansion block and, although she had a key to the flat, she rang the bell. Simon opened the door. His boyish expression disarmed her.

"I missed you," he said kissing her on the lips. "Anything wrong? You look tense. Your message said something had cropped up. The children all right?" He helped her with her coat. "Let me get you a drink." He hurried into the kitchen. Amanda, instead of following him, went to the drawing room and waited.

"Here we are. A nice long vodka and tonic with ice and lemon."

"Thank you." Amanda took the glass from his hand and sat on the edge of the sofa. "How was lunch?"

"It was awful. We just argued. As usual, she made me feel like a failure. I never told you..." He paused.

She held her breath wondering if he was going to say something that might belie what Virginia had said.

"I owe some money. Not a fortune, just a couple of thousand pounds to a family friend. He lent it to me soon after the separation. I was a bit short at the time and had to pay Timmy's school fees. I think this particular friend was hoping for a reconciliation between Sue and me. When he realised we weren't getting back together he took sides. Sue's side, of course." Simon dropped his head. "He told her he'd loaned me some money. Sue was livid and even more furious when she heard I hadn't paid it back straight away. As you know, the little consultancy I do hardly pays the bills. There was an awful row. Oh, I'm so glad you are here." He buried his face on her chest.

Amanda remembered the telephone conversation in Cumbria and wondered if it was related to what he had just told her. She couldn't help thinking about the money he still owed her from the shopping, but felt sorry for him. Her hands gently stroked Simon's head. She didn't want to push him away any more than she wanted to think about his debts or believe what Virginia had said was true.

Later, as they had some supper, she told him what Virginia had both said and insinuated. As Amanda spoke, she hoped Simon would interrupt her and deny it all. He waited for her to finish and then told her he needed her and how lost he would be without her, adding that she was the first woman in whom he had been able to confide. Sue wanted to punish him. Who knew what she might have told Virginia? She had made such a scene about the debt, probably just to humiliate him. Amanda wished she could help him. Divorces were always unpleasant and full of malicious gossip. Why should she believe Virginia and not Simon? She heard herself volunteering to lend him a thousand pounds and wondered if she was doing it to justify her decision to believe him. It was all she had in her deposit account. Simon would do the same for me, she told herself. After all, had he ever given her any cause to suspect he was not truthful?

She stayed the night. They reassured each other silently as they curled up tightly under the duvet. Amanda dreamed that John Blunt and Virginia stormed into the bedroom and accused her of being a home-breaker, but Simon's even breathing beside her when she woke, told her it was only a dream.

★

Spring rain fell heavily on the windscreen of Amanda's car as she crossed the park on her way to Alfred Halford's office. The sudden downpour made the visibility poor. Crossing the park was one of her favourite routes and she normally drove slowly, enjoying the view. Some trees had started to bud and others were laden with blossoms. The lime green, white and pink tones of early spring were hardly visible behind the curtain of water her windscreen wipers were struggling to disperse. She accelerated, accepting that the view was now totally lost to the wall of rain. As she filtered carefully onto Oxford Street, a rainbow appeared, suspended over the grey buildings, now bathed in sunshine. Amanda wished she had left Putney ten minutes later and caught the rainbow over the park. It seemed wasted over C&A. The shop windows were full of spring clothes and bright colours, but people in the street still wore dull-coloured coats and anoraks. On Saturday, when she had accompanied Julia shopping, she had been tempted to buy some new clothes, but had refrained. A week ago, when she had volunteered to lend Simon a thousand pounds, she had underestimated what her bills would be and was now wondering how she would manage with all the extra expenses of the Easter holiday.

She thought of Simon and how evasive he had been lately whenever she mentioned Sue. Perhaps, Amanda told herself circling the square, they were having difficulty deciding what to do about their house and the children. She felt it was better not to pry, but at the same time, she felt uneasy, particularly after what Virginia had said. She knew Simon saw his wife more often than he admitted but felt it was her place to be patient and understanding. Amanda thought of the moments of joy and companionship they had shared and smiled as she remembered the afternoon they had spent at Kew Gardens. They had walked round the grounds and later had sat on a bench, enjoying the warm spring sun that had appeared from behind white clouds. The bench they had sat on had been inscribed to a friend of Kew Gardens, who had died two years earlier. The inscription read: "A thing of beauty is a joy forever". That was true, she reflected, about a lot of things she shared with Simon.

Once she had been to Kew with Douglas to see an exhibition of paintings by a friend at the Kew Gallery. It had been a beautiful autumn day, the grounds and gardens had been ablaze with oranges, ambers, yellows and reds. She had asked Douglas, as they left the exhibition, if they could go for a walk, and he had answered that they had been there long enough. "But not in the gardens," she had added.

"You can come another time with the children. I've got things to do at home," he had replied, leaving Amanda wondering why he had wasted the opportunity to share something so beautiful with her.

Amanda put her foot on the brake, making the man behind her flash his lights. She apologised with a gesture of her hand and started to reverse into the empty space by the meter that she had so nearly missed, thinking about the past. Feeding the meter, she started to rehearse what she would say to Alfred Halford. She hadn't seen him since the party at Tina's. The charity still needed a sponsor for next year's summer ball and Amanda was hoping Alfred's company might be persuaded to help. She looked at her watch. She was fifteen minutes early so she walked slowly towards Baker Street, enjoying the sunshine left after the rainbow. Alfred Halford's office building was large and modern. Before being directed towards the glass lift, Amanda was given a plastic label to pin on to her jacket by a uniformed guard at the door. The lift stopped on the tenth floor, where a girl sat behind the desk of an open plan reception area.

"You're here to see Mr Halford?" She smiled displaying perfect teeth. "Can I get you some tea or coffee? Mr Halford is tied up and will be with you in about fifteen minutes." Amanda realised the whole floor must be Alfred's office.

"Tea would be lovely, thank you." She sat down on the deep sofa, picked up a newspaper and quickly calculated if she had put enough money in the meter.

"Here's your tea." The girl's voice had the same artificial tone as recordings that say: "The number you are calling knows you are waiting". Maybe there was an ideal tone of voice required to keep people waiting.

Amanda read absentmindedly about some new royal melodrama and was going to start on a second article, giving another columnist's point of view, when the voice behind the desk told her Mr Halford was now ready to see her.

She walked into the large office surrounded by windows, overlooking the busy streets below. Alfred sat behind a large desk. On seeing Amanda he sprung out of his chair and crossed the room towards her with the gait of a younger man.

"How lovely to see you again." He stretched out his hand. "Sorry to have kept you waiting. Phone call from abroad." He shook her hand.

"It's very kind of you to fit me in. I know how busy you are and I'll try not to take too much of your time." She was not only thinking of Alfred's time but also of the possibility of a thirty pound parking ticket stuck to her windscreen.

"Come and sit down." Alfred pointed at two armchairs by the window. How sensitive of him, Amanda thought, not to put his imposing desk between them.

"I gather from Patsy that you managed to raise a lot of money with the fashion show. Congratulations! It isn't easy raising money nowadays."

"We were very lucky that it was so well attended and that the dresses donated were so beautiful."

"It was very well organised. I do agree a bit of luck always comes in handy, but at the end of the day there is no substitute for hard work." Alfred crossed his legs and looked at her attentively. "Now tell me how I can help you."

"We're planning next summer's ball and we need a sponsor."

Amanda wondered if she had come to the point too quickly, when Alfred's phone rang. Unhurriedly, he walked towards his desk and picked up the receiver.

"Yes, thank you. I'll take the call." He looked in her direction and smiled. "Won't be long."

She felt encouraged by his tone. Perhaps, with a man like Alfred, it was better to get straight to the point. Amanda noticed that, while he talked on the phone, Alfred was scrutinising the photographs sprawled over his desk. She sat apprehensively opposite him. The dark oak desk created a barrier that hadn't been there before.

Alfred was scribbling something on a piece of paper and it was only when he raised his eyes and said matter-of-factly, "You were talking about sponsorship," that Amanda realised she was the one who felt things had changed between them because of the desk.

"You support a very good cause," he went on, "and we normally allow a certain amount of money per year to be spent on charity. But we would, of course, have to consider whether it is beneficial for us to get involved. Can you remind me who your patron is?"

"The Duchess of Exeter," Amanda said in a half whisper, knowing this wouldn't impress Alfred. "Lady Ashcombe is our Chairman," she added, sensing the wife of a member of the Cabinet would be more attractive to Alfred than a Duchess who dedicated her spare time to hunting. Alfred's expression didn't change. It was difficult to tell whether he was impressed or not.

"Would the name of your sponsor be printed on all the publicity and on the invitations to the ball?" Alfred examined one of the photographs on the desk.

"Yes, of course it would. We normally print the sponsor's name in a different typeface so that it stands out." Amanda couldn't help noticing the photographs were pictures of himself sitting behind the large desk.

Alfred caught Amanda's eye and said, "I'm planning to have a portrait of myself 'at work' done for the board room. My colleagues have been pressuring me to do it for a while. Perhaps they fear I will soon look too grey and will go to posterity an old man." Amanda smiled and, although she was tempted to flatter him by adding that she couldn't imagine him ever looking anything but energetic, chose to go back to the subject of sponsoring the ball.

"We would, of course, like Mrs Halford to chair the ball committee if she can spare the time. I know life is always busy with children under five."

When Alfred smiled, Amanda knew she had said the right thing.

"Let me think about it overnight and discuss it with my junior colleagues. We're having a general meeting tomorrow evening. Ideal time to bring it up. I'll drop you a line soon to let you know what we think of the idea."

"Thank you so much. And thank you for your time." Amanda felt optimistic. It had been an encouraging meeting. As she rose to her feet she looked at Alfred's photographs.

"Who is painting your portrait?" she asked, thinking of Jack.

"I'm not sure yet. I don't know any artists myself. Do you know a good one?" He walked round the desk towards her.

"I know Jack Noel. He painted Tina Karalambos's portrait. You might have come across him at their buffet dinner."

"Never met him, but I do remember Tina's portrait on top of the fireplace. I seem to remember it was a rather good one of her. Do you think he'd be just as skilled at painting an ageing company director?"

"I'm sure he would. He is supposed to be one of the best portrait painters in London."

"I see." Alfred looked at her with interest. "Could you let me have his telephone number? It would save me ringing up Constantine. I spoke to him this morning."

Amanda found herself thinking of the thousand pounds she had impulsively lent Simon and how the commission on Alfred's boardroom portrait would be the last one she would accept from Jack. She opened her bag and looked for Jack's number in her address book.

"Splendid. I'll mention you recommended him," said Alfred.

Amanda felt herself blush. Alfred's remark had been perfectly innocent; being a businessman, he was probably in the habit of always mentioning who had given him a contact.

As Alfred escorted her to the lift he said, "I gather your daughter is babysitting for us this evening, while we're at the theatre."

"Yes, that's right. Kate spoke with Patsy last week. I'd nearly forgotten all about it. She's home for the Easter break and keen to save up for her summer holidays."

"Patsy mentioned she's at university in Bristol."

"I'm afraid she's reading history and not home economics, so I hope she'll cope with Damian. I'll be at home all evening. She can always ring me if..."

"I'm sure there will be no need for that," Alfred interrupted. "If she's half as competent as her mother, Damian will be in excellent hands."

At the door Amanda gave the receptionist a smile. She could tell the girl was impressed by the attention Alfred was paying her. "You'll hear from me soon." He waited till she was inside the glass lift.

As the lift took her to the ground floor, Amanda saw pools of light from the buildings opposite twinkling in the approaching dusk. She felt both optimistic and nervous. She stood a very good chance of getting Alfred's firm to sponsor the ball, but the visit to Alfred's office had also led her into further involvement with Jack and Solange.

Amanda hurried home. She wanted to make sure Kate had left in good time for North London. Patsy had asked her to be early so she could help put Damian to bed while she got ready for the theatre. The traffic hardly moved across the park and it was nearly an hour after leaving Alfred's office that Amanda crossed Putney Bridge. Inside the house she found a message from Kate saying she had left for Hampstead and could she please ring Julia. Amanda was still in the hall when the telephone rang. Anticipating it would be Julia, she rushed to the telephone. They hadn't spoken since her weekend in Cumbria and Amanda felt she owed her an explanation.

"Hello, Julia?" She said cheerfully into the receiver.

"No, I'm sorry to disappoint you. It's me, Douglas."

Amanda was taken aback and there was a long pause before she said, "Hello, Douglas. How are you?"

"Not too well. I've had a terrible cold for over a week and don't seem to be able to get rid of it."

Douglas had always been a bad patient. The few occasions in their married life when he had been ill he had acted like a different person. All his confidence would vanish and he would behave like a child wanting to be mothered and reassured.

Trying not to smile Amanda said casually, "Is Claire a good nurse?"

"I'm afraid Claire isn't here to nurse me."

"Oh, is she away?"

"No, we've split up."

There was a long silence. Amanda eventually broke it by saying in a sarcastic tone, "Have you rung because you want some sympathy for your cold?"

"Kind of. I'm feeling rotten and I miss the children. In fact it's quite lonely."

"Don't talk to me about being lonely, Douglas. Not now."

"I see," he said curtly. "Could I speak to Kate? She rang me at the office yesterday."

"She's out babysitting, but I can give you the number." Amanda couldn't help feeling sorry for him. When she put the telephone down she felt exhausted by the weight of her emotions. She had sensed what he had said in between the lines: 'I'm lonely. I miss the children. Are you still there?'

She knew she couldn't have him back and yet, turning him away was something she had never believed she would have to do. Instead of satisfaction she felt an overwhelming sense of loss. Her mouth felt very dry and she went into the kitchen where she downed a glass of water. The years she had invested in her marriage to Douglas flashed in front of her and, without realising what she was doing, she smashed the empty glass into the sink and burst into tears.

★

When the telephone rang in the Halford's apartment, Kate was in the guest bedroom trying on some cast-offs Patsy had given her. "Never really got my figure back after Damian," she had said, handing Kate a pile of clothes.

"Halford's residence," Kate said alluringly into the receiver as she examined her reflection in the mirror.

"Could I speak to Kate Thompson, please."

"Dad, it's me!"

"Sorry, darling. I didn't recognise you. You sounded so... so grown up."

"Dad, I am grown up. Nineteen! Remember?" Kate paced in front of the mirror with the cordless telephone while she examined the tight-fitting white jeans Patsy had given her.

"Yes, of course you are. I'm sorry. Who are you babysitting for?"

"Some very rich friends of Mum's. He's some tycoon and she is fabulous! So pretty. I've just had the most delicious salad of smoked chicken and avocado, and she's given me a whole lot of her old clothes. You should see them: Armani jeans, Ralph Lauren shirts!"

"How nice." Douglas coughed. "You rang the office yesterday. I'm afraid I haven't been in. I have a terrible cold."

"Oh! So I did. Do you know, I can't remember what it was about."

"Would you like to have some lunch tomorrow?" Douglas blew his nose.

"Tomorrow? Sorry, I'm going out with Sebastian."

"Who is Sebastian?"

"My boyfriend." Kate looked eagerly at the clothes piled on the bed that she hadn't tried on yet and wondered if her father would want to chat for long.

"It would be just the two of us for lunch. Claire and I have broken up."

"Sorry, I really can't tomorrow. Maybe another time, but I'm really busy this holiday, with one thing and another. I'll ring next week, okay? Bye, Dad."

Kate took off the jeans hurriedly and tried the black leather mini skirt. She was glad Claire was gone, but had she been like Patsy, she wouldn't really have minded her that much.

★

The following week after work, Amanda went to Simon's flat. Both Kate and Mark, who were home for the Easter break, were going to be out that evening. She hadn't seen Simon for several days because she wanted to spend as much time as possible with the children while they were home. Kate was seldom in; she was either out with friends or babysitting. Mark still spent a lot of time in his bedroom listening to music, but had looked more cheerful since he had been down to Hampshire to see Tony who had helped him with his summer project.

When she reached Simon's flat Amanda rang the bell. There was no reply. She was early and hesitated before using the key he had given her. Since her confrontation with Virginia, whenever she came to the flat she worried that John Blunt might suddenly walk in. Virginia, whom she still saw regularly once a week at the bridge lessons, had never brought up the subject of Simon again and behaved as though nothing had happened. Amanda often wondered why Virginia had said all the things she had. Perhaps she had only done it out of loyalty to Sue, who was an old friend and, after cautioning her, she had appeased her conscience.

She walked into the kitchen where the table was littered with Simon's correspondence. He had obviously been paying some bills before he left that morning. She pushed a bundle of letters to one side to make room for her shopping when her eyes fell on two open bank statements. She couldn't help seeing that a large amount had been paid to his club and to Turnbull & Asser. She was surprised and couldn't help thinking about all his other debts and the money he owed her. Her train of thought was suddenly interrupted by the front door slamming.

She gave a jump, expecting to see the dreaded John Blunt but was confronted by the figure of Simon carrying a large bunch of lilies. He deposited the flowers on the kitchen table and, picking her up in his arms, whirled her round the kitchen before kissing her passionately.

"I've got the job!" he said breathlessly as he put her down. "I've got the job." Amanda looked up at his beaming face.

"That's wonderful. What is it?" She watched him take a bottle of champagne out of a plastic bag. He looked handsome and somehow taller. He wasn't stooping in his usual way and his shoulders looked broader as he stood uncorking the bottle. The cork popped across the room and Amanda rushed to get the glasses as the froth spilled over Simon's hand.

"I'm taking you out for supper tonight," he said pouring the champagne.

"You don't have to."

"I want to take you out. I've never taken you to a really good restaurant. Today, I can at last afford to do so. What shall it be? French? Italian?" He handed her the glass.

"You choose. You probably know the good restaurants much better than I do." She took a sip of champagne and added, "Do tell me more about the job."

"Later, later while we're having supper." He kissed her. "Now I am going to ravish you!"

He pushed her gently towards the bedroom. Amanda drank more champagne, hoping it would stimulate her to match Simon's euphoric mood. She was apprehensive. She had only made love to a dependable, and at times shy, Simon who had even confided in her that after breaking up with Sue he had become impotent, and that it was only with her that he had regained his masculinity. The Simon who hurriedly was undressing by the window, so full of confidence, seemed like a different person. As Amanda undressed by the bed, she wondered if she would have to behave differently tonight. He normally liked to lie in her arms before making love, but something told her that this evening he wouldn't, and she felt a sense of loss.

On their way to the restaurant, as they stopped at the traffic lights on the Embankment, Amanda looked at Simon. He looked happy and relaxed, just as he had done when he had first walked into the flat with the flowers and champagne eager to celebrate his good news.

"I'm taking you to a French restaurant in Battersea. It's not very smart but the food is superb. It looks like an ordinary bistro, red and white checked table cloths, candles melting over wine bottles and all that, but the cuisine makes it worthy of the Routiers listing. It's run by two brothers. I haven't been there in a while."

Amanda, who had envisaged being taken somewhere smarter, felt disappointed. They rarely went out and when they did, they either went to the cinema or to the small bistros near the flat. Maybe he was worried about being seen by a friend of Sue's if he took her to the more fashionable spots.

As he turned the corner he suddenly said, "It'll be nice for Sue and the children to move back into the house. Renting it out, with me out of a job, was the only solution, and it's been very trying, both for her and the boys living with her parents."

"I thought she was very close to her parents," Amanda retorted, annoyed at his protective tone.

"They're very close. That's half the problem. They mean well, but at the same time are very interfering."

Amanda was silent, sensing that Simon wanted to say more.

"I might have to spend most of next week in Wiltshire. There'll be a lot to discuss and organise this time." He paused and looked at her. "It used to be easy to park around here," he added with a touch of impatience as he manoeuvred the car into a tight space.

The restaurant, as Simon had promised, was cosy and unpretentious. The owner didn't seem to recognise him, which made Amanda think he couldn't have patronised it often. Simon took a long time choosing the wine Amanda now drank indifferently, wishing she felt as excited as he did about the future.

After ordering their food and while they nibbled at an assortment of crudités the waiter had left on the table, Simon took her hand and said, "I'm afraid our Easter plans will have to change. I start work the week before the holidays and won't be able to take time off. In fact, I might even go into the office over the Easter break and try to get acquainted with some of the work. It's a slight departure from what I used to do before. Amanda," he said dropping his voice, "why don't you go and stay with Pat? You did mention she'd asked you all down, didn't you?" He stroked her hand soothingly.

"Yes, she did."

They had planned to go to Wales together while her children spent a couple of days with Douglas. She had paid a small deposit on a cottage and now, disappointed by the news he wouldn't be able to go with her, found herself wondering if she would get her money back.

Waiting for their first course to arrive, Simon talked about his new job and what it entailed. It was still in the banking world, not as good a position as he had had before, but with good prospects. He then went on to mention how his boys would be pleased he had a job again. It had never occurred to Amanda before, that Simon had felt inadequate in front of his sons. He was looking forward to breaking the good news to them personally, rather than let Sue do it for him. He would go to pick them up from school on Saturday after the rugby and tell them. When the main course arrived, Simon asked Amanda about the outcome of her meeting with Alfred. As she talked about the interview, she remembered Jack and her commission and wondered if Simon would mention the money she had lent him.

"I saw Virginia at Belinda's yesterday afternoon when I dropped in with some paperwork. I'm afraid I told her I'll have to give up the charity now that I've got a job."

Amanda felt stunned. That meant she wouldn't see him other than in the evenings.

"I hear Virginia is having a bridge weekend in the South of France," he continued as he put a large piece of duck in his mouth. "I assume you are included? She did say it was for your Tuesday group." He wiped his mouth.

"Yes, she mentioned it last week. We're all invited. It's very generous of her, but I'm slightly worried about the expense. I can't afford the time to drive out there with Helen and Ingrid, which was the original plan, and that means I'll have to fly. I don't know whether I can afford it at the moment."

"Of course you can," said Simon, wiping some gravy from his chin. "I owe you a thousand pounds which I should be able to repay soon. You must go or Virginia will be mortified. She's an excellent hostess and I'm sure won't allow any of you to spend a penny once you're out there. Besides, Provence at this time of the year is glorious. All the flowers will be out. Glorious! I can smell the lavender, just talking about it. I think I'm even feeling a bit jealous." He drank some of his wine and laughed.

It dawned on Amanda how little she really knew about Simon's past. He had never mentioned to her that he had stayed at Virginia's villa, not even after she had told him about the confrontation in Virginia's house. Sue and Virginia were obviously very close if they had spent holidays together. The thought made her uneasy and now she wished she could get out of the invitation.

Simon watched her pick at her food and added, "You'll also have the most delicious food. Virginia has a couple that look after the villa and the woman is a superb cook. It'll do you a power of good, a week in the sun and fresh air." He took her hand and kissed it gently.

She was surprised when she felt hurt by his apparent happiness and optimism and found herself wishing he were once more dependent on her for solace and companionship. He seemed to be urging her to have a good time without him, and instinct made her interpret his encouragement with distrust. As she watched him enjoy his food and wine, regaling her with tales about Provence, she wondered if he would ever need her again for support. She felt guilty at this thought but realised that it had been his vulnerability that had appealed to her. Simon's talk about his long visit to Wiltshire, the cancelled Easter plans, giving up his job at the charity and the suggestions he would now prefer not to use John Blunt's flat, had left her feeling insecure. Their intimacy had suddenly been invaded by his new-found confidence.

★

The following day Simon went to Wiltshire and didn't come back for a week. He rang Amanda a couple of times to say he needed more time with Sue to organise the move. Soon after he came back to London he started his new job. Amanda went to the flat a couple of times but soon their routine changed. Simon had never said that he wanted to leave her or that he had stopped enjoying her company, but he said that his job, his children and his sense of duty required him to return to his family. Sue had decided, now that he had a job, to give the marriage another chance for the children's sake. They were all moving back into the house as soon as the tenants moved out. Simon felt that he had been lucky to find such a good job at his age in the middle of a recession and felt it his duty to give it all his energies. Although he loved her and didn't want to lose her, leading a double life was stressful, he had said, and he felt he wouldn't be able to cope. He had to go back to his wife for the children's sake.

Amanda had waited to feel as devastated and shattered as she had felt when Douglas had left. Instead she only felt humiliation, confusion and anger at her own naiveté.

She threw herself into her work so as to avoid being in touch with her emotions. She kept on telling herself that she hadn't been as dependent on Simon as she had been on

Douglas and that this would soften the pain of another failed relationship.

Looking forward to her impending holiday in the South of France and the company of her woman friends was a solace. She needed time to reflect, away from her routine responsibilities and Putney.

Chapter Ten

During take-off Amanda kept her eyes tightly shut, but this made her more aware of the vibration that shook her body. When she opened her eyes the plane was above the clouds. It was suspended in a perfect blue sky, and the cabin was bathed in a pure bright light that came from a sun one couldn't see. She had asked for a window seat; flying was still an adventure as with Douglas she had rarely gone abroad. Amanda felt herself relax, her arms and legs tingling as the muscles loosened, no longer fighting the fear and excitement of being airborne. She was looking forward to the break. The events of the last few weeks had left her feeling depressed. Virginia had said there would be plenty of time for exploring the surrounding countryside and doing "one's own thing". Helen and Ingrid were most likely, like her, looking forward to visiting the small market towns of Provence and walking, rather than playing bridge.

As she stepped off the plane at Marseilles airport, a sudden blast of heat filled her with the well-being that only sunshine and warmth can give. It had been a long, wet winter in England and, although spring had arrived with its flowers and longer days, the sun would still shy away at regular intervals and the lingering grey days made her wonder whether spring wasn't just an illusion. Virginia had mentioned she would make arrangements for someone to collect her. Amanda looked round the busy airport for a familiar face and soon spotted Helen wearing a flowery print dress and a large-brimmed hat – unmistakably English.

"Helen, how, lovely to see you. But how did you get here?" Amanda had visions of Helen taking a bus ride round Provence to meet her.

"I've rented a car. I like feeling independent when on holiday."

"I bet you didn't particularly feel like driving all the way to Marseilles though. It's really kind of you to meet me. Did you have an awful journey?"

"Not at all. It's a lovely drive to Virginia's. You'll see for yourself on our way back."

They pushed a trolley with Amanda's suitcase towards Helen's car parked outside in the sunshine. "The light's blinding." Amanda took a pair of sunglasses from her hand luggage to protect her startled eyes.

"I think it's the darkness we endure back home for months on end that makes our eyes so sensitive. You'll soon get used to the light. I bet you, in a couple of days you won't be wearing your sunglasses."

They drove the first miles in silence, Amanda looked out of the window, enjoying the blossoming countryside. Helen, conscious her friend was admiring the new surroundings, kept quiet waiting for her to speak first.

"I don't have a present for Virginia. I couldn't think of anything to give her. Any chance we could stop somewhere and buy something? I'd hate to arrive empty-handed."

"We'll stop in Cavaillon. It's on the way. I need to get some sun block from the chemist anyway, and we could have a coffee in a patisserie. I just love the smell of French bakeries." Amanda looked at Helen. She seemed so relaxed and at home.

"When was the last time you were in France?" Amanda wound the window down.

"Last September. I come over an average of once a year. Not always to the South though. I love French food and know my way round quite well by now after so many years of touring. I must say, this 'bridge weekend' is an added bonus. I'm off to Italy in a month's time. Not a bad start to the summer, is it?"

Amanda looked at Helen and realised how little they knew about her. Because she was a spinster and lived alone they all assumed her life was dull and empty. No one at the bridge lessons ever asked her what she did for her holidays or on weekends, assuming that she had gone to visit her sister or taken a walk in Richmond Park. Tina and Virginia's social lives were more often the topic of conversation round the card table. Helen's life, Amanda suspected, was probably fuller and more exciting than theirs. Without a man to worry about, she seemed to pursue her own interests. Had that been her mistake, Amanda thought, to assume that life without a man was incomplete?

"Five minutes and we'll be in Cavaillon! Virginia's house is quite near L'Isle sur la Sorgue. Do you know the area?" Helen put her foot on the accelerator.

"I'm afraid not. I've not been to the South of France since I was a child when I spent a holiday with my parents and my sister near Menton."

"I know Menton. It's pleasant enough and I suppose has the added advantage of being so near Monte Carlo. Provence has a totally different feel to the coast. Pity it's being overrun by outsiders. It's become very fashionable since someone wrote a manual on how to manage French builders. Still, luckily, the French are quite resilient to foreign invasions and, with any luck, apart from farms being turned into million pound summer houses, things won't change too much."

Amanda felt very ignorant beside Helen. She was happy Helen was there. It would make it easier to get away and visit the countryside.

When they drove into Cavaillon, it was five o'clock and the small town had resumed it's rhythm after a sleepy lunch break.

"Shall I take Virginia some flowers?" Amanda followed Helen down the busy street.

"You might as well. She seems to have most things, including two living-in helps and a gardener. Flowers are always a treat and I noticed the shrubs in her garden aren't out yet. Look, there's a patisserie. Let's have a coffee and then we'll find a florist."

The patisserie, as Helen predicted, smelt of warm dough and cooked fruit. They sat by a window with two cups of coffee and two tart au pommes.

"This is the life," said Helen, lighting a cigarette.

"I didn't know you smoked."

"I only smoke for pleasure with a coffee or after a meal. Virginia is very protective of her lungs. Last night after supper, I had to smoke in the garden, which I must say was a bonus. The views round her house are stunning. All rolling vineyards with small hamlets of houses in the distance."

"Has Tina arrived?"

"Yes. We flew out together. When I saw her luggage I had to ask where she was going on from here. Can you believe she's brought three suitcases for four days!"

Amanda laughed.

"Do you think we'll start playing bridge tonight? I had a very early start."

"I wouldn't worry about it. Everyone seems pretty relaxed. Anyhow, it's better to play at night and take the time off during the day. Virginia seems to be having long meetings with her gardener and a brick layer. I suspect she is planning to change the landscape! She seems quite busy with the house, since they haven't been here since last summer. I think we'll have a lot of time to do what we want."

"It must be nice for Virginia to have some company while she's down here organising things." Amanda took a sip of her coffee.

"I think Virginia's husband prefers Dorset to Provence, or so she said last night, and Tina broke the news during supper that they are planning to buy a house in the country too. I can't see Tina in the country, but then she might surprise us all. Apparently," said Helen, stirring her coffee, "Percy's father is at death's door. There was even talk at one point of cancelling this weekend. It's that imminent. I bet Virginia's new stationary with 'Lady' on it is being printed right now. So," Helen put a last piece of tarte in her mouth, "that's roughly all the news chez Hamilton-Veere."

★

Virginia's house lay on the side of a small hill and was surrounded by vineyards. The sun had started to set as they drove up towards it and the beauty of the countryside overwhelmed Amanda. Virginia, who was in the garden when they arrived, came to greet them. She was clearly pleased to see them and to have someone with whom to share the new gardening schemes that she had been hatching all day. After a walk round the garden Virginia took Amanda to her bedroom which was on the first floor and overlooked the vineyards at the back of the house. The room was decorated in a fresh Provençal style. It smelt of lavender, wood and spring.

"Supper's at eight. I'll leave you to unpack. There's plenty of hot water if you want a bath. If you're not too tired, we'll play some bridge later. I'm afraid tomorrow I'll have to spend most of the day in Avignon. I have to choose some new garden furniture."

"I'll fit in with whatever is organised. It's such a treat to be here. I sometimes forget there is anything other than a working life and the city."

Amanda felt invigorated by the news that she would have most of the following day free to explore and wondered if Helen would mind taking her to a market town. When Virginia had left the room Amanda stood in front of the window looking out at the undulating landscape; it was beautiful but soft and undemanding, not unlike parts of South-West England. She remembered the hard rugged beauty of Cumbria and how it had put her fears into perspective. She thought of Simon, her first attempt to love again. She had failed. Had she fallen for Simon to satisfy a need to love and feel loved or to express a true emotion? Her chest tightened. Where had she gone wrong again? Had she been unlucky or had she once again misunderstood the man beside her?

*

Amanda's first day in Provence was spent with Helen in the small town of L'Isle sur la Sorgue. It was Saturday and the market stalls were laden with local produce. Lavender bottles, lavender soaps and lavender bags were temptingly displayed to beckon the holidaymakers. Soon after breakfast Virginia had left for Avignon and Tina had gone with her in the hope she might find some boutiques where she could buy some more clothes. In the late afternoon, they all sat in Virginia's spacious drawing room for a game of bridge and some tea. Tina was wearing a new silk scarf she had bought that morning and looked happy and relaxed, her mission completed. Helen, in contrast to Tina's soigné appearance, had a coarse cotton shirt from one of the market stalls and smelt of the lavender oil she had daubed behind her ears. Virginia looked out towards the patio at regular intervals to admire her new wrought-iron bench; the rest of her purchases were going to be delivered the following morning. Amanda sat enjoying the low afternoon sun with its long shadows. It was difficult to concentrate on the cards. The silence of the countryside, the fresh air and the well-being that comes from having no responsibilities made her sleepy.

"Amanda, you're not concentrating." Virginia's voice was friendly, but reproachful.

"I'm sorry. I'm a dreadful partner today. You look after us too well, Virginia, and I'm feeling so relaxed I can hardly keep my eyes open."

Virginia, flattered by the compliment, was willing to overlook Amanda's shortcomings as a bridge partner.

"Pity Ingrid couldn't make it. She could have relieved you." Helen smiled.

"Poor Ingrid. I'm sure she was dying to come. I can't remember now what feeble excuse she gave. I suspect Dick didn't want her to come." Virginia dealt the cards.

"Probably jealous. Didn't want her to have a good time. Typical of some men. They pretend they want you there, that they can't do without you, but the real reason is they don't want you to have a good time without them," said Helen.

They all looked at Helen. She never spoke about men, let alone what she thought of them. Intrigued, Virginia ventured, "Did you ever have a possessive boyfriend?"

"I had a possessive husband." Helen looked round the table triumphantly, aware none of them expected to hear she had once been married.

"Oh, sorry. We didn't know," Tina said in the tone one uses for condolences.

"Nothing to be sorry about. I married when I was still at university. It was a mistake and luckily we didn't have children. The decision to break up the marriage was mutual; but instigated by me, I suppose. I've had a few longish relationships since, but I couldn't live with a man all the time. Not now, not after so many years of leading my own life."

They all looked at Helen and went back to their cards in silence, each one with her own thoughts about Helen's revelations. Helen and Tina had just scored a rubber when they heard a car coming up the drive.

"Are you expecting guests?" Tina sounded excited, confident that any acquaintance of Virginia's would be worth meeting.

"No one knows I'm down here." Virginia stood up and went towards the window. Helen followed her gaze.

"It looks like an English car."

The car stopped noisily on the gravel outside.

Virginia said, "It's Jack and Solange! I never expected they would come. They said they would be in Paris for the Leger exhibition. How nice of them to come all this way."

Amanda's heart sank. Jack and Solange didn't go anywhere unless there was an ulterior motive. She suspected there had been no reason for them to be in Paris either, and the whole business of an exhibition had been orchestrated so that they would get a casual invitation out of Virginia.

Virginia met them in the hall.

"*Charmant! C'est tout à fait charmant!*" Solange seemed to have reverted to her mother tongue to fit in with the surroundings.

In Virginia's book, a French guest, when in France, always added glamour and a sense of belonging. Virginia was delighted to see them. "Come in. You must be tired. I'm so glad you managed to come."

"It was a last minute decision." Jack kissed Virginia's hand. "The exhibition was disappointing and, as you'd mentioned you'd be here we took a gamble and drove down today. We're on our way to Solange's parents," said Jack, casually surveying the room.

In the drawing room, Virginia opened a bottle of champagne and they all sat round the large stone fireplace. Solange was in high spirits, lacing her English with French, aware it was becoming in the surroundings.

"*Chéri!*" She turned flirtatiously towards Jack. "You better ring Madame Pataou at the Petite Hotel sur la Sorgue and tell her we are on our way. She will only keep our room till seven o'clock. You must ring her at once."

"I won't hear of it," interrupted Virginia. "You'll spend the night. One thing I do have is plenty of room. I'll tell Cook we are two more for supper. That's all settled." She rose to her feet.

"But that was not the idea. We escaped Paris to pay a quick visit to Solange's parents near Montpellier, and we were planning a couple of quiet days here in the Petite Hotel. We just thought we'd drop in on you for a drink."

Amanda watched Jack making his excuses and using all his charm on Virginia and wondered if he sometimes believed the stories he delivered with such candour.

"Come on," said Virginia. "I'm sure Tina, Helen and Amanda would love it if you joined us. Makes it a party. I'll go and tell Cook."

"It's difficult to refuse good-looking women." Jack took Virginia's hand and kissed it again. "But, please, we don't want you to go to any trouble."

★

Before supper, Jack and Solange were shown to their room. Up in her room, Amanda changed into a cool cotton dress. As she looked at her reflection in the mirror, she noticed her tense expression. Jack and Solange's arrival had spoiled what had promised to be a restful break.

Later, as they all sat round the dark oak table, their faces softened by the candle light, Tina joked, "How does it feel to be surrounded by women, Jack?" Her cheeks were flushed by the champagne and wine.

"I love it. It's my work to observe women."

"Constantine is very pleased with the portrait and he's not an easy man to please." Tina looked towards Helen, reminding her that for some women pleasing their men was a challenge.

Helen was enjoying her goat's cheese soufflé too much to be bothered by what anyone said.

"These are lovely rooms!" said Jack. "Wonderful proportions. Far more spacious and elegant than the converted farmhouses that are sprouting up everywhere." He took a sip of wine.

"It was a monastery in the sixteenth century." Virginia smiled.

"Are you planning to have the party indoors?"

Amanda looked up, wondering which party they were referring to.

"Oh, no. Couldn't fit them all in. We'll have two large marquees in the back garden."

Tina caught Amanda's inquiring stare and volunteered, "Virginia and Percy are having an important wedding anniversary this summer. We'll fly back from Crete for it."

It was suddenly clear to Amanda why Jack was there. He had heard about the party and wanted to be invited. An impromptu visit to Virginia would make procuring an invitation much easier. She also suspected that Sue and Simon would be amongst the guests. Virginia obviously felt both she and Helen would fit in better as guests at a quiet bridge weekend than at a party that promised to be the social event of the summer.

"Are you using a local band?" Solange, who had been drinking steadily all evening, joined into the conversation.

"Oh, no. They're coming from England. 'The Metallics'. I'm told by our daughter that it's 'the band' to have, but I have found some excellent caterers in Avignon." Virginia looked round the table. "But now I don't even want to think about it. There's so much to organise in such a short time, it terrifies me. A lot of our neighbours have volunteered to give parties before or after the dance, so that people who are coming for a long weekend have plenty to do." She sipped her wine, clearly excited at the thought of her party.

"It promises to be quite an event," said Solange. "I overheard someone at a dinner in Paris, who owns a house near here, mention they were coming to your party."

"We've been here a long time and know most of the house owners." Virginia smiled, pleased by the news of her reputation as a European hostess.

Jack smiled approvingly at his wife. Solange had become nearly as subtle as he in the art of flattery. He would bring up the subject of the party again tomorrow when he would also admire Virginia's garden. He was confident an invitation would follow when they were back in London. When the pudding arrived and the wine was changed, Solange immediately downed a glass of the cloudy, sweet wine and Amanda noticed that, when she turned to talk to Helen, she was slurring her words.

Solange and Jack had argued all the way from Paris. Money, as usual, had been the subject of controversy. Solange had given her parents money so that they could have the roof of their house repaired and Jack had felt it was not her place to be so generous with their money. In the car she had snapped at him:

"Jose and I do most of the work. I get the business and he does the painting, so I can't see why I shouldn't do the spending too."

Jack tolerated most accusations from his wife except when she brought up the subject of Jose. They both knew that without him the portraits would never get done, but he felt Jose was a secret they both shared and should not be talked about.

"Stop playing the role of dutiful daughter," he had replied. *"You only take an interest in your parent's house because you hope one day it will be yours."*

Jack looked at Solange sitting beside Virginia and tried to catch her eye. He failed as she was engrossed in recounting a story.

"Solange, darling, I wouldn't drink any more if I were you, not after all that champagne," he said.

"But you know I have a 'folie' for dessert wine, *chéri*." She smiled defiantly. She knew Jack didn't like it when she drank more than what was considered socially acceptable. She wanted to annoy him, still angry at his remarks that afternoon in the car.

After dinner they sat in the drawing room. Solange accepted the offer of some cognac and was now slurring her words both in English and in French. Sensing Solange's behaviour was making Jack uncomfortable, Virginia engaged him in conversation, hoping Helen and Amanda would take care of Solange till it was time to go to bed.

"With all the preparations for the party, I completely forgot to mention that a cousin of Percy's was very taken by the portrait you did of the grandchildren and will be contacting

you. He's a Hamilton-Veere as well. Hugo Hamilton-Veere."
Virginia hoped the news of another commission would cheer
Jack up. He was clearly embarrassed by Solange.

"*Chéri*, another commission!" Solange shrilled. "In the car as
we drove down here today, we were worrying about how few
portraits Jack had for the spring. Except for Mr Halford's,
there's nothing else and then by the time we pay Jose and
Amanda their commission…"

Amanda felt her heart had stopped beating. She was numb.
Without looking up she knew all eyes were on her.

"I think it's time for you to go to bed." Jack rose quickly to
his feet and swept up Solange from her chair. "Thank you so
much for a lovely evening." He looked at Virginia.

"*Charmant, tout à fait charmant*," Solange mumbled over her
shoulder as Jack ushered her towards the stairs.

There was an embarrassing silence that seemed to last an
eternity, and Amanda felt both hot and cold.

Helen came to the rescue. "Aren't these beams fascinating.
Not at all like the ones you find in England."

Virginia discussed the architecture of the room with Helen,
looking at Tina but ignoring Amanda's presence. Jack walked
back into the room and made his apologies for Solange's
behaviour, saying her mother was very ill which made her
nervous, and the drive had tired her out. She hardly ever drank
and, when she did, talked absolute nonsense.

Up in her room Amanda lay awake for a long time
wondering if it wouldn't be better to tell Virginia and Tina the
truth about her arrangement with Jack. She would explain why
she had accepted the first two commissions from him. She
needed to pay for Mark's holiday. They would understand. But
how could she explain the commission for Alfred Halford's?
She knew she hadn't done anything dishonest and yet she felt
like a common thief. Maybe the best thing was to say nothing
and wait for the consequences.

The following morning at breakfast the topic of
conversation was Virginia's garden. Jack and Solange, clearly

embarrassed by the previous night, said they would have to leave. They had decided to pay an immediate visit to Solange's mother to put her mind at rest. Solange looked quite composed and was totally immersed in her new role of the anxious daughter. Soon the women were feeling sorry for her, and Tina even remarked on how nice it was to see someone so concerned about their parents. "But then, of course," she had added, "Mediterraneans have a different approach to family life."

Amanda could feel she was being politely shunned both by Virginia and Tina and was grateful to Helen, who suggested they drive to Goult after lunch.

For the rest of the weekend Amanda was politely ignored by Virginia and Tina. They didn't ask her any questions but, at the same time, avoided spending any length of time with her, except for meal times and round the card table. The last two days seemed to drag on forever in this unpleasant atmosphere. Helen came to her rescue whenever possible, suggesting short drives to the nearby villages. It was with relief that Amanda boarded the plane to London.

★

Back in England, spring had finally arrived disguised as summer. It was warmer than it had been in Provence and the London streets were full of smiling faces. Restaurants and coffee shops had put their tables and chairs on the pavements, where those with time on their hands sat enjoying the warmth of the sun. Building sites had become sunbathing platforms, where men in shorts sat enjoying a longer lunch hour than usual. Commuters sitting in traffic jams looked disgruntled, their windows down, wishing they could enjoy the sunshine somewhere else other than in their overheated cars.

At the newsagent's on her way home, Amanda overheard a group of women with pink sunburnt arms discussing the ozone layer with the authority of three scientists. She bought an evening paper and made her way home, wondering whether she should ring Jack and confront him on the telephone or whether she should go straight to his flat. Amanda considered her position. Belinda had rung her a day after her return from France, to tell her she had received some distressing news from some of the committee members. Amanda had understood immediately that Belinda was referring to her commission on the portraits.

In her office, Belinda had said, "Amanda, you've been nothing but an asset to the charity and we're very grateful to you for all your hard work. I am only too aware you've put in very long hours for which..." she had paused, "you do not get any reward. We're also aware of your financial position since your separation and, although strictly speaking, you haven't done anything dishonest, accepting a commission for putting someone in touch with one of our sponsors is very awkward and could give Care Campaign a bad name if it leaked out. Mr Halford is, after all, in the public eye."

Amanda had apologised aware that at this point it was better not to justify her actions.

Back home, as she looked for the front door key buried somewhere at the bottom of her bag, Amanda decided she would go and confront Jack at Hyde Park Villas. If she rang him, he would make excuses.

In the hall Amanda saw Kate's rucksack. It was Wednesday. Kate never came home in the middle of the week.

"Is that you, Mum?" She heard Kate's voice coming from the kitchen.

"Yes. Is everything all right, darling?"

"No." Kate's voice was muffled by a sob.

Amanda dropped her coat and her previous worries and rushed into the kitchen.

"Oh, Mum!" Kate thrust herself into Amanda's arms and, burying her face on her mother's chest, cried with the abandon of a child. Amanda stroked Kate's hair and kissed the top of her head. This gesture made Kate cry even more. Amanda then understood that Kate had needed the release of a good cry for a long time and, although worried for her daughter, was relieved she had chosen to come home and cry in her mother's arms. She hugged her and rocked her gently. How much easier it was to love the child in Kate rather than the young woman.

When there was a lull in the sobbing Amanda said, "Let me make some tea and perhaps you'd like to tell me what's happened."

As she plugged in the kettle, Amanda looked at her daughter with the corner of her eye and had to control herself not to hug her again. With her face flushed and swollen from crying and her aggressive expression washed away by the tears, she looked once again like her baby.

"Yesterday," said Kate blowing her nose, "I had an terrible argument with Sebastian. I think it's over." She sniffed. "Men are all swine! Pigs!" she said emphatically, looking in Amanda's direction.

"Not all of them." Amanda stirred the tea.

"Oh, Mum! It's been so horrid since Dad left. It must have been so hard for you." Kate was back in her arms crying. "I'm sorry, Mum. I've been so upset by everything, but I didn't mean it when I said it was all your fault."

"I know you didn't mean it."

While they drank their tea Kate told Amanda about what Sebastian and she had argued about and, by the time they had had a second cup, Kate was considering a reconciliation and bringing him home for the weekend. Kate's mention of men being swine made Amanda think of the letter she had received from Simon on her return from France. He had suggested they meet again. He was now living with his family in Wiltshire but spent a couple of nights in London in the middle of the week. Amanda hadn't replied to his letter. Hurt by his lack of tact, she had crumpled it up and thrown it in the bin. She should have seen the signs in Simon. Behind the charm lay a weak man. It had made her realise she had failed once more in her choice of men.

Chapter Eleven

The following morning, after Kate had left for Bristol, Amanda drove to Jack and Solange's apartment. She was about to ring the bell labelled "Noel" when a couple opened the door and let her in to the communal entrance on the ground floor. She hesitated before going up the stairs, wondering if it would have been better to have announced her arrival on the intercom. As Amanda stood outside Jack's front door rehearsing what she was going to tell him, she heard his voice pitched in a higher tone than usual saying, "Oh, for heaven's sake. Do you think I'm really going to worry about your threats."

Anticipating one of their heated arguments, Amanda stood waiting to hear Solange's voice. Instead she heard a man's voice, in what seemed to be a thick accent, saying, "You are not getting away with it this time. You owe me fifteen thousand pounds. That's a lot of money for me. In my country I can do a lot with it. I'm not frightened of you any more. Not like in the old days with no work permit. It was easy for you to use me in those days. But now I'm like you, the same rights."

"Come on, Jose." Jack's voice had a conciliatory tone. "It has been difficult lately. You know there isn't the same amount of money around as six years ago."

"We've been busy, with important portraits. I'm not as stupid as you think. I can tell we are painting important people. They must pay you well, so where is my part of the money?" Jose was shouting.

Amanda wondered if Solange was in the apartment. It suddenly occurred to her she might suddenly appear up the stairs and find her eavesdropping.

"There are lot of expenses when you paint important people, Jose." Jack went on, "The studio has to look right. Solange and I have to entertain a lot. It isn't as simple as you think to find rich people to sit for you. We've even had to employ someone to help us with our contacts."

"I don't believe anything you say. You always lie to me, think I'm an ignorant peasant. Look how you live. You don't need all these expensive things to find clients. You are just using me. Well, it's over, finished!" He stamped his foot. "I've gone up a bit in the world since you found me painting on Bayswater Road, with no money to pay the rent and thinking I will be sent back home. It's different now. I have English friends. They tell me what I can do. One of my friends works for newspapers and he said I can sell my story for a lot of money."

"Stop being, pathetic, Jose. What would the caption for the story be?"

Jose's voice rose. "You see, you still treat me like a dog. Little Jose, keep him in the attic. But let me tell you what, the caption of the story will be *Artist who paints royalty and society people is a fake. Jose Karel is the real artist* and the article will then say how you and your beautiful wife spend money going to parties to find your prey and then get Jose to do the portraits and paying him nothing. I should be the famous one. People will know I am the real artist. But I think I will take the money from the paper and go home. My girlfriend likes my country."

"And what makes you think your story is that exciting? There are lots of stories offered to newspapers every day."

"My friend has a friend who does 'showbiz scoops'. They have already talked about it. If you don't pay me what you owe me, I will sell the story to them today."

Jack's voice was agitated. "Jose, as much as I'd like to help you, I simply don't have the money. How can I give you fifteen thousand pounds when we have an overdraft three times that?"

"That's it! You see. You never intended to pay me all my money. Always excuses, saying you give me the rest later. I've had enough. I'm going now to see my friend, John Riley with my story. His friends will pay twenty thousand pounds."

"Come on, Jose, for Christ's sake. You know you'll get the money eventually."

Amanda heard footsteps coming towards the door. She ran into the lift and pressed the button that took her to the ground floor. She hurriedly left the building and went into a telephone booth in the corner of Bayswater Road, from where she had a good view of Jack's terrace. Within minutes she saw a short, dark man leave the building and Jack following him into the street. They were still arguing, Jose gesticulating and Jack looking tense. When Jose made his way towards the Bayswater Road, Amanda decided to follow him and confront him. She would explain her position and try to persuade him not to sell his story to the papers. As Jose walked hurriedly toward the main road, he looked briefly in the direction of the telephone booth where Amanda was standing and then continued down the road. He was obviously planning to ring John Riley and, when he had seen there was somebody in the booth, had decided to go elsewhere. Amanda looked in the direction of Jack's terrace to make sure he had gone in and, when she saw no sign of him, she rushed down the Bayswater Road after Jose.

The street was busy and she couldn't find Jose amongst the lunchtime shoppers. Her mind was in a whirl. What would she do if she had lost him? She'd never find him in the telephone directory and, anyhow, she didn't know his address. She rushed down the street bumping into people. Her heart was pounding. In a daze, she searched for Jose's figure amongst the crowd. If Jose went with his story to the papers, the name of Care Campaign, and most likely hers too, would be dragged into the scandal. Out of breath, she stopped at a pedestrian crossing and saw Jose on the other side of the road. He was making his way into a pizza parlour. Without waiting for the pedestrian lights to change to green, she crossed the road and followed him into the restaurant. Amanda searched for Jose amongst the people sitting round the tables but couldn't find him. As she was wondering whether he had gone to the gents, a girl with a strong foreign accent came towards her and asked:

"Table for one?"

"Yes, thank you."

The girl pointed to a table where a Japanese couple were sharing a large pizza.

"Is the ladies room at the back?" asked Amanda.

"Downstairs. I'll get you a menu. Can I get you something to drink in the meantime?"

"Yes, an orange, please."

"We don't have orange."

It suddenly dawned on Amanda that Jose was most likely using the telephone downstairs.

"Do you have a public telephone anywhere?"

"Yes, by the toilets."

Amanda started to make her way towards the back of the restaurant.

"What about your drink?" said the girl. "We don't have orange."

"A Coke! A Coke would be lovely," said Amanda, who disliked Coke intensely.

She rushed down the stairs and saw Jose was on the telephone. She passed him slowly, trying to overhear the conversation.

"The one of the Duchess was also my work. It's all my work!" Jose was saying earnestly into the receiver.

Amanda went into the ladies and stood in front of the mirror. Her eyes looked small and her mouth tense. She looked frightened. She washed her face with cold water. Perhaps it wasn't too late. If she spoke with Jose she might persuade him to change his mind and tell his friend not to go ahead with the story. Amanda brushed her hair and put on some lipstick. Despite applying some colour to her lips her face looked drawn. She smiled at her own reflection trying to loosen the muscles round her mouth. The smile was twisted and forced, more like a smirk. I'm no good at pretending, she told herself. Pat always says I wear my heart on my sleeve.

When Amanda left the ladies, Jose was gone. She rushed upstairs, cursing herself for wasting time brushing her hair and pulling faces in front of the mirror. Upstairs, amongst the diners, she looked for Jose and couldn't find him. The waitress who had, greeted her when she had walked in from the street was now making her way towards her.

"I left your Coke on the table with a menu," she said with a tired smile.

"Have you seen a short, dark-haired man leave the restaurant?" asked Amanda. The girl looked round the tables with a confused expression. Amanda felt silly. The place was full of dark-haired men and they all looked the same height, sitting at their tables.

"Here," said Amanda, opening her bag and taking out her purse. "Let me pay you for the Coke."

"But we aren't allowed to sell drinks without food. We have a restaurant licence." Amanda looked out at the busy Bayswater Road, where Jose was most probably about to disappear from sight, vanishing into the crowd.

"I'm sorry, but I'm in a terrible hurry. Why don't you order a pizza and give it to someone else. I'll pay for it." She gave the puzzled girl a ten pound note and rushed out of the restaurant.

Out in the street she hesitated. Should she turn left or right? It's like gambling, she told herself, the outcome is in the hands of providence and so she turned right, simply because being right-handed it seemed the more natural thing to do.

'I've lost him,' she thought, the tears pricking the back of her eyes. She hurried her step and then slowed down, aware she might be walking the wrong way. Just as she was wondering whether to walk in the opposite direction she saw him getting on the bus. She rushed towards the bus stop but the bus had started to move. Amanda ran as fast as she could, clutching her bag under her arm, aware of her uncomfortable shoes and the hard pavement under her feet. When the bus stopped at the lights, she jumped on it. Jose was sitting at a window seat, and there was no one sitting beside him. She took a deep breath and tried to compose herself. A bus was not an ideal place to have a conversation with a stranger, particularly if one was about to ask him a favour. Her hair was hanging loose over her face and she had lost her hair band as she had run to catch the bus. Amanda remembered feeling it slide off. It had seemed so unimportant at the time, but now that she was safely on the bus she regretted not having picked it up. She sat two rows behind Jose and decided that once he got off the bus she would approach him and introduce herself. He looked a meek, gentle sort of man, not at all intimidating. She held on to the railing; the metal felt warm and damp from someone's sweaty hand. It was a hot day and the bus was stuffy. She felt like opening one of the windows but refrained, not wanting to draw attention to herself. The bus continued down the Portobello Road and towards the run-down end of Ladbroke Road. Two stops after the railway bridge Jose got off the bus and Amanda followed him. She had never followed anybody and was aware she wasn't too good at it. She either got too close or lagged so far behind that she lost sight of him. Soon, Jose turned off the main road and made his way down a street full of dilapidated houses. The road was empty, and Amanda's footsteps echoed on the pavement. Jose stopped outside one of the houses and put his hands in his pocket. He's looking for his keys, thought Amanda. If I don't approach him now I'll have to ring the bell and his name might not be on it.

Jose started to make his way up the steps when she caught up with him and said awkwardly, "I'm sorry to trouble you, but is your name Jose?"

He looked at her suspiciously and took his time before saying, "Jose Karel is my name. How can I help you?" He was standing by the front door holding the key in his hand. Amanda followed him up the steps.

"My name is Amanda Thompson. I know Jack Noel," she said abruptly.

Jose frowned as he stood upright in a defensive gesture.

Aware she had said the wrong thing, she blurted out, "He's not a friend. He is... He is... It's difficult to explain. I need to talk to you. It's important. I know all about who paints his portraits." Amanda lowered her voice.

"Who are you? Are you press?" Jose looked worried.

"No. I used to work for Jack. I can't talk here." She looked around furtively. "Is there anywhere we can talk?"

"Did you follow me? How do you know my address?" Jose stood with his back to the door, as though barring the way.

"Please don't misunderstand me. I followed you because I've got to talk to you and, without wanting to sound melodramatic, I'm on your side. I'm also very unhappy about Jack's lies."

Jose seemed to relax a little.

"Would you like to come up to my studio?" There was a pause. "We can talk up there," he said eventually.

"Thank you," said Amanda. "I hate imposing this way but..."

He opened the door and let her in. The floor of the entrance hall was covered with uncollected mail. Jose walked over it saying, "People come and go quickly in this building."

She followed him up the stairs. On the third landing her legs started to feel heavy.

Sensing she had slowed down, he turned round and said, "It's all the way up, I'm afraid."

On the fifth floor she stood, out of breath, waiting for Jose to open the door. Before turning the key, he turned and looked at her. He still looked suspicious and tense. She forced herself to smile at him reassuringly. The flat was tidy and light and the walls were covered in paintings. Amanda noticed not all of them were portraits.

She stood in front of a landscape by the door and said, "Is this Greece?"

"No. It's the north of Romania where I come from." He moved along to the next wall and in a solemn tone said, "This is my favourite."

Amanda stood admiring the barren landscape in front of her.

"Is this Romania too?"

"Yes, this is the view from the outskirts of my village. Very beautiful."

"Do you prefer to paint landscapes?"

"Of course, but I have always made a living out of my portraits. Maybe one day I will be able to sell my other paintings too."

"I'm no expert, but they look very good to me. The colour is so subtle."

"Thank you." Jose smiled to her for the first time.

Amanda felt sorry for him. She thought of Tina's portrait and the insipid Mrs Hobdon's and pictured him working all alone from photographs and sketches Jack gave him: unrecognised and underpaid. She followed him to the other end of the room where a bed covered in a blanket doubled as a sofa.

"Can I offer you something to drink?" Jose made his way to a small kitchen area by the window.

"I'd love a glass of water." She watched Jose take a jug of water out of the fridge.

"It's tap water, I'm afraid, but it is cold," he said, pouring it into a glass.

"Where do you work?" asked Amanda looking round the flat.

"I'll show you. The studio is upstairs. When Jack started to use me on a regular basis he found me this flat. It has this very light room on the top. Let me show you."

Amanda took a sip of water and followed Jose up a spiral staircase behind the kitchenette. The room upstairs had a big skylight and smelt of paints and turpentine. It was also uncomfortably hot. Jose went to a small window and opened it.

"It's hot in summer and cold in winter," he said with a sigh.

Amanda remembered Jack's airy studio with its comfortable sofa and large loudspeakers. All Jose had was a radio with a cassette player propped on a chair. The dusty floorboards were covered in paint and the atmosphere was stuffy. When Amanda saw the easel that stood in the centre of the room, her heart beat quickened. On it, she saw the preliminary sketches of Alfred Halford's portrait. Although the sketch was very loose, Alfred's stern face came alive on the canvas. She looked towards Jose, wondering if he had noticed her shocked expression. He was looking in her direction, but his round, dark eyes told her nothing. Her mind was racing. Not only would Care Campaign's name be dragged into the scandal but so would Alfred's.

"Jose!" She turned, giving her back to Alfred's piercing eyes. "Jose, why I've come is to ask you please not to sell your story to the papers. Many people will get involved in the scandal. You see, I work for a charity and Jack has painted... sorry, you have painted, the portraits of some of our members and now..." she said, pointing at the easel, "one of our sponsors. I helped Jack get these commissions." She lowered her eyes. "He pays me for the work I get him."

"You're lucky you got paid," said Jose.

"But I never knew till today that you were the real artist. Had I known, I would never have got involved with him. I shouldn't have done it anyhow, but I needed the money. My son wanted to go on holiday and I couldn't afford to send him. I will lose my job if this story comes out and the charity will lose many of the people who support it."

"I'm sorry," said Jose wearing the same expression.

Amanda couldn't tell if he felt sorry for her or if he was merely being polite.

"I will also lose my friends," she said in a louder voice, hoping to get some reaction.

"I'm sorry, but it is too late to change things now. I have given my story to John Riley. He is a 'stringer' for an important gossip columnist and he thinks we can make good money out of it. I need the money. Jack hasn't paid me for any of my work for a long time and never will now."

"I know. I know. It's terrible. Maybe I could borrow the money and pay you myself." Amanda wondered for a moment if Julia or Pat could lend her the money but soon realised that, in her panic, she was fantasising as she would never be able to repay it.

"I'm sorry you are in trouble. Jack is trouble for everyone who deals with him. He owes money to the framer too. Always the working people, never his smart friends."

Amanda wondered in which group Jose thought she belonged, Frustrated and realising that Jose wouldn't change his mind, she said, "Why? Why did you do it? Why did you work for him? You could have painted under your own name."

"'Jose Karel'! It's not smart like Jack Noel. His clients think he is a kind of Lord Byron. They like to think the charming Jack has done their paintings. Me!" he said, shrugging his shoulders. "Who wants me? But maybe now they will want my paintings. Now that I'll have some money, I can go back home and paint the things I like painting."

Amanda looked at Jose's small figure. Everything about him was rounded: the head, the face, the eyes, even the slightly hunched shoulders. His expression was sad and resigned. He looked defeated. Perhaps Jack had taken from him any self-esteem he might once have had. Amanda wondered, in her despair, if Jose's determination to sell his story had come about because of the money owed to him, or whether it was a way of regaining his dignity. Perhaps John Riley, the journalist, would be more easily persuaded. He didn't hold a grudge against Jack in the way Jose did. By the time she had reached Jose's front door she had made up her mind to find John Riley.

*

After a restless night, as soon as a lozenge of light filtered through the crack in her bedroom curtains, Amanda got out of bed. She opened the window and found the air outside was fresh and smelt of spring. The sky was bright and dawn pink. It promised to be another glorious day. This gave her courage. Without having any breakfast, she walked over to the newsagent's and bought the tabloids on sale at that time of the morning. She had to locate John Riley and decided to ring each newspaper until she found him. Back home she made herself some coffee and forced herself to eat some muesli. She had been unable to eat since her meeting with Jose. Her stomach felt knotted and the thought of food made it worse. It was too early to ring the newspapers and she was wondering whether to tidy the front garden when the telephone rang.

"Amanda Thompson?" It was a woman's voice.

"Yes, who am I speaking to?" Amanda wondered who could ring so early. No one from the charity ever rang before nine.

"It's Sue Banks, Simon's wife."

Amanda was so taken aback she couldn't find anything to say. Sue filled in the silence by saying, "I'm sorry to ring so early, but I know how busy you are and I wanted to make sure I caught you before you left the house." She stressed the word *busy*.

"Not to worry. I've been up for hours. It's such a glorious morning it seemed a shame to waste it." Amanda thought she must sound foolish babbling about the weather.

"Quite." There was another pause. "I'm ringing you because I gather my husband owes you some money and I was wanting to make arrangements to repay it."

Sue's measured voice made Amanda feel like "the other woman" and she found herself saying in an overeager tone of voice, "Oh, there's no rush."

"Isn't there? We heard from a friend you were in financial difficulties and involved with some artist, and thought it would be better if there were nothing outstanding. Would a cheque made out to you and sent to your address be the best way of doing it?"

"Yes, thank you," was all Amanda could manage to say, humiliation rendering her nearly speechless. "Yes, thank you so much."

She put the phone down realising that everyone by now must know about her taking the commissions. Perhaps Virginia had mentioned it to the Bankses with the ulterior motive of discrediting her. Whatever the reason, it was humiliating, and Sue had taken advantage of the opportunity to embarrass her even further. The thought that Simon might have suggested that Sue ring her filled her with anger. Was he deliberately trying to hurt her because she hadn't replied to his letter suggesting they continue their relationship? Fighting back the tears she found herself dialling Julia's number.

"Oh, Julia. I'm sorry to ring so early."

"I'm here. Been up for hours. The children all right?"

"Yes, thank you. Julia, Simon has dropped me. I'm such an idiot. I feel so humiliated. I should have known better. His wife is not only probably prettier but also has money. What did I have to offer? Why did I believe him when he said he was happier with me?"

"Because," interrupted Julia, "he probably was, but chose to go back to what he knew and be unhappy again. A lot of people forsake happiness for security."

"I feel so humiliated."

"I know, but you are coming along just fine. Soon you won't feel you need a man to feel happy and secure and then the right one will come along. You'll see."

*

Amanda spent all morning ringing the various newspapers trying to locate John Riley. By midday it seemed nobody had heard of him. As she had started to wonder whether she had got the name wrong, she came across somebody who said that a John Riley did work for them occasionally and gave her a number where she might find him. That afternoon when Amanda finally got hold of Riley, he said he would be in Birmingham for a few days as he was working on a "door step" job but that he would see her when he came back. He wanted to know why she wanted to see him. When Amanda had said she'd rather wait till they met, he had been insistent, saying he couldn't waste time. He was very busy at the moment. When she mentioned she was ringing him about a story someone called Jose had given him, he had replied, "Ah, the one about the posh painter! Well, meet me at The Judge on the corner of Fleet Street and Aldwych."

On Friday morning Amanda took the bus to Fleet Street. Inside The Judge the smell of ale and tobacco mixed with the stuffy atmosphere peculiar to crowded unventilated rooms made her take an involuntary deep breath. The pub was full. People stood at the bar and talked noisily round small wooden tables. The women wore high street business suits, chic but somewhat different to the exquisitely tailored ones worn by the women on the charity circuit. The men varied, some had the well-groomed appearance of city businessmen and others looked more casual in corduroy jackets and anoraks. John Riley had said, "You'll find me at the far end. I'll try and get a table near the fire exit."

Amanda looked at the wall of bodies she would have to fight past in order to get to the back and suddenly wished Julia was there. Julia, with her imperial manner, would have swept through the crush effortlessly, making the noisy crowd open up like the waters of the Red Sea.

When she eventually reached the far end of the room Amanda looked for the John Riley she had conjured in her mind. She was looking for a man in his fifties wearing a blazer or a suit. When she saw no one that answered that description she looked at her watch wondering if she had arrived too early. Feeling self-conscious she went up to the bar and was about to buy herself a drink when a young man in a creased cotton jacket came up behind her and said, "Excuse me. Are you Mrs Thompson?"

"Yes," said Amanda.

"Thought it might be you. You looked a bit lost and now you look taken aback." He laughed, showing yellowing teeth. "I'm John." He stretched out his right hand. "John Riley."

"Oh, I'm sorry. I imagined you would be older."

"Ha!" he laughed again. "I'm nearly too old for this job as it is. No one can keep this kind of life up after thirty." He shrugged his shoulders and pointed at a small table where he had left several newspapers. "Get you a drink?"

Amanda, noticing the bottle of wine on the table said, "A glass of wine would be lovely. Thank you."

"I'll get you a glass." He got up and disappeared towards the bar.

Amanda noticed his worn-down shoes and slightly frayed corduroy trousers. Could this tired, dishevelled young man be the one who had the power to ruin her life? Soon he was back carrying a glass, a bottle of wine and three packets of crisps. He placed a new bottle of wine beside the half empty one on the table and, after filling both glasses, tore open one of the bags of crisps with his front teeth and placed the packet in the centre of the table.

"Help yourself," he said. A smell of cheese and vinegar filled the air between them. Amanda watched him eat half the packet of crisps before he looked up at her. "So," he said reclining, "What's your story?"

Amanda watched his lanky body flop like a rag doll over the chair, filling all the available space on it, his legs stretching under the table towards her.

"The story?" said Amanda.

"Yeah, the story. I thought you said on the phone that you wanted to talk to me about the posh painter Jose knows."

"Why I'm here," said Amanda, "is to find out how much you know about it and to..."

"I can't tell you that, lovey. You tell me. My boss has already negotiated a price for it with the news editor of *The News*. They seem to think it's worth something, so," he gulped half his glass of wine, "if you have anything interesting to tell me, it might be worth something to you, too. Rubens has asked me to spend as much time and money as I need on this story. He obviously thinks it's worth it."

"Rubens?" Amanda felt faint and took a long sip of the wine that tasted of vinegar like the chips.

"Yeah. Nick Rubens. You know, the gossip columnist."

"He's your boss?"

"Yeah. I'm his stringer. Only started working for him a few weeks ago. He's quite a slave-driver. Expects me to come up with a juicy story a day. Blow me down though, if this quiet little geezer that goes out with my ex-girlfriend tells me his life story and there it is. My lucky break! Just what Rubens likes. A bit of dirt in high places."

Amanda felt dizzy. The room seemed airless.

"Are you all right, love? You've gone pale. Can't be the wine. You've hardly touched it, unless..." he laughed, "you had a few beforehand."

"I'm fine. Just... to tell you the truth, I'm worried by what you've told me. That's why I'm here. I know the painter..."

"Now, let's start at the beginning." John took a long drag from his cigarette and inhaled the smoke. "Why did you want to meet me in the first place?"

Amanda looked round the pub. It was unlikely anyone she knew would be there, but she felt nervous.

"Come on," he said, following her gaze. "It's confidential, whatever you tell me and, for all you know, it might be worth something." He winked. "Do you know the painter?"

"Yes," said Amanda abruptly. "I know him, but why I'm here is to ask you not to go ahead with the story." She took another sip of wine and, to keep her shaking hands occupied, found herself putting a handful of crisps in her mouth.

"I see." John's body was sliding further down the chair and his legs sprawled under the table were now nearly touching hers. "Why don't you want the story out? Is he your hubby? I thought Jose mentioned she was French."

"Yes, his wife is French and the painter deserves to be discredited, but the awful thing is that a lot of other people will be discredited too for no good reason."

Warmed by the wine, Amanda told him her story, pausing only to drink and eat some crisps that now tasted of onions. When she had finished, Riley said, "Let me get some more wine."

Amanda looked in disbelief at the two empty bottles. She could remember having two glasses, maybe three, and yet Riley looked completely sober.

With a third bottle of wine between them, he said, "Look, I'm sorry for you, love, but I'm afraid it's a good story. It's not every day one gets a chance to work for the likes of Nick Rubens. Highly impressed with the Jose/ Jack story he was. He seems to think it is worth fifteen to twenty grand. Not as much as Jose expected, but still, can't complain. Look, I haven't had a good story for months now and this comes along just like that. This guy's painted royalty, and it turns out he's a fake. It might even fetch more. Anything to do with royalty at the moment sells. Every since Fergie and Camilla, they can't get enough of it. If it's sold abroad, it'll mean even bigger bucks."

Amanda pleaded with him, aware she was wasting her time. It was, after all, his livelihood. Why should he help her?

"Don't look so glum," he said as he emptied the last of the wine in his glass. "People have short memories. They'll soon forget reading *Poor housewife ponced for posh painter*. There'll be another story next week and they'll forget all about you."

"But you don't understand. I'll lose my job! I need my job! And what about the charity?"

"Yeah, it's tough. But all's fair in love and war, as they say. I'm just doing my job."

"What will I tell the Halfords?" she half muttered to herself.

"Halford!" John's eyes became alert. "Alfred Halford, the industrial tycoon? Jose never mentioned he was involved. Now that'll make it even better! What's his story?"

Amanda realised she had said too much. Jose didn't know the man he had started painting was Alfred and now, because of her own indiscretion, Riley would no doubt mention his name in the story.

She drank more wine and blurted out pleadingly, "The Halfords have nothing to do with this. Mrs Halford helps me at the charity, that's all."

"Did you get her for him to paint too?"

"Not at all. She has been very helpful to the charity and has become a friend," said Amanda, realising that the man she had come to ask for help was rapidly becoming an added threat to her. She now felt cornered by his inquiring eyes. Realising that prolonging the conversation would only make things worse, she finished the wine and left, making some feeble excuse about being late for another appointment.

Out in the street, her mouth still tasted of vinegary crisps and her head was spinning from the wine. She walked aimlessly towards the river. The orderly seclusion of the Temple made her feel detached and protected from the bustle of Fleet Street and the likes of John Riley and Jack. She sat on a bench by the fountain near Lincoln Hall and tried to think of what to do next. Watching the men in their dark suits and black gowns crossing the courtyard, she wondered whether she should resign before the story came out, to save Belinda the added embarrassment of having to ask her to leave the charity. She thought of her children. What would they think? They were bound to find out. Would they understand that by trying to give them a better life she had got into trouble? To her surprise she found herself wondering what Douglas's reaction would be, how would he judge her? Did his opinion still matter? Would she never be free from wanting his approval?

To whom could she turn? Julia and Henry were away in Spain. She knew Pat would be unable to help and Simon, in whom she had once confided so freely, had severed any remaining tie between them with his wife's phone call. The realisation of how few people there were to turn to filled her with anguish. There were only a couple of friends she could confide in. She thought of Julia and how her relentless loyalty redeemed the rest of her. In her mind's eye she searched for another friendly face and thought of Patsy who had always been warm-hearted and straightforward and wondered if she could tell her the whole story without being judged too harshly.

A barrister in his black gown walked passed her and smiled. She felt like running after him and asking for his advice. Instead, she watched him walk towards Selwyn Hall and noticed the newspaper under his arm. This made her think of Nick Rubens and she wondered whether he would remember who she was if she rang him.

She walked slowly towards the river. Her mind, in contrast to her footsteps, was racing. Different ideas came into her head. She suddenly remembered that Belinda had mentioned an invitation to a charity function at the Carlton Towers that Friday.

"I won't be able to make this," she had said putting the card in her out-tray. "I bet Nick Rubens will be covering this do. It's smarter than anything we could ever put on."

Belinda often asked her to go to functions on her behalf, but this time she hadn't, meaning the invitation was clearly not transferable. If she tried to reach Nick on the telephone he might not remember who she was, but if he saw her it would be different. He was bound to have a good memory for faces. It would be easier to plead with him in person. Amanda reached the Embankment realising she was planning, for the first time in her life, to gatecrash a party.

★

Amanda got off the bus in Knightsbridge and walked down Sloane Street towards the Carlton Towers. The shop windows were decked in inviting summery displays and the mannequins were dressed for garden parties in flowing, colourful, print dresses. The evening was bright and sunny and the adjoining square smelt of summer. She caught her reflection in one of the shop windows and realised that Tina's black crepe dress looked wintry and out of place in the warm June evening. It was too late to do anything about it and, even if she had given some thought to her clothes earlier, she knew there were few things in her wardrobe that would have been suitable for a smart cocktail party at this time of the year. When she walked past a chemist Amanda decided to buy a flesh-coloured pair of tights and change in the ladies room in the hotel. Without black legs, the dress might look less wintry.

In the lobby of the hotel she saw a sign that said "UNIAID Party: First Floor". Amanda made her way up the staircase. On the first floor she heard the sound of voices coming from a room on the right and felt relieved that she was being spared the embarrassment of asking her way to the party. She followed the sound of voices and, with an air of confidence, walked past a footman dressed in uniform. She had never been into the Carlton Towers and didn't want to look lost.

At the raised doorway that led into the large reception room, she stopped. She suddenly felt she was rooted to the spot and became almost breathless with fright. She was about to gatecrash a party for the first time in her life. She tried to regain her composure, telling herself that not to look conspicuous one had to look relaxed. The room was full of people surely no one would notice a woman in a wintry black dress. She took a deep breath and was about to make her way into the reception room when a footman standing inside the doorway intercepted her and said, "What name shall I give?"

Amanda froze and stopped short. The man in the smart gold-edged uniform was waiting for her to say something. She faltered. "My name is Amanda Thompson," she said in a whisper, hoping no one would hear.

"Mrs?"

Amanda nodded.

"Mrs Amanda Thompson." Her name was propelled into the room by his booming, resonant voice.

In a daze Amanda stepped forward. Two smiling women and a man were lined up waiting for her. Amanda shook their hands and just as she was wondering whether to say something, the voice of the announcer filled the room once more.

"Lord Beckitt."

Amanda noticed her hosts had lost interest in her. An ex-minister obviously required an immediate greeting. She slipped into the crowded room, relieved her name was already forgotten. A waiter holding a tray full of glasses stopped in front of her. Amanda took a glass of champagne, hoping it would help her recover from her clamorous entry into the room. Invigorated by the champagne, she moved from group to group trying to find Nick Rubens. She avoided any eye contact with other guests in case they should ask her how long she had known their hosts and she would be forced to explain who she was. She continued to circle the room looking for Rubens. A waiter with a tray full of appetising eats stopped in front of her. Just as Amanda was about to put a quail's egg in her mouth, a short woman dressed in a summery organza dress said, "Aren't these absolutely delicious?"

"Delicious," replied Amanda, hoping this wouldn't encourage one of those meaningless small talk contests that can take up most of a cocktail party.

"Every year I look forward to this party. It somehow seems to mark the beginning of the season."

Amanda smiled while she slowly chewed her quail's egg, hoping that with a full mouth she wouldn't be expected to do too much talking. Another tray of minute and appetising eats were displayed in front of her. The food was designed so that one could chew, swallow and satisfy one's hunger without any need to stop talking.

"Were you here last year?" the woman asked while she swallowed a miniature spring roll.

Then, just as Amanda was wondering how to reply, she saw him. Across a sea of heads, at the other side of the room, stood Nick Rubens.

"Excuse me." Amanda smiled apologetically in the direction of the organza dress and, with her heart pounding, made her way across the room where, underneath a chandelier, Nick Rubens stood holding court surrounded by a cluster of guests. Amanda stood behind the small group, trying to give the impression she was waiting for her turn to have a word with him. Rubens smiled in her direction meaninglessly, confirming Amanda's fears that he hadn't recognised her. A smart couple joined the group. Rubens, who was talking to someone else, stopped in mid-word and greeted them.

"Hello, darlings. Wasn't sure whether I'd see you tonight. I'm glad you've made it. I have a few questions to ask about your last musical."

Amanda looked in the couple's direction and recognised one of the richest men in England. Aware she was surrounded by the rich and famous made her even more self-conscious. She couldn't just butt in; she would have to wait for one of them or Nick to include her in their conversation. Nick Rubens, with his trained eye, looked in her direction, aware that she was there to be noticed. He smiled at her again, this time more demonstratively. He is not sure where he's seen me and is smiling in case I'm someone important, thought Amanda as she smiled back at him. The couple were now the centre of attention in the little group standing round Rubens. Amanda, a few steps behind, felt her jaw getting rigid as she kept on trying to smile casually in their direction. When the couple had gone, Nick took a few steps in her direction.

"We've met before." He looked at her attentively, in the way good listeners do.

"Yes. At Mosimann's. The Care Campaign function."

"Nick, darling. You said you'd pop in last night and you never did." A blonde woman with long legs and a golden tan was kissing him on both cheeks.

"I know. I'm sorry. You know I never miss your charity functions, but there was a Royal Performance I had to cover. I did send my stringer along with the photographer though. You'll be well covered."

"You are an angel." She was gone as swiftly and flirtatiously as she had arrived.

Nick looked in Amanda's direction and hesitated. After the introduction he knew she was no celebrity and seemed less keen to resume their conversation.

"Mr Rubens," said Amanda, summoning up all her courage. "Could I talk to you privately? It is important."

"Nick, darling." Another glamorous woman had joined the group and was kissing him.

Amanda sipped her champagne and waited for her to leave. No one else in the group surrounding Rubens had taken any notice of her. They were all too dazzled by Nick's presence and the celebrities that at regular intervals came to greet him. She felt self-conscious and left out, standing on her own. Brushing off another well-wisher, Nick took a step towards her. He looked irritated.

"Now what is this important thing you've got to tell me?" He forced a smile.

"It's about Jack Noel."

"Ah! Jack. Charming fellow, charming fellow."

"Yes, but he is a fake," she whispered. "You see, I know the whole story. I must talk to you about it."

"Are you telling me it's old hat?"

"No, but I've come to see you to explain why it mustn't come out."

Rubens raised his eyebrows and looked at her with interest for the first time. "What's your interest in Jack?"

"Well, as you know, I work for Care Campaign and... " she faltered.

"Of course, some of the patrons were painted by him, weren't they, or so they thought. Well, I suppose they will be surprised to find out it was the Romanian. Although I think he is rather good, don't you?" His tone of voice indicated he was hoping the conversation would soon come to an end. His eyes were wandering round the room and Amanda could sense his impatience.

"I feel terribly responsible. I introduced Jack to Alfred Halford and we are hoping his firm might sponsor our next ball. It will be terrible for the reputation of Care Campaign if all this comes out."

"Alfred Halford!" His face lit up. "Well, it isn't often that old fox is deceived by anyone. That makes it even more exciting."

Amanda realised the conversation was going the wrong way.

"Let me explain. The story mustn't come out." She paused. Rubens was looking at her with mock amusement. "It would be truly terrible for the reputation of Care Campaign."

"You are very loyal to your charity, but no one can blame you for a few recommendations done in good faith. It's a bit of a shock, I suppose, but Jack is charming and everyone likes him. People will soon forget. I gather his French wife is rather pushy. I bet she put him up to it in the first place."

"The thing is," she blurted out, aware she was about to lose him to an approaching mini celebrity, "the thing is, I have been paid a commission by Jack for the portraits he did of the patrons. Some people in the charity know this. If the story comes out they will assume I knew he was a fake and was..."

"Ah, now you're talking! A bit of money under the table! Your concern makes more sense now."

"I'm not concerned for myself but for the charity and the people who trusted me!"

"You live and learn." He gave her an economical smile. "We all have to make a living somehow, I suppose. The way I do it is finding good stories like this one."

"Mr Rubens, would you please consider..."

"Nick, I've circled the room twice looking for you. How are you, old chap!" A middle-aged, robust man stood by them. He gave Amanda his best smile, assuming if she was with Nick she must be "someone".

"Good to see you, John!" Rubens patted the man's square shoulders and gave his back to Amanda. Amanda felt numb. She was no longer embarrassed or self-conscious, nor cared if people knew she was a gatecrasher. There was a vacuum inside her that seemed to protect her from any other emotion. She felt defeated, like at the end of a race when exhaustion makes one forget the outcome.

When Amanda left the Carlton Towers she made her way towards the park. It was still light and the air was warm. She walked towards the gate overlooking the north side, listening to the noises of the park: the song of birds, the rustle of leaves, the whispers of lovers, cyclists on their way home. When she reached the gates of the park, her thoughts turned once more to Patsy. She was the only person left to confide in. Now, when the story came out, Alfred's name would also be mentioned. She had to go and see Patsy to warn her.

*

When Patsy opened the door, she was wearing a tight Lycra leotard with black leggings. She had a bandanna round her forehead and her smiling face was glistening with perspiration.

"Hi there. Come in. You've arrived just in time to save me from the last five minutes on that exercise bike. Damian will be one next month and I still haven't got my figure back." She patted her thighs.

Amanda followed Patsy's sylph-like figure into the drawing room. She hadn't been to an exercise class nor had had the time to ponder on the shape of her thighs since Douglas had left. Her life had been too eventful. Looking at Patsy's shapely bottom, she promised herself that, as soon as her life regained some form of normality and she once again had a routine, she would do something to tone up. But at the moment, unless she managed to stop the story of Jack getting into the papers, she would probably never be able to afford a holiday again, let alone worry about what she looked like in a bathing costume.

"Sit down. You look tired." Patsy collapsed on the sofa stretching her long legs across it. "What's wrong, lovey? You look worn out! Let me get you a drink and you can tell me all about it. You did sound rather worried on the phone."

Amanda hesitated.

"You're not going to worry about drinking in the afternoon, are you? You need some colour put back into your cheeks and I deserve a few calories. What will it be then?" She sprang to her feet.

"Thanks. I'll have some wine."

When Patsy left for the kitchen, Amanda got up and walked towards the window that overlooked Regent's Park. She remembered the view she had seen in the winter when she had met Patsy for the first time. The park had been obscured by a blanket of mist. Today it was a palette of colours. Her life had changed as much as the park since that first visit. For years her life had been predictable, safe and familiar. Now, each time she returned to a place, she was aware of how much her life had changed since the last time she had been there.

"Here we are. A white wine and a nice long vodka and orange." Patsy handed Amanda her glass and collapsed on the sofa beside her. She took a long sip from her drink. "That's better! Now tell me what's wrong!"

Amanda looked down at the carpet not knowing quite where to start.

"Whatever it is, it's really worrying you, isn't it? You'll feel better once you get it off your chest and have some of that wine," Patsy said encouragingly.

"Patsy, you remember who Jack Noel is, don't you?"

"Sure I do. Alfred mentioned him the other day. He said Jack was doing a portrait of him for the boardroom. I don't think he's done it yet, at least I can't remember Alfred saying he had. But then I don't take in everything he says." She laughed. "Alfred mentioned it roughly at the same time he told me he'd be sponsoring the next Care Campaign ball. I remember that clearly, because he was so pleased I would be on the committee. You know, he loves it so much when I do grown-up posh things. All thanks to you." She patted Amanda's leg. "But what's this guy Jack got to do with your worried face."

"A lot." Amanda took a long sip from her wine. "Jack is a fake. He doesn't paint the portraits; someone else does it for him."

"You're kidding! You mean he didn't do the one of Tina?" Patsy sat up.

"No. Nor the one of Virginia's grandchildren, nor the Duchess, nor any of them."

"You wait till Alfred finds out!"

"He mustn't find out, Patsy. That's not all. Jack offered me a commission if he got any portrait work through me. I said no to begin with, but then I needed money for Mark's holiday and I said yes. He gave me a commission for Tina's portrait and he was going to give me one..."

"For Alfred's." Patsy interrupted.

"Yes."

"Well," Patsy paused for a moment. "It's not a crime, is it? I mean, it happens in business all the time. I can see it'd be better if Alfred didn't find out. Well, you know what he's like! And he thinks of you as someone all straight-laced. Not that you're not, but you know what I mean."

"Patsy, he'll find out now," Amanda was on the verge of tears. "Jack only does the sketching and takes lots of photographs. The real painter has sold the story to a journalist. Oh God! It will be such a mess. Your name, Tina's name. I'm sure Care Campaign will feature somewhere too. They're so good at digging everything out. I tried to stop the story coming out. I even went to see the journalist. There is nothing I can do. *The News* want the story. Jack's painted royalty! And now they know I work for the charity and took money from Jack. Constantine's name... Alfred's name... " her voice petered out. "I'm so sorry to burden you with all this." Amanda clasped her face in her hands. "I didn't know who to turn to. My friend, Julia, is out of town. Oh God! It's such a mess. If I only had some money I'd pay Jose. At one point I even thought of borrowing from you, but I knew I'd never be able to repay it."

"I'd lend you the money, but Alfred, for all his generosity, is so tight his bum squeaks. He never lets me have any cash, and when the Barclaycard statement comes, I always have to go through it with him." Patsy, who rarely looked pensive, was silent for a few minutes before adding, "But the truth is he'll hit the roof if his name gets dragged into it and if he finds out about your commissions, it's goodbye to sponsorship for Care Campaign."

Amanda, on hearing this from Patsy, felt even more helpless and distraught. "I'm sorry," she said. "It's all my fault, getting you all involved in this way."

"Look, cheer up." Her face brightened. "Didn't you say *The News* had the story?"

"Yes."

"Well, that might change things." She reached for her address book by the portable phone. "I know the new editor rather well." She smiled. "From the old days before Alfred, of course. I think he owes me a small favour. He might not see it that way, but let me try."

★

When the phone rang in Tim Curwen's office, he was about to leave for lunch. "A Mrs Patsy Bingham for you. Will you take the call?" The protective voice of his secretary came through the intercom.

Tim hesitated before saying, "Put her through."

"Hello, Tim."

"Well, well. If it isn't La Halford."

"I used Bingham because I wasn't sure you'd heard."

"How could I be in the dark when my smart rivals keep on mentioning you in their gossip columns. How are you keeping?"

"Fine, and yourself? Still happily married?"

"Yes, and we've finally had our boy after the three girls."

"Congratulations! We've had a boy, too. Damian. He's a poppet!"

"Motherhood! Riches! What next? Lady Halford maybe?"

Patsy giggled. "Don't be silly."

"Mark my words. Your old man's done enough in the right places to get a peerage."

"I'm told newspaper chiefs land up with titles too."

"Well, who's going to be first then?"

"Tim," Patsy said softly, "I need a favour."

"Yes, what can I do for you. No one ever rings me just for a cosy chat these days." He laughed.

"I'm told you've got this story about a painter called Jack Noel."

"That's right! And now you mention it, I remember your old man was one of the people conned by him with a few others."

"He never did a portrait of Alfred," Patsy said defensively. "It was only being considered."

"I get it. I get it. You'd like me to leave your old man out of the story." He paused. "Well, I must say he's a good name to drop into the scandal, but I dare say, for old times' sake we could do without him. Plenty of other faces involved, as far as I can remember."

"Tim, you can't print that story."

"And why not?" Tim sat down. "Is there anything else I don't know."

"No. Just that a lot of my friends are involved and it would make a lot of people very unhappy, particularly my Alfred. I don't want him to know."

"I see. Protecting our friends in high places nowadays? Gone up in the world, have we? I'm afraid, Patsy, it's a great story. Royalty involved and all that. I'm afraid I can't help you."

"Tim, please. It really is important that it doesn't come out."

"They'll all recover from it. They normally do."

Amanda was following Patsy's side of the conversation and sat rigid. She kept looking towards the door, terrified Alfred might come home. Patsy, who had been walking up and down the room with short light steps, occasionally smiling in her direction, suddenly stood still. Her expression, usually so cheery, became menacing.

"Okay, then," she said. "Do you remember the holiday we all had in Marbella together?"

"Which holiday?" Tim's voice was impatient.

"You remember the one! I was with Ralph, my photographer bloke and you got off with my friend, Pam."

"Yeah, what about it? It happens every day. Look Pats, I've got to go. I'm meeting someone important for lunch."

"Well, if I remember correctly, you had a nice time with my friend, Pam, and you were a happily married man at the time."

"So what!"

"So... I kept some great photos Ralph took. D'you remember the ones? You and Pam in your birthday suits round the pool? You licking ice cream off her you know whats?"

The editor of *The News* went pale. "You're bluffing!"

"I'll send you some copies. It'll remind you how good-looking you used to be. You should show 'em to Mrs Curwen, though I wouldn't fancy her chances of ever becoming 'Lady' Curwen when the other papers see the photos."

"Blast you! Leopards don't change their spots, I see. All right then. We won't run the story. But that's it, no more favours after this one. Got it?"

"Fair enough. I owe you one now. And thanks, Tim."

Patsy beamed at Amanda and threw the phone onto the sofa. "I don't think we need worry about the story any more," she said triumphantly.

"But what if Rubens goes to someone else with it?" Amanda looked incredulously at Patsy.

"*The News* have bought it, so he can't. It happens every day. You wait till I tell Pam the story," she giggled nervously. "I still keep in touch with her. She lives in Paris." She raised an eyebrow. "Also with an older man. Let's have a drink to celebrate!"

"I don't think I could." Amanda felt faint. "Patsy, did you really keep those photographs after all this time?"

"Of course not! I threw them away with the rest of my snapshots before I got married. I wouldn't want Alfred to see them. Now, what about that drink? You must keep me company. I feel a bit shaky myself. I'm not that thick-skinned. I got a bit nervous for a moment talking with old Tim."

When Patsy left the room Amanda walked towards the window and looked out at the sunny park. The light outside was softer than it had been when she had first arrived, the shadows longer. Her life had changed again, but the burden of anxiety still weighed heavily on her shoulders. She had carried it for too long to be able to shed it with the same speed with which Patsy had made her phone call. Regent's Park looked inviting with its myriad colours, but she longed to be back in Putney, walking the familiar streets with their red brick houses. She wondered if Julia was back and if Kate would be home that weekend. She felt like being at home gardening, tidying her house.

"Here we are. Let's drink to peace of mind and old snapshots!" Patsy stood behind her, smiling. "Cheers." She raised her glass. "But before you go, we'd better think of what we'll tell Alfred about why Jack can't paint his portrait."

★

When the telephone rang in Jack and Solange's apartment, Solange was in the bedroom packing. Jack stood in front of the window looking at the park and wondering whether they would be able to fit everything in their car. He picked up the phone and said, "Hello," with a flat and distant voice.

"Jack, is that you?"

"Amanda, what a surprise!" His voice regained some of its habitual confidence. "We've been meaning to ring you since we got back from the South of France, but if you remember, Solange's mother was unwell."

"I remember." The sharp tone in which Amanda said this was not wasted on Jack.

"I'm afraid," he continued, "she is still very poorly. In fact, we're leaving for France today to see her."

"I'm sure you are. Look, Jack, you can stop pretending. I imagine you're leaving because you don't want to be here to read Jose's story in the papers."

"What are you talking about?"

"You know damn well what I'm talking about. I know about Jose and I know about you and the way you work."

There was a silence. "Look, Amanda, you did quite well out of it."

"Is that what you think? If that story comes out, I'll lose my job and most of my friends. It's to avoid that, that I've managed to stop it being printed. It wasn't easy and I only did it to save my reputation."

There was another silence and Jack was very tempted to ask Amanda how she had managed to silence Jose, but her tone of voice told him it was better not to ask.

"Jack," said Amanda, "before you disappear, you will do something for me. You will ring Alfred Halford and tell him one of your heart-rending stories about why you can't go ahead with his portrait. Tell him you've broken your right arm in several places and it will be a long time before you can pick up a brush again, or any other excuse you can think of. Have a safe trip!" She put the phone down. The realisation that she wouldn't have to speak to Jack ever again made Amanda sigh with relief.

*

Amanda walked out into the small patio that led to the garden and everywhere round her she noticed the signs of neglect. The flower beds were dotted with healthy weeds, the outside of the windows needed painting and the patio hadn't been swept since September. The warm sunshine and the hope that she might not lose her job after all, gave her renewed energy and filled her with optimism. Her children, despite the divorce, had done well with their studies. She was still living in Putney, had made new friends and she had learnt more about life and people in ten months than she had in the past twenty years. She bent down and started to weed the flower beds, enjoying the sensation of pulling out the intruders in her garden. Looking at the chipped paint on the window frames, she decided not to go to work for the rest of the week and attend to her house and to Mark, who was going to work on a kibbutz for two months at the end of the week. Tony had organised it all and Mark was very excited and looking forward to the experience. She would drive down to Pat's for the weekend. She felt like getting out of London for a couple of days and also wanted to thank Tony for all the help and support he had given Mark. Kate's window was open. Her radio was on and a melodic tune filled the garden. Kate's taste in music seemed to be improving and there was also clearly a Sixties revival. Amanda hummed the familiar tune while working on her flower beds. Kate was getting ready for a barbecue and Sebastian was coming to pick her up. Amanda was looking forward to meeting him. The last two times he had been round to the house, she had been out. There was talk of Kate and Sebastian setting off inter-railing together with a couple of friends halfway through the summer. When the doorbell rang, Amanda got up and wiped her hands on the back of her jeans and waited for Kate to open the door.

"Mum, come and meet Sebastian." Kate stood by the kitchen door holding her boyfriend's arm. Sebastian took a step forward and shook Amanda's muddy hand.

"It's very nice to meet you Mrs T." His voice was confident. He was tall and had good posture, which she found rare in young people.

"Shall we have a drink inside?" Amanda bent down to pick up the rubbish and weeds she had piled on a cardboard box.

"Let me do that for you," said Sebastian, as he bent down to pick up the box.

In the kitchen, while she poured some wine into three glasses, she examined Sebastian, who was now emptying her rubbish in the bin. He was an attractive young man, and he was much cleaner and neater than she had expected him to be. She was used to Mark's shaggy friends with long hair and crumpled clothes. There was also a slightly pompous air about Sebastian. It suddenly dawned on Amanda that he was a younger version of Douglas. Looking at Kate, Amanda wondered if daughters were destined to become their mothers, even when they spent their lives struggling to be themselves. She felt like hugging Kate and protecting her. She looked so happy and in love.

"Cheers," said Sebastian in a loud voice, raising his glass towards Amanda.

"Cheers." Amanda smiled back at him and reminded herself that she should be glad Kate was inter-railing with somebody like Sebastian. He was the type that would keep Turkish officials and vendors well at bay. He would take care of Kate, if nothing else because it would make him feel important.

"When are you planning to set off on this trip Kate sounds so excited about?"

"I thought in about three weeks. It will give us all some time to save some more money," said Sebastian.

Another telling sign, thought Amanda: "I thought" not "we thought".

She looked at Kate, who looked stunning in the bottle-green top Patsy had given her. She had tied her hair up and it made her look much older. Amanda was overcome by emotion as she watched her daughter standing beside Sebastian. Would she suffer the pain of being left one day too? How could she protect her?

She turned her face towards the window so that Kate wouldn't notice her worried expression and caught her own reflection: that of a woman whose youth was hanging by a thread. Would it be easier had she been an older mother? Would she worry less about Kate's mistakes?

"I think we'd better be going," said Sebastian, emptying his glass, "or we'll be late."

Amanda stood by the door and watched them walk down the tree-lined street. Maybe Sebastian was more conservative and in control than she had expected, but that needn't mean he was really like Douglas. She must let go of her fears.

★

On Saturday morning as Amanda was about to load her overnight bag into the car, a letter with the logo of Care Campaign was dropped through her letter box, together with some bills. She opened it, not knowing what to expect, but prepared for the worst.

> *Dear Amanda,*
>
> *We have just received confirmation from Alfred Halford's company that they are willing to sponsor our Ball for next year. Mr Halford pointed out in his letter how much he enjoyed dealing with you. He found you both professional and receptive. I thought you would like to know that despite the recent difficulties you've encountered, you have been a great asset to our charity and we hope we will have you with us for many years.*
>
> *Kind regards,*
>
> *Belinda Ashcombe*

As she drove out of London, Amanda touched the pocket of her linen jacket where the letter from Belinda lay neatly folded. It was hot. She wound down her window and the breeze that came in refreshed her. Douglas, Jack, and her fears, like the winter, had gone and here at last was summer.